The Problem Solver: Collection

Ron Mueller

Books by the Author

Fiction Series
The Alex Evercrest Series
The River Front
The Girl on The Grill
Missing
Maggot
Racist
Votive Candles
Windy City
Country Road
Pool of Blood
Sins of the Daughter
Body Parts
The Skull Collector
The Vanishing
The Shadow Fighter
Moonshine
Grief's Trajectory
The Magic Touch
Northern Lights
Alex Evercrest Heroine
Alex Evercrest Collection Two
New Direction
A Family Affair
Disruption
Aftermath
The St. Lebuinnus Church Murder

A Brian O'Neil Novel
Hawaiian Phoenix
Moon Curser
Death Broker

The Problem Solver Series
Solutions
Drug Lords
Border Crosser
The Problem Solver Collection

The Taelo Series
The Early Years
The Golden Feather
Journey of Discovery
Dangerous Passage
Condor Clan Slingers
Circumvention
The Journey of Sages
Collection
Future Leaders Journey

A Taelo Story:
White Swan and Quiet Pheasant
The Child's Name
Floating Cloud
Quiet Rabbit
Busy Bee
Little Otter & Talking Wren
Broken Spear
Burley Bear & Meadow Flower
Taelo Story Collection

Science Fiction

The Savitar Series:
Journey's End
Savitar
Confluence
Savitar Series Collection

Bram Nielson Series
The Fold
The Message
Fold Wormhole
Negative Fold
Ripples in Time
Bram Nielson Collection

Single Science Fiction Books:
Current Past and Future
The Event
The Door
Viajante 7

ℰ๐ *The Problem Solver: Collection* ๕ଛ

Ron Mueller

Around the World Publishing LLC
Cincinnati, Ohio

ISBN 13: 978-1-68223-974-2

Distributed by: Ingram
Cover Picture by Bruce Rolff – Shutterstock.com
Cover Design by Ron Mueller

Table of Content

Introduction

It is a troubled world. The human species has, like no other, risen to dominate the world. The rise is marked with amazing beauty and grace. It is also marked by cruelty to other humans and a disregard for the negative impact they have on their only home, the earth.

The beauty found in poetry and writing, the beauty found in paintings and sculptor is more than countered by the wars, the intentional environmental destruction, and the barriers each separate country imposes on its peoples and the neighboring states.

The belief of limited resources, the behavior of greed, the desire for wealth and the desire for control are all factors in the behavior exhibited by those who surface at the top of the heap. The ability of various leaders, in a myriad of areas, to convince those more interested in their immediate family well-being allows those interested in domination to rise to positions of influence and power. Often their belief is that they have been ordained to be in charge or alternately they are smarter and should be in the lead.

The rise of the rule of law has created a situation where fairness is managed by laws developed by the representatives of the people. Even in the situation found in the United States that has three branches of government designed to maintain the system of fairness to all, slavery, and women's right to vote were initially missed. More recently the rights of gay or lesbian people are in question.

Human greed, cruelty, misbehavior, and disregard to the environment seems to increase asymptotically with the rapid rise of the population.

Justice is not always served. This situation is managed by a secret organization that funds and directs the actions of *The Problem-solver*. This is a person whose principles, judgement, behavior, and actions guide him in how to resolve problems that otherwise would be left unchecked.

The problems are many. The problems are anywhere in the world. The problems are solved in the best manner that The Problem-solver determines.

See if you agree with the problem resolutions, that this Problem-solver, *Ian Sinclair*, has chosen for his various assignments.

<u>**Solutions**</u>

1 The Beginning

*H*igh above, a single red-tailed hawk rode the uplifting warm draft. Ian imagined that the sun shining on the surface of the cliff above the small babbling brook heated the air to provide the hawk the means to stay afloat. His flight seemed endless and effortless. He imagined feeling the air lifting him and allowing him the freedom of such flight.

The cool water rushed across his feet, as he carefully bent to lift a rock and catch his next Iowa shrimp. This was what Ian called the crawfish he had skillfully gathered and put in his basket. Ian was a nature boy wandering the woods and fields in the wild area where he lived. He wandered far and wide.

He knew all the places where some good treat was available. Up on top of the hill was a pond full of his Iowa oysters, better known locally as clams. He would wade into the pond and find the clams with his feet, put his foot under them and then lift them up to his extended hand.

In the spring he would walk through the moist, leaf covered forest areas and gather the morel mushrooms. He ate them fried with a little olive oil and accompanied with eggs from the chickens his family raised.

The mulberry trees sporting their long, sweet berries were the next providers of a great treat. He would eat as many as he picked for the rest of the family.

The yellow-pink blush raspberries with their refreshing and juicy sweet slightly tart taste were next in line to be sought.

Then high summer provided tons of blackberries if you could survive the pain of the thorns that stubbornly defended them.

He grew up poor but well fed and happy.

Nature provided treats. Ian extended this to the world around him.

He came to realized that nature provided but it was the human that horded and selfishly made it hard for others to be relaxed and enjoy life.

People seemed to have a shortage mentality.

Perhaps in the early history of humans, it made the difference of survival or death. However, now the population had reached into the billions of peoples, and it seemed to Ian that it was now the time where the human could focus on letting everyone enjoy life.

This mind set colored his perspective.

It seemed to Ian that like the sun, humans should warm the air and let people float like the hawk rides the warm air as glide the air.

They should learn to enjoy.

In spite of this positive outlook, Ian was pulled into a life he had never envisioned for himself.

He was destined for something that countered all of his philosophical and humanistic thoughts.

He would become the antithesis of his generous practice and outlook. He would live both the yin and the yang as he passed through the world.

In 1967 Ian volunteered for the Navy to avoid being drafted.

The US government was drafting young men into the army to fight in Vietnam. Ian had to look up Vietnam on the map to learn where it was located. Then he wondered how such a tiny nation could possibly be a threat to the US.

The draft directly impacted him, and he decided he should study the history of the Asian region.

He learned that the French had screwed the country and its peoples for more than three hundred years. They had exploited the Vietnamese people and taken the products, the minerals and even the women back to Europe.

Many women stained their teeth purple to be less attractive to the French.

After World War two the Vietnamese patriots, yes patriots, soundly defeated the French in the Battle of Dien Bien Phu forcing the French to withdraw from Indochina.

But the Vietnamese were screwed one more time by having their country divided at the 17th parallel with promised elections to follow.

Ian learned that the US in its own paranoia with communism, saw the Vietnamese in the north as a communist threat and seemed to organically slip in to replace the French.

Ian sadly learned that his hero from his younger years, President Kennedy made the first commitment of US support to a series of corrupt South Vietnamese government dictators.

Ian wondered how this war would have turned out had Kennedy lived.

His actions greatly diminished him as a hero figure to Ian. Kennedy had worried about a re-election that he did not live to see.

Ian knew that President Johnson inherited a mess, and his ignorance and hubris led him down the slope to his own demise and earning him a place in history as the leader who killed more people than any other figure in history.

The Gulf of Tonkin incident, which led to a major US escalation of its involvement confirmed to the North Vietnamese that in their second phase of revolution, the US was now substituting for the French.

It truly became the American War.

Damn the French and damn the clueless US Admirals and Generals advising a President that was afraid to acknowledge that the US screwed up in supporting a series of corrupt South Vietnamese governments.

Ian thought again how stupid the US leadership had been and that if they would have come to stand with him in the pitch-black dark surrounding, he and his fifty-caliber machine gun, they would have reached different decisions and made different commitments.

He decided the safe place was to be in the US Navy.

He volunteered.

His enlistment contract was for six years. It included training as an Electronics technician, training as a Nuclear Reactor Operator, and admittance to the NESEP program where he would become an engineer and an office.

The Electronics school training was invigorating for Ian. It was rapid, practical learning and application.

During this period, he had a brief romance but realized that he would not marry while in the military. He just did not have the control over his life that he felt he would need to be a good husband.

He was given temporary orders to the USS Gunston Hall LSD 5 located in San Diego while he waited on the opening to the Nuclear Power school just outside of San Francisco. The ship was a World War Two left over being used to train navy crewmen.

He had just gotten onboard when he learned of the deployment of the ship to deliver three of the USS New Jersey's sixteen-inch gun barrels.

The New Jersey was off the Coast of Vietnam where it was providing artillery support to the troops.

Ian took it in stride.

He was after all on a ship.

Three barrels for the New Jersey was the max weight capacity for the Gunston Hall.

The battleship fired nine barrels!

Ian focused on his duties. He had a knack for fixing things and soon all the electronics gear on the ship was performing at top notch.

The gun barrels were delivered.

The next assignment for the ship was a surprise to everyone. The ship was to house and manage the deployment of three "Tango Boats" to open the rivers of South Vietnam. The three boats consisted of two mortar and machine escort boats. The third boat consisted of a large tank of napalm and a giant squirt gun that fired a six-foot sausage of flaming napalm the distance of about three football fields.

It was what Ian thought of as the boat from hell.

The Gunston Hall was outfitted with eight fifty caliper machine gun positions.

The captain wanted each of the ships departments to volunteer to man one of the fifty caliper machine gun positions.

Ian's department was assigned the right bow position. No one was willing, and the department had no volunteer.

Ian stepped forward and said he would do it. He also volunteered for the fifty-caliber machine gun on the landing craft escort boat. The landing craft boat served as an escort with the duty to save the tango boat crew if it capsized during the transition from the sea to the river mouth.

The transition from the ship to the river mouth was always made in the dark of night. For Ian, the dark was absolute. The dark was both a friend and foe. Ian fought a constant battle with the dark.

For Ian there was the dark of night, the darkness in his mind and the darkness of his soul.

The last darkness bothered him greatly.

Later it would be the dark of night that too often would trigger memories of being in a lush green, bountiful, country where the children could be seen frolicking in the river and families prospered but where the patriots of that country were fighting against the US and that meant him.

The situation and the part Ian played in it was the darkness of his soul.

He wondered if there was really a God that would forgive him?

He had at one time almost gone into the priesthood. Some inner doubt had surfaced as he pursued the seminary route and he had taken a different path.

At that time, he had not foreseen how different his path would be.

It was the darkness of his mind that generated such bitterness at the misery, the suffering and death he participated in perpetrating on people only wanting to live in their country undisturbed by outsiders.

He and his fifty-caliber machine gun were there to deliver the bitter fruits of death.

In the dark of the night, the scene was always the same variation.

It always would pull him in.

At the mouth of some unknown river, he would once again be on station behind his fifty-caliber machine gun.

He stood alone in three hundred and sixty degrees of absolute darkness. It was a dark, a dark as black as ink in a bottle. The exception was the trillions of stars in the sky. These were constant reminders of the small points of hope he apprehensively held.

No moon was a blessing to Ian. There seemed to be less fighting in pitch black of a moonless sky.

The moon was not the beginning of a lover's scene. It was the beginning of a recurring nightmare.

Ian recalled the quiet as he strained to pick up any sound.

The sound he was most concerned about was the sound of the bullet that he would never hear.

The one that would kill him.

He knew it would be the single answer to the stream of fifty caliber bullet rounds he sent out.

In the future, his mind reproduced the salty odor of fermenting sea weeds. His face felt the warm coastal sea breeze. His hands felt the double handle grips on the fifty.

His recurring nightmares felt real, smelled real, tasted real and produced the sweat he experienced when standing in the sun.

He was there. There, off the coast or there at the river's mouth or there escorting the Tangos.

His mind and body thought he was there.

He was always alone on station, except for the ammo boxes, the post mounted fifty and beside it a post mounted thirty caliber.

He was either on the bow of the ship or on the back of the escort landing craft.

He was always with the fifty.

It became part of his soul.

It was still with him; and it would forever be with him.

On station, he listened intently for any sound, any advance warning of enemy action. It was an enemy he almost never saw. An enemy that sent mortar and machine gun fire his way.

He never fired unless he had a target.

His station used less ammo than any station on the ship, but Ian knew he was more deadly. His fifty did not fire unless there was someone that he could see at the receiving end.

He shot only at a shooting enemy.

Each night he relived the listening.

Listening for the bullet meant for him.

He knew that he would never hear the bullet that killed him, but he strained to hear its sound.

He listened with a mind draining intensity.

Ian knew that a part of his mind was broken, and he doubted it would ever heal.

The fifty caliber didn't have any nuclear power, but it had brutal, penetrating, flesh tearing firepower. Its five-inch, powder filled shell casing launched its copper coated kiss of death, which ripped through most armor and still maintained its ability to cut a person in two. There was no way to argue or bargain when the fifty found its mark.

He stood alone in the dark. His fifty, with its red tracers delivering the kiss of anguish and death.

It was a two-way street, he dished it out, but the incoming could take him out.

He knew, when the fight began, there was no one but him at the fifty. He would stand alone, and he always prayed that the enemy wouldn't find him.

He prayed, not as kneel down, and pray in church, but as in, God dammit don't let the bastards figure out where I am, type of praying.

He thought of it as a vulgar, desperate prayer for survival and he prayed often and fervently.

He would take vulgar praying over the bullet meant for him.

In the darkness, the rapid pulsing of the fifty, the red stream, his cotton ear plugs and the sharp metallic flavor of gun powder on the back of his tongue were so real that he knew he was back in the dark.

He recalled and could feel the heat from the red-hot barrel of the fifty.

He saw the red tracers racing toward the target and their sweeping motion as he painted the target area. He could not see, but he felt the carnage he was delivering with the lead being hurled at a velocity of twice the speed of sound.

Those on the receiving end never heard the bullet that killed them. It killed in silence except for the occasional brief screaming of the victim.

Ian had put his emotions on hold. They were frozen in the frigid, blackness deep in his mind.

He was truly alone when he had his finger on the trigger. So alone that he didn't even think.

He just listened to the roar of the outgoing bullets and the bullet meant for him. He listened and the sounds were of ghosts screaming.

The ghost of the bullet that didn't find him then had followed him home and now haunted him in his sleep.

His ghosts were both real and imagined. He was not sure which had the most denizens. He knew the ones in his mind were beyond what he could count. Their screams were persistent, incessant, and unrelenting.

He had survived.

Most of the Tango boat crews had not. He felt relief at having lived and guilt at his survival.

He now saw through different eyes and thought with a very different mind.

He had joined the Navy to avoid the battle in Vietnam. The "contract" he signed was to become a Nuclear Reactor Operator and then go on to college to be an Officer.

He wanted to become an Engineer.

He now was back in the US, in his apartment. It was morning and he was soaking in sweat. His pillow and bed were one wet puddle.

He had survived but Hell had come home with him and visited almost every night.

He remembered his mother's quiet voice telling him, "you get back what you sow."

He was one of the lucky ones. Lucky to have only the ghosts that haunted his mind.

For him there were no heroes. There were no parades. There were many dead, there were many horribly injured and many more mentally affected survivors.

They had all been useless cannon fodder.

He knew the US lost the war and so did all the Vietnamese. There was enough death, misery and bitterness living on, in both countries.

He later learned that the US dropped more bombs on that small country than was dropped in Europe during WWII. It spread defoliant chemicals called agent orange to defoliate the jungle and created a legacy of birth deformation and cancers to those exposed.

He was one of those exposed to Agent Orange.

He did not like to think about the misery and millions of deaths he had participate in perpetrating on the people in that small distant country called Vietnam.

Though it was over, for Ian the memories were part of his continuing mental landscape. There was the daily vision of the bright sunlight, the deep blue sky speckled with puffy white clouds. There was the breeze blowing his hair and cooling his skin.

There was also the black in the back of his mind and the noises of pain and suffering coming from that unfathomable darkness.

He feared the rattling of his mind. He imagined that everyone talked to their mind, but no one ever publicly admitted it and fewer probably had a mind that talked back and taunted them about their weakness.

He knew few people that had the kind of dissonance thundering inside their minds as he did. He kept this dissonance under his control and spoke to no one about it.

He knew his mind was damaged. He certainly was not going to let any Navy psychologist test him. He hoped time would be the therapy he required.

He developed a level of control that allowed him to appear normal to the people around him.

He could split and control his personality and be whoever he needed to be when he needed to be. He could be himself or be we and bounce around as needed.

He created his reality the way he needed it to be. He knew he had to get out of the Navy and travel the rest of his life journey in his own way.

He no longer fit the mold of the normal person.

He got out of the Navy and went on his own to get an engineering degree.

He went to junior college to get started.

Good luck seemed to find him, and he was accepted into Stanford.

He was older than most students on the campus and a loner.

He was studious and liked the quiet of the library where he could observe people remotely. The rows of books spoke to him about the depth of the human experience.

The quiet allowed him to maintain control.

The library was an oasis for his mind.

It was at the library where he met the woman of his dreams.

Not his dark dreams but the dreams of hope. She was the one he had always hoped to find.

She walked in while he was studying at the first table past the entrance. He could not take his eyes off of her. When she left with a clutch of books, He stopped his studies and followed her to the Student Union. There he mustered his courage and approached her and in a quavering voice asked her out to dinner.

Months later she told him that his intensity had scared the Hell out of her, but she was somehow compelled to accept his dinner offer.

Less than nine months later, during a thunderous rainstorm that was flashing lightening and scouring the earth with hail, and soul piercing thunder as if it were trying to stop him, he proposed to Lesley Madison.

He looked up at her slender physique and almost black eyes that were perfectly set on either side of a trim nose that clearly complemented her slim face framed by black hair, and almost fainted when she said yes to his marriage proposal.

Her acceptance made him the happiest he had ever been. Bright, warm sunshine pushed the darkness to a corner of his mind.

Lesley was almost the same age as him. They had both been on their own for ten years but were still close to their families.

They decided on the date and location for the wedding. Then they went through the meet the family routine.

They went out to dinner with her parents. During dinner, her mother began asking about his background and his time in Vietnam.

That night Ian had one of his sweat-soaked nightmare dream sessions. Ian thought he had that part of his brain under lock and key, but it made its presence known and assured him that it would always be there.

Ian stepped aside as the wedding planning went into full swing.

The December Maui destination wedding insured that only the very closest friends were selected. This was Ian's idea and Lesley immediately accepted. It was his way of limiting the stress that might trigger another undesired flash back.

He received an unsigned congratulations letter with a "Wedding Bonus" from a mysterious benefactor.

It was a check for twenty-five thousand dollars!

Ian had no idea who might have sent it. He put it away. He had no clue who would send him such a sum. It remained a mystery for quite some time.

Maui was the perfect location. Wailea Beach, with the subdued waves and periodic black lava rocks jutting out into the water provided the perfect romantic place for a wedding.

The weather cooperated and the rhythmic sound of the small morning waves washing up on the beach set the beat for the wedding vows. Ian kept looking from his bride to the sun rising over Mt Haleakalā as he listened to the pastor leading him through his vows.

His blissful happiness made him worry that it might be the calm before the storm.

He would always remember the early morning wedding on the beach and their getaway on a sunset catamaran ride. The sun setting below the horizon between the island of Maui and Lanai painted the clouds yellow, orange and red.

The rainbow coming out of the side of the Mauna Kahalawai volcano would forever be imprinted in his mind.

To him it was a clear sign that he was blessed.

He mentally laid this scene over the black door holding his darker memories.

The honeymoon was followed by two more years of going to school. He would ride his bike to the University, swim a mile each morning and then go to class for the day.

That experience was therapeutic.

He began to repair his mind as best he could. Lesley was a gentle warm breeze blowing on him. Energy surged within his mind and he had the strength to build a stronger wall between the dark area and the new area filled with a warm embracing light.

Every mind-numbing mile he swam also helped him gain control.

Then with no warning, his life took another surprising turn.

It was not yet time to be interviewing for a job, but he was approached in the student union and given an invitation for dinner to talk about a unique opportunity. He had no clue who was doing the inviting.

He talked it over with Lesley and they decided he should go and listen to what the offer might be.

Later that evening he sat in the restaurant looking across the table at a non-descript, plain looking balding man with almost grey eyes.

He looked at the succulent, rare fillet mignon topped with fried onions and mushrooms, thin slices of spicy fried potatoes and five white spears of asparagus. It was a dinner that seemed to communicate a warning of what was to come.

The person sitting across from him made a job offer, not for the Engineering degree that he was working so hard for. Instead, it was for his military experience, his hand-to-hand Aikido skills, his marksmanship, and his apparent ability to control his mental state.

He had somehow become noticed by an organization that remained nameless. The offer included paying for his educational expenses and for future services rendered. Services rendered meant solve the problem given to him in any manner that suited him, but the solution had to be final and had to stick.

There was a sizable signing bonus and a payment after each solution.

Grey eyes looked at him with a smiled and told him that he should go ahead and cash the thirty thousand dollar check he had been given for his wedding.

Ian asked some clarifying questions. It was clear he was being recruited as a sleeper agent. He now knew who had sent him the thirty thousand dollar wedding gift. He said that he would think about cashing it if he chose to accept the hand of the devil.

He also realized the offer was much better than he would get for his Engineering degree.

When he thought about the meal, he saw how appropriate it was to the offer he had decided to accept. The meal was a bloody piece of warm red meat, topped with fried legumes, often associated with the death and a vegetable that came straight up out of the ground, like the fingers of a white skeletal hand reaching out of the grave.

In this case Ian figured it was his soul that was being recruited.

He again asked about the conditions and whether he could continue his education.

The reply reaffirmed the fact that his continuing education was a good thing and would be looked upon favorably.

He should go on with life as normal.

Occasionally he would be called on to solve problems that could otherwise not be solved.

He would choose and implement the solution and then return to his normal life.

Ian accepted the terms and conditions. He was not sure it was real. There was no contract, no signatures, no contacts, and no medical physical was needed.

At least Grey eyes had a firm handshake and looked Ian directly in the eyes. Grey eyes was the selling point for Ian.

Grey Eyes had not looked away from him during his questioning.

He went home and described the situation to Lesley. He told her only half of the story.

He told her about the half that dealt with their personal bank account and the payment for their educational expenses.

Lesley was inquisitive about what Ian would be doing for this mysterious organization but quit asking when it was clear she had gotten all she would get from him.

For a few days he wondered if it had been a trick of his mind but a week later, he received mail with the information of his two new bank accounts. There was a personal use account with enough money to cover the cost of living and of going to his University for the next two years.

His second account showed a one-million-dollar balance.

That was alarming!

He had access to more money than he had ever dreamt of. The problems he was to face must be large and potentially expensive to execute.

It seemed he had sold his soul and apparently it was worth a million dollars.

He wondered if the devil had grey eyes!

He had questions but he had no contact to call and ask. He had been told to, "Spend whatever you need to be successful at solving the assigned problem. He was not to be limited by money. When the time comes you will be given more instructions and the connections you need."

Ian Sinclair, a lean two hundred-pound, six-foot two frame, with sandy blond hair and sky-blue eyes was now officially a "*Problem Solver.*"

He again wondered about the type of problems he was to solve.

Being the old guy in all his classes meant that Ian was most often on his own.

Those few who somehow learned about his involvement in Vietnam and wanted to make an issue about his time there quickly learned that trash talk did not affect him. He ignored the people that wanted to get his goat. He was just surprised at how many there were that were trying.

The one physical confrontation with three very physically fit bullies ended in their humiliation as he used one hand to face slap all three of them into submission as he repeatedly threatened more harm if they continued. When he was through with them, they were totally humiliated, and he made them apologize for their rude behavior.

The laughter of the crowd that gathered and watched had the effect that there were no other incidents.

He became known as a deadly fighter! He learned of this and wondered how a hand slapping performance made him deadly.

One of those watching was Lesley.

She came up afterwards and gave him a hug. She knew that he had kept himself in check. She had found his wet pillows and had learned about the internal mental self-control he exerted.

Now she had witnessed him constrain himself when confronted by the three bullies. It comforted her to know he had such strong self-control. She knew that he could have just as easily killed his attackers.

She quietly told him she loved him.

Ian let her warmth flow into him, and he put the blanket back on top of the darkness in his mind.

He had come so close to killing the three that it took him almost a month to feel back in control.

That day he took her hand and they walked to the student union for lunch.

When the final year began, Ian knew he wanted more and that once he left the University environment he would never return.

He decided to continue and get a master's degree.

He thought about his problem-solving agreement and wondered who to contact.

He decided just to register.

He did and was accepted.

He waited to see if there would be any communication from his mysterious employers or if his bank accounts would be closed.

He got his answer when his personal bank account went up enough to cover his expenses for graduate school.

He was not too surprised to know he was being monitored. He wondered how close the monitoring might be.

He had no idea what he would do with a master's degree in Control Systems but that is what interested him. He had a great thesis sponsor which made the experience fun.

He put the control theory and logic to use in controlling his mind. He realized that the thesis was about his mind, and he would need to control it if he were to remain functional.

The blackness seemed to shrink but it still periodically flared.

He had learned to control and edit his dreams.

He could now stand in the dark, alone, and listen.

He no longer sweat profusely in his dreams.

There were still those rare nights where he knew he was into his full nightmare mode. On those nights he would lose control but now his body would wake him up.

His master's degree became focused on "Ian's" mind control. He did not share that part with anyone, least of all his sponsor.

Lesley graduated and went to work for a local law firm. She was well thought of and was soon on her way to be the first woman partner in the firm.

He continued to focus on his master's degree thesis.

He interviewed with several oil companies, several power generation companies, jet engine builders and one consumer goods company.

The lowest salary offer was the one he took.

The top company in Cincinnati made the offer to put his control system master's degree focus into use.

It was a big enough company that it also seemed to have the broadest opportunity for him.

Lesley and he made the move to Cincinnati and rented a home in the Finneytown area near the company's technical center and the Ivorydale plant location.

A week after getting to Cincinnati, he received his first problem solving assignment.

He held the message in his hand. All it said was "Come when you are ready."

It was simply a set of driving instructions to a Maine location, a help phone number and a cryptic statement that put fear in my heart; "trust no one."

It gave him a date to be there.

He told his new boss his first of many lies, "A sick Aunt in New Hampshire needed his help."

Only three weeks after their arrival, Lesley took him to the Cincinnati Airport and to drop him off.

She looked at him doubtfully as he for about the fourth time explained that all the information, he had been given was the time, the place, the type of clothes to wear and a phone number to call for any additional help he might need.

Lesley shook her head, gave him a hug, and whispered, "I love you, please be careful."

It was hard for him to turn and walk away. He turned and waved as she got back in the car to drive away.

He then enter and flew to the specified destination.

2 EMF

*T*he airline check in counter seemed to recede as Ian walked toward it. The friendly and smiling check-in agent seemed to look through him and know that he was a fake person.

His senses were steeped in adrenaline.

He was having trouble controlling his mind.

He was sure the people managing the security line could sense that he was on an iniquitous problem-solving journey.

He felt beads of sweat on his forehead.

His self-assessment was that it was not a good beginning.

His boarding wait was dark and foreboding. He momentarily found himself in the dark once again off the coast of Vietnam. Sweat was now beading on his forehead.

The laughter of a young girl playing with her younger brother brought him back from his dark mind into the boarding area. He spent the rest of the waiting time following the innocent play of the two.

They were the light that pushed back his darkness.

At boarding time, he got on as soon as he could. He had an aisle seat immediately next to the young mother and her two young children.

He was pleased to hear their continued play and laughter.

Once they were into the air, he closed his eyes and let the laughter guide him through the dark and into a light slumber. He slept through the landing in Bangor.

The two children still in good humor and chattering with each other woke him with their questions about the landing. They provided the foundation for his continued self-control.

He stood and helped their mother get all her carry on organized so she could take the two off the plane. He carried her roller bag and followed them off. The two kids ran ahead to a man who he figured was their father. The father gathered the two in his arms and lifted them for a hug.

Ian put the bag down at his feet. He mentally thanked them for escorting him through the darkness.

He had always thought of Maine as a state almost the size of Texas. Instead, it was half the size of his home state of Illinois. Ohio where he now lived was thirty percent bigger than Maine.

He was sure the map somehow distorted Maine's appearance. It stuck into Canada like a thumb pushed there by Vermont and New Hampshire.

What surprised him was that more people spoke French in Maine than in any other state of the union.

He also learned that it had broken ties with the Commonwealth of Massachusetts to become Maine.

It was the state with the fewest people east of the Mississippi.

His awareness of the state's low population was augmented with the knowledge that it suffered one of the highest suicide rates of all the states.

He was not sure what all the superfluous information that he had learned was worth but he had tried to learn as much as possible about his first problem solving assignment.

What kind of assignment was he into and why had he received the "don't trust anyone" warning?

The address he had been given was at least two hours away from the airport.

He went to the car rental where he ended up with a full-size blue Chevy Capri. Nice car and more than he needed.

He had done his homework and had figured out the location of the address he had been given. The grey-haired attendant processing his car rental paperwork was friendly and with a yellow marker highlighted the map to the area of the address.

He was not sure how he was supposed to feel. He was a little baffled and surprised at how little information he had been given. Or should he say he had been given no information just directions?

He had a flash back to standing alone in the dark. He was certainly alone this time. He had a phone number, but he knew better than to call for general information.

He almost made a wish for the fifty caliper and the red tracers but thought better of it.

On this assignment he carried no weapon.

An hour after leaving the airport, he arrived at Skowhegan, Maine. He turned north on State Route 201. Then it was a right on a very narrow County road 43. It was so narrow that it was almost a one lane road. It was the kind of road where cars shared the single lane and went slowly by each other with their right wheels on the shoulder of the road.

The instructions then said take a left onto Rice's Corner Road, a right on Longley Rd, then go to the end. Not only was he all alone. He was sure he was lost in the backwoods of Maine.

He took the narrow single lane, white gravel road and listened to the crunching sound the tires made as he proceeded slowly as the lane took a slight uphill pitch.

The mix of large maple and oak trees provided a canopy over the lane.

Ahead, through the woods, the four windows on the side of a reddish-brown two-story brick house, crowned by a dark green shingled hip roof and a red brick chimney on the far end, became visible. It reminded Ian of the farmhouses of the rich farmers north of the Flint River, back home in Iowa.

It was truly a large and spacious well-built farmhouse. It presented itself as the lord of the yard in which it stood.

He parked the car in front of the veranda. He stood next to the car and admired the one-story veranda with its six white pillars supporting a roof that matched the roof of the house. It was an impressive house with five windows on each floor level. Ian estimated that the brick structure was probably at least one hundred years old.

As usual he was early. He would have time to reconnoiter the farmhouse, the barn, and the surrounding area.

He walked slowly around the front yard to admire the well-kept grounds and skillfully cut lawn.

The huge barn to the rear of the house drew his attention. He decided to get a better look and walked the fifty paces to the barn. The barn's hipped gambrel roof towered at least ten feet higher than the house.

The barn's double doors reached from the ground up about twelve feet to the bottom of the level where the hip roof started.

A new large commercial master padlock fastened through a heavy-duty hasp insured that no one would enter without a key. The lock hardly mattered. He could get into any barn, but he didn't need to get in at this moment.

The barn immediately brought back memories of him standing at the upper loft door of a similar barn taking bales of hay from a sloped conveyor elevator and throwing them back into the barn. It took him back to his youth and....

Back to Sam. Sam who was still back in Vietnam. Sam who had died in his arms.

Damn the barn.

Sam, his old farm buddy, and he would take turns being in the back stacking the bales of hay in the dust and switching to the elevator receiving end when they needed an "air break."

Sam who would never throw any bales of hay again.

He turned and walked back toward the house with tears in his eyes.

He walked out around the fenced perimeter of the grounds and continued to get a feel for the layout of the farm homestead.

The fencing was expertly done, and it was clear to Ian that it was well maintained. It was built with walk out areas that allowed an agile human to walk out of the fenced area but kept horses and cattle in.

Ian made a trip around the perimeter of the fencing that went around the main house area. He was impressed by the farm and its layout and the upkeep it apparently received.

He returned to his car, retrieved his coffee, and climbed the six steps up to the veranda and sat down on an Adirondack chair that faced out toward the car.

He had decided to relax and wait to see who would arrive next.

About an hour later he heard the crunching of gravel from down the lane. A few moments later he watched a black ford sedan with what he took to be government plates approach slowly and park beside the Capri.

He noted the black and white contrast of the two cars. He took the last sip of his coffee as he watched the passenger door open and a dark-haired brunette in a fashionable dark blue dress and matching jacket got out.

He was surprised to see a woman. He knew her looks would turn the heads of all the guys in any room she entered.

The driver's shoulder holstered gun caught Ian's eye as he retrieved his suit jacket from the back seat. He clearly looked like an ex-football player. His side-to-side walking gait put him in the camp of guys who think they own the path they are walking on.

He figured him for a bully.

His haircut screamed Marine, but Ian doubted he had ever served.

The most striking thing was how formally both were dressed.

She was wearing dark blue high-heeled shoes that matched her outfit.

He had spit polished black dress shoes and as he put on his dark sunglasses looked every inch to be one of the men in black from the movie of the same name.

It was clear to him that these were two professional operatives and that the two must not have expected to be coming out to a farm. If they had known, they surely would have dressed differently.

He mentally posted a gold star to the group supporting and communicating with him. They were very sparse but very effective in their communication.

Ian stood up and tucked in his long sleeved dark green plaid shirt, into his blue jeans. He looked down at his neatly polished brown leather work boots before proceeding down the six steps of the veranda.

The woman stepped around to the front of the car as if to have a clear shot at him. She had a plastic laminated identification card in hand as she introduced herself simply as Mary.

Her hazel eyes perfectly centered on her face seemed to penetrate Ian's gaze and made him wonder what lay behind them. Her knowing smile seemed to say, yeah, I know I'm good looking, take a look. And he agreed that the rest of her body was worth looking at, but he purposely avoided the invitation. He was loath to feed her ego.

Her card identified her as a CIA employee, it had her picture, title, clearance level and employee number.

John stepped up next to Mary and presented a similar card.

Impressive, Ian thought. Maybe he should show them his driver's license, but he thought better of it.

He just smiled and thanked them.

He thought of it as the country boy meeting the city slickers.

This he thought would make for a great movie scene.

He introduced himself. He just gave his name. He had no title, no clearance level, no agency. What else could he do?

Mary asked him about his assignment details.

"To be here at this moment, at this time," was his reply.

"And to trust no one," was what he thought as he looked at the two and as he maintained a neutral expression.

Mary's look clearly implied she thought he was holding out.

What are your assignment details, he inquired looking steadily back into her gaze?

Her gaze might be penetrating but he had looked into the business end of a forty-five and been on the business end of a fifty caliber. Her gaze did not match up to his. His ability to look beyond her exterior seemed to affect her. She was the one that looked away first.

Ian could not suppress a chuckle when they both gave the same answer as he had given them.

"Ok, let's go sit on the veranda chairs and swing and relax until someone who knows our assignment shows up," he suggested.

He went to the trunk of his car and took out the Styrofoam cooler he had purchased when he stopped at the small mom and pop grocery on the way to the farm. He carried it up to the veranda.

It was close to lunch time; the sky was a sparkling blue and sun had warmed the Maine air to where it was actually a comfortable November day. A bit on the nippy side but in his flannel shirt he was comfortable.

A sliced loaf of hard brown bread, a package of what he called "farmer's" salami to distinguish it from those thin little slices of "Italian cut" ones, some provolone cheese and a small jar of mayo made for a good sandwich.

A bag of red delicious apples provided a dessert. Together with a bottle of water, they could all share an impromptu picnic.

He only had one cheap plastic knife, no plates, and a roll of paper towels.

Both Mary and John accepted the offer of a sandwich and an apple. He put the sandwiches together and handed them out with a paper towel.

The conversation was minimal.

He was surprised that the two seemed uninterested in walking around to get a feel for the place.

Mary and John sat and made small talk.

He just listened.

It was clear to him that they had worked together on some previous assignments. Clearly, Mary was the brain and probably the deadly one and John was the brawn. He was also deadly but seemed less sharp than she.

He decided, neither was to be underestimated. He would heed the "trust no one" warning.

As he listened to their talk, it was clear they had already discounted him. It appeared that they had classified him as being no threat.

He liked it that way. He was just a friendly peaceful guy. The dark part of his mind just laughed.

He smiled and made a second set of sandwiches.

After lunch, as the cooler went back into the trunk, the crunching of the gravel announced the arrival of another vehicle. This time it was a plain white panel truck that looked like it would deliver some article like a mattress or some large box.

He watched as the rather thin, but steely-eyed grim-looking driver with a dark black beard that looked two or three days old got out and walked around to the back and opened up the double doors.

Four men dressed in different combinations of sports jackets, slacks, and loafers but all looking like college professors climbed out. They stretched and looked around.

He then watched as Mary and John came down from the veranda.

He walked up to the group just as Mary and John arrived.

"You must be the ones assigned to provide security. My name is Randy, and I am in charge of this operation," the driver of the truck addressed him.

He seemed irked as Mary replied.

Mary became the spokesperson for the three of them.

He stood silently by and listened and observed. It was clear the driver was the person in charge of the farmhouse and the coordination of the activities.

He seemed to know Mary.

Randy introduced the four other men as the geniuses behind a breakthrough invention.

Their security was of the utmost concern. He looked at him and made the point that the three of them were there to provide protection.

He then led the way into the house.

He stopped the group in the main entrance area. Pointing up the stairs he told Mary she had the main room with the private bath. John and he were to pick out any of the other three rooms. He would take the third.

Then he led the remainder of the group past the stairs and began to describe the layout they would all share. It was clear each would have one of the rooms on the first floor.

It was brains on the first and brawn on the second floor.

He learned that the four men had come to the farmhouse from some secret lab and would be doing some field testing of a new device.

They were perfecting a small EMF generator.

The breakthrough was in the size and power of such a device. Scientists had been working on an EMF generator for years. It was a fascinating project that captured Ian's imagination, but he was not to be part of the development.

He was on the brawn team.

It was clear that he, Mary, and John were the brawn as opposed to the scientists being the brains. They were to ensure the safety of the four.

He decided to go upstairs and pick out his room. He picked the one at the opposite end from Mary and John. Randy would be between him and the two.

Mary took the lead in establishing the protection routine. Someone would take a periodic walk around the perimeter of the area around the farmhouse. Two people would always stay with the four that were to be guarded.

She was fair about the design and had each of them take a turn around the perimeter in sequential order while the other two stayed back in the house.

He complemented her on her protection design. He suggested they also periodically swing out to the limits of the farmhouse area boundaries.

A few days later the first snow blew in. It was a heavy dense snow that seemed to fall in clumps versus snowflakes. By the time it was his turn to make the afternoon round of the grounds, the snow had accumulated to the point that it reached the bottom of the Impala's door frame. He estimated they had about ten inches of wet heavy snow.

Randy said that the snow was typical Maine weather for that time of the year.

The gas fireplace warmed the area he considered as the family room. It was the one room in the house where they seemed to spend the most of their time. The tour of the property was once an hour.

The coffee pot was the main attraction that made the kitchen the most frequented room. Coffee was always being made and consumed by everyone.

Ian spent as much time there talking to the four scientist as talking to Mary and John.

He also got to know Randy, the driver of the white van who was the manager of the operation at the house.

Randy confirmed Ian's assessment of Mary and John. He had worked with both of them before. His unpolished description of each of the two made it clear that he did not like or trust either of them.

He categorized Randy as a maneuverer that always made sure he was in the right place and position for any given situation. He was a survivor he did not rush in but followed shortly after those who did rush in.

His assessment of the situation was that there were three dangerous people and he, watching over four inventors focused on inventing something they would later want to step back from and claim scientific innocence because of their invention's destructive nature. It was akin to the development of the nuclear bomb but on a lower tier of the political scene.

A few weeks later he and Randy set up a table out in the field on the far end of the house. They put a garden tractor battery on the table and connected it to a radio control unit mounted on an aluminum box about the size of the battery.

Everyone gathered along the fence to watch the demonstration. The winter weather had ensured everyone was bundled up and had their woolen hats pulled down over their ears. The woolen scarf around Ian's neck kept the bitter cold being delivered by the light breeze from hitting the back of his neck.

One of the four professors had the controls. He looked around and asked if everyone was ready and then began his count down from five and pressed the control button.

High in the sky there was a flash that resembled a faint light blue Fourth of July firework flower burst. The delicate light blue flower burst against the dark blue of the early December sky. Its faint color gave lie to the power the device delivered.

Almost simultaneously some smoke rose from the EMF unit on the table. The control transmitter in the professor's hand burst into flames. This was followed by the explosion of the tractor battery on the table.

The entire group, including himself, dropped down on their knees in an attempt at self-protection.

After recovering from the scare, the four scientists gathered in a circle and were doing a kick dance and moving in a circle as they celebrated their success.

When the group got back inside the house, they discovered the power of the EMF device.

It became painfully apparent.

Every computer that had been on was fried.

The refrigerator and stove were fried.

The fluorescent lights were fried.

And what he thought of as the worst damage, the coffee maker was also toast.

He laughed at the brains who could think up such a weapon but forgot to protect their own equipment or think about any other damage they might perpetrate.

Perhaps they had underestimated the power of their device.

Randy was not a happy camper. He chewed out the four "geniuses" for being so "stupid."

His attitude surprised Ian.

He listened as Randy made several phone calls requesting computer replacements, ordering a new refrigerator, stove, coffeemaker, and an electrician to fix the lighting.

He was not sure who Randy had called but he must have had a team of supporters to act on his request.

The four geniuses spent the next several days in animated discussions. They were encouraged by their success and were building a new set of devices.

They all spent a cold night as they huddled under double blankets.

Randy's order of replacement equipment arrived the next day, and the electrician repaired the lighting and got the heating back on.

He, Mary, and John kept their protective vigil.

He suggested to Randy that they throw the main electrical disconnect to the house when they were getting ready for their next EMF test.

After about a dozen additional tests a prototype the size of a pint of milk was declared ready for production. It could be pointed to a specific location and when the button was pressed a faint blue blossom would appear and the EMF wave would wipe out the electronics located in that vicinity. It could now be aimed at a focused location and not take out everything in the area.

Ian imagined the disruption such a device would have in a battlefield environment. He could envision downing helicopters and jet fighters.

The field tests were over. It was time to move on to the next phase.

He, Mary, and John stood on the Veranda as the four "geniuses" boarded the white van and departed.

It was December twentieth when Mary and John led the white van out of the driveway and he followed behind.

The snow began to fall heavily as they made their way to the main highway.

The three of them had been instructed to take rooms at the Towne Motel for the night. They were to come back the next day to "scrub" the house and make sure there was no traces of what it had been used for.

He made a side trip to a hardware store to buy some materials he thought he would need.

Mary had suggested they have dinner together that evening.

He had given an excuse about not feeling all that good and declined. He let Mary and John know he would meet them the next morning at the farm.

Later that night Ian drove back to the farmhouse. He parked out by the road and walked in the back way. He entered the house through the basement.

He was there to set up the farmhouse in case he was to be part of getting the place cleaned up.

This was part of "trust no one."

The "trust no one" warning was blaring in his mind.

The term "clean up" had raised bumps on the back of his neck.

He immediately heeded his premonition.

It was well after three in the morning and the snow was still falling heavily when he got back to the hotel. He was sure all his tracks at the back of the house would now be covered and invisible.

To say it was a short night would have been an over statement. He got a cat nap in and then returned to the farm and parked in front of the farmhouse veranda. He was sitting in his car, half asleep, with the engine running to keep warm as he waited for Mary and John to arrive.

Suddenly, he saw a light blue flash go off.

The car engine died.

He realized he had been caught flat footed.

He swore under his breath.

He had been waiting with the engine running to keep the car warm.

The EMF weapon had just been used to incapacitate the car.

If the car had been off, he would never have known.

He reached over and manually opened the lock to the car door. He stepped out and closed the door and watched Mary and John approaching up the long lane on foot.

They had not driven in!

They were walking up along his car tracks. They were making sure only one set of car tracks would later be found.

Ian had guessed right. It was clean up time and more than the house was scheduled to be cleaned up. He figured that he was to be cleaned up as well.

He did not have a weapon and for an instant he wished he had one.

This was going to be trickier than he had planned.

It was apparent these two were coming in for the kill.

He hoped they planned to do him in once they were inside the house.

"Is the house clean," John asked.

"I haven't been in to check it out yet," he lied. He had it set up for his personal safety.

He noticed Mary was carrying her purse which she normally left in the car. He knew that was most likely where she had her weapon.

It was clearly clean up time, and she was packing.

"Well let's go in and make sure the place is clean before we abandon it," John said as the two got to where he was waiting for them.

He felt a sense of relief. They were both within his fighting range. If they made a threatening move, they were dead, but they just didn't know it.

He fell into step besides them.

He could tell John had his favorite weapon in his shoulder holster.

"Yep, clean up time," he thought again.

It surprised him that this was going down in this fashion. Two CIA operatives were going to do him in.

He had followed the advice given him at the beginning, "trust no one" and he was prepared.

It just made no sense to him.

He guessed that the EMF breakthrough was so important that anyone knowing about it would be eliminated.

This meant that the Mary and John were as hot as he was.

Who and how was the CIA going to handle them?

He thought he knew how and had already made the preparation to handle that situation.

He sensed some disharmony between Mary and John.

The three were supposed to be on the same side.

They had been the assigned guardians of the top-secret EMF program.

They had eaten together, talked and enjoyed each other's company.

In any other scenario they would have been friends.

He guessed the CIA had decided to eliminate him since they probably couldn't figure out who he was and who his support happened to be.

Hell, he didn't know either.

He had been given no warning about this specific situation, but he had heeded the warning, "trust no one."

If he survived this situation, he would heed that warning for the rest of his life.

He always monitored the ebb and flow of the activities around him. He had sensed this situation and was prepared.

"Well, the EMF program was very successful. Is that one of the field devices you're carrying," he inquired.

"Yeah, this is one of the prototypes. I picked it up this morning at the lab. It's one of the six ready for production testing. The next move is into the production phase.

Some production engineers will create the battlefield versions from the prototypes. The production will be handled at a secret facility somewhere. We are all out of that loop," John replied.

He noted this was more than John had said for most of the time they had worked together.

John was nervous.

He probably didn't like what he was about to do and since he had one of EMF devices it was also obvious that he was lying.

It was also immediately apparent to him that the lab was not too far away.

It was clear to him that John had orders to follow the production phase of the project.

He had no such instructions.

He knew his assignment was over but there were a few details that were yet to get done.

"Yesterday before we left, I noticed a computer in the main workroom," he volunteered.

He knew there was one there because he had put it there during the night.

Everything was supposed to have been cleared out," Mary said in a surprised tone.

They were now on the veranda stairs.

He played polite as he had always done and let Mary go ahead of him. Then he let John go up as well. Mary had the keys to the house and opened the lock.

They all walked in.

"I am going to miss this place," he said as they walked in.

"Not me, too simple and too old for my taste," John replied, "Let's go see about that computer."

"I'll wait here," Mary said as she sat down on the steps leading upstairs.

"See, I told you there was a computer in this room," he said loudly as he stepped into the room.

He immediately turned and caught John in the act of pulling out his gun. He grabbed the gun barrel by the silencer and put it up under John's chin and simultaneously pulled John's trigger finger twice.

The surprised look at that last moment told him that John had realized his mistake. If they ever met in the next life, Ian would have to ask him about it.

He caught John and pulled him over to the desk chair. He turned the chair, so it looked like John was looking at the computer screen. The computer screen could be seen from the door, but the chair was tall enough to obscure John's dead condition.

"Hey, Mary come look at what's on this computer," Ian said in his best impersonation of John's voice.

He hoped the voice impersonation was close enough to get Mary to come back. He figured she had stayed back so she would not have to participate in his assassination.

A moment later, Mary came slowly through the door with her gun drawn and at the ready. He was sure she was worried about John shooting her.

He didn't wait for her to get into the room but shot her through the door as she cautiously entered. His first shots hit her shooting arm causing her to drop her weapon. Then Ian stepped out from behind the door and shot her twice between the eyes.

He heard the voice of his Aikido master, "never talk when you are going to kill someone. Just do it."

She looked just as surprised as John. Too bad! He had gotten to like her and for a brief moment felt some remorse.

After checking both of them to make sure they were dead, Ian went quickly into the kitchen and turned on the oven as high as it would go and left the oven door open. He then went quickly down into the basement.

He had stapled an aluminum foil lining across the rafters in the basement to hide his body heat signature.

He wanted to hide his movement if there was some drone flying overhead watching.

He suspected that somewhere high in the sky a drone would be monitoring the situation in the house. It most likely had been sent to eliminate all of them. He was sure it would be watching the heat signature of the people inside the house.

If there was a drone monitoring the house he hoped that whoever was on the other end would take action before John's and Mary's heat signatures cooled.

He hoped those watching would see the three current heat signatures. The heat from the oven was intended to provide a third heat signature. Three people were scheduled to die, and he was planning to make sure that was how it would be interpreted.

He went across the basement to the exit at the far end. It was one of those exits with two exterior slanted doors covering steps leading to the outside. These doors were made of quarter inch thick steel plate. He planned to spend a few more hours in the stairwell until it got dark.

In anticipation of a bomb blast Ian put in ear plugs and flattened himself against the stairwell stone wall. The stair well was roughly eight inches wider than that of the wooden basement door.

If the drone didn't rocket the house, then Ian would burn the place down before he left.

He was prepared to wait for several hours. After that he would leave by the back route.

The CIA did exactly what Ian had anticipated.

The missile from the drone created a large crater where the house had been.

It was lucky he had been standing against the wall.

The force of the explosion ripped the door to the basement steps off its hinges and pinned him, like a salami between two slices of bread, to the wall.

The steel doors leading to the outside flapped up and then the one over him fell back down as the other one flew out toward the now slightly backward slanting barn. It had survived the bomb blast, but it would never stand straight again.

Looking through where the door hinges were peeled back but still holding the door Ian saw a huge crater.

The entire house was gone!

His car was gone!

He wondered how far it had gone or whether the force and heat had just evaporated it.

The force of the explosion had almost taken the barn down as well.

All was good. He was alive! He was temporarily pinned against the wall, but he was alive and hidden from the drone monitoring the area.

Ian was standing in the only remaining portion of the farmhouse. He was pleased the builders had built such rugged steps down into the basement.

His ears continued ringing like an insistent caller on the phone. The taste of the dust mixed with the faint smell of explosive, partnered with the vision of the hole that had once been a house, let him know that it was a miracle that he was still alive.

He reached into his pocket past the EMF generator and retrieved a chocolate power bar. He took a bite as he thought through the next steps he would take.

The CIA would presume him dead along with their operatives. Nasty leaders he thought.

He wondered about his team.

Ian leaned back and relaxed.

Being alive at this moment was the ultimate experience. He was high on adrenaline and luxuriating in the feeling.

His assignment was almost over. Putting his hand on the EMF generator in his coat pocket had triggered the need to undertake one more task that needed to be done.

He needed to get the rest of the prototypes and if possible, destroy the computers and notes associated with this project.

The action he was about to take might even save the geniuses' lives.

His legs grew numb, his back had found all the stone protrusions of the wall, and his nose was running. The sun was clearly on its way down and the cold was winning the battle against his body heat.

He figured it was time to move out. He made his way through the woods and used a pine branch to cover his tracks. Another snow would totally eliminate all signs of his passing.

He reached the small highway and found John's car.

He checked the GPS and selected *last location*. He hoped it would lead him to the new lab location and the other prototypes.

He followed the GPS instructions and map to the last location. The building looked to be an abandoned two story dark red brick factory with a long row of tall windows with eight by twelve-inch glass panels.

It had once been some sort of factory or warehouse. The fact that all the windows were intact indicated that it was in current use. The two roof mounted cameras slowly rotating back and forth verified Ian's initial assessment.

The place was active.

He drove past. Once out of sight, he parked the car. He found a gun and badge in the glove compartment with John's name on it. He left the gun but decided the badge would be handy.

He watched the cameras. They went slowly back and forth like water sprinklers would do when watering the lawn. Avoiding them would be as easy as avoiding a lawn sprinkler.

He timed the rotation and then walked briskly across the parking lot and within seconds had picked the lock leading into the building.

He scanned the area inside for surveillance cameras. He felt uneasy about not finding any. On the far side, of the large room full of old equipment and construction debris, was a new looking grey steel door.

He crossed the room and carefully tested the door. It was not locked. He opened it slightly. The door opened into a shiny newly remodeled area.

He could see two guards sitting on chairs, in front of a glass double door, located down the hall. The red tiled floor and burnt orange glazed block walls and bright light created a pleasant warm atmosphere.

He chose the direct approach and walked boldly down the hall.

"How are you guys doing," Ian asked as he walked toward them?

He pulled his badge from his belt.

"Just call me Captain John," he said showing them the badge with John's name on it, "Just checking on the security arrangements. How are you two doing?"

"No one told us about a security check," the smaller one of the two guards spoke up.

"They aren't supposed to tell you about it. If they had I would fire them," he said as the two visibly relaxed.

His behavior seemed to fit what they expected from someone giving a surprise inspection.

Where are the devices you are guarding," he continued the ruse?

"We were only told to guard the door. I guess the stuff you are asking about is inside," the larger of the two answered.

"Well, let's go and make sure everything is safe and where it should be," he said opening the door and holding it for them.

As the second guard stepped through he took the guard's gun from his holster. The first guard was just turning around when he told him to freeze. The guard was starting to react as he put the gun in the guards face and pushed the smaller guard past him.

"We can all get out of this with our lives if we act calmly," he said in a quiet tone and took the gun from the guard's hand.

"Now sit down in those chairs and don't make a move," he commanded.

His voice and threat seemed to work.

After opening several drawers, he found some blue painters' tape. Not the optimal material but it would hold them for a little while.

After securely taping their arms to the chairs and telling them not to struggle. He loaded all the computers, and anything he recognized as coming from the farmhouse onto a large flatbed cart.

"Now stay put for a short time. You don't want to come after me. It would cost you your life. Wait about thirty minutes and then see if you can get free. I will leave your weapons down the hallway." Ian said as he pushed the cart with the prototype EMF generators and the computers and notes out of the lab.

His handlers would get all but one of the EMF generators and know of his survival. Hopefully, they would not know about the one that he decided to keep for himself.

The CIA would wonder about the individual that had taken the devices and sabotaged the project. They would never find out who that person was because he had already been eliminated.

Alone, invisible. And great to be alive!

And it was Christmas. He would be home in time to celebrate with Lesley and enjoy a quiet New Year's Eve party.

He was interested in what this solution would be worth.

He would be monitoring his bank account.

3 In the Heart of Russia

*I*an looked up the escalator leading to the luggage area and felt a surge of warmth as he saw Lesley.

Almost immediately his mood changed from the grey funk he was muddling through to a sunny, warm spring breeze feeling. Her smile was sunshine, and her hug was a furnace of warmth on a cold winter day.

When Lesley asked how his trip had gone. He simply replied that it had been very successful. *"And I am alive,"* he thought as he took her hand and led the way to pick up his luggage.

Lesley led the way to their car, and he threw his luggage into the trunk. Since he was not sure of the way back home, he took the passenger seat and Lesley drove home.

Their home!

He was scheduled to officially start his work on the week between Christmas and New Year's Day. His HR contact had emphasized that this gave him a one-year head-start on his health insurance and retirement benefits.

His new boss agreed, so he spent one day in his new office before the New Year. There was one other person there and maybe a dozen in a building that normally held a thousand people.

He was a new Engineer but older than most of his coworkers and almost as old as his bosses.

His experiences gave him a very different perspective. He wanted less talk and more doing. His engineering department was short staffed for the amount of work and the projects that needed staffing.

His work focus and attitude served him well.

His first assignment put him in charge of modernizing a power and steam generation facility at one of the manufacturing sites. He was glad to have the challenge of the work. Working with the project team brought him into an environment that strengthened the barrier to the dark zone of his mind.

He and Lesley were in their early thirties. Lesley was worried about waiting too long to have children.

He was a little hesitant but looked forward to becoming the loving dad.

A few months later, when little Ella came into the world, he was extremely happy.

She was not only beautiful, but she also slept through the night!

She smiled and gurgled. She was a happy baby.

He knew life was good.

The Cincinnati spring was warm, and the trees grew green, and the flowers bloomed.

Ella seemed to go from diapers to walking in the blink of an eye. Her rapid progress in getting potty trained was welcomed by him.

Then his next problem-solving assignment came to him.

A courier delivered a package to his home. He carried the package to the dining room table and opened it.

There was an American passport with his picture issued to Dr. Demyan Kuzmenko that immediately caught his attention. Demyan was an American Professor at the University of California. He was first generation American, born to Russian emigrants.

The enclosed documents were official Russian paperwork authorizing his travel through the tundra area to observe the condition of the wolves being released and to track them to understand the condition of the repopulation program. He could find no flaw in the paperwork but then he also was no expert in what official Russian paper work looked like.

The instructions also instructed him to go on vacation on the Black Sea in July.

The instructions identified the problem as a missile development program being done in the heart of Russia that needed to be eliminated. The development lab was located along the Irtysh River. Ian had never heard of the Irtysh River, but he learned during research that it along with the Ob River made it the seventh longest river in the world.

He discovered that the river ran from China, through Kazakhstan and north through Russia to the Arctic Ocean. He was glad that the assignment was during the summer months.

During his preparation studies for the assignment, he learned about the Battle of Irtysh River fought in 657 A.D. between the Tang dynasty and the Western Turkic Khaganate. The Tang won and controlled the region for hundreds of years.

He stopped and laughed, about the fact that he wondered how any of this historic stuff would help him.

He was being sent into the land of the devil bear and he was learning Chinese history.

He found a travel guidebook that followed the river and gave him a better feel of the area. The vegetation along the banks of the river varied between marshlands, coniferous forests, and marshy wetlands. To his amazement the guidebook showed the warehouse district where the development lab was located. He was not absolutely sure of the specific warehouse where the development facility was located but he got the lay of the river waterfront.

He made his travel arrangements.

He arranged to do a workshop in the Zwichau manufacturing plant in East Germany. This would put him a short train ride away from the Black Sea.

He would carry out his legitimate business and then proceed to his problem-solving assignment.

He scheduled vacation for Demyan on a beach on the Black Sea near the town of T'bilisi.

The work session at the Zwickau plant took exactly one week. He said goodbye to the plant manager as Ian Sinclair.

He took the taxi to the train station and boarded the train to T'bilisi. He traveled into T'bilisi as Ian Sinclair but checked into his hotel as Demyan Kuzmenko.

The next day he boarded the train to Omsk. It would be a long train ride, but it would be less conspicuous than using the airline.

Omsk, a beautiful city of more than one million people, was one of the largest cities in Siberia.

The problem-solving assignment lay another hundred miles to the north. This was the part of the journey that was Ian's biggest concern.

He was a professor from the US studying the success or failure of the "wolf population re-wilding" effort being carried out in hopes of reducing global warming. It sounded farfetched, but it provided the cover he needed to go wandering around the wilderness. Ian had all the official paperwork to authorize his movements. He hoped his team had done a good job in making the documents look official and real.

He left Omsk on a river freighter traveling north toward Tobolsk.

The missiles were being developed in one of the local ship building plants located there.

Ian would need to determine which one and then figure out how to penetrate the security that would be in place. He had no illusions about the huge risk he was taking.

He would "trust no one." This was his takeaway from his first assignment.

The boat ride would take him by the shipyard-warehouse thought to house the missile development program. He spent the slow trip upriver sketching the river side scenery. He hoped anyone watching this strange Russian American would see that he was truly interested in the landscape and the animals seen along the riverbank.

The ship's Captain stopped by several times to "practice his English" and to see how his main passenger was enjoying himself.

Ian wanted to be able to look closely at everything along the bank without being too obvious when the boat went by the shipyards. He would closely scrutinize the shipyard looking for the weak spots in the security.

The boat he was on would make a four day stop at Tobolsk to unload goods and take on additional consignments.

He inquired about a bed and breakfast that he might utilize while he waited for the boat to continue.

One of the riverboat crew recommended a house a few blocks from the river.

He inquired about the price.

The crewman thought it would be around a thousand rubles, maybe a little more but he said it was worth it just for the food that was offered with the room.

He followed the instructions of the crewman.

He was sure that there was someone that would be watching but he did not sense or see anyone following him. He spotted the small sign for the bed and breakfast pointing inward between two multistory older homes.

He followed it back to an open central courtyard.

Ther he took in the neat arrangement of large, tiered pots forming a central cone four pots high and then an outside circle of pots three tiers high that filled the gaps between three sturdy benches made from three-inch-thick oak or some similar hardwood.

The older white-haired woman with a headscarf tied under her chin immediately caught his eye. She looked a lot like a grandmotherly "babushka."

He knew little to no Russian, so he handed her the note the captain had written and in English asked if she had a room available to rent.

"You have a Russian name, but you speak English. What kind of mother would raise her son and not teach him his root language?

Yes, I have a room. Follow me," she said in broken English as she gave him back the card with the ship captain's note.

You are right. I should have learned some Russian, but my mother was American, my father was Russian.

"Follow me. If you like the room, you pay in advance. How long will you stay," she asked?

She wiped her hands on a wet cloth and led the way into the house.

"The boat I am on will take about four days. I only have a few days before I need to go into the wilderness to see how the wolf population is doing," Ian replied.

"You hunt wolves," she asked?

She slowly climbed the four flights of stairs to a room that was just below the roof rafters and had a window that looked out toward the courtyard. It lined up almost directly with the walkway that he had walked in to reach the courtyard.

"The bathroom is down one floor. It is shared by one other room. Do you want it," she asked?

"Yes, this is fine. How much," he asked as he put down his knapsack.

"Twelve hundred fifty ruble per day and you get a hearty breakfast," she replied.

This was within the range the sailor had mentioned. She seemed to be giving him a fair price.

He liked her attitude. She seemed to know he was not who he was trying to appear to be. He just wondered what she thought he was up to.

"Is there a simple restaurant where one can get a decent meal," Ian asked as he took out his leather bag where his money was kept?

"Tonight, I am cooking Beef Stroganov and cooked vegetables.

You are welcome. The cost is two hundred rubles.

There is a sandwich store about two blocks from here and a small restaurant across the street from it. You will have to go several kilometers farther if you want anything else," she replied as she watched him take out his money.

"Let me pay you for a week. I would love to eat at your table tonight. Tomorrow I will walk around and get a feel for the neighborhood.

May I sit out in the courtyard and finish up some of the sketches I have started," he asked as he took out his sketch book?

"You hunt wolves, and you draw," she asked in a speculative voice and raised her eyebrows as she took the money.

"No, I study the wolves. I draw them too. I am studying the efforts of repopulating Siberia with them. My name is Demyan," Ian said as he showed her some drawings of wolves in the wilderness.

Then he flipped to the river scenes.

"Ah, you are a strange one. You have many talents. I am sure you are also a master storyteller. I am called Raya," she said with an amused look.

"Demyan, I will call you to dinner in about an hour," she said as she turned to leave.

Ian unpacked his belongings. His camera and sketch pad were his field tools. His clothes were basic hiker's shirt and pants. His official paperwork rounded out the contents of what he carried. He was traveling light, and everything was of local make.

He had left a suitcase in the train station in Syerdlovsk with his western clothes. He would go back there after solving his problem and transform back and be a westerner on his departure.

He leaned out the window and studied the roof. The buildings were close enough together making it possible to get away if it proved necessary. He planned to look this over more closely after it got dark.

He took a change of clothes and went down to the bathroom. He hoped she provided guest towels.

A quick shower, clean clothes prepared him for the evening.

He took his pencils and sketch book to the courtyard.

He put a few obligatory pencil strokes to the wilderness drawings. Improved a few riverside sketches and then went to the drawings of the shipyard.

Periodically, he looked up and watched Raya working in the kitchen. There didn't seem to be anyone else in the house. After dinner, he would ask about a tour of the house. He needed to get a better understanding of his surroundings.

He did a sketch of Raya doing her cooking in the kitchen. It was an eye-catching scene framed by the open door and window opening into the courtyard. Raya was focused on cutting vegetables. The sound of her knife rapidly cutting through the vegetable augmented the blur of her rapidly moving hand.

He would give the sketch he was creating to her before he left.

Soon the great smells coming into the courtyard from the kitchen made him want to come to the table. He was eager to get inside and eat whatever Raya was cooking.

Finally, Raya came to the courtyard door and announced that it was time for dinner.

Ian closed his drawing pad and eagerly followed her in.

There were only two places set at the table.

"Yes, I have no other guests. My husband died about six months ago. He was the one who went to the riverfront bars and recruited the men to stay at our house. It has been hard, but I will get by," Raya said as Ian sat down at the place she indicated.

Ian got an inspiration that he thought would help Raya. He would act on it tomorrow.

It would provide the perfect cover for him to wander along the waterfront.

"Would you be willing to provide breakfast and dinner for anyone just wanting to eat here," Ian asked quietly?

"Yes, for a price; just like I charged you. And if they stay here, breakfast is included but dinner is extra," Raya said firmly.

Ian showed her the picture he had drawn of her cooking in the kitchen.

"That is very good. "May I have it," she said as she held the notebook in her hand.

"Yes, I will give it to you when I am done. I am going to make a series of small ones.

I will put down your address, the cost of staying here and the cost for dinner. It will invite people to eat here even if they chose not to stay.

Tomorrow, I will put them in all the bars along the river that are within reasonable walking distance," Ian said as he watched her reaction.

"Why would you do this," she asked looking suspiciously at Ian.

"Because you are my Raya," he said.

He was playing with the meaning of her name, which in Russian meant friend.

"You are a good storyteller, and you seem to have a good heart," she replied as she picked up her plate and took it to the sink.

"Would it be possible to take a tour of the house? And may I sit in the living room or maybe at the kitchen table to do some work later," Ian asked as she returned trying to give him more food.

"No, thank you," Ian said as he kept her from serving him more.

"Yes, I will show you around. You can use the living room and the kitchen.

However, after nine you must be quiet. This is the time I go to sleep. If you make too much noise, I will let you know," she said as she took the food back to the stove.

"Let's do the tour now and then I will come back and clean the kitchen," she said as she led the way toward the front of the house.

Ian followed her to the entry that opened to the street. This was opposite the entry leading to the courtyard.

It was quite a large old home, with an entry foyer with a sitting room to one side and a formal dining room on the other. The other entry to the dining room was from the kitchen. Stairs went up from the sitting room side of the foyer.

The master bedroom was over the dining room and there were two more small bedrooms and a bathroom on the second floor.

The next floor up had three small bedrooms and the bathroom Ian had used earlier. The backstairs came up opposite the bathroom. The stairs then went up to the floor where his room was located.

"Your room is the biggest and has the best view," Raya said as if she had been asked.

"It is a very big house. I noticed there was only one way into the courtyard in back. Is the courtyard yours," Ian asked?

"Yes, long ago there were no other homes around this house. Over the years the owners sold their property. When our family got the property, it was surrounded as it is today and only the passageway out to the street is still ours…mine," Raya said correcting herself.

It was clear to Ian that Raya was still adjusting to the loss of her husband.

Later in evening after Raya was asleep, Ian tested the roof and crossed along the peak to the other building. He located a steel vent pipe on an inward corner of the building and located the fire escape that went down to the street by the entrance walkway.

Ian easily jumped the walkway gap and checked out the other building where he located another fire escape.

He was making sure he had several escape routes just in case he needed them.

The next morning after a sausage and egg breakfast, Ian took his sketchbook and began wandering along the waterfront.

He was sketching as he went.

He stopped at each place, ordered a coffee and then he showed the proprietor or the person that seemed in charge the six-by-nine-inch drawing advertising Raya's Bed and Breakfast and asked them if he could post it. He was well received in most places, and he left a good tip at each.

He slowly made his way up the river all the way to the boat building site he suspected held the missile development effort.

He easily picked up the surveillance cameras following him and noted their locations. It was obviously the place he was looking for since it was the only warehouse along the waterfront with surveillance cameras.

He was glad to have a legitimate reason for walking the area. By lunch time Ian was about a kilometer downriver from the building of interest. He had just put up an advertisement when two muscle men collared him.

"You are not from around here. What are you doing here," the bigger one asked as he held him by the arm?

"I am Demyan Kuzmenko, a US citizen. I am on the way to study the wolf population in the Tundra," he said as he lightly pushed on the offending arm.

The hand was removed.

"Please show us your passport and do you have papers authorizing you to be here," he asked?

"Yes, but who are you," he asked as he looked directly into the eyes of his inquisitor?

He wanted the two to see he was not going to be pushed around.

The other guy was just standing by in a more or less relaxed posture, but his hand was near his chest.

"We are FSB," the bigger one said with the voice of authority.

"Do you have any papers," Ian said looking him straight in the eyes.

The hand near the arm pit moved into his vest pocket and pulled out a badge.

It was apparent that both men were armed and that they were truly official.

Ian reached into his jacket pocket and pulled out his passport and the papers describing his mission.

"What do you look for when you are studying the wolf," the larger of the two asked after a moment of reading?

"I see if they are surviving, if they have young pups, I count the size of their packs," Ian explained.

"It's a great way to get away from the wife," he joked.

That seemed to lighten the moment.

"How long will you be here," the quiet one asked?

"I am waiting for the freight ship I am on to unload and then take on their next load. When they are done, I will move on with them to the Gulf of Ob. The captain estimated unloading and loading would take about four days," he replied.

"Why are you putting up signs for Raya's Bed and Breakfast," the smaller of the two asked as he looked at the drawing Ian had just posted.

Ian said he was staying there. He had learned that Raya's husband had died and that she had lost most of her business. This was his good deed to help her.

"This is very generous of you. Let me warn you not to drink at Egor's pub. That is the place they "recruit" river hands on Sunday nights," the smaller quiet one advised.

Ian had been to Egor's pub to put up a sign. Egor had not let him do it. Ian could easily believe Igor would be in that kind of business.

He thanked both of them for their advice.

Ian ordered a beer and went out to a table that looked down the street toward the boat dock. The two FSB agents got into a black car and drove back toward the boat building facility with the cameras.

Ian could not find any surveillance cameras this far away. He was sure the two had come down looking for him after the camera crew had observed him.

He was also sure that his passport number would now be getting checked out. He was counting on his team to be good with the paperwork, but he was going to proceed as quickly as possible.

He continued walking and looking for more restaurants and bars.

He approached the boat building facility down a road that came out exactly at the front gate. He found two bar restaurants one block away from the main gate. He visited each and put up the advertisements.

Then he walked one street away as if looking for more restaurants.

Ian walked one block past the end of the facility and turned down toward the river. There were several waterfront businesses as well as bars.

He stopped in a bar with a river front drinking area and ordered a beer. From this vantage point he could study the upriver side of the building housing the missile system.

The downriver side had another boat building facility as a neighbor. Ian had scouted it from the downriver side and found it to be wide open. He would go tonight and approach from that direction to see if there was a way in from there.

He doubted there would be.

A wayward log floating down the river revealed what Ian had feared he would find. The log floated in toward the dock area. It must have triggered a sensor.

A spotlight on the roof came on. It revealed a machine gun emplacement on the roof.

The two guards there just monitored the log and watched it bump into the end of the pier and then float on down the river.

The light went back out.

Ian noticed the black car leaving the facility and slowly driving away past him. He got the license number and watched it go straight on down the street. He could see the bridge across the river, and he saw the black car drive across.

He retrieved his hidden duffel and made a call to a phone number that had accompanied his problem-solving orders.

He needed to know where the two guards resided, so he asked his team to get him the addresses.

He walked back to Raya's Bed and Breakfast. His phone rang as he entered the walk to the courtyard. He stopped and listened as the information he needed came through.

"You have already been successful. I have two new guests. Each paid for a week, and they plan on staying for several months. Tonight, dinner is free for you," Raya said with new energy in her voice.

"I am glad that I could help," Ian said as he received a hug from her.

That evening Ian left by the roof and climbed down the fire escape of the first building.

He went to the waterfront and found a cab to take him across the river to the address he had been given.

He took a cab to a nearby address. He paid for the cab and asked him to wait on the main street and gave him money to wait.

The address to the security guard's house took him to a small Tudor style home located down a smaller street.

He walked down the street to the address. No dog was present so the doggy treat he had brought along would not be needed. Ian made his way around the house and noted there did not seem to be an alarm system.

He found the door lock easy to pick and thankfully the door hinges were well oiled.

There was just enough light for him to see. He looked for the familiar place to drop the wallet and all the official cards. Sure enough, there on an entrance table was the ID card and a second key card.

He pocketed the two and left the same way he had come in. The back door locked as easily as he had unlocked it.

He picked up his shoes and went to the corner where he slipped them on and walked to the main street where he took the cab back to Egor's pub.

Total elapsed time six minutes and a few seconds.

"Not bad for a novice burglar," He thought to himself.

He had picked Egor's place out of spite.

He went in and ordered a beer.

He then started a raucous fight by declaring one of the boatmen a coward and that he had an atrocious smell.

He tripped the attacking boatman and sent him flying across the table of two men drinking beer with chasers.

Once the fight started, he faded to the background and left just as the police arrived in force.

He walked to the gate of the shipyard. He had a hooded sweatshirt on. He was sure they would later be able to easily identify him. But for now, he hoped they would be slow in their reaction.

The key card got him in, and he proceeded to look both ways down two crossing hallways. There was a light coming from one of the rooms to his left. He quickly proceeded to the room with the light. He figured it would be the night watch.

Ian looked in and showed the guard facing him the ID card he had in his left hand. He stepped toward the guard and just as he was about to say something. He hit him in the side of his head with the heel of his hand. The guard was still standing as Ian made his way past him and caught the second watchman as he turned in his chair.

Both guards were out. He put each guard back in his chair and taped them in and then taped both back-to-back. He finished the job by taping their mouths shut.

He had brought his own supply of duct tape. He hoped to use all of it. The more he used the fewer people would die.

There was a layout of the warehouse on the wall. Ian studied it and found there were three additional night watch offices and the riverside gun tower.

He made his way to each watch office and quickly incapacitated the people that he found there. He felt very good to have taken out the three offices without any real resistance.

It was obvious these folks did not expect anyone to try to break in.

He approached the roof cautiously. He carefully cracked open the door leading onto the roof. He could see the square platform of the gun tower.

The gun tower guards were sitting looking out toward the river and quietly talking.

The flat roof was a tar and gravel surface. Ian did not want to try to cross to the tower. He was sure he would make too much noise.

He would instead see if he could get the guards to come to him.

He coughed and then he let the stairway door slowly go closed.

Both guards stood up and walked toward the door. When the first guard opened the stair way door, Ian pulled him all the way in and closed the door. He launched the guard down the stairs.

He then let the door go and pulled in the second guard and hit him in the throat just hard enough for him to momentarily be unable to breathe.

He went sliding down the metal stair railing and quickly taped the wrists of the recovering guard.

"Relax and breathe slowly," he said quietly.

The second guard had recovered and came charging down the stairway as he tried to get his gun free from its strapped down position.

Ian reached up and pulled him toward him and hit him on the back side of the neck. The guard went out cold.

After securely taping the second guards' hands behind his back, He pulled both down a well waxed tile hallway to the closest surveillance office.

He made sure everyone was still well secured before making his way to the missile development area.

Ian knew that his action would have little impact on the development of smart missiles. He was sure his mission was more about tweaking the Russian leaders about the vulnerability of one of their most secret projects than stopping the actual development of the missiles.

He wiped all the computers' memories, their file allocation tables and then magnetized them.

He loaded all the computers, and all the records he could find, the missiles and their guidance system into one of the large river boat hulls.

He then filled the hull with a supply of dry lumber and doused everything with gasoline. He launched the boat with a cloth napkin burning on a piece of dry lumber with its tail in a puddle of gas.

Ian figured he had about ten minutes before there was a huge fire ball floating down the river. He pulled all the guards into the hallway leading to the front door.

He then used the can of gasoline he had found in the development area and poured a stream along all the hallways and the watch rooms.

He was ready to finish the job. He pulled all the guards outside and across the empty street. He then threw a burning wad of paper into the building.

Ian walked up away from the river as the place went up in flames. It lit up the entire neighborhood. At almost the same time the boat on the river burst into flames.

It was a grand scene.

The missiles exploded in a climactic scene that mirrored a fourth of July river barge fire and explosion of all the fireworks on the Ohio River that Ian had witnessed.

He returned to the building he had climbed down by Raya's B&B. He climbed back up and went into his room.

He was not staying.

The entire neighborhood was now up and running toward the fire.

He gathered his things. He took the drawings of Raya and penned a note thanking her for a good stay and put it on the kitchen table with a significant tip.

He went back up to his room and left by the window. He went to the other building.

The FSB guys must have done their homework. Ian caught a glimpse of them coming up the narrow walkway toward Raya's B&B.

He went to the drainpipe at the corner of the building and slid down. He walked by the end of the entrance walkway. The black car was sitting at the corner. It had the keys in it. He got in, turned on the car.

He saw the two come out to the street as he drove away. He drove across the bridge and headed toward Syerdlovsk. He hoped the two would not have the police chase him.

"There goes our car. Should I call the police for help," the larger of the two asked?

"Are you kidding, he would end up killing them. He was in my house and took my security card. I thought he seemed very sure of himself when we confronted him. I wonder who he is?

He could have killed all the guards, but he made sure they were all safe before setting the fire. I really hope he gets out, so we don't have to answer any questions about why we didn't bring him in when we first stopped him and why he was able to take our car," the quiet one replied.

Ian drove carefully and was pleased that there was no pursuit. He reached the train station area of Syerdlovsk.

He found an old, abandoned house and drove the car into the garage. He caught a cab to the train station, got his bag, changed into his business suit, and took the train back to T'bilisi.

Two days later he flew from T'bilisi to Frankfurt and caught a flight to California.

He was looking forward to getting home, so he caught a red eye special to Cincinnati and arrived early on a Saturday.

Lesley had the coffee brewing and after a hug she fixed breakfast.

Ella was still sleeping.

Ian gave Lesley a kiss and thanked her for a great breakfast.

Lesley sat down and said she had two surprise announcements.

The first was that she knew of a home that was part of a divorce agreement. It was up for sale at a bargain price. She had gone and taken tour and said it would be perfect for them.

Ian of course agreed to go look at it when she asked if he would go with her later in the day.

The second announcement was that she was pregnant.

Ian sat and let the news soak slowly through.

Lesley was expecting more excitement and asked if he was OK with that.

He stood up and pulled her to him and gave her a hug and a kiss.

Of course, he was. He was slowly covering the black space in his mind with more glowing warm blankets.

4 Of Elephants and Ivory

*I*an was significantly older than most new company hires. His ability to operate successfully on significant projects on his own soon had him traveling the world to manage improvement projects or to coach site leadership to make production improvements.

He became a coach to multiples site leadership teams that he strategically selected. Three sites were in Asia, three were in Europe and three were in the Americas.

His sites were top performers in their key business success measures. He was sought after by many other sites.

He found it ironic that he was known as a master at helping the sites solve their organizational and production problems and that he was a problem solver in what he called his dark world side.

Lesley, through her legal connection found what she saw as a unique opportunity to buy a home in Indian Hill one of the premier communities that surrounded Cincinnati. The house was part of a divorce proceeding. The home was up for sale to facilitate splitting the assets in question.

He went along with Lesley's suggestion, and they purchased the home at a depressed market value. Lesley thought she was spending well beyond their income, but he seemed to have a bank account that always grew to meet his needs.

The home was decadent in his evaluation, but Lesley loved it. This was all he needed to know. There was enough money in his bank account that they could have paid out right for it, but he chose not to be too obvious about his financial situation and took a thirty-year mortgage out instead. Lesley said she would later pay it off.

He was sitting in the great room watching Ella and Matt. Ella was now three and Matt had just turned one. He stood up and walked around the great hand tucked rug in the center of the great room that the kids were sitting and playing on.

He looked up at the vaulted ceiling rising a good twenty feet above him and the sectioned twelve-foot-high windows running around the entire room. Through the windows he took in the waterfall cascading down from the hot tub perched like a small volcano over the main pool.

He smiled and quietly said, "Decadent."

Just beyond the pool was an immaculate putting tee. The special spongy green grass seldom needed cutting. Ian thought of the irony that he didn't like or play golf, but he often stood where he was standing and watched Lesley practicing her putting.

Decadent.

The tennis court on the other side of the great room was not quite as useless to him. He played a little with Lesley though she almost always easily beat him at the game.

Decadent.

His plush recliner sat directly in front of a six-foot-high fireplace framed in by sturdy thick shelves on both sides. It took up the entire back wall.

He looked down to the floor in-front of the fireplace at an inlayed picture depicting a merry gathering with people eating, talking, and dancing.

Decadent.

He thought about the inlaid drawings in the floor of each of the main rooms that depicted the purpose of that room.

Decadent.

Really decadent but he had to admit to himself that he enjoyed all of it. He would, however, never get use to this opulence.

He thought about the poverty he had grown up in and contrasted it to his current lifestyle.

He was getting good at changing diapers. Ella had been out of diapers after just a year. Now it was Matt, he was diapering. Matt was just turning one, but it was clear to him that Matt would not be as quick as Ella at getting out of the diapering phase.

The kids so far were fall babies.

Matt was a happy baby, but he refused to sleep for the entire night. Ian was often sleeping with Matt on his shoulder on the great chair in front of the fireplace when Lesley woke him in the morning and asked if he was ready for some coffee.

The rhythm of their lives seemed to have settled into a nice consistent pattern.

This worried him since he saw and followed all the problems happening in the world. He knew it was only a matter of time before he was once again activated.

And his premonition seemed to come true on the following day.

He was listening to the news about the elephant ivory poaching in Africa when the announcer said, "We need a problem solver to resolve this problem."

His breath stopped as if he had been hit by a lightening stroke. This could not be a coincidence. How would he know if it was a message to him?

Not long after the newscast he received a brief message by phone. "Watch the news about poaching, the message is for you."

He wondered where in Africa he would be going.

A box arrived and in it was the information about his next problem-solving assignment. The passport that was in the box let him know that he would be Mathew Parker. He was to be a cameraman and field editor for the pictures he took. The information included the kind of cameras he would be expected to be able to use.

He called around and found a camera shop that was willing to give him training on the cameras that he was expected to use.

Lesley asked about his sudden interest in photography and he told her about his next problem-solving assignment. He was to disrupt the Ivory trade in Tanzania.

He felt relieved when all Lesley said was that he should be careful.

It triggered his own internal comment of, "and trust no one."

His research into the ivory trade was disheartening. He discovered that more than thirty-three thousand elephants were killed for their tusks each year. It was hard for him to imagine that number.

He had not realized that there were that many elephants to begin with.

He compared this with the automobile accident death rate in the US at thirty-seven thousand out of a driving population of two hundred million licensed drivers.

There were not that many elephants!

The customers for the ivory were mostly the wealthy in Asia. Ivory made a strong social statement for them.

Much of the money made by the ivory traffickers financed the insurrections taking place in the countries of Africa.

Much of it enriched the local strongmen.

And much of it went to greedy individuals.

Ian saw it as a soulless endeavor that had a market of thoughtless buyers.

The only trade worse than that of trafficking animal parts was that of trafficking drugs.

Both were evil practices. And both relied on willing, paying customers.

A few days later, Ian received an invitation to participate in a National Geographic documentary on the poaching of the wild game of Africa.

The invitation was addressed to Mathew Parker.

He was surprised that he would be part of such a prestigious team. He was pleased to receive a formal invitation. This was one of the few times he showed Leslie something about his problem-solving assignment.

She held up the invitation and said she was impressed and gave him a kiss on the cheek. He knew that was a way for her to say thank you.

He was really nervous about how well he would fit on the film crew team. Ian didn't have a clue what he was supposed to do but this would be the cover for any other action that he took.

He wondered what the team that he would support had been told.

He always wondered who his supporters in the world of problem solving might be. He had one and only one meeting with the one person he thought of as his handler. It had been several years now, and he could not even recall this handler's looks.

But his two bank accounts had been kept full.

His personal account had several million in it and his business account never went below a million.

Money was not an issue.

The instruction was to stop the poaching of elephants on the Maasai Mara National game preserve.

He flew into New York to meet the National Geographic team. He had been invited to a dinner meeting by the team leader, Andria Miller.

They had talked briefly on the phone and he had gotten the impression that she was not enthusiastic and had questioned his presence on the team.

At the dinner Andria came right to the point. "You came very highly recommended. In fact, it was a deal that I could not refuse. Tell us a little about yourself and your specialty," she pointedly asked.

From the tone in her voice, it was clear to him that she had been pressured to take him onto her team.

He had no specialty in this field, and he was not going to try to fabricate one. He chose to plead ignorance, admit to no skill and put himself at the mercy of the team.

"I am Mathew Parker, I solve problems. I don't have a clue about what you all do but I am willing to learn or if you want, I will carry your bags. I have been assigned the task of determining how to stop the poaching of elephants that is taking place."

You and your team are documenting a leading problem in the world, the poaching of Elephants and Rhinos. I am to analyze the problem and if possible, produce short-and long-term solutions to this problem. I can't think of a better way to understand the situation than to be out in the field with professionals like all of you," Ian replied to Andria's question.

"You have been accepted on the team as a cameraman and film editor. I hope you are up to it. Mike will give you the basics of handling a camera. You better get good in a very short period. I would hate to fire you when we are out in the field and have you standing in the middle of nowhere by yourself," Andria fired back.

Ian wasn't sure if she was serious or just joking. By her looks and tone, he figured she was not joking.

"Sure thing, I will make sure the lens cover comes off before I start taking pictures," Ian replied with a grin.

He was glad that he spent the last three months on his photo lessons and on all the equipment being taken to the field. He felt confident he knew the basics.

He hoped he would have the eye for taking the film shots this group was famous for.

"We have two more days before our flight. I can go over all the equipment we will be taking and give you the basics of it all," Mike volunteered.

"Thanks Mike. I think that's a great idea," Ian replied even though he gave a mental groan.

His first impression of Mike was positive. He would make sure that Andria got a good report on his capability.

"I thought you were going to help me with the copy and the editing," Mary Everston spoke up from her side of the table where she was sitting next to Mike.

"I will be pleased to do that as well. I hope you do that before Andria sends me out for close shots of the lions," Ian said.

He looked over to see how Andria was taking in the team conversation.

Her neutral facial expression spoke volumes. He was sure she had been told to take him on and do the best she could.

Her look warned him not to play poker with her.

He would, however, work on winning her over.

It was a busy two days as Mike went over all the equipment with Him. He had taken lessons on every camera that Mike went over and was sure in his ability to handle them.

He also went over editing with Mary. Her lessons were basic, and Ian listened carefully.

Editing was totally new to him. It was clear that one needed a mental vision of what made a good scene and picture. He focused on and worked on remembering Mary's criteria for a good scene.

What came clear to him was that getting close in detailed shots made the editing easier. He was not sure what Mary's report back to Andria would be.

Two days later the team left New York on their way to Africa via Germany.

A long twenty hours later after a layover in Frankfurt, the team landed in Dar Es Salaam, Tanzania.

There they took a short hop on another flight to Dodoma.

It had taken almost two full days to get to this destination. The trip seemed even longer than the two days of flying.

He would have had to search diligently to find an ounce of humor in the travel worn team at the time of their arrival.

He was in an upbeat mood. The team was well versed in world affairs, and they were good conversationalists.

Only Andria remained quiet and stand offish.

Their local guide met the team at the airport with a flatbed truck. There was a ton of equipment that went on the flat bed. A separate van stood by to transport the team.

Even with several local laborers, it took almost an hour to load the truck and carefully secure all the equipment being taken to the field.

Andrea and Mike presided over the loading.

The team finally left the field two hours later and headed out on A 104. The city of Dodoma slowly receded behind them as a long tiring ride loomed ahead of them.

He rode in the front seat of the van with the guide and driver. He engaged them in conversation about the elephants and rhinos. He was interested in hearing about the elephant's movement and the actions of the poachers, and the rangers involved in protecting the elephants.

He learned a great deal during the long and bumpy ride. He would periodically hear a quiet conversation in the back of the van but most often the three in back were sleeping.

The team's destination was an old plantation ranch near the town of Ngorongoro, located near Lake Magadi.

A smaller lake just south of Lake Magadi was where a small herd of elephants were known to reside.

By the time they arrived he had gotten a much better sense of the poaching situation.

It was almost a purely economic issue. There was little work and the pay for legitimate work was miniscule. Poaching was a way to make some rather significant money. Individuals could earn more on one poaching trip than they could if they worked a normal job for the whole year. In a country with thirty-percent unemployment, poaching was an attractive activity. It kept many families fed.

There was not much he would be able to do about the current economic situation. His solution would be purely short term.

The leaders of the country had to turn elephants into a tourist trade and take care of the long term.

He took in the panoramic view of the rambling, high walled, one-story ranch house, with a grass thatched roof against the backdrop of the waist high patchy green and tan grasses that stretched as far as the eye could see and were dotted with high Marula and Baobab trees in all directions.

He immediately fell in love with the location. He felt connected with the original builders of the ranch house. He felt a part of the terrain and the land beyond.

He felt a sense of belonging.

The ranch site itself was an oasis ringed in by old Marula trees that shaded the house. It appeared the small cottage behind the house had been added some time after the original ranch site construction. It was much closer to the ring of trees than any other structure.

The yellow golf ball sized Marula fruits could be seen hanging on the branches of the trees. A water well with an old-style crank and a bucket tied to a rope was located between the house and cottage. The external cooking area came into view as the Land Rover and flatbed truck came to a stop.

He stepped out of the van and absorbed the feelings, sounds and the sweet aroma of the fruit. It felt right, smelled right and the rustle of the grasses and the twitter of birds sounded right.

He closed his eyes and became a willing sponge for all the feelings.

The interior of the ranch house was very open, and the natural upward flow of warming air kept the main room cool. The kitchen was outside by the water well and was accessible through a central hall. The bedrooms went around the main central room. The team was given a tour and shown the choices of bedrooms.

The small cottage behind the main building was reached by going past the detached kitchen. An alternative way was to approach it from the parking area.

He chose to bunk in the cottage because it would make it easier for him to come and go at night if the need came up. He felt lucky that no one contested him for the cottage.

Over dinner, the team discussed doing a reconnaissance of the area to get a bearing on the approach they would take to get the film footage for the documentary.

He spent the evening preparing himself in how to use the small handheld camera and a larger shoulder camera.

He had asked his problem-solving support team for a long-range sniper rifle and a healthy supply of C4 but neither had yet arrived.

The next morning after a light breakfast, he and the rest of the team boarded an open-topped Range Rover.

He took in the wide expanse of the savanna and again let it overwhelm his mind. The grass land was sprinkled with the tall Baobab trees. A sprinkling of gazelle and zebra and an occasional giraffe came into view as they drove slowly across to where their guide thought a small herd of elephants had lately made their home.

he was standing in back with Mike. They were both holding onto the roll bar. The view was breath taking and the ride exhilarating.

He pulled out his field glasses to investigate a flash of light in the far distance. He closely studied two trucks that could be clearly made out in his binocular. He noted their license plates and the brand of the two trucks.

"Those are probably the trucks of some poachers," the driver replied to hiss question of who the trucks belonged to.

"Where do they come from," he asked the driver.

"I think this group comes from Singida, there is a small airport there that is used by the group. There are three competing poachers who hunt in this area. Another smaller but very powerful group operates out of Makuyuni," the driver volunteered.

"They each come from a different community where they have almost complete control. The rangers fear to confront them. Three rangers have been killed. Many of the rangers are afraid for themselves and their families," the driver continued.

"Do the poachers compete with each other or just for the animals they take," Ian asked?

"Yes, they compete, but they have more or less divided the preserve into three areas to keep from confronting each other too often. The strongest group is the one from Makuyuni. They are better equipped and have the most aggressive leader.

"How many elephants are there on the preserve," Andria asked.

She was sitting in the front seat and had been listening to Ian's line of questioning.

There are probably around a few thousand. It is hard to know exactly," the driver replied.

The driver pointed ahead to a small group of elephants as they came into view. There were two males, several females and two small ones.

The driver stopped the Land Rover.

Ian hopped out and picked up his small handheld camera. He walked slowly toward the elephant group.

He stopped at one pile of elephant dung and took a handful and spread it strategically on his closes. This was a camouflage trick he had learned when he was growing up on the farm in Iowa. By the time he was done rubbing on the dung, he was close to the small herd of elephants. He hoped he smelled like one of them.

The youngest bull elephant came rather quickly toward him to investigate. He stood very still but continued to shoot the film of the young bull coming toward him. The young bull stopped just short of him. He seemed surprised that the animal before him had not moved and probably that he smelled like one of his group.

Ian kept the camera rolling.

He could hear Andria frantically shouting in the background, but he could not hear what she was saying.

The young bull elephant reached slowly out with his trunk and sniffed Ian's clothing. He snorted, turned, and walked back toward the rest of elephant group.

He assumed he was accepted by the elephant herd and followed. He felt he was getting some great footage. He was up close as Mary had repeatedly suggested for great shots to edit.

He checked to make sure he had the lens cover off. He turned to look back at the Land Rover and held up his lens cover and waved.

He could see that Andrea was using binoculars and that Mike had set up his tripod on the hood of the Land Rover.

He raised his camera higher and separately showed her the camera lens.

He hoped she would appreciate his joke.

For the next hour he followed the elephants and took footage of their interaction. He was certain that the individual animals somehow communicated with each other.

The two small elephants repeatedly came over to him. They seemed curious about what he was doing and played with him and his equipment. He enjoyed their interaction and felt comfortable after one of the female elephants came over and seemed to accept him in a friendly manner.

He was doing a running commentary as he walked along with the herd. After being checked out a second time by one of the females, he seemed to be accepted by the rest and ignored.

The Land Rover followed slowly along.

He decided that he had gotten some great footage and that it was time to go back to the Land Rover.

"Ok, I am sure that will be great footage, but you scared the hell out of me. Do you have a death wish," Andria asked as he approached?

"No, that is why I left when the lioness came out.

Elephants and I are friends, we have the same aura," Ian replied with a smile.

"I thought you were concerned I didn't take the camera lens off. I was just trying to make sure that I didn't get fired in the middle of the Savanna," he continued his teasing.

"I don't know about aura, but you smell worse than an elephant. "You smell like shit," Mike spoke up as he backed away from Ian.

Ian burst out laughing, "Yes, I do indeed."

"Let's get you back for a shower and see what you have in the camera," Andria said as she made a face and held her nose.

The drive back went much faster than the ride out to the herd.

He hopped out of the land rover. He handed his camera to Mike and headed to his shower.

A short time later he stood quietly just inside the doorway as he listened to the complimentary comments being made by the team about the footage he had taken.

"OK, today you redeemed yourself. I love what you got us. I still don't know why you are with us but if you get more of this type of footage you are golden with me," Andria said as she raised her Bud in a toast and waved him in.

He went to the cooler and got one for himself.

"I don't have a clue about making a documentary, but I do know how to get up close and personal with all animals," Ian said, as he clinked her bottle and gave her a wink.

Though most women would consider him bashful, OK in looks, and only one could claim to have been in bed with him, he loved to flirt with all of them.

Ian was truly a one-woman man, and his thoughts were always with her.

However, he always teased.

Andria was taken back a wee bit.

He just smiled.

"Look at the footage I got of Matt. I didn't understand what he was doing when he walked toward the elephants but look, he scooped up some poop and spread it all over himself," Mike commented as his footage played across the screen.

"I love it. The two of you have some great stuff for me to begin my work. We will be able to make some great footage from all of this. I'm sure you got at least fifteen seconds of fame here," Mary said jokingly.

She had never gotten so much material so quickly. She felt there was almost enough to write and narrate a whole story.

"I am going to drive into Makuyuni to look around. Is it OK to take the handheld camera with me," Ian inquired?

He wanted to see if he could locate the poacher's headquarters and any warehouse operation that might be processing the ivory tusks.

"I'd love to go with you if you don't mind," Andria replied.

"The company would be welcome," was his response.

Her presence would make it easier for Ian to look around. Two of them would be less suspicious than if he went by himself. Also, it would make it more legitimate for him to be taking pictures.

He got into the driver's seat, and they headed out to Makuyuni. Andria began to ask questions about his background and experience.

Ian really did not want to spend much time on himself, so he asked about what projects she had done recently and what she hoped to accomplish on this current venture.

The deflection worked.

Andria talked for the rest of the drive into the town about her hopes for the Elephant and Ivory documentary. She hoped that it would provide a breakthrough for her.

She had dutifully supported other team leaders. This was her chance at getting the spotlight on her.

She thanked him for the footage he had gotten that day.

He smiled and replied that he did not want to be left to walk back to his cottage. He also now understood her attitude to having a novice photographer on her team. She needed a clear win out of this documentary.

Makuyuni was a small town at the juncture of A 104 and B 144. It had one huge complex where several trucks like the one the team had seen in the preserve were parked. It seemed clear to him that this would be where the black-market Ivory would be kept. There were several large one-story metal warehouse like buildings.

He continued to where several local bars seemed to be clustered.

"That one looks most appealing to me," he said as he pointed out a corner bar with some outside seating.

"Sure, let's have a drink there." Andria said as they got out of the car and walked toward the bar?

"Oh, I figure in about five minutes we will be greeted and be asked to meet the leader of this poaching operation," he added with a smile.

"You have got to be kidding," Andria replied with a surprised look.

"We'll see was his reply," as the waitress brought them their beers.

Almost precisely on the five-minute mark, Ian spotted two men dressed in casual but trim suits walking up the road towards them.

"I think our welcoming committee is coming to greet us. Relax and let the events flow. I think for now everything will be friendly," he said as he took a sip on his beer and continued to watch the two approaching figures.

Both had light tan suits, no tie, and well-polished black shoes. They looked comfortable but he thought they were over dressed for the small town they were in.

"Good evening, Mr. Mugato, the leader in this area, asked us to inquire if you were with the National Geographic film crew. If you are, he is extending an invitation for you to come to his home and have a drink out by his pool," the taller and younger of the two said cordially.

"We indeed are with the film crew. We would be pleased to meet Mr. Mugato," Ian replied casually.

"Please follow me. It is only a short walk to his estate," the shorter and older of the two said quietly.

Ian was surprised at the almost perfect English both men had spoken.

He looked at Andria and saw a look of surprise. She was a little more hesitant than he had expected.

She whispered to him asking if it would be safe.

He smiled at her and put her hand on his arm. He stopped long enough to pay the bill and leave a generous tip. Then he led her along behind their two guides.

Their two guides turned the next corner and ahead of them was a gated property with a huge home in the middle.

There were two armed guards at the gate.

A small walk-in gate was opened, and they were escorted into the inner area.

It was a meticulously kept lawn.

The bushes were shaped into elephants, giraffes, and lions.

The grass was lush and green.

They were led through the center of the house. It opened out onto a large veranda with a pool in the middle.

There was a table set with drinks in a large gazebo between the house and pool.

The entire estate was eerily out of place in this small village in the middle of a nature preserve.

He figured its manicured lush environment must cost a small local fortune to maintain. He was also certain it was but a drop in the money bucket that this poaching leader made.

"Wow, I didn't know we would find a place like this in these parts," Andria said as she sat down.

It was clear to him she was impressed.

He took in the posture of the two guides, or whatever their real capacity was, as they stood by between the house and the Gazebo.

A moment later a slender man, with blond hair and blue eyes, walk from the house toward them.

"Good evening, it is a pleasure to have you come for a drink," he said pleasantly as he took Andria's hand and brought it to his lips.

Ian stood and waited for him to extend his hand.

The dead fish hand immediately sealed his impression of a person not to be trusted.

He sat down as Mr. Mugato explained that he was not black but had taken the name to fit in with the local population.

Ian wanted to comment that the house and compound were probably also built to fit into the local culture, but he kept quiet and listened.

Mr. Mugato began by asking how the filming was going and if there was anything he could do to help.

"Where would we be filming," he asked casually?

"Well, we really don't have any place. We found a small herd of elephants that we will get back to tomorrow," Andria said in reply.

He was quiet for most of the conversation.

He sipped his drink and thought about how he would proceed in solving this poaching problem.

His actions would only temporarily slow the poaching problem. Until the market for ivory and various rhino parts was brought under control, poaching would continue.

He took note that there were no cameras and apparently no motion sensors used to protect and monitor the compound.

Finally, his drink was done, and Andria seemed ready to leave.

"Well, I think we better call it a night. We will be going out early tomorrow. Thank you for your hospitality," He said as he stood up.

Mr. Mugato thanked them for stopping by and invited them back the next time they came to town.

"He seemed pleasant enough," Andria said as they drove back to the ranch house.

"Yes, poaching is making him rich. He has dozens of local workers processing the elephants he kills. The big building nearest the highway is his processing warehouse," he explained to her.

"Are you sure he is the ringleader? He seemed so pleasant," Andria asked as they arrived at the ranch house?

He didn't bother to reply but wished her a good night and retired to the small cottage.

The small pebble he had wedged in the door was gone. The door to his bungalow had been opened during his absence. He entered cautiously and quickly turned on the light.

There was a rifle case on the bed.

"You may need this for your hunting," was neatly written on a note. The rest is in the two boxes under the bed.

Ian opened the case and found a long range, scoped rifle. In his book it was a sniper rifle. He pulled it out and felt its heft. He returned everything back into the case.

He went to sleep wondering when the rifle had been delivered and who the deliverer might be. Somehow this person was connected with him on this particular problem-solving assignment.

He went out before breakfast and sighted in the rifle. It was a .308 and fired a bullet almost the same size as the fifty caliper he used in Vietnam. He quickly got use to the drop and chose the longest range possible to site in.

He repeated his sighting shots three times. He then cleaned it, put it in its case, placed the rifle in the back of the Land Rover with the cameras and his backpack.

He then went in and joined the rest of the team for breakfast.

The early morning sun was behind the team on the drive out to where they hoped to find the small herd of elephants.

The terrain was interspersed with a variety of trees with exotic names.

He especially liked the Baobab tree because of the stories told by the driver of "the tree that eats maidens" and another story about the impact of the white man who shot the python that lived in the tree.

The driver explained that the python lived in the tree and answered the prayers for rain for the local tribes.

A white hunter shot and killed the python thinking he was doing good.

The locals realized that there was no way to pray for rain and a long drought followed. To this day, when the wind blows through the branches of the Baobab tree, the hissing of the python ghost could be heard.

The driver then told the story about the Baobab tree falling in love with four attractive young women that often sat in its shade. When the maidens got married the tree became jealous. During a raging thunderstorm, the tree opened up its trunk and took the maidens in to shield them from the storm but then never released them. To this day, during windy thunderstorms the crying of the maidens can be heard coming from the Baobab tree.

The driver explained that the people feared the ghosts of the python and the maidens more than the sounds of the wild animals and that they believed that those who pick its white flower will be killed by a lion.

He looked at the Baobab trees they were driving by and assured the driver he would not pick any flowers or do anything to upset the Baobab tree.

He said he liked the Buffalo Thorn tree better because it was supposed to protect the person under it from lightning and the Marula Tree because his elephant friends loved to eat the fruit of the tree.

Andrea looked up from where she was sitting in the front and raised her eyebrow and mouthed a, "Really"!

He turned his attention back to the horizon. He was on the lookout for poachers as the team proceeded across the open range. In the far distance he saw the glint of sun on glass and instructed the driver to head toward it.

He took out his rifle and peered through the high-powered scope to where he had seen the glint.

"Hey, where did you get that beautiful thing," Mike commented when he saw the rifle.

"I thought you left it on my bed yesterday," Ian said with a straight face.

Then he went on as he saw Andrea paying attention.

"I had it sent ahead, just in case I wanted to do some hunting."

As Ian looked around, he saw two trucks heading in the direction of the glint.

"Stop the car for a moment," Ian instructed as he sighted in on the trucks.

His first shot was a little high, but his second shot hit the front tire of the lead truck. The third shot aimed at the front tire of the second truck was easier because both trucks had stopped.

Andrea's reaction was to ask what the hell he was shooting at.

Ian replied that he had shot out the front tire on both of the poacher's trucks. He pointed out that these poachers were heading in the direction of the elephant herd that the team was looking for.

"Now that we have stopped them, let's go over to see what those guys are up to," he suggested.

The driver responded to Ian's suggestion, while the rest of the team looked at each other and remained silent.

They arrived as the tire for the first truck was removed.

"Stay here. I am going to have a small talk with these guys," he instructed the team as he jumped out and walked toward the two trucks.

"How are you doing," he inquired in greeting as he got as close to them as possible.

The six men standing and watching the changing of the tires turned toward him. They were not too happy and were suspicious of his presence.

"Where are you headed in such powerful trucks," he asked as he stepped into the group.

"You should not be asking questions," the one that seemed to be in charge responded.

"You are right. I really came to tell you that if you do not leave when you get the tires fixed you are likely to die today," he said quietly.

There was absolute silence for a moment as the men looked at each other.

"Take him," the leader commanded.

As the men rushed him, Ian waited to the last moment and then at very close range he hit the first one in the throat, the second got straight fingers to the eyes and the third got a stiff palm to the nose the fourth and fifth both got fists to the sides of their temples, and all went down immediately.

It was over in almost the blink of an eye.

The leader was pulling his gun from his holster when Ian's knife pierced his eye and went into his brain. The leader dropped to his knees. He was dead before he hit the ground.

The two who were changing the tires turned with their tire irons in their hands. Ian shook his finger and told them they could choose to die, or they should get back to work and get their friends out of the park.

"Do not come back," were his final words as he turned and walked back toward the Land Rover.

"What in the hell was that" Mike asked as he turned back with him.

He had jumped out and was on the way to help. Ian liked him for that.

"Who are you," Andria asked as they got back to the Land Rover?

He didn't reply but took up the rifle and looked toward the location where he had spotted the glint. He suspected the glint came from a scoped rifle.

He spotted it. He immediately took a step to his left. He could hear the bullet hit the Land Rover.

He hoped no one was hit.

He took careful aim, squeezed the trigger, and immediately took a long step forward and to the right. He waited a few seconds and carefully took a second shot at the far away target.

There was no replying shot.

He jumped up into the back of the Land Rover and instructed the driver to drive to the large boulder where the shots had originated.

He kept his eye on the figure on the top of the rock. There was no movement.

"Stay here, I will make sure everything is safe," he instructed.

He walked carefully up to the boulder and went around back and up to where the shooter lay dead.

Ian looked around. From his vantage point he could see the small herd of elephants milling around a small watering hole.

The shooter's Land Rover was behind the rock. he pulled him down and strapped him into the passenger's seat. He would have him delivered back to Mr. Mugato later that day.

He returned to the Land Rover, grabbed his camera, and associated equipment.

It was clear to him that the events that had just transpired had shaken Andrea. He would explain later, at the moment he had something totally different in mind.

"I am going to visit my elephant herd and get you some additional film footage," he said as he scooped up some elephant dung and spread it over his clothes and equipment.

A mother rhino with her young was standing just opposite of the elephants. The young rhino chasing the long-legged white cranes and other smaller birds made for some great footage.

He began filming immediately.

The young elephant bull again came over and checked him out. He seemed to remember him from the day before and seemed friendly.

The baby elephants in the herd came over and played with him.

The mother came over and made sure Ian was being friendly and not threatening the little ones. The babies must have only been a few days old.

He sat down on a small boulder, and they came over to him and seemed curious about the equipment.

He got up and frolicked with the baby elephants who probably outweighed him by a few pounds. He hoped Mike was taking this footage of him playing with the baby elephant.

Once again, he made his retreat when a mother lioness and two younger lions came to the watering hole. As he left he got some great close-up shots. The lioness was not showing any signs of threatening him, but he figured it was getting time to eat lunch and he did not want to take the chance of having to run with camera in hand.

Ian returned to the Land Rover and handed his gear up to Mike.

"I have some great footage, I can't wait to see it on the screen," Mike said enthusiastically.

He seemed to have forgotten the truck and the sniper incident.

He could tell by Andria's silence that she had not.

"I don't think she will go to town with me again," he thought to himself.

"I will see you back at the ranch," he said as he headed toward the boulder where the dead shooter was located.

He did not turn but could hear the team depart.

He drove the dead poacher's vehicle toward the town. He left the Land Rover about a mile from the ranch. He placed a call to arrange for it to be driven back into town.

He left the key on the driver's seat.

He jogged slowly back to the ranch.

On his arrival back to the ranch, he went to his cottage and took a quick shower.

As he left the cottage a quiet voice at the edge of the darkness called out.

"Mr. Matt, I have been instructed to give you some help," a small wiry black man said as he stepped into the light.

He had not expected to be personally contacted and carefully took in everything surrounding him. He was ready if attacked.

"Thank you, yes I can use some help," he responded.

He shared where the Land Rover with the dead shooter was located. He instructed the person offering help to take it back and park it where it would be visible to as many people as possible.

He had painted a message on the truck, "Stop the killing of your animals, they are worth more alive. Tourists with money will come to see them."

"Don't let anyone see you. Please pass the word that death awaits the poacher," he instructed him.

"The word is that Mr. Mugabe is planning to have you and the rest of the team killed," the wiry man continued.

Ian thanked him for the help and the information. He then turned and walked into the main house.

Everyone was reviewing the footage for the day. He knew he had done good work because even Andrea said something in praise. He had figured that she would never speak to him again.

"Folks, something has come up and I will need to leave you tomorrow. I apologize if this puts you short," he said to the entire team.

There was the general, "Oh no, what are we going to do?"

But no one made much of an effort to change his mind.

He thought he saw relief in Andrea's face as he made the announcement. It was clear the day's action had affected all of them.

He was on the way out when she stopped him just outside the door.

"I don't know who you are, but I know you love the elephants as much as I do, and they seem to accept you. So, I will accept that you are on the good side. Take care," she said as she gave him a quick hug.

He hoped she would feel that way in a few days when she read or heard the news.

He packed his bag. He had his own small camera with him. He also took his sniper rifle. Then he asked the driver to take him to town.

He first went to the warehouse where he verified it was full of ivory.

He located the truck fueling area.

He then liberally soaked the interior of the warehouse with gasoline. He soaked the interior of all the trucks with gas. He then poured a trail of gasoline away from the warehouse to a lone large boulder at the corner of the lot.

He crouched down behind it and lit the gasoline trail. It quickly snaked its way back toward the warehouse and parked trucks.

The upward draft of air and giant flames lighting up the dark of night surprised him. He had been expecting it but none-the-less shrank down as the heat wave reached him.

He watched as first a group of guards came rushing out of the compound around the house. Mr. Mugabe came out in his robe. He was escorted by his two bodyguards.

Ian would have preferred to solve his problem in a fairer fashion but chose to use his sniper rifle.

He took aim, slowly squeezed the trigger, and watched as a small hole appeared on Mr. Mugabe's forehead. His body took two more steps before falling to the ground. His bodyguards looked around with their guns drawn but there was nothing to see.

He was sure that Mr. Mugabe's demise would ensure the safety of the documentary team.

During the ensuing confusion, he went to Mr. Mugabe's garage where he found a Ferrari.

He made sure it had a full tank of gas. He then opened the garage door, walked to the gate, and opened it and then proceeded to slowly drive away from the town toward his next problem-solving session.

Two weeks later Ian had eliminated the leaders of the other two poaching organizations that had used that area.

This would only be a temporary solution to the problem, but it was the best He could do on one trip.

He was the problem solver, but he realized that some problems would take repeated corrective action.

His trip had been cut short. He felt he had been effective and successful. He had come out alive and was eager to return to Lesley, Ella, and Matt.

He hoped the documentary team also felt he had contributed to their success.

5 *Three Bad Pennies*

*T*he trip home was longer than the trip out. He had too many hours to replay the events of his problem-solving mission. The blessing was that the fate of the elephants was not a major newsworthy item. The upheaval he created did not make the international news.

His greeting at home helped him erase the darkness of the problem-solving events. Ella ran into his arms and Matt seemed happy to see him.

Lesley gave him a hug that woke up his passionate side.

Once again, he raised the barrier to the dark side of his mind.

His real day work life was a travel pattern that took him to Asia, Europe, Mexico, and Brazil.

He coached production leadership teams at multiple sites in all these areas.

This meant extensive travel to the production plants that were located around the world in more than seventy-five countries.

He spent almost fifty percent of his time traveling.

He tried as often as possible to schedule his travels six months out so that he could also schedule a good home life.

Lesley had given up her legal work and was now working from home managing the money in their personal account. She built a portfolio of stocks and bonds. Most of her investments were long term but she had a select portfolio that she was constantly trimming and adjusting. She was now making more money than when she had practiced law.

It was almost a year after his Elephant and Ivory documentary that Lesley announce that she was once again pregnant.

Almost simultaneously he received the next problem-solving assignment.

He decided he would have to give up having children.

The CBS evening news announcer, in a street interview about the scheduled exchange of prisoners between Israel and Hamas, commented that they really needed a problem solver to handle the tense situation in the region.

"We need a problem solver to correct this nonsense of three of the world's worst terrorists going free," was the quote attributed to a person on the street.

He had the habit of recording the news so he could listen to it at his convenience. He replayed the interview a few more times until he was sure it was a message for him.

It had been almost two years, so he needed to convince himself. There was little doubt about the message. It was the kind of problem he would be called in to solve.

The solution was simple. Executing it would be a challenge.

He did the research into the situation.

The Gaza Strip was sealed off by both the Israeli and the Egyptians.

The living conditions for the common person living there was described as challenging.

It was also likened to one large prison complex.

The perpetrators who had been found guilty of several car and bus bombings and the bombing of a coffee shop were to be exchanged for one Israeli army soldier being held hostage.

These three and about six hundred other detainees were being exchanged for the one Israeli hostage.

He wondered who in Israel would negotiate such a deal. Then he thought about his role in this, and he saw that someone was using the currency they had and would arrange for a quick devaluation of three of those being exchanged.

The bad pennies were to be erased and the other one hundred and sixty would provide the shielding that would quickly diminish the impact of the assassination of the three.

He was being called on to provide a very specific solution.

He made a few calls.

One call was to arrange a weeklong workshop at the Cairo production plant. This would be the legitimate means of getting into Egypt. He then made his hotel and flight reservations.

A second call was to his unknown support team asking them to connect him with a way to get into the Gaza and to have the proper weapon available in Gaza when he got there.

The team response was to arrange a meeting between him and a news reporting team. He would go with them into the Gaza itself.

He let Lesley know about his upcoming trip would last a little over a week.

She must have sensed that there were two purposes to the trip because on her departure hug, she cautioned him to be careful. She wanted her kids to have a father present at their birthdays.

His flight left Cincinnati and went to Frankfurt. There he caught a flight to Cairo.

It reminded him of his flight to the Elephant and Ivory engagement. This flight was not as long, but Ian felt less sure about the situation.

On his arrival to Cairo, he took a taxi to the hotel that had a view of the Pyramids. He had been to the hotel on a previous trip to the Cairo manufacturing plant and liked its location and view.

The next morning, he sat and watched the sun rising between two of the great Pyramids. He held the long-stemmed glass of orange juice up to the sun and enjoyed the view of two pyramids pointing up to a light blue morning sky while being wrapped in a pinkish orange light just below the blue. The orange juice in his glass took on a golden glow. Instead of rose-colored glasses he had a glowing orange colored glass.

He wondered about the beauty.

Was it the calm before the storm?

He enjoyed a casual breakfast on his veranda and wondered about the history of the Pyramids. Grand in their nature, they none-the-less looked tired to him. It made him pause to think, they were several thousand years old.

Sometimes he felt their age.

He arranged for a tour of the city via the concierge. He also arranged for a cruise on the Nile.

Then on his return he would spend the day taking a tour of the Pyramids, and the famous Cairo Museum.

This was all part of his cover. He wanted to make sure his activities were known to the hotel staff. He also needed a way to be gone for a few days and that absence needed to go undetected.

He walked out to the main street and flagged down a passing taxi. Since he wanted to utilize his tour in a tricky way, he didn't want to use one of regular hotel cabs. Once downtown, he caught the tour bus going to the Nile Delta River cruise. His tour would take place in a few days, but Ian was able to use his tour ticket for the bus ride.

Once he got to the Nile River Cruise pick up location he found another bus going to Rafah, Egypt where he planned to join up with a network news crew.

Upon his arrival in Rafah, he went to a bar often frequented by western reporters where his news crew was to be found.

He was looking for a specific news crew that was short one cameraman.

He stopped at the bar and listened to the conversation at several of the tables. There was a news crew drinking at one table that was discussing the loss of their camera man. He sat down at the next table and ordered a beer. As he listened, he was able to verify that their cameraman had fallen ill.

This was the crew he was looking for.

"Pardon me, I couldn't help but overhear that you are short a camera man. I am a qualified cameraman and would love to support you if you are going to cover the hostage exchange," Ian volunteered.

"I'm Lindi, join us and let's talk about it. What's your name," the only female at the table responded?

"I'm Matt Miller, pleased to meet you," Ian said giving them the name on the passport he was now carrying. He had hidden his other papers in an empty lot in the city. He carried another passport for his legitimate business purposes.

"This is Luke our editor and Brad our driver and equipment manager," Lindi went on with the introductions.

She then proceeded in an attack mode of questions.

"I haven't seen you at any events with any other crews," Lindi made the statement in an obvious attempt at rattling his confidence.

"I have seen you, but you are on camera. I suppose you catalogue the looks of all the good-looking camera men," Ian replied in a teasing tone and with a smile.

"I thought you wanted this job," Lindi said with an obvious fake surprised look.

"I thought you needed a cameraman," Ian said acting as if he was going get up to leave.

"Hold on you two. Sit down. We do need a cameraman. Lindi is just trying to make sure you know how to handle the camera," Luke spoke up.

"What have you done and where," Luke went on to ask?

"I'm not a professional cameraman. I am more of an adventurer. However, I have been on several safaris and have helped the camera crew and participated in the editing of the films. You can find me on several of the credits on American Geographic Animal World films," Ian replied truthfully.

He had indeed been on those safaris and done the camera work for a short time a few years before. That was a problem-solving situation that involved Ivory poachers.

"Ok, are you able to leave early tomorrow morning and go with us into Gaza," Luke inquired.

"How are you getting into Gaza," Ian asked with a look of curiosity?

"We already had our equipment sent in and have arranged for a van while we are there. We were to go in today but, John, our cameraman came down sick. We spent the day looking for a replacement but there are none available locally," Luke volunteered.

"This must mean my pay is at a premium," Ian said with a smile as he lofted his beer.

"That will depend on the quality of your work," Lindi and Luke both said almost simultaneously.

"Fair enough, if I make you look good, I expect a bonus," Ian said looking at Lindi.

"I hope you mean money," Lindi replied with an obvious look that implied Ian was trying to be improper?

"I'm too old to think of anything but money," Ian said with a smile.

"Ok, I am going to call the tunnel manager to see when we can get transported in," Luke said as he stood up and left with phone in hand.

Ian had come prepared for the participation he had gotten "hired" for. He was sure the sick cameraman had been approached and was suitably rewarded for being sick.

He was now on the way in but needed to equip himself with the appropriate weapon to carry out his problem solving.

The exchange of the prisoners for the one Israeli soldier was to take place in two days.

Late that evening, the film crew was met by a guide that took them to the Egyptian side of the tunnel entrance. The entrance appeared to be the entrance to a prison cell. It was locked with a brand-new lock. There were no guards around and our guide had the key to open the lock.

Once the crew was in the guide pushed the lock closed from the inside.

The crew scaled down a ladder into what appeared to be a dimly illuminated well. There at the bottom was a cart that looked to Ian to be very much like a large Red Flyer wagon that he had as a kid. It had a bench running lengthwise for the passengers and a cross seat at both ends for their guide. The "Red Flyer" was designed to go both ways.

The wagon was attached to a rope that disappeared out in front of them into the dimly lit horizontal tunnel.

The guide sat on the front side and pushed a button that activated the rope. The ride across the border into Gaza went slowly but smoothly.

On the far end Ian and the rest of the film crew were helped out of a well like structure and led to their hotel accommodations. They checked in as if they were any normal hotel guest.

They were in Rafah on the Gaza strip.

Early the next morning, the team went out taking background footage and interviewing various groups.

His role as the cameraman allowed him to get a good lay of the area. They drove up to Highway 242 to understand the layout of the exchange area.

Lindi walked around and picked out the spots she would stand as she made her observations and comments during the exchange event.

Ian concluded it was going to be a very good spot for his problem solving.

The team returned to touring the area and interviewing various people they randomly picked.

He was also looking for a very specific kind of rifle. During their background filming he spotted it in a small gun shop in which he had been told it would be found. He now had the location of the shop relative to his hotel and was pleased that it was only a few blocks away.

That night after everyone retired, he went out the window of his room and went back to the gun shop. The back door was easy enough to open and Ian quietly made his way into the front of the shop.

The rifle he was interested in was on a wall rack. After carefully checking that there was no alarm, he lifted it from the rack. He placed a similar looking rifle from a lower rack into the one he had just emptied. He made sure he had the number of cartridges he planned to use.

He hoped the gun switch would not be noticed for several days.

He retreated back the way he had come.

Back in his room, he made a few key modifications to the camera equipment.

The rifle components were the key parts of a popular 308 caliper sniper rifle.

He took the rifle barrel out of the gunstock and mounted it onto the camera. The rifle scope mount integrated naturally to the camera base.

The rifle scope looked like a camera lens.

The barrel of the rifle looked exactly like the base of the camera.

The silencer appeared to be part of the lens adjustment.

He was pleased with how everything came together.

The camera shoulder mount became the support that took the place of the gunstock.

He sighted the scope in for three hundred yards, as best he could without firing the rifle.

When he was done the camera unit appeared almost the same as before. A close look would give it away, but he was betting that the attention would be on the bus with the prisoners and not on his camera.

He would allow himself one sighting shot and two shots per target. He practiced loading his rifle several times until he could do it while keeping the camera operating. He knew his actions needed to be those that a normal camera man would take.

Those being released back into Gaza would be walking across the border along Highway 242.

There would be only one person going toward Israel and several hundred coming into Gaza.

He was only interested in three of the people coming from the Israeli side.

He hoped to be able to take the three out before anyone noticed or understood what was taking place.

In the morning, the film crew drove up to the exchange area. He suggested parking the van in a spot by one of the few trees growing in the area. It was also in the back of the area away from where the majority of the crowd was already gathering.

Not far away someone had set up a generator to provide power for a refreshment stand and power to a black van.

The news team got into position. Then Lindi wanted to get in closer.

He suggested that he stand in back and capture her from long range. This would allow him to zoom in when appropriate or scan around the crowd to get a better feel overall.

Luke liked the idea and supported him.

As things would have it there seemed to be a delay of the exchange. By noon it was obvious some major issue was at hand. A crowd had gathered, and it was slowly growing and becoming more agitated.

Lindi did several interviews of people in the crowd. This allowed him to move about and become part of the scene. There were several other news crews doing similar interviews.

The folks in the Gaza were all waiting for those being released.

The black van presumably holding the Israeli soldier remained in position.

Finally, as the sun hit its zenith, as the heat of the sun was peaking, the restless crowd was holding loud and chanting curses at the Israelis, the buses were sighted. The crowd got louder when the buses were seen arriving at the exchange point.

The crowd began chanting, "release our son's." This went on in a continuously repeating pattern.

The exchange was about to happen.

He checked his field of vision. He would have clear shots, but he wanted to be a little farther away from the crowd and have the crowd between him and the targets.

The noisier the crowd the better it would be for him. A cheer went up when the bus doors opened, and the first group came out.

He scanned the passengers stepping off the bus. None of the targets were in the first group coming across. There were five buses in all. Each pulled to the crossing area and let out its load of exchange prisoners.

After three buses had unloaded and a steady stream of men had crossed over into Gaza, an Israeli on a loudspeaker requested the Israeli soldier be released.

The side doors of the black van opened, and a single figure stepped out and into sight. He had his hands bound behind his back with wire ties. He walked slowly but steadily toward the exchange point. Held hostage for almost five years, he was now being exchanged for a rather large number of prisoners.

Most of those being exchanged were minor players captured on the battle fields. Many were wives and children of the prisoners being released.

Three were terrorists of the worst kind. The three had killed more than sixty people with car and bus bombs, the bombing of a coffee house and the bombing of the first responders coming to help in the first bombing.

These three continued to be the talk of the terrorist scene. They had been tried and found guilty. They had become heroes to the depressed peoples in the Gaza strip.

He saw them exit the bus in the next group being let out to walk across.

"Luke, I am going to get to a better position," he called out as he moved over to where the large generators were running.

Luke waved approval and gave thumbs up.

Ian wanted the noise to cover his shots.

The three got off the last bus and were coming across together. Ian wanted to thank whoever had arranged the release in such a manner.

This made his problem solving much easier.

The three were walking side by side, smiling and waving to the crowd like heroes.

He watched as the lone exchange prisoner made it across the border to the security of the troops awaiting him on the Israeli side. The exchanged soldier got on the last bus and the bus immediately departed.

He took one sighting shot at a rock close to where the buses had made their drop off. He noted where the shot hit and calculated the drop and the drift.

He then aimed and tagged each of his three targets with shots to head and heart. He noted each drop to their knees and then fall forward on their faces as if kissing the ground. He did not wait to evaluate the results.

There was a roar from the crowd as they thought the three men were kissing the ground but then the three fell over. The crowd rushed forward to where the three, lay dead.

The barriers across the road were put back into place and the Israeli's fired machine guns above the rushing crowd.

Ian twisted the barrel and pulled it loose and dropped it down the generator's vertical exhaust. He then continued his duty as camera man and maneuvered for a better angle.

The rush of the crowd to the three that had been killed and the ensuing confusion allowed him to completely eliminate all evidence of his weapon or involvement. The pieces of his sniper rifle were dropped in various trash containers, vehicles and behind rubble.

By the time the team gathered at the van, he had eliminated all evidence of any of them being involved.

"Luke, Lindi, I think this is a good time to leave by the tunnels and get back to Egypt," he encouraged the team.

"Yes, you're right, if we don't get out now, we will be stuck here for a long time as the people go on a rampage in retaliation for the killing of their heroes," Lindi said as she got into the van. She wondered where the shot had come from.

He smiled as he realized that Lindi and her team were totally unaware of their participation in one of the more daring problem-solving efforts he had undertaken.

The team had all their gear and belongings, so they went straight to the tunnel they had crossed over in. They were lowered down. Then they put all their gear into their buggy and rode it across into Egypt. As their guide opened the lock on the door exiting into Egypt, Ian heard one of the operators announce the tunnels had been shut down.

"Just in time," went through his mind.

"Well, you did a good job as our cameraman. How about a flat three thousand for the job," Luke asked as they sat around that evening at dinner.

"That sounds fine, but I don't want it personally. It would just mean I would pay more taxes. How about you sent it to the United Appeal Organization for me," Ian suggested to them.

"Wow, I guess I read you wrong," Lindi said in a contrite way.

"No, you read me right the first time but now it's too late to change your mind," Ian said with a smile as he winked at her.

The next morning Ian caught the tour bus coming back from the Nile River tour. It was the one he was ticketed on. He got in and took it back to Cairo. He sat near the driver talking to him about how much he had enjoyed the river cruise and then gave him a big tip as he got off the bus in Cairo.

He flagged down a taxi and proceeded to the Cairo Museum. The taxi driver would also remember him because of his generous tip.

He spent the day following the history of Egypt from the first Pharaohs to the present time. He found it interesting and a great way to decompress.

The news of the shootings was the conversation of many people on tour at the museum. Some thought the Israeli had done it, but the analysis of the bullet wounds indicated the shots had come from the Gaza side.

There was total confusion about the situation.

When he returned to the hotel, two Egyptian officials greeted him. They were both dressed in very nice black suits and showed him their GDSSI badges.

They had a few questions about where he had been for the last few days. He showed them his ticket to the Nile River cruise, his ticket to the Museum and the ticket to the Pyramids. All were appropriately punched and dated. They looked at each document and then thanked him and left.

He was sure they would be checking out the details. He had anticipated being checked and was glad he had made a point of giving good tips to everyone during his trip.

He once again had breakfast with the Pyramids as the main view and read about the mysterious assassination of the three terrorists.

There were claims the Israeli's had hired the killings.

Other's thought the parents of the slain had hired the killing.

He would never know who had been behind setting up the situation, but he knew who had solved the problem.

He had eliminated the three bad pennies.

That day he kicked off a root cause problem-solving session at the Cairo manufacturing plant. He was eager to get this work done and then get out of Egypt. He never liked staying close to where he had done his other problem-solving.

The site workshop was a resounding success. He was pleased but he was more pleased when he got out of the cab and walked into the airport.

After flying for more than fourteen hours, He got off the plane in Cincinnati somewhat exhausted.

Then he got to the up escalator and saw Lesley looking down at him as he rode the escalator up to the luggage claim area. He immediately closed the door to the problem-solving session and the dark part of his mind and felt the glow of her warming radiance.

He took her in his arms and let the warmth of goodness flow into his soul.

6 Pirates

*I*an was relieved to be home. Ella ran to him, and the warm bundle of joy warmed his soul. Matt was happy to come to him and he once again felt connected to a normal life.

Lesley let him know that their next had started to kick. It was clear to her that their next would be an active bundle. She took his hand and guided it to where the kicking was taking place. His smile seemed to be what Lesley had been wanting to see.

He returned to his normal travels around the world. He was now sought after by various production plant managers across all the businesses of the Company. He held several work improvement workshops in the central office work areas as well.

Work pulled him back into its fold and his travels distracted him from the machinations of the dark side of his mind.

His brief foray into darkness slowly receded to the point that it almost seemed it was his imagination. He controlled the dark space with the love and light of his family.

In November, Sean, the name Lesley chose for their next child, arrived. From the very first it was clear that Sean was to have his own way. He was not to be denied. Lesley seemed to give Sean preferential treatment. Ella was going to a pre-school and Matt was in a daycare center.

The family had a string of sequential birthdays. Ella's was in September, Matt's in October, Sean's in November, Lesley was on Christmas.

His birthday in April was the outlier. He thought that ironically appropriate. In his mind he was an outlier to the rest of the people he thought of as normal.

He was beginning to see a pattern in the frequencies of his problem-solving assignments. There seemed to be a breather year and then the next major world issue triggered the next assignment. He was happy that it was not every world issue that triggered an assignment. He wondered about how many other problem solvers there were besides himself.

He was sure he was not the only one.

The call for the next problem-solving session came to the secure phone he kept in his work desk. The work desk was located in his home library which also served as his home office. The instructions were simple; take care of the pirates. Be at the Taj Mahal and join Maurice and Ted Daimler on their continuing trip around the world.

He was a little taken aback. "Hey, give me more than that to go on," Ian said as the message on his phone ended.

He did his research on the pirates and found that Somalia was the most active pirate area. There were other pirates but none as aggressive as the ones in that area.

They had made global news by capturing a giant container ship and they had also risked taking on a US Navy destroyer.

They seemed formidable and unstoppable.

He decided that he would need heavy fire power on this problem-solving assignment.

His memories of the pulsing of the fifty-caliber machine gun surfaced and he could hear the laughter coming from the dark corner of his mind. Yea, I know I am crazy, but you are trapped in my mind, Ian laughed to himself.

Lesley always seemed to sense when he was going out to do normal work and when he was about to go out on his problem-solving forays. He probably gave it away by the way he prepared for the problem-solving sessions.

She reminded him that she loved him and that he had a family to come home to.

He smiled and thanked her for giving him armor and amour.

Lesley laughed and gave him a loving light slap as he got into the cab taking him to the airport.

The flight to Mumbai, India went through New York and Frankfurt and took a good two days of solid travel. He was tired as he got off the plane in the early afternoon.

Then he got on a night train to reach the Taj Mahal where he was to meet up with Maurice and Ted.

He was fairly exhausted as he stepped off the train in Agra at five in the morning. He had taken a sleeper on the train from Mumbai to Agra but had gotten no sleep.

The station was blanketed with a sea of sleeping people wrapped in mostly light grey blankets. The sleeping bodies looked like a beached grouping of seals.

He followed a narrow path between the bodies and got out to where the taxis were lined up waiting for customers. These were three wheeled tricycle type of taxis. He and his baggage took up every bit of space.

He had reservations at the Obero Amarvill hotel. The ride took what seemed like forever to him. After checking in and taking a quick morning shower, he went looking in the breakfast area for Maurice and Ted Daimler.

He recognized them from the photos he had been sent. He approached their table and introduced himself. He said that a mutual friend had mentioned that the two of them were in Agra and that he should look them up.

They invited him to join the two of them for breakfast.

He knew enough about their friend to be able to converse and tell stories about him for hours. They never detected that he really had no clue who this mutual friend might be.

Maurice invited him to join her and Ted on a tour of the Taj Mahal.

He had researched the Taj Mahal and knew it was one of the world's ultimate expression of love. It was built as a symbol of love for Mumtaz Mahal the favorite wife of the Mughal Emperor, Shah Jahan.

It had cost a small fortune. It cost the equivalent of eight hundred million in current US dollars. Some writer referred to it as "the teardrop on the cheek of time."

He liked that sentimental perspective.

He had also learned that tourists were often disappointed by their guides and the number of vendors and children mobbing the tourists in the desire to sell souvenirs.

He accepted Maurice's invitation and suggested they arrange with the hotel to provide them with a car and driver and a guide. He made sure they understood he was paying.

The Taj is said to bring people together. He worked hard on getting an invitation to join them on their continuing tour around the world. By the time they left the Taj, he had an invitation to sail with Maurice and Ted on their sailing boat the "Lazy Lady."

He had achieved his first goal. He now had to figure out how to get all of his gear onboard the sloop.

The three of them completed the Agra visit by touring the Red Fort.

Afterwards they went to dinner and enjoyed a mix of Indian cuisine that provided them with the conversation of what each specific dinner course happened to be.

Moving on board their sloop was tricky. He needed to get a host of armament on board and hidden in case they were searched.

He had created the cover of being a biologist traveling around the world collecting samples. He joked he was emulating Charles Darwin who had developed the theory of evolution. He was developing the theory that bugs ruled the world.

Maurice said that it was no theory. She claimed she could validate it as a fact.

He asked about the possibility of taking his samples onboard.

Ted and Maurice quite happily agreed. They boasted that the Lazy Lady, a Bavaria Cruiser fifty-five had ample space. He should make himself at home and could use both aft bedrooms to sleep in and to store his bug collection.

One bedroom became his weapons storage space. All of the boxes were labeled as samples. The top half of each box did indeed have a wonderful collection of bugs. The bottom half of each box contained a variety of weapons including a shoulder rocket launcher.

Maurice pointed to the map under the tabletop glass. She traced their trip from San Francisco up by Alaska and down the Russian coast to Japan, then on to Taiwan, the Philippines and most of the southeast Asian countries. The trip had been more than she had ever dreamt it would be. She then pointed to Karachi, Pakistan the next destination upon leaving Mumbai. She pointed out the route beyond Karachi that would take them to Sur, Oman and then to Bosasa, Somalia.

He would try to keep all of them from becoming hostages of the pirates that controlled the coastal waters off of Somalia. He figured it would be there when they sailed along the Somalia coast that he would need to be ready for almost anything.

Maurice asked whether Ian would like to join her and Ted for a last shopping trip in Mumbai?

He thanked her for the invitation but declined with the excuse that it was the perfect time to move all his belongings on board.

When Maurice and Ted went shopping, He took the liberty to modify the "Lazy Lady" by mounting four small ceramic torpedoes tubes on the hull well below the water line. These could not be seen during normal sailing. He loaded the totally ceramic torpedoes in all four of the remotely controlled tubes. He had another four torpedoes stored in the bedroom. The system had specifically been developed to pass any metal detection sensors he might encounter.

He arranged the "bug boxes" so only the top was convenient to examine. The very top of each box had only bug specimens stored in them.

As they left Mumbai the following day, Maurice took the "Lazy Lady" out past Colaba point where she promptly engaged him to do the sailing.

He had practiced his sailing but was not use to a boat as well equipped and so powerful. During the six-day trip from Mumbai to Karachi, he took the time to sharpen his sailing skills.

He also took time to get to know Maurice and Ted on a more personal level. Both Maurice and Ted complimented him on his sailing skills.

He readily accepted their praise and continued stretching the Lazy Lady in her dance with the wind. He wanted to be able to know his limits when the time came to put the Lazy Lady through the sailing navigation challenge he figured they would face.

Ted was a retired cabinet maker. He had started by making tables and chairs and expanded to bedroom furniture. His biggest sellers were Adirondack chairs. He stated that his success was also his disappointment. The chairs were not of interest to him and no challenge to produce. He had built his small company into a profitable business and was now in the process of passing it on to his sons. He was still involved but the sons were now running the day-to-day business. Ted laughed and said he was now reaping the good training he had given his sons.

Maurice must have been a stunningly beautiful young, woman. She was now a beauty in her later age. She knew she was good looking and liked to flirt. She and he got along very well. He could flirt with the best of them. She was a product of Minnesota farm life and proud of it. She would have become a chef but joked that Ted had kept her barefoot and pregnant and never given her the chance to graduate from culinary school.

He loved flirts and loved to flirt with them.

He was a one-woman man and true to Lesley but as Ian often joked with Lesley, "he had married her because he loved her, not because he was going blind."

Karachi was an interesting stopping point and he went on tour with Ted and Maurice.

It seemed to him they were always visiting tombs. The Pyramids were tombs, Taj is a tomb. In Karachi, the three of them went to visit Mazar-e-Quaid the tomb of the founder of Pakistan. They took in the Masjid-e-Tooba, the largest single dome mosque in the world. Late in the day they went to Bagh Ibn-e-Qasim and enjoyed the park and then went to dinner.

The next day Maurice and Ted went off on their own to do some more sightseeing and shopping.

He stayed with the Lazy Lady. He wore his swim trunks and sat out on the pier fashioning C4 into small floating mines. He did not want the Lazy Lady to get any C4 contamination. It was clear to him that no one was watching and if they asked, he would say he was preparing potato balls for dinner.

When Maurice and Ted returned, he volunteered to cook dinner. He had purchased a large fish that looked somewhat like a red snapper. He had scaled it and rubbed it with olive oil and salt. He placed it on a large flat pan and surrounded it with yam, Brussel sprouts, a few tomato wedges, and asparagus. He lightly salted all the vegetables and put slices of butter around them. He covered the lot with aluminum foil and put it in the oven.

The dinner was a huge success. The entire fish was consumed and only a few succulent vegetables escaped uneaten.

A local white wine brought back by Maurice from her shopping trip also suffered extinction.

He accepted the praise for his cooking. When the time came, he hoped to be as successful with his problem solving.

He, Maurice, and Ted left Karachi after a couple of days. As they sailed toward Sur Oman, Ian put the Lazy Lady through every maneuver he could think of. Both Maurice and Ted commented that they had never stretched the Lazy Lady like Ian was doing and followed by saying they enjoyed every moment, and he should continue to demonstrated her capabilities.

He knew that they had entered into the Somali pirate zone. He was glad that they had not faced any threat from pirates on their way across.

He volunteered to take care of the "Lazy Lady" while Ted and Maurice did their sightseeing. He continued to prepare for the encounter with the pirates that he knew they would soon be running from.

He guided the "Lazy Lady" out of Sur, Oman and sailed on course for Bosaso, Somalia, the largest port city in Somali located in the Gulf of Aden. From this port onward they would be in the heart of where the pirate activities took place.

He asked Ted if he was concerned about the threat of pirates.

"I have a 308 with a scope and will defend the "Lazy Lady" from any pirates. They will be in for a surprise if they mess with us," was Ted's confident reply. Little did he know that his boast would be put to the test.

Ian didn't try to argue with him.

He figured that Ted must not have paid much attention to the news accounts about the capabilities of the pirates. They successfully attacked large freighters. They more or less ignored the threat of the British and American Navies. They took on all ships no matter the capability.

He had the "Lazy Lady" loaded with a huge amount of armament and he still felt he did not have enough and wished for more and perhaps some help.

They made Mogadishu without incident, and it ended up being a quiet stop.

Not much was going on as far as he could tell. He became more nervous than ever.

Where in the hell were the pirates?

The coastline of Somalia consisted of miles of barren beaches and flat dry areas almost treeless plains beyond them. The sea remained calm, and the "Lazy Lady" cut through the water as smoothly as a sharp knife through a properly cooked tender steak.

Ted and Maurice planned to stop at Kismayo where they would stay for seven days while they took a locally guided tour to the Lag Badan Bush Preserve and another tour in Kenya to see the Boni National preserve.

He thanked them for the invitation to go with them. He said he preferred to baby-sit the "Lazy Lady." He was surprised that they were going to leave it unattended except for the oversight of the people renting them the dock mooring space.

He was sure if he did not stay the boat would be gone before they returned. His presence was protecting the Lazy Lady from being taken over at the pier, but he wondered what the situation would be when they left.

After Ted and Maurice left, he went into Kismayo and walked the few shopping streets.

He wanted to see if there was an obvious place where the pirates sat and talked about their adventures. He was trying to determine who the pirates might be and where their boats were located.

Finding the pirates and finding their boats was not as hard as he thought it would be.

The pirates operated very much in the open. Their boats were anchored out off the beach. There were about a dozen power boats anchored off there. It was not apparent to him which boat was a pirate boat and which boat was a fishing boat. He guessed the boat's purpose really depended on what was available to catch.

The "Lazy Lady" was anchored in the port and could easily be seen from the beach area. The fishing boats were all bottom anchored just off the beach. Apparently, there were common bottom anchor points where multiple boats ended up in clusters.

As he walked down the pier to the "Lazy Lady." A newly anchored ship just outside the harbor caught his eye. Once on board, he took out his high-powered binoculars and scanned the new arrival.

He took this as an ominous sign. It was too much of a coincidence for the ship to show up and anchor offshore.

To him the new arrival looked like a support and supply ship. He had watched the news and seen such a ship being pointed out. It was a floating armament locker for the pirates. It provided the "pirates" who were usually local fishermen in need of work, the arms, and the guidance to raid the targeted ship in question. The arms ship stayed off the coast away from the control of local authorities. They were the control center and the local fishing boats became their attack arm.

He added this new arrival to his list of places to place his c4 explosive surprises.

He prepared the sleek long waterproof satchel bombs with remote controlled fuses. Self-setting explosive pins allowed for easy attachment to a wood or fiberglass boat hulls. He arranged eighteen satchels on the deck. The goal was to place these satchels on the hulls of the anchored pirate vessels.

As he waited, the dark of night chose a snail's pace for its arrival.

He kept himself busy by preparing an additional half dozen charges for the ship now anchored outside of the harbor. He planned to attach them with metal piercing self-anchoring pins.

These did make a small explosive sound which gave him some concern.

When it was finally dark enough for him to move into action, he pulled the "Lazy Lady's" small skiff alongside. He quickly loaded the satchels and placed all of the charges into the skiff. He then quietly paddled toward the closest cluster of pirate boats.

The night turned pitch black and was a perfect backdrop for his endeavors. He quietly lowered the skiff's anchor and slipped silently into the water. He made sure the anchored boats were unattended. He attached the first satchel. The explosive charges that fired the nails in sounded like thunder to him but went unnoticed above the normal background noise of the lapping waves. The installation of each satchel two thirds of the way back from the prow of each boat was quickly accomplished.

He moved the skiff around to make it easier to deliver the satchels to all the anchored boats.

In less than two hours he was on his way out to the anchored ship. The ship stood out like a beacon in the pitch-black dark of the night. The ship was aglow in red and white lights. It was clear to Ian that they were not trying to hide or go unseen. It was also clear that there had been no intervention from anyone on the coast.

He used the small electric motor to get him in close to the ship and then used a paddle for the final approach. His goal was to get to the ship's hull undetected.

Once he was inside the curve of the hull, he got in the water and placed three charges along the front third of the hull.

The prow would be blown off and the ship would not be able to travel in the forward direction. The crew's only hope would be to throw the ship into reverse and head backwards to the beach and run the ship aground.

He held his breath as he paddled quietly away from the pirate ship back toward the harbor. When he arrived at the "Lazy Lady" he took a deep breath.

He pulled the skiff up on deck and dried it off. He finished cleaning up the deck and finally went down into the galley and fixed himself some breakfast. It had taken the entire night to accomplish his preemptive preparation to deal with the pirates.

He hoped not to need to use any of the explosives he had placed but felt there was a good chance that he would need to use all of them.

He had deployed the preemptive defense. He knew the challenge would be to get Maurice and Ted into preparing their on-board defenses.

He sat out on the deck and watched the sunrise over the pirate command ship. After his morning coffee, he went below and went to sleep.

A couple of days later the harbor fuel tug came by and asked if he was interested in buying fuel. He was unsure of who might be associated with the pirating, so he checked the fuel before taking the nozzle to put it into the tank.

The person in charge of the fuel boat quietly told him to watch out for pirates. They were watching.

He gave the fuel nozzle back to person in the fuel boat when he had topped off the Lazy Lady's fuel tanks. He paid and included a generous tip. He thanked him for the warning.

After fueling up he went through checking all the sails and cleaned out all the lockers.

The next day he got everything ready to go. He took a swim off the side and checked out the hull to make sure no one was doing to the "Lazy Lady" what he had done to them.

Everything was as he had set up. He repositioned two torpedoes to point aft and left two pointed forward.

A few days later as the sun was going down behind the distant mountains, he saw Maurice and Ted walking down the pier as they returned from their tours and came on board.

Ted was standing and looking at the setting sun, bemoaning the fact they would lose a day due to their late return.

Ian suggested they could leave immediately and make up most of the time. He would be glad to take the first eight-hour shift.

"The fuel, water, and food are all stocked. The sails inspected and the deck hand is ready. We can dine on a grilled steak, have some wine, and watch the sunset as we sail," he said giving them a smart salute.

"Oh, that sounds like a lovely idea. I will toss a salad and get the steaks ready for the grill," Maurice said as she went down below.

"Ted, you should see this place. It is cleaner than it's been for years," she yelled back as she walked into the main dining, cooking, and seating area.

Well, let's weigh anchor," was Ted's response.

"Let me make sure we are clear of any pier rental issues. Then we can cast off," Ian replied as he jumped onto the pier and walked to the rental office.

"Be careful when you leave. You know this is a dangerous area for pirates," the agent said quietly.

He thanked him for the warning and wished him well. He also rewarded him monetarily as he realized that there were honest people in every corner of the world. It was a tough world to be left alone to live peacefully.

He walked briskly back to the "Lazy Lady."

"We are ready to go. I will take her out and get her into the wind before dinner," he said as he untied the ropes from the pier.

Tom replied that it was great that Ian was taking the first shift on the helm. He wanted to get a quick shower before having dinner.

The engine came to life and Ian backed the "Lazy Lady" into the channel and pointed her at the mouth of the harbor.

He was not expecting anyone to follow. He took note that no other boats left the area. He was sure the action would take place at sea, away from any authorities and away from their home base. Those watching him would most likely be glad he was leaving before sunset.

Once out of the harbor he he flipped the switch to raise the main sail. The wind caught and he could feel the "Lazy Lady" come to life. Next, he raised the jib and felt the next surge of power.

He then let out the spinnaker and the "Lazy Lady" was skimming swiftly through the water.

"What in the world are we doing," Ted asked when he came out on the deck with the steaks he was planning to grill.

"About ten or twelve knots," was the answer knowing Ted did not mean what speed.

He was trying to get as much speed as possible and put well out to sea.

Then the pirates would need to chase after them.

There would be no give in his treatment for those who chased them. He wanted them to be trying to take the "Lazy Lady." He was counting on their desire for a quick capture to allow him to take them out.

The sun was setting over the coast as the steaks reached their peak and the mouthwatering aroma drifted out to the helm.

"Everything is ready in here," Maurice called from the kitchen area.

He set the tie on the wheel and went below. He filled his plate with some salad, corn and selected a small steak.

"I am going to sit out by the helm," he said as he grabbed a beer and went to the seat in front of the wheel.

The wind and sails were having a steady love affair and "Lazy Lady" glided smoothly through the water. The sun's last rays were casting an eerie purple, grey glow over the land to the starboard side and a Cheshire moon was making a faint glow across the water.

"This is the life," Ted said as he sat down on the starboard bench.

"Yes, it is, and I love it," Maurice said as she walked up and sat down.

"It is gorgeous, and I wish beauty by itself would keep us safe. The reason I have the "Lazy Lady" at its top speed is to get as far away from the harbor as possible. I expect the pirates living there and the command boat anchored outside the harbor will be out hunting us down by morning," he said between a couple bites of steak.

"I will get my rifle and shot gun ready," Ted said.

"I didn't see any pirates," Maurice said looking questioningly at Ian.

"I know they will be out after us by morning. Two people warned me back in the harbor. I also spent time observing the command ship. I suggest we get prepared to defend the "Lazy Lady"," he replied quietly.

"What do you suggest," Ted asked?

"We will most likely get overtaken by tomorrow afternoon. The pirates will most likely come at us from three different directions. One group will come from behind and two from the front," Ian replied.

"What can we do," Maurice asked quietly?

"Yes, a great question. I need to make a confession so you can better understand my response. I am known as the problem solver. The pirates along this coast are the problem I have been sent here to solve. Usually no one knows I have been around but, in this case, there was no place where I could safely leave you. However, you will be safer with me than by yourselves," he confessed to Maurice.

"I wondered about your bug collection. Now I probably know some of what you brought on board. I am a little pissed you waited until now to let us know what we were getting into," Ted commented.

"I was told you had rejected help and rejected changing your route," Ian replied looking him square in the face.

"I guess we did do that," Ted replied.

"Now here is what we will do," and he went on to tell generally how they would fight the pirates. He purposely left out most of the defenses he had set up.

Maurice would take over the helm when the pirates arrived.

Ted would then use his 308 to nag the oncoming pirates.

He did not tell them of the torpedoes, or the satchel bombs he had put on the pirate boats or about the bombs currently under the seats they were sitting on. He felt it would stretch them more than they could handle. They were still unsure they would be attacked. He was not sure about their ability to act.

After Ted and Maurice went down to get some sleep, he began to prepare for a full battle. He put the radio controls that would trigger the bombs in a storage area at the base of the helm.

Maurice would take the helm from midnight to four. Ted would take the four to eight shift. He would return to the helm at eight.

He took in the spinnaker and the "Lazy Lady" dropped twenty percent in speed. When attacked Ian wanted to make a show of making a run for it by resetting the spinnaker.

Time crawled for him. He arranged the C4 floating bombs in the locker under the seat. These could be dropped overboard and set off by remote control. He wanted to use them last if they still needed to run for it.

After getting everything as ready as he could, he went below to get some sleep.

"Call me if anyone shows up," Ian said as he left the deck to Maurice.

It seemed only a few moments later that that he awoke with a gun in his face.

"So much for planning," he thought as he was herded out onto the deck.

"I'm sorry, I fell asleep at the helm and the next thing I know I am looking at the barrel of a gun," Ted said as Ian joined the two on the bench.

He leaned forward with his hands around his knees and looked up at the leader. He groaned loudly as if in pain. He needed to act quickly if they were to escape. The explosive charge kit was below the bench. He chose to take immediate action.

"What's wrong," Maurice asked in a concerned voice.

"It must have been the steak I ate last night," Ian replied with another groan and this time he fell off the bench and leaned back with his chest on the bench.

He slipped his hand into the bench. He grasped what he needed.

He did a sweeping floor kick and brought down two of the pirates. He jumped up as the third pirate was raising his gun. Ian stepped in, spun, and hit the pirate in the face with his elbow. He pushed the gun down and shot the leader in the foot. He guided the leader's gun hand and shot the two that he had floored. He then dropped the activated c4 charge into the boat tied alongside. An explosion was followed by screams from the boat and then silence. His final action was to guide the gun below the leader's chin and pull the trigger.

The entire action had taken less than fifteen seconds.

Maurice and Ted were sitting with stunned expressions on their faces.

He quickly dumped the bodies over the side and cut the rope dragging a part of the pirate boat hull.

He looked at Maurice and Ted and said that the steaks were great. They still had not moved from the bench on which they had been sitting. He decided that he would give simple to understand orders.

"Ted, catch the wind and set all sails. Head due east," he barked.

"Maurice would you be so kind as to make all of us a pancake breakfast; I would enjoy two eggs over easy to go along with three pancakes and three sausages," he asked as he guided her to the steps leading to the galley.

This helped the two to come to life. They were clearly still in shock, but they were now doing something they could do in auto mode.

He went to the rear locker and got out a deck brush, a bucket and proceeded to clean the blood off the deck.

"I'm sorry, I fell asleep. I didn't even know it until they jumped on board," Ted apologized as he guided the "Lazy Lady" eastward.

"It happens. I should have anticipated a single boat being sent after us. I missed it and it almost cost us. There won't be any more mistakes today.

Let's focus on the rest of the pirates. They may not hit us today because they probably received radio communication of our capture and went back to port.

But they will be back in the next few hours, and they will not be happy. Lock the helm and let's all get a good breakfast," he said as he finished getting the water off the deck.

The pancakes, eggs over easy with two sausages were great. he complemented Maurice on her breakfast.

He was thinking through the next encounter. The pirates would be more aggressive when they came at them the second time and they would come in overwhelming numbers.

"We're in trouble aren't we," Maurice asked after Ted left to be at the helm.

"Well, we are now at more risk. I will need to bring the pirates close, so they bunch up. Then I can take them out in one big bang. However, what I am concerned about is whether they come in firing their guns," he replied.

The sun was setting when he saw the pirate chase boats. He decided it was time to take control.

"Let me have the helm. Maurice, go below. Go into the shower and sit down. Ted, I can use you up here if you are game," he said looking at him.

"Sure, I'm game. What do you want me to do," was the quick reply.

"When I give the command, I want you to take down the spinnaker. Then immediately be ready to reset it," Ian said as he scanned the horizon for more boats.

They were coming in from three directions as he had anticipated.

He kept the "Lazy Lady" going at full speed until the two front groups of pirates began to converge.

"Take in the spinnaker," he commanded as he cut the helm and took a forty-five-degree tack to the wind. This brought the boom into the middle of the boat. The Lazy Lady leaned to one side.

He was headed straight at the starboard group of pirates. He then turned ninety degrees and headed back toward the portside of oncoming pirates.

All of the boats were now closing fast, and they were beginning to bunch up.

Once again he turned the helm and the "Lazy Lady" groaned as he turned her sharply back along the original path.

He was watching the pirates, and they were all cheering. They knew they had their prey captured.

Ian then took a 180 degree turn and now the wind was at his back. The two groups now in front were almost together and coming in fast.

"Let out the spinnaker" Ian said and as it filled, he let the mainsail boom out to catch the full tail wind.

"And unload your shot gun on both sides of the boat," he shouted at Ted.

The "Lazy Lady" jumped swiftly forward.

The oncoming pirates were caught by surprise.

Ted was blasting away as they went through the mass of small speed boats.

Ian cut between the groups and sped out past them. The three groups converged behind the "Lazy Lady."

The shooting had caused them to hesitate in the chase, but they were almost immediately coming on as fast as they could.

"Take the helm but do it from the bench area," he yelled at Ted as he pressed the buttons on his control panel. The sea behind them exploded. The air blast caught up with them and the noise was deafening.

The huge wave traveling out from a cratered center was almost ten feet high. There would be no survivors in the group behind them.

"Can I come out now," Maurice asked as she looked back at the fire and smoke where all the boats had been.

"You don't play fair do you," she continued?

He looked at her and just raised his right eyebrow.

He told Ted to sail the Lazy Lady as fast as he could. The danger was not yet over.

Late in the day Ted pointed to a large ship overtaking them.

Ian looked through his binoculars and noted the small one-inch gun mounted outside the con tower area.

The first shell hit the water just to the starboard side of the Lazy Lady.

The second hit just to the port.

He understood the message and told Ted to let down the spinnaker and begin to let down the main sail but be prepared on his command to immediately reverse the process.

He watched as the ship approached. The third shot did not happen. He figured they wanted the boat in one piece as much as they wanted the passengers for ransom.

When the ship was about a football field away, he pressed the button that set off the explosives he had placed along the bow of the ship.

He watched as the entire front of the ship blew off. The result was as powerful explosion as he had ever experienced.

The first smaller explosion that he had triggered was followed by a series of explosions and the boat lit up the entire sky behind them. He speculated that his explosives had triggered the explosion of gunpowder and the armament on board the ship.

He shouted for Ted to hoist the main and put up the spinnaker.

The Lazy Lady took a leap forward.

He watched as what was left of the ship was going full speed astern and heading in toward the shore. It did not appear that it would make it.

He had not used the torpedoes or needed the shoulder mounted missile launcher. His supply of C4 floating mines was fully intact. Plenty left for any other pirates that might come after them.

"Is it over now," Maurice asked once more?

"Yes, I think it's all over for now. We have several more ports where some minor pirating is going on. If you don't mind, I will go with you to the Cape," he replied as he sat down to enjoy the sunset.

Ted was still at the helm.

Maurice replied that he could travel with them at any time to any place. She had never dreamt of so much adventure and would not want to have it without his presence.

A few days later after reaching the Cape, he said goodbye. He had taken down all his armament and had brought it to the pier and sent a message to his support team to retrieve it.

His flight from the Cape to Cincinnati took a full day of travel. His greeting once he got home once again brought him back to the land of the living.

He wondered what the next problem-solving assignment would possibly be.

7 Hydra

*O*nce again he blocked the dark side of his mind and let the bright creative part take over. Lesley gave her love, and the kids were the sparklers of the constant fireworks of life.

They constantly lit up his life at home. Girl Scouts, Boy Scouts, coaching soccer, basketball, and baseball absorbed him in the tumultuous flow of a great life.

His home could not have been more rewarding or fulfilling. The fact that he lived in a decadent home, in an affluent community, only served to remind him to give back to the community.

At work he assumed a coaching and developmental role that was not going to take him to the top of the organization but one that allowed him almost total flexibility in the type and timing of his work. He was always welcome at the sites he coached, and he was used broadly across the company.

The yin and yang of his life did not escape him.

Instead, it made him cognizant of his behavior and actions. He focused on the principles and values that he supported and wanted his kids to embrace.

He treated everyone as equally as he could.

He also applied his beliefs to himself and the morality of his behavior.

This would have been much more difficult had he been more deeply religious. He truly believed in some advanced, superior helping hand but if there was a God, he or she was not a controlling one, nor one focused on reducing the evil loose on the world.

He was not about leaving the righting of wrong to the next world. He truly accepted the role of being a problem-solver.

How he solved the problems he was sent out to solve had never been questioned by the organization that funded him and his problem-solving sessions.

His family was not put at risk by his nefarious problem-solving actions and therefore he continued to standby waiting for the next problem to be solved.

He was listening to the evening news on NPR about the shootings of young people in Norway when the announcer made the comment "This is a terrible solution to this situation. We just need a better problem-solver, one that provides a fair solution."

He knew he had been given the signal to deal with the Norwegian shooter who had killed seventy-six people in what the shooter called a preventive strike. In fact, he had slaughtered mostly innocent bystanders and killed teenagers attending a summer camp.

In Ian's view these were actions of a very disturbed mind. The shooter claimed he was sane. Various specialists examining him for the court gave conflicting views.

Normally the defense would have been seeking the doctor who would proclaim their party insane, and the prosecution would have been looking for one to give the opposite opinion. In this case the roles were reversed.

Because of the way the Norwegian law was written, the prosecution felt they would have better long-term control over the time the killer would spend locked away if the outcome were to send the shooter to an insane asylum. They would be able to keep him there forever.

The defense knew the maximum time if he was sane was twenty years with a chance of parole.

He was not sure how anyone would grant parole to someone who killed more than seventy people.

He agreed with the commentator either solution was less than desirable.

At least in this assignment he would blend in with the local population. On the last several assignments his presence was immediately obvious.

On this assignment his work could be focused on solving the problem versus figuring out how to blend in.

He began by reading all the material that had been printed about the shooter. He was unique in his singular, fanatical view, and his ability to filter out any information counter to his thinking.

However, Ian knew that people normally developed their views in interactions with other individuals.

He wanted to know the people who had helped the shooter develop his current view. What he found was an alarmingly large network of people with similar views. This was a solid network spread across Europe with outposts in the US, Australia, and Canada.

To kill the snake, you must cut off its head. This snake had many heads.

He recalled the story of Heracles in Greek mythology where he killed the Hydra of Lerna. He also recalled that Lerna was the fabled entrance to the Underworld or Hell.

The story and its many parts were very appropriate and applicable to his problem-solving assignment.

Currently only one head was exposed to the public, but he had found many heads ready to take similar actions.

The assignment began to look and feel more complicated than he liked. This multiplicity made the job much more difficult. He preferred simple confrontation and elimination. His investigation led him to conclude action would need to be taken in rapid order against each head of each cell of the loosely affiliated organization.

Like Hercules in the Roman version of the story he would have to cut off and cauterize the stump of each head.

The arrogance of the individuals involved was a benefit to him. They were very open and vocal about their views and though they thought they had hidden themselves behind fake names on the internet, he was able to quickly find their home addresses and their real names.

The internet is a very open environment and hard to hide in. He was not a professional hacker, but he knew how to follow the threats back to IP numbers and he had a program that analyzed patterns and correlated them to specific IP locations. He also had the support of a team that thrived on traveling through the depths of the Internet. With their help he had a very complete story for every head of the Hydra.

Once he identified a specific individual, he dug into their work life and their recreational activities.

A work accident scenario when possible was the easiest to execute. However, recreational activities like mountain climbing, hang-gliding, off-road cycling, sky diving and deep-sea diving appeared on the list of recreational hobbies that these individuals participated in. These activities also made for perfect accident scenarios.

The Hydra had nine heads and this organization currently had nine cell leaders. A husband-and-wife team led one cell. It was impossible to tell which one of the two was the actual leader. He hoped they did their sky diving from a plane piloted by one of their cell members.

He spent almost a month doing his research and developing a plan of action.

He planned a legitimate business trip to Rome, Italy for his day job. Afterwards, he would begin the cycle of problem-solving.

He then scheduled a series of train and plane rides that took him to Gdansk; Poland, Rostock; Germany, Edinburgh; Scotland, Copenhagen; Denmark and Oslo; Norway.

He would assume a different identity for each problem-solving event.

He would strike rapidly and continuously in a path from Poland, to Germany, England, Denmark, with the final action in Norway.

His final travel point would be back to Rome to complete his legitimate job and then return home.

Each leg of the trip was booked under a different name and nationality. This was going to be an arduous round of elimination. He hoped to keep everything he planned to do in a strict organized executional order.

Once again Lesley seemed to know that he was not only going to Rome for the work he did for the company but that he was on a *Problem-solving* assignment. She knew that when he went into his research and study mode it was to ensure that he had the knowledge and depth of understanding that ensured he would safely return.

Lesley always asked her mother to spend some time at their house while he went on one of his longer assignments.

"Please be careful. We don't need the money, just you. Do what you must but come home, where you are loved. The kids need you," Lesley whispered as she gave him a departing hug.

She knew that he had earned many millions of dollars that had greatly enriched them, but she felt that he didn't do it for the money but because he had agreed to do it so many years ago.

He knew that he would be a problem-solver to the end of his days. The yin and the yang of his situation would forever pull at him.

The light fought the dark.

The light was on the winning side and Ian hoped that it would continue its reign.

The trip to Rome turned out to be pleasant. The person sitting next to him on the flight from JFK to Rome was an Italian romance writer. She shared how she developed and wrote her stories. She was the image of the perfect grandmother. Once she began to spin her story, Ian began to see a sexy goddess weaving an unbelievable story of lust and passion.

He constantly had to shake his head to clear his vision. He had to separate himself from the words and see the person who was using them.

Upon arrival he went to the manufacturing plant as scheduled to carry out the legitimate part of his trip. He spent his first two days of a workshop getting some improvement work started. The teams doing the improvement work would then have the remainder of the week and the following week to implement their improvement solutions.

He would return to either help them make more improvement or to validate their accomplishments.

The workshop was a perfect cover for what he needed to do.

On the third day, Leonid Grazinski, his name for the first part of the trip, boarded the plane to Warsaw, Poland. Leonid had dark hair, a full beard and wore large black rimmed glasses.

It was a short flight. Upon landing Leonid went to the car rental counter and got the keys for the car that he had reserved.

He drove out of the airport to a local super market where he bought two fifteen-liter water containers.

His next stop was a garden shop where he bought three large bags of pine wood chip mulch.

Then he got on the highway to Gdansk.

On the way he stopped twice to buy gas. He paid cash each time.

Upon reaching Gdansk, Leonid drove immediately to 839 Walowata where the husband-and-wife team lived. He wanted to verify firsthand what he had already verified on the web.

He drove to the backside of the house and carried the wood chips and gas cans to the side of the house.

This was the riskiest and most exposed part of his activities, and he hoped those watching would not remember him once the event took place.

Then he, posing as a Polish government official went to each of the work locations where the two worked. His official looking papers got him an interview with each. He had come up with a story about missing family members and trying to find their relatives.

His brief conversations or departure interviews as he thought of them verified the conclusions he had reached from his research. Evon and Jeran were not nice people.

They both shared a fairly cold and hard view about everything around them. Neither was very interested in understanding what had happened to their long-lost relatives.

He was being thorough because the solution he was about to execute was irrevocable.

The interviews did not last long.

He left after the interviews and went to a local park to have a late lunch sandwich and to wait a few hours for the couple to go home.

The park he chose had a path around a lake. He followed the path and observed the quiet lives of other people doing the same.

Were any of them on similar assignments as he?

"Thank heaven they have no children." He thought as he contemplated his next actions.

He was now into the part of the job he disliked and dreaded. The solution he had selected was rather brutal and final. On this problem-solving round all solutions would be final.

On the mission into the heart of Russia, no one had been killed. It was on the opposite book end of his current solution set.

The research into these two targeted individuals pointed to a more permanent solution.

Darkness provided the cover he needed.

He removed the beard. If by chance someone did see him, he wanted them to see a clean-cut face and no glasses.

One of his major concerns was how close together the individual homes were to each other. He took note of the fire alarm box on the corner. He would pull it once he was away from Evon and Jeran's home.

Entry into the house was a simple matter. The backdoor was open.

He carried two syringes of nikopeen. This would knock out a person for at least two hours and was practically undetectable. Additionally, it would be undetectable since the individuals would be lumps of ash when the fire was put out.

Evon was at the sink and never knew what happen. He approached her from behind and put one hand over her mouth and the syringe into the vein in her neck. Evon went limp and he quietly laid her down on the floor.

Then he dropped a plate and let it shatter on the floor.

Evon, are you all, right?" Jeran asked from the next room.

The lack of response immediately drew Jeran to the kitchen.

Ian stood out of sight in the small entrance alcove.

Jeran entered and bent over Evon. He quietly uttered her name as he knelt beside her.

The night stick made a nasty thudding sound as he brought it down on Jeran's skull. The needle to the neck vein followed immediately.

He arrange both of them in their beds in the bedroom. He then brought in the wood chips and gasoline.

He covered the two with wood chips. He sprinkled the gasoline around the room and under the bed. He then went around the rest of the house sprinkling gasoline.

He then carefully lit a cigarette and put matches in the ash tray in such a fashion that he could light one match and let it act as a fuse. This would give him a few moments to get out of the house and down to the corner before the fire ignited.

Initially it would look like an accidental smoking in bed fire.

He knew if the authorities were thorough, they would discover it had been deliberately set. He hoped they would not be looking too hard.

He was at the corner where the fire alarm was located when the very visible whoosh of the initial ignition took place. The sound was rather subdued, which he decided was a good thing. He waited a few moments until the entire house was on fire and then pulled the alarm. He knew that everything in the bedroom would be totally engulfed. Nothing would remain.

He walked casually to his car that he had parked two blocks away.

The drive to the airport was uneventful. He turned his car in and went to catch his next flight. He was on his way to Berlin.

He left Poland as Dr. Martin Schindel. He was on his way home to Berlin. Martin had grey hair and mustache, long sideburns and dressed as a throwback to the seventies. He was quiet and other than his clothes he went unnoticed by those around him.

Once in Berlin, he picked up the car rented to Dr. Schindel and drove to Rostack where the next event would occur in a warehouse.

The third target, Adalmar Pfeiffer, worked as a high bay forklift driver at a warehouse. He was scheduled to meet a fate similar to the one where he had "accidently" killed a Turkish co-worker by backing up and crushing him in between the forklift and the wall.

His research into that event convinced him Adalmar had gotten away with premeditated murder.

He parked the rental car across from a gas station about six blocks from the warehouse. Dr. Schindel entered the bathroom and came out looking like a fifty-year-old dock worker wearing a worker's uniform. He left his car and walked the six blocks to the warehouse.

He arrived for the night shift.

The time was close to midnight when he made his way into the warehouse. If everything went as planned, he would be on the way to Edinburgh by one in the afternoon of the next day.

The security cameras on the top of the building scanned slowly back and forth. This design was efficient but left many holes in the video recording. But few people broke into a warehouse so why spend money on sophisticated equipment was how he reconciled the low tech being use.

He entered during the blind moment of the security camera sweep. He would leave later through another of these video holes. He would never be seen.

In a sense, he would be a true ghost.

There were only a few other warehouses close by.

He had scanned for their security cameras and had stayed out of their scans. He did not want to accidently show up on any other videos.

Once inside, he climbed to the top of the high-rise racks. He was able to observe the forklift operators and determine the rack aisles Adalmar worked.

Adalmar worked three high-rise aisles. His job was to place and retrieve pallets from the holding racks and then to deliver the pallet to a conveyor running across at the front of the aisle.

He chose the middle aisle as the scene for the accident. His plan was simple. He would push a pallet out from the very bottom rack. He would block the forklift pickup holes to prevent Adalmar from immediately picking it up. Adalmar would need to get off his forklift to either spin the pallet or clear the pickup holes.

He loosened the railing holding a pallet at the very top. He blocked it, so it would not fall. Once Adalmar was in the right position he would release the pallet.

Adalmar was oblivious to the preparation. He was busy picking and placing the pallets as scheduled and posted on the video screen on his high-rise forklift.

Ian first prepared the drop pallet and then climbed down and prepared and positioned the bait pallet.

The ease by which he was making his "accident" arrangements made him wonder how many other industrial "accidents" were murders?

Adalmar drove his forklift in for his next pick up and was blocked by the bait pallet.

Ian dropped the nuts and bolts from the top rack in to convince the investigators that it was an accident and then pushed the pallet out as Adalmar was crouching below in an attempt to turn the bait pallet. He looked up in alarm as the nuts and bolts landed around him.

The ensuing crash was thunderous in Ian's ears but from his vantage point it was obvious no one else had heard anything. The scene below was straight out of the Wizard of Oz. Only Adalmar's lower legs and feet were visible.

He hoped it would be hours before Adalmar was discovered.

He went through a roof vent opening and immediately to the corner of the building. He made his descent as the camera slowly scanned past the area. His coming and going would be invisible if anyone studied the footage of the video.

He returned to the airport and took a room as Shawn McGregor. He now sported a white beard and curly grey hair.

The next morning the departure from Berlin to Edinburgh went smoothly. He joked with the airline attendants and bantered jovially with the passengers around him as he boarded the plane to Edinburgh.

Once on board he fell asleep for the entire flight.

Edinburgh was one of his favorite cities and generally the Scottish attitude was very much to his liking.

He went to the pub most often frequented by Bryce Guthrie to see if he would show. He wanted to verify Bryce's next outing.

Bryce had invited his friends via his web site to go riding. He knew Bryce was planning to go out riding the next day.

Bryce was very much into the extreme end of the resistance movement and his definition of those who should be dominant was very limited. It was limited mostly to him and his immediate, following.

Most Scots would have found themselves excluded. His blog was revealing in its lack of logic and extreme dialogue against almost everything. It was clear Bryce wanted to be recognized for being a tough guy, who resisted any kind of authority.

Ian finished his beer. He spotted a notice from Bryce on the pub's bulletin board announcing the ride for the next day.

He decided to get familiar with the trail Bryce was planning to ride. He drove out to the area and found a shop that rented bikes to be used on the trail. There were several trails available to ride. The difficulty of each was posted in the shop on a map showing all the trails. The trail Bryce had mentioned was the most difficult one.

However, a trail rated as easy went within fifty yards of the most difficult one. He rode out on the easy one to the point where the two trails came together the closest.

He hiked up the slope to the more difficult trail.

Not far away was the point where there was a bike jump from between two boulders to the path below. The jump was actually blocked but Bryce had challenged those coming to his outing to take this jump.

Ian was here to make this jump Bryce's last one.

The following day, he went out early and again rented a bicycle and took the easy trail. He pulled his cycle into the brush out of view again at the point where the two trails were the closest together. He then climbed up the steep rocky incline to the trail Bryce would be on.

Timing was going to be the crucial element of his plan. he had learned that Bryce normally out rode the group of cyclists he went out with. He would push himself to the extreme just to prove his dominance. He always wanted to be in the lead.

Ian was hoping Bryce would take a lead of at least ten to fifteen seconds.

The layout was a jump of about eight feet from an opening in a crevasse. It went down to the trail just below it. The easy bike trail was another fifty yards below that point. There was a non-jump way around, but Bryce loved the jump.

He installed a trip wire that would flip Bryce off his cycle and hurl him down below. There he would be waiting to apply the final touch if needed.

The "accident" happened just as planned. Bryce went over his handlebars and hit the rocks below with a sickening crunch. Ian gave a quick twist to Bryce's head to finalize the accident.

The bicycle had come over the wire behind him. Its front wheel smashed on the rocks and bounced just beyond the body.

Ian quickly climbed up and retrieved the trip wire and descended on the opposite side of where the following riders would come.

If one of those following chose to follow Bryce on the jump route, they would land on his body.

He did not wait to see what would happen.   He went straight down the trail back to where he had left his bicycle. He rode at a rather placid pace around his easy trail and returned to the rental area.

The emergency vehicles were just going out to the scene of the "accident" as he turned in his rented bicycle.

He inquired about the ambulance.

"Some hot shot tried a jump that was closed and died on the rocks below. The jump has been blocked but this guy always goes around the barricade," the clerk volunteered.

"I hate to say it, but he had it coming. He ignored all the safety signs and barricades," the clerk continued as he processed the cash payment.

Ian took his receipt and quietly left the scene.

He headed back to the Edinburgh Airport. He entered the large back stall of the bathroom as Shawn McGregor. When he came out, he was Felix Madsen.

Felix was trim, had blond hair, was clean, shaven and sported a neat casual outfit.

The next stop was Denmark where a swimming accident was about to happen.

He considered Denmark as a very friendly country.

He had been there many years ago as a young sailor and had toured the countryside on a bicycle.

He had almost sneezed himself to death when he was overcome by the pollen from the blossoming mustard fields. To this day, he was adverse to large expanses of yellow blossoming fields. The yellow blossoms were beautiful to the eye but deadly to the nasal passage.

His time in Denmark had remained as one of his favorite memories. Perhaps it was the corn liquor and beer he drank with the Danish friends he made that colored his mind.

He had learned via his help team that his next target, Nels Jensen, had the habit of taking a daily early morning swim across the small harbor in front of his home. He would swim out and then return to the dock.

This solution approach was very simple. He had devised an inflatable sock tube to be slipped over one or both legs. It could be quickly inflated with air to pin the leg in. Some lead weight on a cable would then pull the bag and the swimmer down and he would drown.

Once Nels had drowned Ian would deflate the tube and release the body. Slipping the tube over the leg like a sock ensured no signs of foul play would appear on the body.

He arrived in Copenhagen. He drove to a local hardware store and bought the lead he needed and then drove to Esberg. The more than one-hundred-year-old Guldager Kro Hotel had caught his eye.

He had called ahead to make sure they would accept his diving gear when it was delivered. He had sent a week's payment in advance. The proprietor was happy to make the acquaintance of Felix Madsen when he arrived.

There was a deep dive scheduled to go down to a sunken World War II German Cruiser. This gave him a specific real excuse to buy the gear he needed for this solution. The specialty bag was in his suitcase. The weights required to pull the swimmer under were available at the various shops selling diving equipment. However, that would be very obvious to a good investigator.

Instead, he had purchased the lead ingots to be melted in doing pipe and equipment joining. The ingots were just the right size. Three of them would pull any adult under.

Later, hewould return the weights to the store and get his money back. This would ensure the weights would disappear and never be available even if someone figured it out.

It took two more weights to counter the buoyant effect of the specialty bag. The balloon holding all the weights was rigged to exhaust all the air when the lead weights were released.

All that escaping air would be visible on the surface of the water as the air bubbles broke the surface. This he felt would be as low risk as he could make it.

Nels was consistent in his swimming routine. Ian watched and timed him swimming out and return. The next day he would be waiting for him in the water.

The next day he dropped the anchor of the power boat he had rented to go fishing. He was just outside of the small harbor where Nels swam. He lowered his equipment over the side and put on his wet suit and dual air tanks. Once in the water he pulled his equipment into place.

Nels walked out of his house and dove into the water. He was unaware of anything unusual.

From below Ian carefully maneuvered to intercept Nels's path. It was crucial to remain almost directly ahead of Nels and come up in time to slip the balloon over his legs. He managed to capture only one leg just up above the knee.

The instant inflation and immediate downward pull took Nels off guard. He was already drowning by the time he began to struggle. Ian followed him down to the bottom. There a tank of compressed air waited to provide the air to refloat the weights.

He brought Nels back up near the surface and released him. In this way if he sank back down it would be a natural sinking.

He gathered all his equipment and swam slowly out of the small harbor to the small power boat anchored just beyond the opening. He put everything into the boat and headed back to the dock where he had rented the boat.

On his return he was able to show three fish that he had "caught." They had been caught in the harbor the day before by a fisherman that sold them to him. He had purchased them for the specific purpose of showing his success when he returned the boat.

It was only seven thirty in the morning. The sun was making its appearance as it painted the fluffy clouds above to an orange and pink hue.

He returned to the Hotel and went in for breakfast. Afterward he called to cancel his dive with the excuse of a head cold. This was always an acceptable excuse for not going on a deep dive.

He checked out and returned to Copenhagen. Along the way he returned the lead weights and disposed of the two floats by cutting them into small pieces and dropping them into several random dumpsters.

Then it was off to the airport to catch the evening flight to Norway.

The local news reported the drowning of a local swimmer.

He knew that his next solution, if successful, would make global news.

The research into the psychiatric clinic where Andrew Brenic would be held made it clear it was designed to keep the inmates in, but it lacked the most basic defense against someone focused on breaking in. After all, who would want to break into an insane asylum?

His plan was to act on the first night Andrew arrived at the facility.

He arrived a few days before.

He was Lars Ringdal an inspector with the Norwegian Southern and Eastern Regional Health Authority.

The document he presented explained he was to examine the facility where Andrew would be kept.

The internal operation was rather simple. However, there were lots and lots of cameras; too many for Ian to come in invisibly. While on tour, he noted the model and make of the camera recorders. He needed a replacement set of storage media. The recorder model brand being used by the clinic still used DVD's.

Ian asked about the surveillance procedure. He was shown the DVD storage files. They were kept in chronological order. Each camera had its own DVD storage drawer. The DVDs were replaced during the beginning of the morning shift. Before leaving Ian managed to lift three blank DVDs. He would use these to create fictitious video footage to put on the DVDs that he would leave behind.

He only needed to replace the few DVD's recording the hallway and the room Andrew would be in. He also needed to replace any DVDs on which he now currently appeared.

Andrew was to be transferred from the prison where he had been held to the psychiatric center on a Sunday afternoon.

The media was great at showing Andrew being brought out to the transport van and quickly being escorted away by several police car escorts.

Ian was prepared and ready to carry out his problem-solving actions. The DVD for Andrew's room would show him quickly fashioning a noose from his under clothing and then using his bed frame to commit suicide by slow strangulation.

The figure in the DVD was a dead ringer for Andrew. It would be almost impossible for even an expert to realize the rouse.

In real life, Ian would provide the hands-on guidance Andrew needed. A mild version of nikopeen would incapacitate Andrew long enough for him to suffocate from the noose. It would be almost un-detectable. He put this into Andrew's drinking water and the coffee brought to him when he arrived.

He was in the security area making his official observations. This allowed him to change out the DVDs from the previous visit. The disc set for the evening's event was in his briefcase. He would change this out after completing his task in Andrew's room.

After all the arrival excitement died down and the facility went back to a normal operation, there were two guards left to watch their new and only prisoner in their wing of the facility. Like almost all in this profession they drank a continuous cup of coffee. Ian put a mild sedative into their coffee and quickly had them sleeping in their chairs in front of their monitor displays.

He then went down the hallway to the room in which Andrew was being held.

The water and coffee sent to Andrew had kicked in and he lay on his bed unable to move but his eyes were open.

Ian looked directly into them and mouthed "I am the devil sent to bring you home."

He gave him a brief smile as he put the noose around Andrew's neck.

Andrew's immediate look of alarm and his attempt to speak made it clear he understood his fate.

Ian moved him around, so the frame of the bed could function as the gallows and lowered him, so he was suspended by his neck.

The noose was immediately effective. Andrew actually managed to put up a slight struggle before passing out. The autopsy examination would verify strangulation from hanging.

Ian made sure the deed was complete before returning to the observation booth and replacing the appropriate DVDs.

The entire event had taken less than ten minutes.

He left the observation area and dialed the guard station from the supervisor's phone.

He left it ringing. He knew that one of two guards would awaken and then sound the alarm when they realized Andrew had hanged himself. He figured that it was very likely the two guards would lose their jobs.

He went immediately to the Oslo airport and returned to Rome.

There he returned to the manufacturing plant to review their improvement progress.

Two days later he boarded a flight back to the US as Ian.

The flight home re-opened the door to the world of light. He could hear the laughter in the dark, but it was muffled out by the warmth of his thoughts about Lesley, Ella, Matt, and Sean.

The dark laughter gave way to a child's giggle. The light came with the warmth that only love could provide.

He knew there would be other problems sent his way but for the immediate future he was going home.

He took a deep breath and closed his eyes as he thought about home.

8 One Bad Sheriff

*L*esley came out and welcomed him home. Ian gave her a big hug and a kiss. They walked hand in hand. A cup of coffee and some small talk later put Ian in his normal state of mind.

Ian marveled at the rapid pace of change the world seemed to achieve. He realized that it was not necessarily that more was happening, though he thought that might also be happening, but that technology had made discovery and communication occur so easily and swiftly.

People were communicating around the world with each other. The ability to take pictures with one's phone had dramatically changed what people were able to document.

The proliferation of news channels meant that he had to recorded several news channels to keep up with events and spent several hours scanning them for the signal that would activate his problem-solving actions.

He focused heavily on the family. He was into Boy Scouts with Matt, into set building in support of Sean's participation in his high school acting. He supported Ella by taking her to her music lessons.

Waiting during her lesson gave him time to review the events of the day. He would listen as he walked around her piano teacher's yard. Mrs. Henry, a widow, was an avid gardener and grew a variety of plants and flowers around her home. He had asked permission to walk around the outside of the house to admire her handiwork. This simple request had put him in a very good relationship with her.

It was in the yard that he learned of his next assignment. He was listening to the news on his i-phone when the call for a problem-solver occurred. He stopped and looked at the blooming roses with their skirting hem of sweet alyssum. The automatic porch light seemed to sense the greying of his mind and chose that moment to blink on. He realized that he would need a similar blink of inspiration to handle his next assignment.

He waited until he was back home, and the kids were all in bed. He let Lesley know that he would be in the library listening to the news. He sat periodically sipping his cup of chamomile tea as he listened to the commentator give his report on the local sheriff that was challenging the President about the treatment of prisoners. He noted that the sheriff was quite disrespectful, and he seemed to Ian to be a bully and blowhard.

He was surprised that such a person had won multiple re-elections. His personal arrogance and the ignorance that he exhibited gave Ian a bad impression of the people of the area.

How was it possible for them to vote for such a person unless they too were ignorant? The majority of the people in his county supported him and his tough stance on crime. His war chest had millions of dollars in it, and he felt righteous and just. He was praised, supported, and admired by those on the far right.

Then the commentator mentioned that it seemed that the sheriff was the problem that needed solving.

Ian listened to several different stations. This was not something he wanted to misinterpret. It was also an assignment he did not want.

What was he to do to one mean sheriff, an elected official?

He noted that it was almost a year and a half since his last assignment. The assignment pendulum must had struck home.

The research led to the realization that the sheriff was not one of the normal "bad" guys. He was a little beyond himself in self-admiration.

Ian was sure that when the sheriff looked himself in the mirror and he saw superman, the man of justice. He certainly could not see the image of an apparent ignorant bigot.

This was not the normal go get the bad guy assignment. He knew he would need to develop some new approach.

He studied the action of the sheriff's department. He found out about their consistent actions against the Latino or black groups. In each case the claim was that a complaint had been called in. The sheriff's office also held periodic special immigration sweeps in the Latino areas of the city.

The Sheriff subsequently destroyed many of the records that pertained to these cases. Challenges to his actions took on a, "he-said she-said," type of legal argument. He guessed the sheriff had learned this from the old saying, "No body, no crime."

As he thought about the situation, he concluded that if the sheriff thought in this manner, he really was a criminal in sheriff's clothing. He knew the sheriff was not the first and that there were many wolves with sheep's clothing in politics.

The rhetoric coming from the sheriff and his office sounded exactly like the lines used during the racial discrimination practices in the south and across the country during the civil rights movement. He was a little amazed at the politeness and almost the silence of the black community.

Surely this group could see actions previously taken against them that were now being practiced against the Latinos.

He was also surprised at the judge giving the plaintiff's the same council given the black community during the civil rights days about having to prove that the police department was following a discriminatory policy.

Did she not read or know any history?

The official records only corroborated 10 or 11 stops for the last three years. This was ludicrously low.

Of course, who was keeping the official record?

He was sure the sheriff was rewarding all the record keepers well.

He decided he would go and get firsthand knowledge about what was happening in the sheriff's territory.

As always, Lesley knew he was off to some problem-solving assignment and reminded him that they could be considered wealthy, and he did not have to take any undue risks.

The flight out to Albuquerque was one of the most uncomfortable flights he had experienced. It was a small plane with small seats. He sat in the first seat on the left. This was the side with only one seat in the row. Across the aisle there were two seats. The plane was full, and the cabin was too hot.

He closed his eyes and thought about what he had learned from his study and analysis of the situation.

He had interviewed past colleagues of the sheriff, and they pretty much confirmed the sheriff was a; "no nonsense," self-principled, always right individual. The sheriff had shared that he often lay awake at night thinking of new ways to make the news. When last on a nationally televised event he accepted the "honor" of having his office compared to the KKK.

It was clear to Ian that he was dealing with a sadistic narcissist that was a criminal that stood behind a badge.

His abuse of power, misuse of public funds, racial profiling, election law violations, failure to investigate sex crimes, unlawful enforcement of immigration laws had cost Doan county over one hundred forty million dollars in fines and out of court settlements. And the sheriff continued to be re-elected, which said something about the people in that county.

The small city of De Luca was just fifty miles from the Mexican border. It had a rather large Spanish population and was the second largest county in the state by population.

Ian asked his team to provide a reliable contact that he should seek out to learn first-hand about the situation

Randy Everly was a transplant from Wales. Randy's red hair and red skin complexion made him stand out from the other people around him. His parents had immigrated to the US in the thirties and had been one of the families that endured the westward migration and had ended up in Arizona because of a raging dust storm. They had struggled to make their life in the dry land outside the city of Los Cruse.

He was one of six children and was the only one still in the area and working the ranch his parents had established. He joked his ranch 'Dry Marsh" was a ranch mostly in name. He now raised a few head of cattle but made his primary income from raising sheep, selling wool and lamb meat that he sold via the internet. He was also the author of a cookbook, "A lamb in Every Pot."

Ian met Randy at a local Mexican grill in the parking lot. He walked up and introduced himself as Tom Easterly and then agreed with Randy that they should continue to continuing their discussions in the air conditioning and a cold beer.

He found Randy an interesting character. He wondered if Randy's out of place appearance gave him any problems.

It was clear from their discussion that Randy had struggled with the attitude of many of the people in the county.

More than two thousand local residents were specially deputized participants who paid for their own uniforms, badges, and other policing equipment. They were an on-call posse that did the bidding of the sheriff. Even the governor of the state was a member of this group. It was great press for him, and it assured he had a sure number of votes from this fringe group.

A few supporters were so engaged and into participating in this checking and giving a helping hand to the police that there was an elite four hundred who had outfitted themselves and patrolled the streets on a daily basis.

It was mob law at its best.

Randy had documented them at work and had video he shared with him.

Ian commented that it seemed that the county was very close to a gestapo state.

Randy agreed that it was democracy at its worst.

He felt the majority of the people did not support the behavior that had become common and was currently in control. But most of the people did not go to the poles and vote.

"The supporters who supported such action must have blinders on or they have sold their souls," he commented to Randy.

Ian was experiencing a slow burn because though the sheriff may have gone rogue and though the sheriff seemed to be a son-of-bitch, hard-boiled, iron fisted even severe to the community at large, he had a long history of law enforcement. He had been re-elected multiple times, so he seemed to have the support of the "gracious" though very biased people of his county.

What action could be taken against such support?

The county had recently paid out more than eight million dollars in a settlement to the family of one individual who had died at the hands of the sheriff's deputies. The internal cameras recorded the "snuff like film" event. The police officer claimed that the gun had gone off accidently. He was still on the police force even though he had faced additional charges of unnecessary brutality since that time.

There were two other similar deaths. But the people were not white, they were Hispanic. Thus, there was no follow up action against the police perpetrators.

Ian was sickened by such accepted behavior.

"What a country. The most militarized country in the world, with the most per capita prisoners in the world," he thought as he continued to ponder his problem-solving dilemma.

Randy suggested he witness the local sheriff's men in action. He said there was a road work crew scheduled to do some work on the following day.

He shared that the crew worked for one of his friends who had complained that the sheriff's men seemed to have his company targeted. Many of his work crew were of Spanish heritage but all were American citizens born here to families that had lived in the US for all their lives.

Ian agreed to meet the following afternoon and rode out to where some road work was underway. They parked at the far end of where a variety of pickup trucks and cars were lined up on the side of the road. They then walked back to where the work was being done. A patch of struggling, scraggly trees and some cactus provided some shade and cover for him and Randy to remain out of sight.

He was glad for the shade on such a hot day. It was like sitting in an oven. They were sitting in the shade, but it was of little comfort.

The work crew blocked Hope road as they got ready to lay gravel down on the driveway.

It was so hot the sweat dried before it formed

A slight breeze wafted a gust of heat into his face, and he turned his attention to the road work.

He wanted to see firsthand if the sheriff's department would check the road crew for papers. About three o-clock two patrol cars stopped and began checking. He caught all of it on tape and got great audio as well.

"You know the drill. Line up and show us your work documents," a large egg headed officer said as he lifted his hat and ran his hand across his hairless head.

Every one of the workers had their US passports with them. Ian took note. He did not regularly carry his passport!

"Ah, Pedro, I think I have an outstanding parking ticket on you. Stay here until I get back from checking it out," a second officer commented.

"You boys have so many names it's hard to tell you apart. Not enough to just have first, middle and last. Gotta add mama's name and any other ones you think of. You're lucky though, it wasn't you," the second officer said as he handed Pedro's passport back.

It was obvious Pedro was angry, but he kept his cool and put his passport neatly back into a zip lock bag and into the side pocket of his old cargo pants.

He knew better than to confront the police.

Now Ian understood the protestors who carried signs calling the sheriff, "Ar-payaso" or clown in Spanish. It was also obvious that there was no love lost between the men standing in the hot sun and the police officers.

"The supporters who supported such action must have blinders on or they have sold their souls," he thought adjusting his hat to hide his face from the sun.

He mulled over possible ways to handle the situation. He was in a fix, a true conundrum. He knew he was out of his element.

After the deputies left, he and Randy interviewed the workers and documented how they felt. Several had served in the Marines and the Army. They felt conflicted and angry.

When asked how they would change the situation they suggested getting rid of the sheriff and all his deputies.

Ian sympathized with their attitudes and about getting rid of the sheriff.

He knew he was facing a wall. He then got the idea of looking deeper into the sheriff's family tree and looking for the family rogues.

Every family had some.

What were the rogue's personal behaviors and were there any really bad ones?

He really doubted he would find anything there, but it was worth the effort.

How about family driving habits?

He really was trying to find a low-key approach to dealing with this problem. This was more difficult than dealing with really bad guys like killers, terrorist, and drug dealers. Some would say the sheriff fit into all those categories except the last.

Ian wondered if the sheriff was a teetotaler.

When he got into more of the sheriff's personal records the pattern of self-righteousness just got worse. The family did, as all families do. They gave no information to a stranger.

He got nowhere.

For once Ian wished instructions and guidelines came with the assignment.

He decided he was personally too involved.

It was time for another approach.

He sat and looked down at the floor. He needed some sort of inspiration. He needed a different perspective.

He called Leslie to see how her day had been. Hopefully, she was having a better day than he.

Leslie was excited. She had volunteered to work on the democratic presidential election committee.

This caused him to think about how this country was supposed to work.

There were elections.

The sheriff was coming up for re-election. He had a strong war chest.

His opposition needed a strong campaign. He wondered how much money he could put into a Super PAC aimed at unseating the sheriff and all his cronies across the state. To date his bank account had been limitless. Ian had used millions of dollars before, and the account always came back to its original sum of one million.

He would put up the money, but he also needed a strong candidate for Sheriff and a person to run the state campaign.

The next morning at breakfast he asked Randy if he would consider running for sheriff. Randy said he had considered it but that he did not have the financial means to wage an effective campaign.

He tested Randy by offering him financial support that would exceed what the sheriff had in his war chest.

Randy said that if he had that kind of support, he would challenge the sheriff.

He then asked if Randy knew anyone that could mount a state-wide challenge to the current administration and had the contacts that could run such a campaign?

Randy replied that he did not but that his friend who owned the construction company probably did.

After making the initial plans, Ian stated that he would arrange the financing but would remain anonymous.

The two went to the bank and arranged a bank account.

Ian called his support team and requested they set up a Super Pac called a New Tomorrow. He gave them the bank, the account number and routing number. They were to keep the account at one million until the county and state elections were over.

It was time for him to go home.

Perhaps his unknown sponsors had hoped he would eliminate as many people as he had done on other problem-solving sessions. All had been bad people but none as this One-Mean-Sheriff.

Ian had to be satisfied by the feedback he got when his personal account went up by the normal amount plus a bonus.

His flight home was significantly better than the one he had experienced on the way out.

As he looked up to the top of the Cincinnati airport escalator and saw Leslie waving at him, he put his recent experience to the dark side of his mind.

The side of his mind that flourished in sunshine and happiness took over.

9 War Lord

*L*esley was a radiant guiding light beam that kept him focused on staying sane. He continued the fight between the dark and the light, but he had mastered the dark's most overwhelming impact. He was aware of the need to keep his mind in control and fought an almost daily battle.

Lesley had also been the rock that guided the family's development.

Ella had gone to college and was unsure of what to do. Lesley had recommended she seek a degree that would lead to a solid long-term employment. Ella decided on a Finance and Accounting degree.

Matt at first went into game programing. Then he went into communications because he saw it as a way to get to the front office of big companies. Then he went back to programing. He was in one university or another for a good ten years.

Sean, who had perfect SAT and ACT scores got accepted by every Ivy league university and was sought out by about a dozen state universities. He picked Harvard and while there he also pursued his first love that was singing by getting into the Hasty Pudding's Crocks. He traveled twice around the world during their summer road tours.

During this time, he continued his professional management career and had become a leader in their internal global organizational improvement program.

He also had many problem-solving assignments on a roughly one assignment every other year cycle. It remained the one practice that other than Lesley, no one else had a clue about. Lesley knew he took the special assignments that would have been labeled as extremely politically incorrect. Her one constant message to him was to come back alive.

He was never called on to solve simple problems and he was not called in to solve every problem. He was not sure what the criteria was that resulted in his engagement. However, most problems required him to seek out some new perspective of why the problem was not being successfully addressed.

He and Lesley were experiencing the empty house syndrome.

Lesley had joined a reading club.

She actively campaigned for her favorite politicians. Some were Republicans, and some were Democrats. She focused on the actions the specific person supported. She demonstrated what it meant to be an independent.

He was kept busy at his day job. He also was writing both fiction and technical books. His other endeavor was to spend time at the gym trying to stay in shape.

He was sitting and watching the news when he was pulled wide awake when the announcer ended his reporting by stating that there must someone who could solve this problem.

He had missed what was being reported and had to replay the news. It was then he saw the atrocities being shown. The report was on the child armies being used in Africa. The scene was of one person being punish for some infraction by having one eye blinded with a red-hot poker. A second scene was of a person accused of stealing having the offending hand cut off.

He took in the news from several other sources. His first level of understanding was to get the different reporting perspectives.

He then went on the internet to study the history of that African region.

He discovered that the recent history of Africa in the last two hundred years was so violent that it seemed unreal to him.

There seemed to be no end to the pain.

No end to the injustice.

There were white on black atrocities and total domination.

There was black on black and tribe to tribe atrocities.

An Aids epidemic seemed to go unchecked across the continent.

The continent experienced a series of drought and starvation.

Numerous countries had corrupt leaders who sent billions to their bank accounts in Switzerland and neglected the people they were supposed to help.

He wondered how this continent could have been the place where the human race got its start.

How it could have been the host of one of the great civilizations of the world and then descent into the hell it had become in modern times.

One of the more current disseminators of tyranny and cruelty was the warlord, Julian Kerney. He wielded a self-styled cruel justice.

He used child soldiers and supported a thieving raping army. He was in control of a large region of Uganda.

To Ian it was clear that this warlord was without a soul. Or perhaps he indeed was the son of Satan.

He had these thoughts as he watched the news. The scene he was viewing, captured by someone's cell phone, was the punishment session after Julian had over run and taken over a non-supportive village. He lined the young men up.

Those that begged for their lives he shot.

Those who did not beg had a hand or foot cut off.

Those he thought defiant got both hands cut off.

One particular young man who remained defiant after losing both hands had his eyes gouged out. It was clear the war lord relished the role of being the applier of the cruelty he seemed to embrace.

A cruel egomaniac would be too kind of a description.

It was clear to Ian that he was crazy.

What made this particularly poignant was the fact that this crazy warlord had children carrying out his orders. The majority of his army was made up of children between the ages of seven or eight to about fifteen or sixteen.

These "soldiers" were desensitized and were brutal to their captured victims. The ax man cutting off hands and feet was perhaps all of twelve or thirteen.

Ian wondered what type of people they would grow up to be.

It was clear there would be only one solution.

Unfortunately, Ian did not have any faith that the solution would change the course of events in the world that was currently in practice.

It would only delay or perhaps divert the problem.

The warlord was constantly surrounded by his guards. Since he was the target of the Uganda army, he was constantly changing his location.

Kerney thought himself to be king of the territory he controlled. He was next to god in dispensing the punishment. His headquarters was located in an abandoned prison left behind by the British when they left the region. He held many of his enemies in the prison.

Ian was sure that he made it their hell on earth.

His ego made him take periodic chances at getting caught by doing impromptu interviews and inviting journalists to tour with him.

Ian decided being a journalist seeking an interview that would be broadcast globally was his best chance at getting close to the "general."

He approached this war lord by sending him his credentials and detailed his objective to tell the general's side of the story. This approach had worked with one of the leaders of a Mexican drug cartel.

Ian knew that vanity was one of the most common weaknesses of megalomaniacs and he planned to leverage it to the hilt.

The wait for a reply was relatively short. Ian used the time to learn more about Kerney's mode of operation and the territory in which he operated.

He was invited to Kampala for the interview.

Once again, he let Lesley know that he was on a business trip and that he would probably be gone for a little over two weeks.

Lesley raised her eyebrows and reminded him that she wanted him back in one piece.

He chuckled and told her that he had always come home in one piece.

His travels took him to Rome and then on to Kampala. He had packed two sets of travel bags. One set was going to get stored at the Kampala airport. He had been instructed by Kerney to meet his escort at the curb outside of the arrival terminal. Ian was glad that they had not come into the airport to meet him. He located the nearest locker. He was happy to see that it had a combination lock. He put one of his suitcases into it.

Ian felt that walking out of the doors of the airport was like walking into a sauna. The hot air made breathing hard. He looked around. He had been told someone would meet him. A tug on his sleeve caused him to look down and to his left. A youngster about ten or twelve years old stood looking at him.

"Mr. Mathew Parker, I am Peter, and I am here to escort you," he said politely.

Ian recognized him as one of the young soldiers shown in the news report participating in cutting off hands and feet. A shiver ran through him.

Peter waved his hand to someone waiting in a van.

"You must be part of the Lord's Resistance Army." he stated in a calm voice. He was surprised at how calm, friendly, and polite Peter appeared.

"Yes, we are to take you to the hotel. We will return to take you to dinner with our leader at seven this evening," he replied as he opened the back of the van. He took Ian's suitcase and put it in.

The driver opened the sliding door and Ian got in behind the front passenger seat.

"Can you tell me something of your experience in the LRA," he asked Peter as they drove to the hotel.

"No, we have been told to be polite but not to be interviewed by you or to answer any questions," Peter replied.

"I understand, then perhaps you can tell me about the city as we drive through?" he replied. He realized if he were able to get something from either of them, they would most likely be in trouble.

"Yes, being a tour guide is my other job," the driver volunteered and began to describe the highlights of the city.

The driver kept a running commentary about the sites he drove by. He expertly maneuvered through traffic and shortly arrived at the hotel.

Peter guided him to the check-in counter. He reminded him to be in the lobby a few minutes before seven.

The three-foot-long brass clock hands of a built-in wall clock, behind the lobby desk, let Ian know he had about two hours to shower and relax before dinner.

He thanked Peter for meeting him and getting him to the Hotel.

He went up to his room. There he took a long hot shower and then took a short nap.

Shortly before seven, Peter and the driver of the van once again met him. It was a short drive to the restaurant.

Peter accompanied him in and made the formal introduction.

"It seems you are more of a photographer than journalist," Julian Kerney stated when Ian was introduced.

"I guess the photography gave me the most visibility, but I am actually a journalist at heart," he replied as they followed the waiter to a table in the back corner.

"You may address me as Julian. What should I call you," he continued?

"Most people call me Matt or Mathew," Ian replied. This was the name he had taken for this mission. He always kept his true identity secret but used some identities multiple times.

"I have always enjoyed the better things in life. I know you must think me cruel and barbaric, but I received my degree from Oxford in philosophy. My field behavior is a necessary evil of keeping control in this part of the world," Julian said as he ordered the wine.

"I took the liberty to order a beef Luwombo with a side of Malewa covered sweet potatoes as the main dishes. I think you might find an order of Nsenene and Nswaa interesting appetizers," Julian continued.

It was clear to Ian that he was being tested.

Julian was watching to see what his reaction would be.

He knew what the Luwombo would come wrapped in a banana leaf. He asked Julian what meat would be served in the Luwombo.

He then commented that he hoped the Nsenene were crispy and not chirping or hopping about and that the Nswaa were as delicate and tasty prepared in the Ugandan way as compared to the Southeast Asian way.

"It all sounds good to me," he finished with a smile.

"Tell me what you have been doing since your time filming elephants in the Congo," Julian said as the waiter poured the wine for tasting.

Ian's story was partially true, but a great deal was complete fabrication. All of it was plausible. He shared that he had traveled to Egypt to report on its grand history - true. He had sailed the East Coast of Africa - True. He had spent several years writing a book about the region which was not yet published. He had done nothing of the kind but had plenty of material to do so and it was a good time filler. He was not sure Julian heard a word he said but his eyes were watching his. If Julian were looking for signs of lying, he would see none. He was a consummate storyteller and believed all of his own stories.

He could pass a lie detector test with no effort.

"Well, you have come to me because you see potential fame and fortune in featuring a cruel war lord like me. Is that not the case?" Julian continued.

He was baiting to see if he would flinch.

"I am not sure about fame and fortune but an in-depth interview and a written article about you, what you seek and about your followers, will most likely be picked up by all the agencies. It will help feed my growing family and will not hurt my reputation for getting the unusual story," he replied and took a sip of wine.

"And it will not matter if it does not happen because if all the dinners are this good, I will be quite satisfied," he continued as he put his glass down.

He actually enjoyed the appetizers of grasshopper and termites. It was clear Julian had been trying him via the appetizers, but he had experienced similar fare in Mexico.

The conversation then turned to Julian and his vision of the world he would create when he came into full power. He painted a vision of a country at peace under his leadership.

While Ian listened, he realized he was dealing with a self-centered cruel narcissist. What concerned him more was that Julian thought himself sane and rational. This was one of the more intense interactions with a narcissist that he had ever experienced.

He was happy when he was finally escorted back to the hotel. It was good to get away from Julian. He was toxic and inevitably jerked on his hate gene.

Few people had ever affected him like Julia had.

He was the product of a good family, was very smart, he was well educated and ultimately evil.

Ian placed him in a category where only the devil would be worse.

Julian had extended an invitation for the next day to tour the countryside with him.

He had accepted.

The car that picked him up looked like any other black limousine. Julian was sitting in the back on the driver's side and Peter was sitting across from him facing the rear.

The backdoor was opened by a person that got out of the passenger's seat.

Ian thanked him and sat down facing forward.

He then greeted Julian and Peter.

The acceleration and handling made it clear that the limousine was heavily armored. He figured it was both fully armored and bullet proof. It was following a truck with eight heavily armed soldiers and one who was seated behind a roof mounted fifty-caliber machine gun.

A similar truck followed behind.

The backseat of the limo was spacious. Peter was responsible for handing out water or any other drink that might be asked for.

Julian explained he would be making multiple stops to talk to "his" people.

At every stop there was a crowd to cheer him.

Julian put on a good show of being a kind and thoughtful leader.

At each stop, Ian took notes. Interviewed a few people in the crowd and shot a myriad of pictures.

"I have planned something special for your visit. Trials were held, and judgment passed on a group of criminals. I have scheduled their punishment for this afternoon. You will witness firsthand how humane and how just I can be." Julian said as they were driven to lunch.

A shiver ran through Ian. His job was to eliminate the problems at hand. He was not squeamish on how to do this with the bad guys. To stand by and watch innocent men and women get mutilated and killed was more than he wanted to experience.

Time had run out. He would need to act more quickly than he had planned. His plan of action had to be right after lunch.

"We have rounded up the leaders of the opposition. They have each committed an atrocity against their fellow Ugandans. The elimination of these leaders is crucial for the peace of the region," Julian explained when Ian asked about the crimes that had been committed.

"After lunch we will go out to the execution site to witness the verdicts and the punishment," he continued. The punishments will be delivered by those who have been most offended.

Ian knew then that whatever he was going to do would happen in the limo.

He was not going to stand by and witness the injustice that would occur.

His solution would have to happen before the executions and maiming that would be carried out.

"Where is Peter," Ian asked as they entered the limo after lunch?

"He is one of the executioners and went on ahead to get things prepared," Julian explained.

This was a relief for Ian. Even though Peter had committed many atrocities, he was as much a victim as those he was about to execute. He was a boy whose mind had been bent and deformed by those around him.

Ian had a job to do, and he would do it.

It would be easier with Peter out of the picture.

He appeared to be unarmed. He had two wooden pencils, his pad of paper and a camera. This made him a very dangerous person.

He was aware Julian was armed. His driver also carried a shoulder pistol and had a shotgun mounted on the door. The person in the front passenger seat was also armed.

It was a situation that three people who were very confident in their safety were about to die.

When he went into action, he gave no warning. He drove the first pencil through Julian's ear and out the other side.

There was a look of surprise on Julian's face.

At that moment Ian hoped Julian realized his world had come to an end.

Julian gave out a startled gasp and then slumped forward.

The person in the passenger seat was bringing his gun around as Ian drove the second pencil through that person's left eye and into his brain.

The driver was just turning to see what was going on when Ian drove the same pencil through the driver's right eye and out the back of his head.

Without pausing, Ian pulled the driver into the back seat.

Ian rolled over into the front seat and got behind the wheel. He was glad the windows of the limo were darkly tinted. His next move was to get away from the armed escort. He followed the truck in front until they got to a major intersection.

He knew the airport was just a few miles away. He had a departure ticket that would take him out of the country. He had anticipated the need for a quick departure and had a departure ticket for every day of his stay. This had become his departure day.

He took a right turn and roared away from the trucks. It was clear they had not expected the departure of the limo. He took several turns through the back streets before making a run for the airport. He lost the escort early on and did not see them as he drove into the airport.

He put the limo in the back of the long-term parking lot behind a small truck.

He locked it and then walked away toward the airport. The limo was well hidden and could only be seen from the runway.

He hoped it would not be found for several days.

Once in the terminal, he went to the lockers where he had put his extra suitcase. Then it was on to the airline counter where he checked in his bag. That day's departure flight was on time. He walked slowly toward the gate and stopped at several shops to look around. He arrived at his gate as the first-class passengers were called. He presented his ticket and went on board.

He sat looking out of the window of the plane.

He had solved the assigned problem but the thought that a young Peter might be the next Julian did not escape him.

It was a solved problem with the solution very much wanting for a better one.

10 Family Wedding Vacation

*I*an was in love.
In love with his family.
In love with the woman of his dream.
He marveled at his fortune. Even after almost forty years, he still fought his demons from his time in Vietnam, but the family members were the bricks in a wall behind which he kept the demons that still haunted him.

His professional management role in a world class company ensured that he had experienced challenging work. He traveled too much globally but still managed to play a key role in his family's activities.

Lesley kept the family active, engaged and growing together. She also kept him stable.

She was his foundation.

His second problem-solving profession was always in play. This was a side of his life that Lesley knew about but she really had never totally understood. She never probed too far into the dark side of his problem-solving profession.

She knew that his problem-solving provided for what she considered incredible wealth. She was the money manager for the family and the millions that had accumulated over the years was as much her doing as it was the constant influx he added.

He and the family were in LA for a wedding of one of his nephews.

Lesley had suggested they include some vacation in with attending the wedding.

Everyone agreed that it was a good idea. It would be the one recent vacation where the whole family would be together.

Everyone would meet in LA.

It was a direct flight from Cincinnati to LA. Lesley and he were treating, and she had booked business class seats for everyone including Ella's husband, DJ.

It was a first for everyone and they enjoyed their time in the business class section of the plane.

Sean, who currently lived in LA, met them at the airport. During the drive to the hotel, the luxury of the flight out was the highlight of the conversation.

Sean made the point that he was owed a business class flight.

Lesley laughed and said the next time he came home to Cincinnati he would get his wish.

When they got to the hotel and checked into their rooms the conversation changed to how grand the rooms were. He and Lesley had one grand suite, Ella and DJ had another and Matt and Sean shared a third.

All the rooms were comparable.

They all had a kitchen with a table, an entertainment area with a couch, a large, curved screen television, and a lazy boy chair.

The bedrooms all had two twins.

A full breakfast in the hotel restaurant was included.

He thought about the wonderful years his family had given him. He still had his demons from Vietnam, but he had been blessed to participate in raising Ella, Matt, and Sean.

Each had provided a unique experience.

Ella was so well behaved and confident in her abilities that she had never challenged either him or Lesley as she grew. He gave her a rating of zero for preparing him and Lesley for the challenges that Matt and Sean gave them.

Ella attended the Ohio State University and there met DJ. She had refused repeated marriage proposals, but DJ kept returning. Dennis J Nin, better known as DJ, had found the woman of his dreams, and pursued her until he finally succeeded with his sixth proposal of marriage.

Ian really liked the consistent perseverance DJ had shown.

Matt was the personification of a good guy. He was always thinking about making and keeping good friends. This did not always work to his advantage but his focus on his abilities and a fundamental belief in people was all he needed to guide him. He became an Eagle Scout but rejected the Scouts when he learned the scouting organization was biased against gays. He loved school and had degrees from three universities.

From day one, Sean excelled in school. He was the top student in his high school class. He had perfect scores on his SAT and ACT. He had universities across the country who tried to entice him to attend.

He chose Harvard.

Upon graduation he had called to let him, and Lesley know that he could not accept some of the highest paid employment offers that had been extended. He thought the financial companies making the offers were acting counter to his principles. He instead chose a non-profit offer that was substantially below the ones he received from the large financial firms.

Ian was proud of all three.

He had to wipe away tears of joy as he thought back through the wonderful years. The three had all become principle centered; principles of honesty, integrity, fairness and of treating everyone as you wished to be treated.

Sometimes the highest good feelings are a warning for the greatest pain.

His senses were at full alert. He was worried and had no basis for the worry. This made him worry more.

Ella provided the best calibration for the wedding that they had all attended.

She made the point that the wedding was bigger than hers, but it was nothing like the weddings that her uncle gave his daughters.

She reminded us how he had thrown a first-class wedding for all three of his daughters.

She placed the wedding they had just attended between her really small one and the ones Uncles's daughters had been given.

Lesley and he had kept Ella's wedding small.

Lesley and he had a small wedding, but they were still in love and together.

They both felt the wedding was the beginning and should not overshadow the long journey ahead.

The day after the wedding Sean, who was currently living in LA became the family tour guide.

He first took the family on a morning walk on the beach that ended up with a coffee at Starbucks.

He then took the family to the top of Mt. Griffith.

There the family had a picnic and took in the view of the LA valley. The sea formed the far boundary that met the U shape range of mountains forming the sides of a steep bowl around the city.

He enjoyed both the morning beach walk and the time on top of Mt. Griffith.

Sean had provided the right way to enjoy LA.

The family watched as the sun turned the clouds a yellow, orange, and red hue. It slowly met the ocean and seemed to melt into the water.

He then invited the entire family out to dinner but admitted to not having a place in mind.

Ella volunteered a place one of the police attendants at the wedding had recommended. He had given her a card with the address.

Sean took the card and entered the address into the Google map App.

He was in the front passenger's seat.

Matt was sitting behind Sean.

DJ sat behind him.

And Lesley and Ella were in the very back seats.

"Tell me again how you got this card," he asked Ella.

"Oh, I was admiring the variety of food, when this guy approached me and began a conversation," was the reply.

"He was probably hitting on you," Sean replied.

"Hey, that is great if I can still get that kind of attention," Ella joked back.

The GPS was set to the address, and they were on the way. The grey of the evening was threatening what was left of the day. Sean drove slowly down the mountain toward the restaurant.

"No matter where we are going it will take forty-five minutes minimum," Sean commented.

Having lived in LA for a year he was the resident expert.

Things went quiet for a while and Ian noticed everyone but the two in front were snoozing.

He smiled and mentally agreed that up close LA was a sleeper.

"Hey, this doesn't look like a very nice part of town. The GPS shows us getting there just around the corner," Sean commented.

Ian's senses came fully awake. This was the feeling he usually had during his problem-solving sessions.

Sean turned the corner and went into the drive of the restaurant. The parking lot was full of people drinking and laughing.

As Sean turned into the drive all the people out drinking turned to look at the van and began to come toward it.

"Turn around and get out of here," Ian barked at Sean. Sean seemed to sense the same thing he did and backed into an empty space and then headed out toward the street.

The crowd surrounded the van and began beating on the windows.

"Don't stop. Just drive," Ian said as he pushed down on Sean's accelerator leg. The van sprang forward, knocking people down on both sides. A few ran along sided pounding on the side of the car.

Inside the it was absolutely quiet.

The traffic at the main corner was going to be a problem. Three guys with knives in hand were running the van down. They were being cheered on by the crowd that was now standing in the middle of the street.

He instructed Sean to keep the van moving slowly. He instructed Matt to slam his door into the guy coming for Sean. Ian opened his door and stepped out into the street.

The person running up the right side of the Pilot gave a big grin as he ran toward Ian.

He raised his knife ready to drive it into Ian.

Ian responded with a back kick and caught the attacker in the chest. He could hear the bones breaking as the attacker flew backward, bounced once on the street, and then lay still.

He proceeded around the back of the van and stomped on the heel of the second attacker that was getting ready to slice the back-left tire. The sound of breaking bones let Ian know that the attacker would not continue the pursuit. When that attacker reached for his gun Ian delivered a round house kick to his temple. He could hear the snap of neck bones and figured he had just killed the second attacker.

He then called out to the attacker that was just recovering from Matt having slammed the door into him.

The attacker responded by waving his knife back and forth.

Ian stepped toward him and in toward the car.

As the attacker lunged Ian twisted.

The attacker was good. Ian felt the knife slice cleanly through his jacket.

The attacker would draw blood, but Ian guided the attacker's hand and knife so that it traveled up and under the attacker's chin. He then used his other hand to push the blade up and into the attacker's head. The point of the knife exited out top of his head.

"Say hello to the devil," he said as he turned to look back to the mob that was now moving forward toward the car.

Without stopping Ian ran back to the passenger's side and jumped in.

"Get us out of here," He quietly said to Sean.

For a moment there was silence in the car. Then everyone but Lesley was asking questions. He knew she had watched his every move.

"Where did you learn to fight like that?" everyone asked almost in unison.

He was not sure how to explain more than thirty years of the type of problem-solving work that he had done. They knew him as a professional engineer traveling the world fixing manufacturing problems. He was not about to tell them anything more than he needed to.

"You learn many things during training. I learned most of what you just saw in Vietnam," he said giving as much truth to the statement as possible.

He didn't volunteer the years of continued practice that had kept his skills honed. Someday they might all learn about the small fortune his dark side problem-solving work had provided.

Currently he was trying to prevent that by opening a small business. He planned for it to be a very successful, so the extra income could be explained in that manner.

He pointed out that they were not yet out of trouble. They had been set up by a person Ella described as a cop. The people on the street would have the license plate number of the van. They needed to get the van off the road. They needed to change cars.

He suggested they go to Avis or Hertz and rent another vehicle. DJ and I will go in and get a rental. You go on to the hotel and park the van in the basement garage.

Again, there was silence.

Lesley quietly asked if they were going to stay out of trouble.

He replied that they would all be in the clear in a few days, but he wanted everyone on the morning flight to Cincinnati.

Sean reminded him that he lived in LA.

Ian replied that it was about time he took advantage of a business class seat and visited home and spent a few days with his mother.

He and DJ got out at the car rental. As they got done renting a van, Ian asked the attendant if she might have some duct tape. He thanked her and asked DJ to accompany him to help him tape his cut jacket.

He entered the restroom and went into the handicap stall. There he took off his jacket and shirt. He had been feeling bad about getting old and a little pudgy, but it had saved him. The knife had sliced through his jacket and made a shallow eight inch cut across his abdomen. It was a nice clean cut and there was very little blood. Only the fat layer had been cut.

He held the cut shut and instructed DJ to place three vertical strips of tape along the cut. He wanted there to be about a quarter inch between each piece of tape.

DJ did as he was instructed. He asked whether it hurt and whether Ian should go to the doctor.

"It doesn't hurt too much right now. I am sure it will hurt more tomorrow," Ian said knowing adrenalin was still at work.

"Don't tell anyone about this until a few years from now," Ian instructed DJ.

"Let's duct tape my shirt and the jacket while we are at it," Ian said as he took some paper towels and put them over the wound, "Here, give me some of that duct tape."

He and DJ walked out of the restroom and Ian tossed the duct tape back to the attendant showing her his repaired jacket.

"Good as new," he joked.

They walked out and took the full-sized van with bench seats.

They drove to the hotel and went up to their rooms.

Sean let him know that the van was parked in the darkest corner of the underground parking.

"What happens next," Matt asked?

Sean asked if they would be in trouble for leaving the scene of a crime and also fleeing across state lines?

Yes, probably if it gets to that. However, you will be alive to handle that situation. Right now, there are people in the police department and in the gang, we just confronted that want all of us dead.

It was a set up and it probably has happened numerous times in the past. Probably always to out of town visitors who unfortunately accidently went into the gang's main headquarter. Let me handle this and I think it will all come out OK," he said looking at Sean.

"You all head for the airport. I will stay behind to deal with the police. I will call you in the next few days and let you know what is happening," he told everyone.

He needed to get them all out of the way. There were some critically urgent unfinished actions that he needed to take.

"Dad, we can stay and help," both Sean and Matt spoke up.

"I know you could and thanks, but you can help most by making sure everyone is safe at home. Don't let your guard down when you get there. One of you stays up at night to make sure no one shows up," Ian instructed them.

He felt confident he would snuff out any reprisal at the LA end, but he figured you could never be too safe.

After a few hugs and kisses, He got everyone packed and on their way.

Lesley was unusually quiet.

Ian knew he would be doing some explaining once this was over. For now, she was taking her brood to safety and doing so immediately.

She came over and gave him a hug and kiss and mouthed "I love you.

Then she whispered, "Take care but solve this problem for good. This is personal and it is family."

He smiled. Lesley had thrown him a curve ball that he had not expected. He planned to hit the ball out of the ball park.

He whispered back not to worry "I am the problem-solver.

I leave no loose ends."

11 The Family Wedding-The Precinct

Sean had highlighted Los Angeles as the city known for Hollywood and being the movie capital of the world. He had boasted that it was home to Disney Land. He had lauded Stanford as one of the best Universities in the world just south of the city. He said he loved the vibrant night life. He had also pointed out that it had the Getty Center, a Natural History Museum, and a world-renowned California Science Museum.

Ian agreed that it had some very positive features, but he pointed out that it had also earned the nickname as the Gang Capital of America. He went on to share the statistics that LA had an estimated one hundred and twenty thousand gang members!

The 18th Street gang,

The Bloods,

The Crips,

The Hells Angels,

The Mongols, and

MS13 were just a few of the gangs that ran the streets.

He was unclear which gang the family had come in contact with.

He got on the Internet and found the precinct where the attack had taken place. The police station address was only ten blocks from where the incident took place. He wrote down the address and took a cab to the precinct headquarters.

He figured that the gang would have an inside person in the station.

The station was designed so the police sergeant faced the entrance door. Directly behind him was the call center and communication center out to the patrolling cars. To the right a series of desks served as the work center for each police detective.

He walked up to the desk sergeant. He causally looked around at the arrangement of the desks and who was sitting at them and then addressed the desk sergeant.

"Are you still looking for the folks that were attacked by that gang down the street?" he asked.

"Who are you," the sergeant asked as he looked up?

"Well, I am the one they attacked," he replied.

He watched as one of the ladies behind the sergeant picked up her cell phone and dialed. He was sure, she was the inside connection to the gang. He wasn't sure about how corrupt the other cops were but probably most were honest and hardworking.

"They said a whole pack of you attacked them. In fact, they said a rival gang attacked them," the sergeant said as he picked up the phone and dialed.

"Captain, you better get out here and meet the pack of thugs that attacked the gang. This should be interesting."

The precinct where the action had taken place had been contacted with the story that a gang had come in, attacked, and killed several of the club members.

"Good job by the way. You got three of the worst ones," the sergeant said quietly as he looked down at his log. "Be careful, they have eyes somewhere in here," he went on.

"Thanks for the warning, she is behind you. Don't let her leave when the excitement starts. She just called in the dogs," Ian said just as quietly.

Ian received an acknowledging grunt from the sergeant.

The Captain came out of his office from down the hall.

"You certainly left a loud calling card," he said as he approached,

"Where is the rest of your gang?

What's your name?"

Ian gave him his name and he extended his hand.

"Well Ian Sinclair, you and your pack of thugs are accused of attacking and killing three gang members for no good reason. I don't suppose you brought the rest of your army in with you," the Captain asked as they shook hands.

"Sorry to disappoint you but I was the only one they attacked and as you know they did not fare well," he replied quietly.

"Carl, get over here. Get this man's account of what happened at the Eagles nest. Once you have his statement call me. I want to talk to him afterwards," the captain said as he handed Ian over to Carl.

Carl was one of the folks Ian had been watching since coming in. He had been watching when the woman behind the sergeant made her call. Ian figured he was another inside connection.

"Carl, do the folks working here live in the neighborhood," he asked as he followed him to his desk.

If Ian sat down to look directly at Carl, He would have his back to the door and the work pool area. He turned the chair ninety degrees, so his left arm was on the desk and he was facing the entrance.

"A few of us do. Most have moved their families to better school districts, but they are still in the city," Carl volunteered.

"What keeps you in the area," Ian inquired?

"I don't have kids," was the brief reply.

Ian relaxed as he waited for the coming storm he knew would soon arrive. He answered the name, location, and reason he was in town. At this point, the information he was giving was fictitious. He was not about to give them anything useful until the threat of the gang was removed.

The front door of the station opened, and a tall, dark-haired officer was bringing in an individual that seemed inebriated.

"Jorge, what have you got there," the sergeant said as he looked up?

"I think this guy is high on PCB or something. I am going to get his name and facts and throw him in the holding cell," Jorge replied.

Ian wasn't sure about Jorge, but he knew immediately the person with him was the storm. He would be the one to pull an ice pick or some other weapon.

Ian knew from the layout Jorge and the guy he had in tow would come right by where he was sitting.

He pretended to be paying attention to Carl, but his entire focus was on the two walking toward him. At about three paces, the collar stumbled and appeared to be falling into him. He had an ice pick in his hand.

Ian stood up as if to catch him and smoothly guided the hand with the ice pick up into the chest of the attacker.

Ian took a slight step back.

The collar fell flat on his face. It all happened so swiftly only the collar and he saw the ice pick.

Everyone was surprised when they turned him over and found the ice pick sticking in his heart.

"Sergeant," he called out and nodded at him as the lady behind him grabbed her purse as if to leave.

"Mary, why don't you wait a bit," the sergeant said as he took her cell phone from her hand.

"Carl, why don't we go and talk to the captain now," he suggested as everyone was standing around looking down at the lifeless body on the floor.

"Captain, you wanted to talk to me. I just want to know if you are a good guy or bad guy before I talk to you," he said as he closed the door.

"What just happened out there," the captain said as he answered the phone. I could hear the sergeant on the line.

"Who are you? You just took out another of the gang's thugs and in my station," the captain said sounding a little irritated as he hung up the phone.

"I honestly came for a family wedding. At the wedding, someone recommended this especially good restaurant. That someone, I believe, is on your police force. When the family and I arrived at the address for this restaurant, we were in a parking lot not far from here. It was there where the entire clientele came out for the entertainment of the evening. It just turned out to be a very different entertainment than what they had planned," Ian said looking at the captain.

"Your station is compromised. If you check the phone call that lady behind the sergeant made in the last hour or so, you will find she called the gang.

I am not sure about Carl or Jorge.

I suspect Carl.

The sergeant seems honest. Find out how Jorge made his collar.

If you want to clean out your neighborhood, let's go visit the gang headquarters," Ian continued.

"Have you got a death wish? You want to go to the gang's headquarters. Do you know I have been trying to take down this gang for several years now? I moved my family out of the state to a safe location so I wouldn't have to face the threat made on them," the captain said as he ran his hand through his hair.

"I often find that going directly to the source of the problem makes it easier to see and solve the problem. Yes, let's go visit. I am sure there will be some resolution to this situation once they listen to me," Ian said confidently.

"You really must be crazy but your ahead four to one," the Captain said as he made the call.

They both walked out and got into the Captain's car. Jorge followed and went to his patrol car.

"I see you are bringing Jorge as your back up. Do you trust him," Ian asked the captain.

"It won't matter who is backup. If it goes wrong, we could have a hundred people and we would still be dead. The only reason I am doing this is because so far it is four to zero, on your side. Let's make sure the score stays to our favor," the Captain said looking steadily at Ian before putting his car into gear.

Ian was not sure he would be able to keep score that well, but he certainly planned to try. He had no special plan in mind. All would depend on the meeting that was about to take place.

They turned down the street toward the same parking lot he had been to earlier in the day. It was now close to midnight. There was still a small crowd laughing and drinking in the parking lot. They stopped to look at the two patrol cars as they drove in but stayed where they were.

Two very large men came out and approached the car he and the captain were in. "You gotta leave all your weapons out here," one of them said as he approached.

"Ian, you don't have any weapons on you, do you," the captain asked as he took out his weapon and handed it to Jorge?

"Jorge, keep this for me. Be ready for anything. Call for help if things turn ugly. I already called central to let them know what we are up to," the Captain went on rather loudly.

Ian knew for a fact that the captain had not called anyone.

He replied that no, he did not have any weapons.

The two thugs patted them down. "They're clean," one of them announced.

It was just like a movie scene.

He followed the lead thug.

The exterior of the facility belied the opulence of the interior. A long bar extended out to the left of the doorway and another on the right extended away from the door.

Both bars were fully occupied with a mix of scantily clad women hanging on to men that looked like bikers but were probably gang members. A combination of booths and tables filled the space in front of each bar.

It was clear to him that business was good.

The booze was flowing

The food was being carried out to the tables.

The women were doing business.

As he watched a patron snort a string of coke.

He was sure that there was an ample supply of drugs.

They were guided up the stairs. At the top landing they were led straight ahead through a large solid dark mahogany door into a large plush mahogany paneled office.

It reminded Ian of his library office at home, only the interior was more lavishly laid out.

The desk seemed to dwarf the person sitting behind it.

The person stood up and offered seats to him and the Captain. He introduced himself as Francisco De Pena, leader of the Reds. He went on to introduce the two people who had escorted them in as Pepe and Chema as two of his most trusted lieutenants.

"How may I help you," Francisco asked as if he was a friend of the Captain.

"I was just trying to find out what happened today. I hope there isn't a turf issue starting between you and some other outfit. This is Ian, he is helping out on the investigation," the Captain said.

Ian looked around trying to assess the situation. He needed to get the Captain out of the room.

Francisco sat quietly behind his desk sizing up the situation from his perspective. He was wearing a very expensive set of sunglasses even though he was inside.

"Your Zimmerglas sunglasses really stand out. They look great on you," Ian said casually.

"Perhaps the Captain should go see the scene of the incident and you and I can get better acquainted," he said nonchalantly.

"Pepe, Chema take the captain for a tour of the scene. When you are done come back here but leave the captain at the car," Francisco instructed his two lieutenants.

Ian almost stood up to cheer about Francisco's instructions.

Once they had left, Francisco turned to him.

"So, what do you want to talk about?" he said, looking at Ian over his glasses that were now at the tip of his nose. He had almost black eyes. He was really sinister looking as he sat waiting in expectation for what he was going to say.

"Let me come a little closer. The walls have ears and what I am about to say should only be heard by you," Ian said as he stood and approached the desk.

"By the way those are really a nice pair of glasses. Where did you get them," he asked as a way to distract him?

"One of my guests was wearing them and decided I should have them," he was saying as Ian leaned in to whisper in his ear.

"You are about ready to…,"-and then Ian plunged Francisco's desk pen into his ear and pushed it all the way through-…meet the devil," Ian finished up as Francisco slumped forward.

He stepped around the desk and turned the chair around as he had been when he had first walked in.

He studied Francisco's handwriting and on his second try penned a note that looked amazingly like Francisco's handwriting. He knew a handwriting expert would be able to tell it was a forgery, but it would not matter.

He wrote: "I can no longer live with the knowledge of the bad deeds I have done. God forgive me." *Francisco*

He then looked around and found a set of Ivory chopsticks and pocketed them. He went out to the top of the stairs to wait for the two lieutenants. It took longer for them to return than he had expected but he could hear them talking as they mounted the stairs.

"I wonder what that guy and Francisco talked about," the one in the lead asked.

"You know the drill; the guy is getting to the end of his career. He wants money," the one behind volunteered.

"You've got it wrong guys. I am here with a deal Francisco is eager to tell you about. It will change your lives," Ian said as he met them at the top of the stairs.

"He is waiting inside and wants you two to join him."

Ian followed them both in through the door. They had made the mistake of discounting him and letting down their guard.

"Francisco, Chema was wondering what it was you wanted them to know about," he said loudly as he plunged the black ivory chopstick through Pepe's head.

Too late, Chema sensed something was wrong. As he turned Ian stepped up and hit him in the Adam's apple with his stiffened fingers then he grabbed his head and plunged the second chopstick directly through his left eye. He finished him off with a stiff upward palm to his nose. Chema slumped to the floor in a big heap.

He pulled both of them into the chairs in front of the desk. Then put the suicide note on the desk.

He didn't expect anyone to believe it was suicide, but it would give the captain something to talk about to the news media.

He removed all the implements of death and wrapped them in a paper towel from the coffee area. They would never be found. He cleaned up the area, so it all looked neat and peaceful. Then he put a do not disturb, important meeting sign on the door as he left.

He called back into the room as if someone were listening inside, "Thank you Francisco, I look forward to doing more business with you in the future."

He smiled at the faces below as they looked up at him as he walked down the stairs. He walked out as if he had just won the lottery and was on his way to celebrate.

The bar area went on with the drinking, coke snorting and the other activities that were in full swing.

"Great guy, that Francisco," Ian said as he walked out the front door.

"I was just about to go in after you. What happened?" The captain wanted to know.

"Well, Francisco seemed contrite when I pointed out how nasty he had become. He promised me he would seek higher council. I think your problems may be over," Ian said putting his arm around the captain's shoulder.

"I think I have a plane to catch. Can you drop me off at the airport? There is a red eye special I can still make if we hurry," he said as they got into the car.

"So, I should stop asking questions and let you get out of the state. Is that what you are telling me," the captain asked quietly?

"Let's just say, your prayers have been answered. Remember you should always be careful what you pray for," Ian answered.

He went on to suggest that the captain should forget that he had ever visited his precinct.

12 Family wedding-Resolution

*I*an was the last one onto the plane. He had purchased the last first class, ticket. He knew the family was in the back. He needed to think about how to tell them a good story about what had occurred.

Lesley was the closest to knowing what he might have done but Ian doubted she would know just how ruthless he could be.

When the plane landed, he walked out and waited for the family to come out. Everyone was surprised to see him and wondered how he had beat them to Cincinnati.

They wanted to know what happened.

"Well, I went to the police station whose district we were in. It seems they were not aware of what was going on. I talked to the station captain, and he assured me he would follow up on the situation," Ian said as everyone gathered around him.

Lesley gave him a hug and whispered that he was the problem-solver and asked if the problem had been solved.

Ian held her at arms-length, gave a slow smile and quietly told her he always did as she asked.

"How about we stop for breakfast and then go home and relax," Ian suggested. Then I can share more details of what went down. Ian was fabricating the story as fast as he could.

It was lucky Lesley had driven their new van to the airport. It was big enough for everyone to fit in.

Everyone was as tired as he was. Breakfast was a little awkward.

Ian could tell his two sons wanted to ask about the fight.

DJ asked how he felt. Ian was sure DJ wondered how the wound was doing.

Ian knew the look, Lesley wanted time alone with him.

The only one in neutral was Ella.

Ian sipped his coffee and thought about what had happened. He would need to check back with the captain at a later date. He was not sure everything would end with just the taking out the three leaders. There would be some new gang members to take over.

The morning news highlighted the unusual occurrence of a gang land suicide in LA. The captain of the local district was shown walking to the speaker's podium. The captain stood in front of the cameras to make a short statement. He described the situation of the recent killing of multiple members of the Red gang. He then went on to describe what appeared to be a triple suicide by the Red gang leaders.

"A suicide note was found with the three dead gang leaders. It says they are sorry for the grief they caused. I am not sure about its authenticity, but we will keep an eye on the situation and make sure there are no other gang actions in the works," the captain said and then walked off the podium.

It was Ella that looked around the table and said, "really, are we to believe this fairy tale. We know who took care of the situation. Thank You dad. I won't have to worry about my family any longer."

Ian just looked at her as if he had no idea what she was referring to.

The rest of the family looked at her and then at him.

He remained silent. He had decided there was no reasonable way to explain any of it. He quieted the laughter coming from the dark side of his mind and concentrated on the light. He looked around and knew he lived a blessed life.

The End

<u>Drug Lords</u>

<u>Introduction</u>

We will never stop the flow of drugs coming into this country as long as there are customer wanting to buy it.

Prohibition of a specific good has never worked. This is true for the oldest profession, liquor and now drugs. If there is a pull, the flow will continue.

Many countermeasures to the drug flow have been proposed. It will take a combination of all of them to make any significant impact.

The biggest impact would come about if there were no customers.

The next biggest would be that drugs would be so cheap and the margin so low that it would not be a very attractive business.

This is the story of an action directly targeting the primary businessmen that manage the drug flow logistics. They are family men and women. They are a part of the fabric of the society in which they exist.

They are also ruthless to those opposing them and even more ruthless to their competitors.

Their lives are always on the line. They take many lives but often theirs are taken as well.

The financial rewards are great. The price for these "businessmen" often exceeds the reward.

<u>Drug Lords</u>

<u>1 Assignment</u>

*T*he kids were now all out of college.
Ella and family were established in Georgia.
Matt was a programmer.
Sean was now established in California and had a partner.

Lesley and he missed having them around the house. They visited often but the two of them had more house than he had ever wanted.

Ian had come to accept and enjoy the space. He still thought of it as decadent, but he had become accustomed to it and was relaxed and enjoyed the decadent life that he lived.

He spent a great deal of time in his library office.

Massive bookshelves held hundreds of the classics and many of his own writings. He had stopped collecting books. He had transitioned into what he called the world of his children. He was a computer nerd. His use of the internet and Google had become common.

He still loved to periodically pick out one of the books and sit down to read but the majority of his time was on the keyboard of his computer.

His new iPhone vibrating in his pocket had sent a shiver down his back and raised the hairs on the back of his neck.

He knew the message was no coincidence. As he watched the CNN news cast about the beheading of the policemen in Mexico, the news caster had called for someone to resolve the terrorism going on in Mexico.

He knew these words were meant for him.

"Call" was the text on his personal iPhone that had come up right after the news cast.

He knew immediately this would be an assignment that he would not want. He also knew this was not a call to be made from his personal phone.

He thought back to two previous calls.

One had sent him into the heart of Russia to stop or delay the development of an intelligent missile system.

The other call had sent him to the Gaza Strip to eliminate three terrorists being exchanged for one Israeli soldier.

His job was to solve problems that could not be addressed in a politically correct manner.

His targets often ceased to exist.

He usually received his assignments directly from a news broadcast when the announcer asked, "Who can lead us to a solution to this problem?" or some other similar phrase. Such a statement would cause him to replay that segment of the news multiple times.

Usually, he was on his own to respond. He seldom got any directions from his handler. He seemed to correctly respond to most of the calls. He knew this because his bank account always received an appropriate influx.

He sat down in the thickly padded desk chair and opened the bottom left desk drawer of his desk. At the very back was a combination lock box. He pulled it out and placed it in front of him. He keyed in the five digits on the touch lock, lifted the box lid and took out the phone. It was the older phone version that did not have a GPS module. It had only one number stored in its memory. Ian pushed the dial button.

He knew he was a problem-solving junkie. He loved to pit himself against the "bad" guy. He had survived for more than thirty years at a calling that normally meant a short life. He was alive because of his low key, almost invisible way of solving these special problems. When he was in the field his senses were at their height.

He could smell and taste trouble.

His premonition for trouble was mind blowing.

Several times he had gone from plan a to plan b to plan c as the action unfolded. He had always wondered what would happen when he ran out of plans.

He swiveled in his chair and looked out the windows directly at the tennis courts. It was dimly lit by one of the security lights that was on the far side.

He could faintly hear the water fall from the hot tub to the pool on the other side of the family room as he put in the ear buds and then plugged them into the phone. His mouth was dry, and he wished he had his normal tall twenty-ounce thermal mug of Pellegrino and ice.

He hesitated a moment, let his mind relax and then made the phone call.

The silence just before the phone began to Bing, Bing, Bing as it connected was disconcerting. He always imagined this as a call to hell and the person answering it as the devil himself.

Only Lesley was aware of this alternate world he lived in. The rest of his family did not have a clue. He had to fight the overwhelming urge to hang up. He did not want to get into a long, protracted assignment. He was ready to retire from the role of being the on-call problem-solver.

This was not a movie.

There would be no flash of light to erase his memories.

His memories were clear.

His life was the yin and yang, of good and evil, of dark and light.

He had willingly participated in both worlds.

Ian thought again of the two lives he lived.

They were polar opposites and in both-worlds he was the problem-solver.

"It's been a long time," said a familiar voice on the other end of the line.

"Not long enough," Ian replied as he thought about his last assignment that had taken him into the Heart of Russia.

"This assignment will be tough and perhaps long. We have arranged for a leave of absence from your company. We will provide all the help that you ask for. Your account will cover whatever you need."

He thought about his bottomless million-dollar offshore account. On one assignment he had purchased a multi-million-dollar yacht with no questions asked. The yacht had ended up somewhere in the government system.

"Your assignment is to take out the top leader of every drug cartel in Mexico."

"You have got to be crazy. Me and what army," he snapped back?

He was holding onto the edge of his desk as he experienced the world turning black. He was seeing everything in front of him through a tiny white hole that was slowly growing smaller.

He was about to pass out.

He took several deep breaths and slowly the lights came back on. He had a metallic taste in his mouth, and he felt cold all over.

"We know this is a tough one and we have assembled the strongest and best support team you can possibly want. We have also made arrangements to get you included in several key organizations that will give you ample cover."

He remained silent. Backup team! Ample cover! Who the hell did they think he was?

"Great to talk with you, Good Luck, and may the force be with you," the voice on the other end said in a formal manner.

Then the phone went dead.

He looked at the silent phone in his hand.

Who the hell do they think I am, superman?

He slowly put the phone into the box, locked it and put it in the back of the desk drawer.

He got up and slowly walked to the kitchen where he knew he would find a cup of coffee.

He knew that he would accept the challenge. There was some part of him that loved to pit himself against the bad guy. This assignment would be the ultimate challenge.

He wondered whether this would be his "swan song." He hoped not, he had visions of sitting in front of his fireplace with Leslie snuggling next to him reading.

His mind was already kicking into high gear. He could feel his heart beating a little faster and he could smell the leather of his chair as his sense of smell sharpened.

He thought that he could taste the mountain air in the coffee he was drinking.

This primordial reaction to a challenge that would involve eliminating his opponent always came as a surprise. His energy level immediately hit a new high and he knew it would stay high until the letdown that always came at the end of an assignment.

"Do any of these supporting team members have names," Ian had inquired?

"No and you know better than to ask. So, I take it that you have accepted and are ready to go," the devil's voice had responded.

"You knew the answer before I returned your called," Ian had replied.

He knew he would need a workplace outside of his home to prepare for this assignment. In his mind there would be at least six to eight months of research and planning.

He went online to find office space that would be close to home but secluded enough that he would not be noticed.

His search took him to a twelve hundred square foot, second floor office area with windows around three sides of the room. The windows were modern, triple layered gas filled. The floor space was for an open office layout.

He laughed as he thought about the open office layout aspect. There would be no one else but he and his computer in the office.

But it seemed to be what he needed.

He called the listing realtor and made an appointment to meet him at the location and walk the office space.

The tree lined parking area, the well-kept green area, and the office space itself made for a very comfortable work arrangement. After the walk through, Ian bargained with the realtor on the length and the price of the lease. He got eggshell colored, simulated wood vertical hanging blinds for the windows thrown in as part of the contract.

He would have had the blinds put in anyway, but he wanted the realtor to feel as if he was doing his job and that the customer was truly trying to get the best deal possible.

Three days later, he carried in seven flip charts and easel stands. The four-by-eight-foot walnut desk and large black leather office chair was scheduled for delivery between twelve and two. He had also ordered several office tables and half a dozen chairs.

He would pick up his Dell 36-inch, 128 TB hard drive, computer and monitor at the store after the desk arrived. It was an all-in-one computer where the monitor and the computer was one unit. This would be the computer to search the internet and to research his intended targets.

Ian walked around the perimeter of the office as he thought about how to lay out his meager office furniture.

He was on his second walk and about ready to put up his easels when he realized his thinking was antiquated.

He had envisioned using the seven easels as the media to organize the information and to display the plans for the interaction with each of the drug cartels.

He realized he was thinking in yesterday's terms. He realized that he should be setting up a separate computer systems for each cartel.

His personal goal was to survive this problem-solving assignment.

To do so he would need to be at the top of his game.

He scolded himself and told himself he had better sharpen his thinking and shape up fast.

He could not be a fossil he needed to leverage all the latest technology.

He immediately called the store where he had bought the Dell and asked for seven similar but lower end computers. The store clerk said he had just what he needed. They would all be all-in-one computers and he would send them along with the one that was already scheduled to be delivered, and everything would be put on one bill.

He interpreted the enthusiasm in the clerk's voice ensured that he would get what was needed.

All the equipment arrived as scheduled. He had the deliverers put the computers on the tables he had set up around the room. Afterwards he set everything up and made sure everything worked.

He knew he had to create the connection from each cartel focused computer to a central control computer.

He called his on-line support group and asked them to guide him in setting up an in-office network.

With step-by-step guidance, he was able to set up the network in one afternoon. The internal network was not online. Only his main computer would connect to the global internet, and the main computer would not connect to his internal network. His internal network would be totally isolated.

Seven-thirty the next morning, he parked his ten-year-old, dark green sedan with a black leather interior that his Leslie made him park immediately in the garage and close the door when he arrived home.

This was one item he had refused to upgrade. He always bought used cars and refused to drive any of the luxury cars that were par for his neighborhood.

It was one thing to have lucked out in buying the grand palace they called home, but it was another to compete with the neighbors to see who could drive the most expensive car to show who had the most money.

Bullshit! was what went through his mind each time he attended a neighborhood party and listened to the conversations of condescending, haughty, pompous attitudes of superior mental midgets with their hand waving and the rolling of eyes as various groups gathered to impress each other.

The office building was one of several in the industrial park. All seemed to be duplicates of each other and had a row of evergreen bushes around their perimeter.

The gold number printed in the horizontal glass across the top of the doors to his office building provided the only means of telling the difference between the other six buildings in the complex.

Maple trees were the dominant species surrounding each parking area. Two rows of six-inch diameter trees ran lengthwise across each lot.

Except at high noon the parking areas were always shaded. His parking area, specifically meant to be for his building, usually had one car parked in it. He was the only current renter of floor space in his building. He had the entire floor, but he was the only person working there.

He, carrying his light brown leather briefcase that featured a flap buckled on one side, walked slowly toward the office. He pressed his key-fob and listened for the beep of the car horn letting him know that it was locked.

"Stupid habit" went through his mind. There was nothing in the car worth stealing, he thought as he looked up through the heavily leaved branches of the maples to a clear blue morning sky.

His family had no clue as to where his current work location was. Long ago he had given up having a landline office phone. All calls, whether business or personal, came to the same phone. He had made sure to turn off his GPS and turned off the sharing location feature.

It was time to get started on the overall plan for this assignment. After that he would begin the research into each individual cartel.

The parking lot ended about one hundred feet from the building's double doors. He stepped up from the black top surface to the worn, heavily pebbled cement walk that was obviously sealed in some plastic sealer. The pebbles were preventing an otherwise deteriorating surface from getting any worse. The sealer gave the walk an old nostalgic look.

The newly planted yellow and gold marigold flowers edging the sidewalk on the building side provided an elegant touch to an otherwise plain office area. He looked down past the two additional buildings in this section of the park and was pleased with the harmony the flowers, trees and bushes provided.

"Damn," he exclaimed as the right-hand door remained closed when he tried pulling it open. The left-hand door responded easily to his pull.

It seemed to him that every double glass door always had one side locked. Why have two doors if one was always locked? He would need to post a big arrow on the locked door pointing to the open one to remind him which side to use.

He noted that the bottom floor of the building was currently empty. He hoped it would remain that way.

The six-foot-wide, grey, and black granite step slabs held in place by a black steel frame went up the left side of the entrance. Halfway up, the stairs made a ninety degree turn and continued to the second floor. The second-floor landing area and the hallway leading back to the Men's and Ladies restroom matched the granite of the steps.

It was clear that these buildings had been upscale offices at one time. They were still in good condition and well kept. Businesses had moved out as the business expansion had moved from an eastward expansion to a southward one that made its way to the Airport.

Once at the top of the stairs Ian's office area was immediately to the right. He put the key fob up to the lock and heard the opening click.

The doorknob turned effortlessly, and he stepped in and closed and locked the door behind him.

On the far end of the office area, was a dark walnut desk that faced the entrance. It had a very large computer screen standing on it. This was his search, find and research center.

About ten feet in front of it was a duplicate desk that was the command center for the internal computer network. In front of that desk, fanned out across the room in a semi-circle, were tables with another set of computers with their screens all facing the center.

This lay out took up half of the office floor space. The back area was what he considered the work area. He had no people but a boat load of technology. He thought of the semi-circle of computers as his technological employees.

These were employees that got no salary or medical benefits, and could voice no complaints, another words perfect employees.

The first half of the floor was appointed with a large oriental rug, a couch and a large recliner bracketed by two lamps on square walnut stands. This part of the office area looked back toward the two command desks and was clearly a rest and relax area.

In the front left corner of the office, behind the recliner, a refreshment center held a stainless-steel refrigerator, a microwave, a small counter top oven and a coffee or tea maker.

The recliner area was his relaxation and thinking area.

Today he would be focusing on getting an overall plan outlined.

He needed to come up with a plan that contained three key elements: A research element,

       The guiding plan, and

       Flawless execution detail.

The first was the most critical.

The second essential to returning to his good life.

The third critical to achieving his mission of coming home alive.

He walked slowly across the office area looking for any proof that his support team had come in overnight to fulfill his request to get his office shielded from broadcasting beyond the office walls.

He was worried about two major technical issues. The first concern was the ability for web sites he researched to track him to his computer. The second concern was not to have his internal wireless network broadcasting beyond the perimeter of the office area.

He felt that needed to maintain a high degree of secrecy.

He immediately noticed the vertical silver wire that went down each of the vertical blinds. The wires were connected at the top of the blinds with small delicate silver chains. He walked up close and could see that the entire office area was now behind a grounded metal mesh shield.

He smiled as he took in the hip designer feel it gave his office.

"Well done team," he thought as he finished walking around the perimeter.

As he approached his main computer, he noticed that the screen was on and had a message clarifying the six-layer computer isolation from the internet. The cookies he was worried about would never reach the shielded level occupied by his computer.

"Well done again," he thought.

Ian sat down and leaned back into his chair.

He pressed start on his computer and the message the team had left disappeared, and his blank screen desktop appeared.

He opened his briefcase and took out a dozen 18 terra bite memory sticks and put them into the top drawer. He put his old cherished brief case to the side of the desk and then pulled up a detailed map of North America on the computer and saved it onto one of the memory sticks.

He pulled out the memory stick and walked around to the desk immediately in front of him, turned on that computer and transferred the map into the master plan folder.

He focused on the US-Mexico border and tried to contemplate how he might approach his problem-solving assignment.

Starting on the Gulf of Mexico at Brownsville, Texas seemed to be as good as any place. He would then proceed westward along the border to San Diego. He knew there were several cartels along the border and then one in Tijuana.

He would continue south down the Pacific coast side around the tip of the California peninsula and back to Mexico City.

He drew the path across the map.

He took it all in and let it flow through his mind.

It seemed to make sense to him.

He immediately felt a sense of relief as he got his first piece of the plan saved onto a file. In the old days, he would have saved the paper flip chart. Saving it to a file did not seem to have the same beefy feel to it but he knew that it was a more flexible way to manage the information.

He now felt ready to begin the investigation of the drug cartels themselves.

He took a time out to get a cup of tea. This was his preferred caffeine source. Just about any tea would do, but Jasmine and Chamomile were his two mainstays but name almost any tea and he would at least have one sealed bag of it. He always used a teaspoon of local honey, that he bought from a former colleague, to sweeten the tea.

From his easy chair he took in the work area in front of him.

He could have located both computers on the same desk, but he wanted a physical reminder and a physical separator to emphasize the split between his research and his planning.

He could not afford even a momentary lapse in the separation of information.

His internal network needed to remain totally isolated. Each of the internal network computers would hold specific information for one of the targeted cartels.

He knew his life depended on his ability to compartmentalize and separate the information that he was generating about each cartel.

Sitting in his break area sipping on his tea served to give him time to think about his next steps.

He eventually would envision, think through in detail and when appropriate act out every action he planned to take. The break area was as important to him as the two research computers and the internal computer network.

He knew the most important computer in the room was the organic one shielded by his thick skull.

As fractured and damaged as his brain might be, it was what had kept him alive through the many problem-solving sessions he had been on.

Even the dark part of his mind that often taunted him cooperated in making sure he remained alive.

It was time to begin his research into the drug cartels and learn about their leaders. This was where deep understanding of the situation was important. He would need to see and understand aspects of the operations of the cartels that others had either missed or ignored.

His approach needed to go beyond the facts and needed to give him the knowledge that would allow him to execute his plan and live to take the next step.

Utilizing the resources he had at hand, he would study each cartel separately and as deeply as he could.

He activated one of his special GPS free phones and called the support number of his team. He put in a request for all drug cartel information available in any US or ally government data bases.

He then went to Google and began traveling the streets of Matamoros and regions controlled by the Gulf Cartel. After spending most of the afternoon understanding the history and the current operation of the Gulf Cartel, the infighting and positioning of the various members of the cartel the futility of the assignment he had taken on became clear.

He would strike a blow to the leadership of the Gulf Cartel, but it was a hydra with multiple heads, and it would most likely just grow another. His strike on this cartel would be noticed but no matter what leader he took out, there would be another one to immediately rise up to take his place.

He stored his notes onto the thumb drive, stood up and walked to the internal network computer in front of him. He stored the information into the first computer. He made a paper tent label from an eight-by-eleven-inch sheet of paper and with a big black marker wrote "Gulf Cartel." He put the label on the left hand most computer in the arc of computers before him.

He would give each of his electronic lackeys' appropriate names.

It was time for a break and another cup of tea.

After that each additional cartel would get the same deep scrutiny. He allowed for one week of deep study for each cartel.

He continued with his research and planning. He prepared the entire problem-solving circuit.

Then he envisioned his action at each problem-solving location. As he did this, he made a list of the tools, materials, or weapons he would need.

After reviewing and finalizing the materials he requested his support team to obtain and position the materials in the proximity of where each problem-solving session would be.

He walked through multiple scenarios at each problem-solving locality.

He was leaving nothing to chance. He planned for success, but he also tried to imagine what could go wrong and planned for that scenario as well. He wondered what went through the minds of his support team. They certainly must be thinking he was at the edge of falling of the reality cliff.

He concluded a lot could go wrong. He was going in alone against people practiced in the art of eliminating their enemy. It was clear to him that even the Mexican and US governments had stayed clear of a direct confrontation with the various drug cartels.

He had no illusions about the enormous money, power, and influence that the cartels had and that they often flexed their power when confronted by an adversary.

He would be on his own. His success was predicated on his ability to remain a ghost. He would need to remain invisible and move faster than the cartel leaders recognized or figured out the pattern of his problem-solving.

<u>*2 Matamoros-The Gulf Cartel*</u>

*I*an learned that the Gulf Cartel was one of the oldest of the seven major cartels on his list. It had participated in smuggling booze into the US during the Prohibition era. Later it turned to drug smuggling, collecting protection money from businesses, engaged in human transport, and kidnapping. It had solid connections and affiliations throughout the US and Europe.

It was clear to Ian that it was a sophisticated operation. It emulated the big companies on Wall Street. Many of the cartels even had a board of directors.

He thought that was appropriate. They trafficked in drugs and Wall Street trafficked in money.

Some people partook of both.

Both were led by people only interested in grabbing more money.

One had lobbyists working to ensure their money grab looked legal and the other simply ignored the law and did what they wanted.

The Gulf Cartel's leadership was split between two factions currently working together to control the same territory and to fight off the Los Zetas cartel operating in Nuevo Laredo.

He thoroughly studied both factions and with the help of his nameless support team he had identified a protection collection route that one of the leaders consistently followed. The target Ian selected was not the top leader of the Cartel but was a key member on the Board.

He was the unlucky target.

The location of the top leader was currently a mystery. He solved it but decided that the location made it an even more risky one than he could imagine.

Utilizing Google map street view, he drove the same route, taken by this unlucky leader, multiple times, on his visits to various businesses.

Then he slowly and carefully studied the route and decided on the place where he would solve the problem.

The stucco multicolored buildings on each side, with their iron grated windows and doors presented the dichotomy of the environment. Here lived cheerful, hardworking people fearful of the desperate, the jobless, the hungry and the drug runners.

Here lived people who enjoyed sitting outside of restaurants and coffee shops but who were currently under the control of the drug cartels and under the control of the many corrupt policemen. These were mostly good, god-fearing people wanting to live in peace and raise their children.

But the honest policemen had their heads cut off! Honest people stayed in the shadows and tried to stay out of the eyes of the cartels.

He stopped and studied a place that was called, *"The English Coffee Shop."* It featured a rather French like coffee shop layout with white tablecloths over black iron tables with matching black iron chairs. On the sidewalk there were several tables.

A night shot of the street showed the lights coming down from the steel bar covered windows on the second floor affirming them as apartments or homes for the shop owners or renters. This was by all accounts a vibrant neighborhood.

The building opposite the café where the actual explosion would take place presented a clean, red brick wall with no windows. This was a relief to him. His goal was to have no collateral injuries.

After three more examinations of the route, he knew what he would do.

During his research of Matamoros, he saw the ads for a robot fight tournament. He put in an inquiry to his support team to see if he could somehow get on one of the robot fight teams. It would serve as a perfect cover.

A few days later, as he sat at his primary office desk, he got a call on one of his support phones.

"You are now a member of the University of Illinois Fighting Robot Wedge team. You are their last-minute design engineer replacing their "sick" team member, call to get acquainted with the fighting robot team," was the message.

He dialed the number he had been given and waited for someone to pick-up on the other end.

This is Trip Masters, your fight design engineer, he stated his name as someone answered the phone.

"Great to hear from you Trip. I am Dr. John Newton, but I am called Dr. J by my team. My team and I have been working hard to get to the top for a long time

You better be good.

The team that beat us has a unit almost identical to ours entered in the Matamoros competition.

Our design engineer was tops.

You better be good," Dr. J finished his long introduction.

"When can you get to Champaign-Urbana to help us finalize our entry," he asked?

"I can be there in about a day. This seems to be rather close to the competition to be finalizing the designing of your unit," Ian replied as he realized they wanted some real engineering design work from him and thought he actually had robot design expertise.

Dr. J agreed that the finalizing of the design was very late, but they were worried about what they had heard about the improvements by their competition. The team wanted to reassess their current design.

He let Lesley know that he was going to the University of Illinois for a few days. This was, he told her, in preparation for his upcoming trip.

Lesley smiled and joked that it was good to see him seeking to improve his mind.

He drove to the main U of I campus the next day and put up for the night at a local B&B.

Early the next morning, he parked his rental in an almost empty parking lot and began his walk across the campus.

The chh, chh, chh, of the sprinklers and the cool breeze on his face invaded his wandering thoughts.

The dark aroma of the coffee and the sharp strands of light from the sun peeking over the building at the other end of the campus mall began to penetrate his waking mind.

The mall seemed to have been newly renovated and landscaped. The broad sidewalk was a combination of reddish-brown brick laid out in a herring bone pattern surrounded by a rectangular cement frame. Every square had at least one brick in a center square with the name of the person or family that had donated money to fund the renovation. There was space for new donation bricks to be added.

Young eight-foot-high maple trees with tinted hardy orange mums planted at their base were equally spaced around the mall on both sides of the walk. Most trees had an accompanying plaque dedicating the tree to a loved one.

His mind imagined the day these young trees would create an arch over the walk. He could see the fall yellow, orange, and red colors the trees would display. It was a beautiful mental image for the slightly anemic looking young trees.

The Mall, about the size of three end to end football fields, was highlighted with three, equally spaced, round, rose gardens. These gardens and the thick green grass gave a long-term promise of upcoming elegance.

The first big decision of the morning was whether to go clockwise or counterclockwise to reach the building at the far end. The young black policewoman coming toward him crystalized his choice and he walked slowly toward her.

They both stopped when a biker riding the same path enthusiastically let them know she was coming through.

At that moment, the chirping of the birds replaced the chh, chh, chh of the sprinklers as they stopped and the warmth of the sun penetrated the black tee shirt Ian was wearing.

Morning had arrived in full force.

He took in the fresh spit polished uniform and the confidence displayed by the young policewoman. This was probably her first professional job, and it was clear by her thrown back shoulders and smooth confident walk she was proud of her job.

The aroma that accompanied a slow sip of his coffee prepared him for this first encounter of the day.

"Hi, I'm looking for Dr. John Newton," he said in greeting.

"Oh, you must mean Dr. J. Are you the new high-powered fight design engineer I heard him talking about at the coffee shop?"

He's counting on you to make a difference.

The team has come in second in the last two years.

They really want to break that cycle," she rapidly replied.

Pointing to the building at the far end of the mall, she instructed him to go in the first door, go down into the basement. Turn left and then follow the hall until he got to the first set of double doors.

She told him to knock loudly since the door was key card locked and the folks inside sometimes made an awful racket.

He thanked her and walked leisurely toward the building.

The hallway back to the double doors was dimly lit and had a moldy smell.

He wondered how an award-winning team could be relegated to the conditions he was walking through.

The keycard lock guarded a brushed stainless-steel door. Its clean fresh appearance put it at odds with the darker, more worn surroundings.

It seemed to be the right door, so he knocked.

"Welcome to our private playground," Dr. J said as he pulled him in and closed the door.

The transition was amazing. He entered a bright laboratory style room with a stainless-steel countertop all the way around the outside walls and three six by six-foot stainless-steel islands at its center.

The room had a high ceiling and there were numerous machine tools, welders, and metal working equipment situated around the room.

On the center table roughly six by six foot in size was what Ian took to be the fighting wedge robot.

"That is the robot and let me introduce the team that thought of it, designed it, built it and took it to many wins," Dr. J said.

He noticed that Dr. J kept one hand on the robot as if it were a bible as he made the introductions.

"Marty is the electronics genius that designed the control circuits. Samantha is the machine and metal working specialist that cuts, shapes and welds. Henry is the main robot operator. His deft hands and mind have guided our wedge to many victories.

I am the back-up operator. Sam is the team's logistics and set up support," Dr. J continued.

"Thanks for filling in for our design engineer. News has it that his father is dying, and he needed to stay with his family."

"I was told you were the world's best robot fighter design engineer. How come we haven't seen you at any of the competitions," Dr. J inquired?

It was clear to Ian that their design engineer had been offered a significant incentive to have a dying father. He had experienced a similar situation in several previous problem-solving assignments. He knew that in this case, if he were going to lie, it would need to be a big one.

"You haven't heard of me because I play with robots designed not to compete with other robots but designed to kill anything it is assigned to kill," he lied with a straight face.

"Let's study the plans of your fighting robot and list all the fatal weaknesses that we can," he moved the team immediately into an action that would highlight what they knew were fatal flaws of their design.

He pulled a white board over and opened the black marker pen. He listened and put up the weaknesses the team identified. He kept the list to the left side.

Then he began to ask the questions that each identified flaw caused him to ask.

"You know that if you get turned over, you are in trouble. Why not make both sides operate the same," was his first suggestion?

"Your current strategy is to outlast the opponent. Why not kill him immediately," was his next question?

"You count on one of your team members to visually manipulate the robot during battle. Why not give the robot the ability to act and activate its defenses based on the movement and position of its robot opponent," was his final question?

At first there were some defensive replies. Then the team got into identifying improvements to the new ideas.

It was clear to him why the team did so well in competitions.

One of the team pointed out the limited amount of time before the tournament.

He counter that he understood that it would be a monumental challenge but to continue doing the same would be to have the same results as in previous years.

He asked if they wanted to be the world champions.

"I understand the challenge. I will work with Samantha on building the new shell for the robot. You work on the controls and intelligence. Dr. J can work on the weapons," he countered.

He looked at the team.

Dr. J. looked back at him then turned to the team and simply said, "Let's do it."

He was pleased with himself. He had no clue about robotics, but he knew how to envision and empower teams.

He stepped in toward Dr. J and put out his hand palm down. Dr. J understood immediately and put his hand on top of Ian's. The rest of the team followed and in unison the whole team shouted loudly, "Let's do it."

By Friday after spending twenty hours each day and eating in the lab, testing each item as they went, the team was standing around the large table admiring the new robot.

"Look at this beauty," Dr. J said as he stroked the low slung, three-inch-thick plain stainless-steel disc. Samantha had polished the shiny stainless-steel alien spacecraft looking robot to almost a mirror finish.

There was nothing to prevent the opponent from turning the disc over. The tactic of lifting and turning the opponent over was a common attack practice.

This robot wanted that to occur.

Once contact with the opponent was made, the robot drove spikes into the opponent and then climbed on to it. If the spikes did not take hold, they retracted and the whole unit allowed itself to be turned over. The other side was exactly the same, so it waited for the opponent to try the turnover attack again.

However, at the peak of the second flip, the side opposite the opponent launched a thin cable to lasso the opponent. If the lasso caught the opponent, the entire robot would pull itself on top of the opponent and ooze out super glue. The units would be bonded, and the robot began its boring and laser cutting.

The boring and laser cutting would create very small holes. Acid was then injected into the opponent and the party was soon over.

"This is diabolical. How did you ever think of all of this," Dr. J asked as he looked at Ian?

Ian pointed out that he had not suggested any of what was now called nasty and killer ideas. "I only asked questions. You all piled the nasty on," he said quietly.

"We did in fact do that, but we would never have thought of all of this in one package," Henry commented.

"What are we going to call this beast," Samantha asked as she lovingly put her hand on the polished metal surface of the robot.

"Why not *Muerte de Norte,* Death from the North," Ian suggested.

"That is a great name," the rest of the team commented in unison.

"I am going to etch it on the surface of both sides of our robot," Samantha said as she got out her Dremel tool and put a small grinding fixture in it.

"It's time for our road trip to Matamoras and victory. Let's get Muerte de Norte loaded up. We leave tomorrow," Dr. J declared.

"I need to get a couple of things done before I go. I will meet you at the hotel in Matamoros," he said as he got up and headed for the door.

He had discovered the University only paid for shared hotel rooms. He needed to have a private room for himself and decided that all of them should have the same status. He asked his support team to call ahead to the hotel and make the arrangements and to rent the best rooms.

He looked back at the stainless-steel door and then turned to walk up the stairs out to the U of I mall. This time he took the right path around and walked slowly through the meager shade of the young maples as he admired the three rose gardens in the middle. The mall had a few students either hurrying to their classes, sitting on the benches, or sitting out directly on the grass.

He wondered how many of them funded the drug lords he was on the way to punish for providing what the customers wanted.

He returned home before beginning his problem-solving journey in Matamoros. Once he left home it would be several months before he would be able to return.

The two days home evaporated quicker than a window spray on a car's hot glass windshield. He knew his return home would only take as long as a wait in the emergency room when you only had a cold. He knew from experience it would seem longer than he anticipated.

He contacted the support team and gave them instructions on cleaning and emptying the planning office.

Lesley seemed to know that he was on one of his special problem-solving trips. She whispered that she loved him, wished him luck, and told him to be careful.

The sun was halfway on its daily journey across the sky in front of the house and the tree shadows were getting to their smallest stature with clouds seemingly hovering over them like whipped cream on a green tea sundae as he gave Lesley a hug and kiss and walked slowly toward the cab.

The taxi driver was standing with the trunk open, ready for the one blue green medium-sized suitcase he had packed.

Always a light traveler, he never carried more than the one suitcase and his briefcase. Periodically he would choose a slightly larger suitcase for the longer trips or a smaller one for day trips. In this case, he had chosen the medium one because he had prearranged materials and clothes to be strategically located along the entire problem-solving trip.

He felt the surge of energy he always experienced at the beginning of an assignment. The forty-five-minute trip to the airport evaporated in the intense mix of the thoughts and scenarios he played out in his mind. All of his plans were now in his head.

The computer he carried was clean. He knew this because it was fresh out of the box, and he had yet to set it up.

The driver's announcement of their arrival caught him by surprise. He automatically paid and tipped and proceeded to baggage check in.

Ian was glad to see that there was only a light crowd. He had armed his new identity with the appropriate road warrior miles and a diamond medallion status. He went through security in the express lane and was soon on board the tram to the B concourse.

Starbucks was on the right at the top of the escalator leading up into the concourse. He stopped and bought a double espresso and then poured in a healthy amount of cream. He seldom bought his coffee from Starbucks, but he was now playing the part of a typical businessman. The cup in his hand was symbolic, it was the sign of a seasoned road warrior.

He was dressed in business casual. His carry on was only his briefcase and the Starbucks latte.

He wanted to be seen as the high mileage business jerk who gets the aisle seat and gets to board early and suck up the overhead space.

On this trip he had bought the ticket via the internet, under a fictitious name with a credit card that was closed shortly after paying for the ticket.

He loved watching the folks as they got on the plane.

Every mood possible was displayed.

He especially wondered about those folks who came on looking like sour milk or seemed to exude dislike for all those around them.

Then there were the blissfully happy ones or the ones he would not have wanted to play poker with. He always joked with the kids or the mother's struggling to control several at one time. He always wondered how mothers were able to remain sane on such travels.

The flight to San Antonio was uneventful. It gave him plenty of time to go over every action he would take on the first trip across the border into Mexico. He felt reassured for the solid cover of the robot tournament. It made him more invisible than he would otherwise have been.

The intense week at the University had truly bonded him with the team. They provided the same emotional lift that the smell of a young puppy gave him. They exuded wonderment and positive feeling about their future. He hoped that they would reach the peak they were aiming for.

Once the plane stopped at the gate, he immediately stood up and got his bag from the overhead. There was a wait, while sequentially each individual got up, reclaimed their bag, and then proceeded down the aisle. He was content to just stand and wait. He hated to sit in the small seats.

Once out of the plane, he walked briskly toward the exit and the cab stand. He took a cab to the downtown San Antonio river walk.

He walked down the steps to the flagstone walk that bordered the most domesticated river he could imagine. It no longer had river banks but was walled in and reminded him of a long flowing swimming pool bound on two sides with cement, brick and stone walls and lined with gardens of flowers and trees.

The completely domesticated river reminded him of a farm boy in a tuxedo at an elite debutante ball in South Georgia. Both made him uncomfortable. Both were totally foreign and out of place.

Standing below the palm trees competing with tall, large live oaks to provide shade from the uncompromising heat of the sun, he looked for a place to have lunch.

He thought about walking over to see the Alamo but decided to hold onto the memory of the time he and his son had made that trip together.

They had come for an American Idol contest tryout.

No luck on the tryout but it was a great father son trip.

He thought of him and knew he was now happily living with his partner in LA and working from home at what seemed to be a good job.

He spotted a sidewalk restaurant with tables in the shade of blue and white stripped canopies. Several blue and red barges carrying passengers along the river went slowly by and provided entertainment while he ate his spinach salad and nursed his iced tea.

He took another cab to John Friendly's used car lot where "Everyone was welcome and there was a car for everyone."

There he paid cash for a white Chevy Malibu.

At random, he selected a motel for the night. All he wanted was a clean, non-smoking room. It had been a long week with the robot fight team. A good night's sleep would be great.

The next morning, he drove to the East Jefferson bus station across the street from The University of Texas at Brownsville. The school's dark blue sign with large white lettering claimed the distinction of being Texas's south most college.

He wondered which college in Florida was claiming the to be the US's southmost college.

He drove around the back of the bus station to long term parking and walked back on a newly constructed brown brick inlayed sidewalk. He was becoming sensitized to the fact that brick sidewalks seemed to be the new fashion.

It was also clear that the station had undergone a total remodeling and sported a mixed brown, red and speckled black brick veneer.

He had seen what he thought were several entrances on the side where the University was located. He took what seemed to be a main side entrance.

He walked in onto a polished black and white terrazzo floor and walked up to a grey granite ticket counter that was just a little lower than chest high.

Looking around, he located a refreshment alcove at the far end and realized what he had initially identified as entrance doors were really bus loading doors.

The fare to Matamoros was a mere seven-fifty.

The dark complexioned, black-haired young lady with almost black eyes asked to see his passport. She provided him with a form that would serve as a tourist visa and asked him to fill it in.

Her perfect American English identified her as a young Latina that had grown up in the US. She was polite, and her smile gave her the beauty she seemed to know she had.

He finished using the counter to fill in his entry paperwork and then looked over to the refreshment stand wondering if he could get a cup of coffee with the change he had received when he paid for his tourist visa.

He took in the mix of people waiting for the bus as he walked slowly across the granite floor and the outline of Texas, and its major cities marked in inlayed brass.

The majority of people appeared to be Latinos. He was definitely in the minority and that concerned him. He hoped the group of young white, laughing and joking, backpacking travelers would be on his bus.

It turned out he needed to add another dollar to get a large cup of coffee. After the first taste, Ian wished it would have tasted as good as the look of the cup. Instead, it tasted more like the paper the cup was made of.

The wait for the bus was exactly a cup of coffee long and he knew he had taken his time to drink it.

Several other buses had come and gone, and it was clear that most of the Latinos were not going to go south across the border but were taking buses to other destinations. The loud group continued their boisterous ways and were clearly having a great time as they made their way to the bus he was taking.

He stood up and dropped his empty cup into the bin at the end of the row of seats. He was carrying a small backpack and nothing more. The suitcase he had left home with was in the trunk of his car in the long-term parking lot. The clothes he needed in Matamoros were to be delivered directly to the Holiday Inn.

The bus driver was loading the luggage, and the ticket agent was now checking to see that everyone had the proper paperwork ready and complete. She gave him a bright smile as he showed her his paperwork and waved him on board.

He sat in back and relaxed as he listened to the chatter of the group up front.

The first stop and check occurred on the US side before the bridge across the Rio Grande. The bus stopped, and two custom officers came on board.

One was a five-foot-five, body builder in appearance, pixie cut, steel grey haired no nonsense looking officer. Her biceps and forearms would have made any guy proud.

He had no doubt that if she were to lift her blouse there would be a ribbed six pack exposed.

She began to check the passports and visas in the front.

Her companion looked like a portly no-nonsense Curly, of the three stooges fame. His hair was cut short, probably done by himself or a cost-conscious wife. He presented a somewhat unfriendly, gloomy look.

He handed him his open passport and visa. He had looked at the name to reinforce his new persona.

The inspector asked him to open his backpack. It was clear to him that Curly had already made up his mind and was only doing a cursory check.

Only about five minutes passed before the bus was once again on its way.

The next stop was on the Mexican side of the border and the border patrol that came on board repeated the check.

It only took another thirty minutes to arrive at the main Matamoros bus station.

There he negotiated briefly with the driver of a white cab with 766 painted on the rear fenders.

The drive down highway 101 took another thirty minutes.

Two pinto palm trees loaded with their small yellow coconut like fruit, bracketed three flag poles.

One was flying the Mexican red, green, and white flag with the eagle and snake in the center, the US flag to its right and the state of Matamoros flag was on the left.

They seemed greeted his arrival to the off white six story tile roofed Holiday Inn.

The convention center, where the robot fight competition would take place was a tan, yellow colored square building the length and breadth of a football field featuring two pinto palms and a canopied entrance, stood to the right side of the hotel.

The cab dropped him off at the entry foyer.

A hotel porter opened the taxi door as he finished paying the cab driver.

"Hola, gracias," Ian said as he was led into the lobby.

He, dressed in a black short sleeved shirt, steel head grey khaki pants with black oxford shoes, followed the porter outfitted in a black suite, spit polished black shoes and white gloves through the two layers of self-opening sliding doors.

The transition from the dry hot air to the cool of the lobby was refreshing. The bustle of the lobby was quieted by the height of the lobby ceiling and the whir of the rotating overhead fans.

The porter led him to the reception desk where a young lady wearing a blue blouse awaited him.

Ian decided to practice his Spanish by asking about his hotel reservation.

"Hola, mi nombre es Trip Masters. Usted debe tener una reserva para *"Muerte de Norte"* combatir equipo," he said to the receptionist whose name tag identified her as Angela.

"Hola, señor Masters, tiene la habitación de la esquina en el quinto piso como usted pidió," she replied.

"I understand that I have the corner room five hundred one as requested. Thanks.

I would love to do this all in Spanish, but you are way past my ordering beer ability," he joked with her.

"No problem, I am fluent in English," Angela said with a Texas American accent as she flipped over to her second language.

"Por favor, Dígale al equipo que me llame cuando llegan," he asked Angela in Spanish. He hoped that he had asked about the arrival of the rest of the team.

"See you do know more Spanish. Sure, I will have them call you when they arrive," Angela replied with a smile that beamed a brilliant white.

He walked slowly across the lobby toward the two brushed stainless-steel elevators accented by a polished brass waste basket sitting between them and below a wooden framed pair of restaurant advertisements.

He got out on the fifth floor and proceeded to the corner room. He had splurged and rented one of the larger suites.

A four-person steel framed, glass topped table with four white padded chairs around it and a couch, chair and coffee table lay between the entrance door and the wet bar that had three tall white padded stools arranged in front of it.

The bedroom with a connecting bath was through a door to the left of the wet bar.

He closed the door behind him and put his small backpack on the floor and walked toward the wet bar and into the bedroom.

The marble in the bathroom immediately drew him in.

Pink and white marble covered the lower half of the walls and grey and white marble tile was used on the floor.

A wall-to-wall mirror spanned across the top of a marble counter with two pots of paper white flowers between two sinks.

A large Jacuzzi tub with a glass enclosed shower beside it filled the area across from the sinks.

The bathroom was almost as large as the bedroom behind him.

He turned and saw that his suitcase had been placed on a stand at the end of the bed.

He walked across to the suitcase and quickly unpacked. He wanted to get his shorts, gym shoes and tee shirt and do a quick workout in the hotel gym.

The bathroom was calling, and he wanted to enjoy the luxury of standing below the ceiling showerhead featured along with the normal showerhead. He hoped that the overhead shower would put out a heavy stream of water.

Later after returning from the workout, having enjoyed a long hot shower, he stood behind the wet bar counter.

He was surprised to find the two potted six-foot-tall palm trees bracketing the bar were real.

He was impressed to find the bar featured a small refrigerator with two Corona, two Modelo and two Negra Modelo.

There were also various kinds of soft drinks.

A separate wine cooler held a Riesling, a Cabernet Sauvignon, and a White Zinfandel.

His requests had been filled to the T.

He planned to entertain his team in his room.

He was very conscious of and feeling somewhat guilty about the situation he was putting the robot team in.

There was no danger to them, but he was definitely using them.

He had arranged for each member of the team to have separate rooms with a similar layout as his. The charge would go against his problem-solving expenses. He often imagined some secluded accountant trying to make sense of the expenses he submitted. None had ever been questioned and all had been paid.

The jangle of the bone-colored phone at the end of the bar brought Ian immediately back to the present. He had drifted into his problem analysis mode and had been leaning with his weight on his elbows on the bar.

He wondered how long he had been zoned out.

He picked up the phone and could hear the background noise of the hotel lobby.

"Trip," this is Dr. J. "We just arrived and are checking in. They say we have been upgraded at no cost. This is great."

"That is good to hear. Once you get settled, why don't you come up to room 501 and then we can plan where to go for dinner," he replied.

He already knew the restaurant where he wished to go.

He turned to look at the wine and beer glasses hanging behind him from the ceiling.

It would be interesting to listen to the reaction each of the team members would have about their rooms.

He called the concierge and asked if a cart of appetizers for six people could be arranged.

The concierge rattled off his suggestion of Pulled Pork Taquitos, Enchiladas, Black Bean and Sweet Corn Guacamole dip, Mini Chicken Chimichangas, and Quesadillas and a variety of corn chips.

He listened and then simply agreed.

The knock and the pattern clearly indicated Dr. J would be the person at the door. He walked over and opened it just as the rest of team could be heard down the hall getting off the elevator. Their chatter clearly indicated they were excited.

"I am in 502 across the hall in almost as nice a room as this but it does not have the bar. I can't believe we got such great rooms.

Is this your doing by any chance," Dr. J asked as he exaggerated his English accent and peered directly into Ian's eyes?

"Let's just say our benefactors were quite happy to upgrade the team," Ian replied as he waited with the door open for the rest of the team to arrive.

"This is already the best trip I have ever taken, and the tournament hasn't even begun," Samantha commented as she entered the room and stopped still, "Wow and I was just commenting that it couldn't get any better."

He watched as each team member in turn stopped to absorb the elegance of the room.

"What's your pleasure wine, beer or a soft drink," he inquired as the doorbell rang.

"Dr. J would you be so kind as to tend to the bar," he asked as he walked back to open the door.

He stood aside and watched as the server pushed in a large cart, opened the leaves of the cart, arranged the appetizers, and removed the lids.

"It just keeps getting better," Samantha reiterated as she stepped up to the appetizer cart and examined the offering.

He listened to the conversation and realized that eating out at the restaurant that he had planned to go in order to walk the area where he would carry out his problem-solving action was not going to happen on this evening.

The team attacked the appetizers with a gusto and a youthful energy he had forgotten.

He recalled several of the more memorable parties when he was a student at Stanford. He especially remembered the one where a beautiful dark-haired young lady with almost black eyes had escorted him to his dorm. He had pursued her until she had said yes to become his wife.

He suggested that rather than go out to eat, the better plan would be to go to the convention hall, check out the arrangements, unload *"Muerte de Norte"* and secure it in the team's assigned accommodation.

Then come back and eat in.

The resounding agreement confirmed Ian's read on the situation.

A half hour later the entire team walked down the hall to the elevator. Angela was still at the desk as Ian walked up and asked whether they needed a key to get into the building where the robot fighting tournament was taking place.

"Sí, el señor Trip, voy a tener el conserje organizar para alguien que te acompañe terminado," replied with a brilliant smile and a slight nod of her head.

He simply replied, "Gracias."

He led the team to the middle of the lobby, and they chatted about the coming tournament.

The outside of the hotel was now illuminated in the Holiday Inn green color. The lights at the entrance to the convention hall and the interior ones were all on. They were a day early and it appeared they were the only ones on location.

The facility was literally a football field in size but square. Most of the walls were folded back creating a huge open floor area. An eight-foot-wide half inch thick plate metal track led from what could have been taken as a glass enclosed boxing arena toward an area in the back of the facility. This last area had been divided and each team had a separate area to house their robot and their equipment.

The area opened to five truck dock doors.

He suggested the team bring *"Muerte de Norte"* in while he finished checking out the rest of the facility. He asked their escort to open up one of the bay doors before going on his own excursion.

He needed to be invisible in his coming and going. He located the surveillance cameras and looked for the blind spots. He repositioned a few cameras to create the blind spots he needed.

The invisible route out and back in was via the men's restroom. It had an entry from the tournament area and another from the hallway near a side exit door. There was one camera just above the backdoor of the bathroom.

He had a spray that did not blank out the camera but fogged it, so nothing was clear or distinguishable. This could be done from inside the bathroom by reaching out and spraying the camera covering lens.

The team was just finishing unloading and arranging all their equipment when he returned. Together they walked out to the front door where the hotel guide was waiting. The evening had cooled appreciably, and the air felt cool as they walked the short distance back to the hotel.

The younger members of the team were ready to party.

He suggested a quick break to allow each of them to go to their rooms. Afterwards, they could come to his room, and they would order dinner in and celebrate their arrival to the tournament.

The next two days were actually exciting. *"Muerte de Norte"* seemed unstoppable. It had won against each opponent and had only one more fight to win the tournament. The best part was that it had not yet used all of its arsenal, so it had a few surprises that had yet to be exposed.

The lasso technique had not been used.

"This is just fantastic, and I doubted my friend when he suggested we let you on our team," Dr. J commented.

Ian wondered who this friend was and how he was connected with his invisible supporters. He knew none of the details about his invisible support.

"Our final fight is scheduled tomorrow evening. We win it and we take home the trophy and the hundred grand prize," Marty commented.

"What time tomorrow evening," Ian asked.

He hoped it was not during the same time that the problem solution was to be delivered.

"Our match is set for nine pm. It was originally set for eight-thirty but the whole event has been running thirty minutes to an hour behind. Since they want to televise the final bout, they decided on the nine o'clock time frame," Samantha shared.

Ian doubted the time change was accidental. It appeared very coordinated with his plans.

During lunch the next day, he checked for the panel truck he expected to see in the parking lot.

The old dull tan van was parked at the end of the lot as he had requested. Its plain drab appearance and middle of the series selection was intentional. He was intent on making it hard for witnesses to remember it.

It was a relief to know that his support team, though invisible to him, was on the job and helping. He could now spend the day watching the robot fighters in the tournament eliminate each other.

The van had been modified to his specifications. An elevator to lower a flat box shaped robot to the ground had been installed. The elevator was remote controlled and worked off the same transmitter as the bomb robot.

The bomb robot was already on the elevator platform and would be lowered when commanded. The robot was a small flat square stainless-steel box. It was equipped with drive wheels and with a scissor jack lift. A high-grade explosive loaded in a cone shape depression would guide the explosion upward and hopefully keep it contained.

Everything was ready.

He had designed, built, and tested everything prior to having it shipped to where it now sat in the parking lot.

He smiled when he compared the design of the two robot units, that he was a part of designing. He had told the truth when he said that he built killer robots.

Activating the explosive charge was the only step remaining. He would do that once he reached the coffee shop.

"It's great to just be able to watch. *Muerte de Norte* has been so successful it got all the points to carry it to the finals," Dr. J. commented when he returned to where the team was sitting.

"I have a quick errand to run but I will be back for our final competition," he casually commented.

He walked into the restroom behind the refreshment stand. Two young men in jeans and matching green T shirts were commenting on the standings of various teams as they stood at their urinals. He walked casually past them and took the last stall near the back entrance and waited for them to leave.

He opened the rear door of the bathroom and sprayed the lens of the camera mounted on the wall above it.

He then stepped out into the hallway and walked out the back door.

He walked along the back wall of the center and then around to the right toward the front.

When he reached the front corner of the building, he stopped to look up at the position of the surveillance camera scanning the front lot and waited until it was pointed to the other end.

He then walked up to the van and casually got in. The tinted windows would conceal his presence. He took the time to check out his equipment and the robot. He also changed clothes and put on something more appropriate for the coffee house venue.

He started up the van and drove it slowly out of the parking lot. He drove up highway 101 until he reached the street where the coffee shop was located.

He was relieved to find one parking spot three cars behind where he knew the limo carrying the cartel leader would stop.

"Sometimes luck is as important as planning," Ian thought.

After parking the van as close to the curb as possible and once again verifying that the buildings on his left had no windows in them, he climbed into the back and activated the explosive charge.

A quick check let him know the elevator to lower the robot bomb to the street surface was working.

Everything he could do was now ready.

He opened the back doors of the van and stepped out. He could see no one as he took in the scene above the coffee shop. The lights and the black steel bars on the windows indicated they were occupied residences.

They should be OK.

The mariachi music coming from the coffee shop gave the area a cheerful sound and feel.

He straightened out his tan sports jacket, checked out the polish on his black boots and with a newspaper in hand walked across the street toward the shop.

A young waiter introduced himself as Enrico and asked where Ian would like to sit. His perfect English let Ian know that he had already been classified as one of the tourist gringos on vacation. He hoped this young man did not have too good of a memory.

He took a seat outside next to the wall to the right of the restaurant's large glass window. The inside of the coffee shop was already half full. The coffee shop would most likely have a good night.

"What can I get for you," Enrico asked as he cleared the extra place setting.

"Una taza de café y cuernos de azucar por favor," he asked for coffee and a roll in the best Spanish he could muster.

"Buena elección," Enrico replied with a large smile and walked into the shop to get the order.

Google Earth is like watching football at home on the big screen. You get a better view, and you get to see replays," Ian thought as he looked up and down the street as he tried to get oriented.

It was exactly what he expected.

He hoped things would turn out as expected.

He had his back to the wall, a cup of coffee, his sugar-coated crescent, and a newspaper in hand. He relaxed and tried to make sense of his Mexican newspaper.

Not too long afterwards a black Cadillac limo with darkened windows came slowly down the street and pulled into a spot two cars in front of his van that had been blocked by three orange cones.

He thought the fact that one of the leaders of the cartel actually went personally out to periodically talk to his victims spoke volumes about the need for direct feedback to his importance and power.

He had obtained the information on the routes of the bosses via a request to his unnamed supporters. They seemed to have the resources to find anyone anywhere.

Why was he needed?

"Perfect position," he thought as he looked from the van to the limo.

The black limo had not gone unnoticed.

The music was still playing inside, and he could hear the chatter from inside the coffee shop but the conversation at the outside tables seemed to have stopped.

Each person's dinner and coffee now seemed to take all of the attention. No one looked at the limo.

He pulled the small control module from his pocket and pushed the start button. He imagined he could hear the elevator in the van lowering the robot bomber. He put on what appeared to be his reading glasses and took a sip of his coffee. His glasses were polarized, and he was able to see the outline of the robot bomber as it slowly made its way under the car in front of the van, toward the limo.

He watched as a man dressed in a sleek black suite and spit polished black shoes stood up from one of the tables, took a sip of his coffee and then walked slowly across the street.

The driver of the limo came around and as he opened the door, the robot bomber raised up just in front of the gas tank and made solid contact with the bottom of the car. The explosion was aimed and would be contained in the back of the car.

"This will be an evening all of the clientele will remember," he thought as he waited for the businessman to exit the limo.

He took the last bite of his pastry and followed it with the last sip of his coffee.

He was glad he had paid when he had received the order. He put out a generous tip.

"Thank you, senor," a waitress walking by said as she picked it up.

"Asegúrese de compartir lo hará Enrico," he said in Spanish so she would think he knew Enrico, who had waited on him and that the tip was for him.

"Si of course senor."

He was becoming impatient when finally, the driver walked back around and opened the back door and the business owner stepped out and replied to something said from inside the car.

Ian was now at full attention. He hoped the business owner would get across the street before he had to activate the bomb.

Ian watched as the driver of the limo and the businessman seemed to be in a synchronized dance. Each were moving to their designated positions in slow time.

When he heard the slight rise in the engine noise and just as the car was about to move he pushed the fire button.

The blast hurled the business owner up onto the sidewalk. The limo rose three feet into the air and turned into a fireball. Glass came raining down on everyone out on the sidewalk and the four large glass panels on the front of the shop blew in on top of the patrons inside.

The smoke was overwhelming. The familiar taste of spent gun powder was on Ian's tongue and momentarily it took him back to his time behind the fifty-caliber machine gun in Vietnam.

He slowly picked himself up from the sidewalk where he had been hurled from his seat. He picked up his glasses and his newspaper and stumbled across the street to the van.

He was dazed.

The van had all of its windows blown out and as Ian started its engine, he could see that every window above the coffee shop had also been blown out. The car in front of the van had been blown back against the van and had all its windows blown out.

He wondered about the magnitude of the explosion.

He drove slowly away from the coffee shop. His mind raced as he tried to make sense of the blast's intensity. All he could think of, for the intensity of the explosion, was that the limo had been carrying a load of explosives in the trunk. His robot bomber had only enough explosives to penetrate the passenger area and eliminate anyone sitting in the backseat.

The driver would have survived the attack. Instead, everyone outside of the café was injured and the limo was a burning mass of twisted steel and contained two dead people.

The police cars with their alarms blaring approached rapidly and the area became a sea of flashing blue and red lights.

He drove slowly back to the hotel and parked the van in the location where he had found it. He cleared the shattered glass from his backpack and took out the clothes he had left the tournament in and put them on. He left everything else in the van.

He had to use a handheld piece of the rearview mirror to see the parking lot security camera. When the parking lot camera was pointed to the other end of the parking area, He exited the van and walked slowly along the back wall of the meeting hall. The long walk gave him time to recover. He was still in shock, and he figured he would have bruises all over his body.

He stepped into the bathroom. One person was just finishing washing their hands.

He remembered to wipe the entrance camera lens clean.

He stopped by the bathroom mirror and removed some black smudges from his cheek and put his hair in order.

He then returned to watch the remainder of the robot competition.

"You are just in time. The judges are insisting the entire team needs to be present for the final fight. We were getting worried," Dr. J said as he led Ian over to one of the judges to sign him in.

Once in the fight ring, *Muerte de Norte* rapidly decimated its opponent. It was the same as a knockout in the first round of a heavy weight boxing match. The issue of course was that there was not much fight time to broadcast.

"They want to do an interview with each of us," Samantha commented a few moments later.

"Sounds good," he said agreeably as he suggested they meet in his room to celebrate afterwards.

He edged his way toward the bar where he bought a beer and then blended into the crowd and faded away.

He was not about to get interviewed. He needed to stay anonymous.

As he crossed over to the hotel, he noticed the van was gone. He went up to his room and took a long hot shower. The blast had been strong enough that he would have a brick shaped bruise on his back and a bruise on his back side from having been bounced out of his chair. He knew he was lucky not to have been hit by flying glass.

A short time later he heard the team coming down the hallway toward his room. It was clear they were into celebrating their victory.

"You missed the interviews, but we sang your praises," Dr. J commented as he led the way through into the room.

"Let's get the celebration started at the bar and then we can call in our order," Ian replied.

It was early morning before the party broke up. Dr. J thanked him and walked out the door and crossed to his room.

He knew that the robot tournament would be an event he would long remember, and he would find some way to talk about it outside the context of his more lethal problem-solving actions.

The team met the next day at eleven to check out of the hotel. They still had to load "*Muerte de Norte*" into the truck and then begin their drive back to Illinois.

He accepted a ride with the team to the Laredo Airport.

The security checks on each side of the border went smoothly. One of the border agents who had watched the robot fight complemented the team on their victory.

At the airport everyone got out and gave him a hug and thanked him for helping them win the tournament.

"Well team have a great trip back. Maybe I will see you all next year," he said as he gave each of them a hug as they got back into the van.

He turned and walked into the airport ticket area and walked down its length and went down to the arrival area. He caught a cab to the bus station where his car was parked. He waited for the cab to leave and then walked to his car and drove away.

He was on his way to Laredo.

The local radio station reported the death of one of the key Gulf Cartel leaders. The blame was currently being pointed at rival cartels.

The news commentator spent a great deal of time speculating on the war between the rival gangs.

The news featured a witness that stated a large burly Mexican had driven away from the scene in a black van just as the police arrived.

He could not contain a chuckle. He had become a burly Mexican driving a black van. He thought about the difficulty of a blue eyed, white gringo to blend in.

"Blending in well," he continued his musing and hummed the tune to Yankee Doodle.

But the scene of the explosion kept playing his mind. He knew he was not OK. He had been alarmed at the power of the explosion and the people that had been hurt. He was experiencing something similar to PTSD.

He would need to keep a close watch on himself.

He heard the dark side of his mind laughing. He thought of Lesley and the kids, well his "adult" kids and got some semblance of control.

Normally he would have several weeks or months of time between problem-solving sessions.

Not this time.

The series of problem-solving events would be more like an ultra-marathon.

3 Laredo-Los Zeta Cartel

*A*s Ian drove toward Laredo, he let his mind run through his research of the Los Zeta cartel. Their headquarters was in Nuevo Laredo across the border in Mexico.

The Los Zetas were originally comprised of a special forces group that had deserted the Mexican army to become the enforcers for the Gulf Cartel. After some leadership disagreements they had formed their own cartel and fought to control the area around Nuevo Laredo.

Ian had found their current leader Benito Solano-Solano interesting in that he had originally been on the good side but like Darth Vader in Star Wars he went over to the dark side.

Benito had joined the army straight from high school. He quickly rose through the ranks in the special forces unit and became a tough anti-cartel fighter. After losing many of his men because of repeated betrayals by his superiors he decided to change sides.

Benito was a young bright and very capable individual who had been successful in simultaneously fighting the Gulf Cartel, and the Mexican and US governments.

Mexico had a two-million-dollar reward, and the US had a five-million-dollar reward for information leading to his capture.

No one came forward for the reward. No one dared to do so. They knew that if they did, they would never live long enough to spend any of the reward.

Ian considered the Los Zetas to be one of the more dangerous targets because they operated with more discipline and paid more attention to security then most of the other cartels.

It was clear to Ian that both governments knew Benito's location. After all, he had found Benito's main operational compound just outside Nuevo Laredo three miles off Highway 2 using the internet and Google Earth. The two governments certainly had the resources to learn of Benito's whereabouts.

Ian realized that making contact with and taking any corrective action was going to be very difficult and extremely dangerous.

For this occasion, Ian was Martin Lindquist, a contributing reporter to the Boston Herald doing a report on the lives of Drug Cartel Bosses.

The official reason Ian was in Laredo was to try and get an interview with Benito. The "assignment" was to highlight Benito's humanitarian, family, and religious side. This was a different angle than most articles about Benito had focused on.

Benito was known to be a very effective, and thoroughly ruthless leader responsible for the deaths of many people. However, he was credited with donating the money to build the chapel in Santa Barbara in honor of Pope John Paul II.

Perhaps he thought good deeds might still get him into heaven.

Ironically, the church Benito gave money to was now under investigation for the potential use of illicit funds. This to Ian was ironic in that many people go to Rome and visit all the loot that has been accumulated from around the world and "given" to the Catholic Church. No one has thought of challenging their collection or the organization.

Ian stayed a few miles under the speed limit as he drove northeast on highway 83. The three-hour drive to Laredo would give him time to think through the plan and the various versions he had developed for his problem-solving session with the Los Zeta cartel.

Ian came into the Laredo area and took exit 3B and followed his GPS to the Goodwill store at the junction of San Dario Ave. and East Mann Rd. He was surprised at the upscale look of the store. The Goodwill business must be more lucrative than he was aware of.

The day had grown warm, and he was glad that he had dressed light. He parked the car and made sure he had all of his belongings out. He found the Goodwill store manager and followed her instructions on the car donation procedure.

In less than thirty minutes he had made his donation and was ready to walk to The Family Inn across the highway from the Goodwill.

He had chosen the location because of its proximity to the Goodwill store and was pleasantly surprised that it mirrored the pictures it posted on the internet. Ian gave it the name of "The Honest Family Inn."

The swimming pool in the center surrounded by palm trees made the place seem open and relaxing. Each of the first-floor units had a veranda and a four-person table. He was there for at least a night and looked forward to sitting out and reading.

Ian had his team book a room that featured a veranda. It had two queen beds and was quite well appointed. It was much better than he had been expecting.

After checking in Ian went to his room and put on his running shorts and jogging shoes. He put a pair of jeans and anything of value into his backpack and then went out for a jog.

The jog took him down San Dario Avenue alongside US 35. The constant tire hum was at first distracting but soon faded into white background noise. The heat of the day was just starting its late afternoon decline. It was as comfortable as it was going to get.

The cooking smells from the restaurants along the way went from Mexican to the smell of grilled steak coming from a place called the Sirloin Blockade. It all made Ian hungry.

The five-mile jog took Ian towards West Saunders Street where several used car lots offered a variety of transportation. He was aware of the dealer car lots that were much closer and just north of the Goodwill store, but he was looking for a place that would most likely be slower in processing its paperwork.

At a place called Bago's Auto, Ian stopped, took his jeans from his backpack, put them on and walked onto the lot. After a quick look around, he used cash to purchase a late model maroon SUV.

The interior of the SUV was in great shape, and it was evident that the car had gone through a thorough cleaning. The smell of the cleaning fluids was a little overpowering. Ian rolled down all the windows and drove out onto the street.

He drove with the windows open down San Bernardo Avenue to check out the Tornado Bus company and to see if they had a long-term parking area to leave the car. The lot behind the rather small station was available and would cost him fifty dollars for the time he would need to leave the car.

The bus ticket into Nuevo Laredo was only twelve dollars. The time choices for the ride across was either at the wee early hours of the morning, long before sunrise or the one single time at four-thirty in the afternoon. He quickly made the decision to go across the following afternoon.

Ian had the rest of the evening and the next day. He would have preferred to be in Nuevo Laredo earlier, but he had no clue what he would do there at three in the morning. Who had decided on such a time for a bus route?

It was time to go to dinner and then get a good night's sleep. Maybe the ache in his buttocks, caused by being blown out of his chair during the explosion in Matamoros, would feel better after another day of rest. He laughed to himself about having a real pain in the butt.

He chose to have dinner at the Compos Bar and Grill, one of the better rated nearby restaurants. Ian was early and there was at least another hour of daylight, so he considered the outdoor seating, but the view consisted of the shopping strip's parking area or the side of a shopping store across the street.

Inside was a little dark but overall was an acceptable atmosphere. Every item on the menu attracted him. He chose a Lamb and Scallop appetizer, an Ahi Tuna Salad, and a bottle of Pellegrino.

He recalled similar diners where he ate whatever his sons and friends wanted and that was prepared by an eager mother. He always had his glass of Pellegrino.

While he waited on the food, Ian went to the web site of his new identity to continue his transition from Trip Masters, design engineer to being Martin Linquest reporter for the Boston Herald. It's always nice to know your bosses name and what you have been writing for the last twenty years Ian thought to himself as he sat and reviewed his website appropriately named Martin's View.

His support team had created a website that went back multiple years and had some very interesting articles. He smiled as he became sensitized to what a great writer he was.

The next morning Ian stayed and had breakfast at the hotel. The splashing sounds from the water fall and the kids playing on the slides and swings opposite of the swimming pool relaxed him. He sat at the blue green tiled gazebo counter and had a simple breakfast of bacon and eggs, a pancake, and a cup of coffee.

He watched the face of the waitress as she put his over easy eggs on top of the pancake. He asked for extra syrup. After pouring all the syrup on the pancakes and putting pads of butter between them, he broke the yellow of the eggs and began eating the syrup-soaked pancake with a piece of the egg.

After breakfast Ian arranged to check out late in the afternoon and then retreated to the veranda in front of his room to think about his coming problem-solving engagement and to continue his review of Martin Linquest's web site. His very interesting website!

Martin Linquest had been born in Ian's imagination. Building a believable web presence and getting it appropriately posted required the expertise of his invisible support team. He had asked for their support and was given the message to generate the report article outlines and interviews.

Ian figured he should have become a fiction writer. It had taken him longer to generate the years of history present on the web site than the work he had done in getting ready for the robot fight team. He had sent the material into his support group, and they had created and populated the web site. He was sure they could do anything they wanted and put anytime stamp they wanted on any material. The internet was fantasy land to Ian.

Anything and everything was possible.

Martin Linquest was on Facebook, had his own heavily followed blog and had articles in many of the national journals.

Ian remained on the veranda with a slight breeze blowing between the buildings that kept the veranda at a warm but pleasantly comfortable level. The laughter of three six-to-eight-year-old kids in the pool created a peaceful atmosphere.

He skipped lunch and joined the kids in the pool.

Finally, at three Ian checked out and drove to the bus station.

Ian parked the SUV snug to the back wall of the bus station. He paused to look at the orange, red and blue strips painted horizontally on the wall of the station before grabbing his backpack from the right front seat.

His one suitcase was in the back.

Looking around the area he wondered whether the car would remain here for the week. There was little he could do about it if it got stolen.

He got out and walked around to the front of the station.

Three blue bus seats graced the front of the bus station office. They were occupied by an older white-haired man, what appeared to be his wife and a teenager probably fifteen or sixteen.

Ian stood at the corner of the building behind a silver pickup truck. It appeared the three were all waiting for the same bus.

When the bus arrived, it was clear there had been several other stops and some of the passengers looked as if they had been riding for a long time.

Ian gave the driver his ticket and was reminded he needed a valid passport, or a tourist permit as he boarded.

The passenger pick-up took less than five minutes and the bus pulled away five minutes early.

Ian noted as they crossed into Mexico, that the Rio Grande was not so grand, and it had little water in it.

The Mexican border guards boarded the bus and checked everyone's passports and then the bus proceeded.

The air blowing from the ceiling vents made conversation difficult and most of the passengers were quietly looking out the windows.

At the bus station, Ian was about to get into a cab when he spotted a van with the name Fiesta Crowne Plaza with the distinctive yellow circle with three golden horizontal squiggle lines.

The older couple and the teenager were all pulling their suitcases toward it.

Ian walked over and asked if there was room for one more.

The ride took less than fifteen minutes. Ian was taken by the fact that the teenager played some game on his i-pad and the older couple were completely silent. The family connection did not exist.

Ian rode in silence himself but found it hard not to start a conversation. Had he been on a different mission he would have done so but at the moment he wanted to remain as unnoticed as possible.

The hotel catered to the North American tourist. Its distinctive emblem was at the top of a twelve-story brick column enclosed stairs that went up the side of the building.

The older couple and the teenager seemed to rush away from the van as Ian took his time, thanked the driver, and gave him a tip.

The four threes' numbers to the right and just above the height of the double sliding door entrance caught Ian's eye. This was an easy address to remember.

The door opened to an expansive brightly lit lobby.

A receptionist, dressed in a dark blue business dress and matching jacket over a light blue blouse with thin vertical stripes and a gold necklace with a heart strategically hanging in the v above the top of the blouse button, stood below a red brass enclosed oval with the three horizontal stretched triple S symbol above foot high lettering boldly announcing the hotel's name in giant bold letters and in smaller letters below it gave the location, Nuevo Laredo.

The grey and black granite counter Ian was walking toward stretched in the same shape across the entire back of the lobby. The front of the counter had lights shining down illuminating bone-colored panels with white swirls.

Five clocks on the wall to the receptionist's left provided the times for Laredo, Los Angeles, Chicago, New York, and London. The entire check-in area was brightly lit by recessed lights beaming down from ten feet above.

Ian walked up to where the receptionist was standing and was greeted by a smile that lit up her face and flashed her bright white teeth. Her hair hanging down each side to almost to her waist provided the perfect frame for her pleasant sisterly face.

Ian gave her his new name, Martin Lindquist, and handed her his passport.

"Yes, Senor Linquist we have been expecting you. We have the style of room you asked for with a king-size bed, a work desk, a separate table, and a nice chair to sit in. I hope you like it," she said as she found his reservation and checked him in.

Ian took the elevator to the seventh floor and went to his room where he unpacked his suitcase, hung up his clothes and put his personal computer into the safe. He put out the various reports and memos that solidified Martin Linquest as a real person.

He expected that some time on this trip his room would be searched.

Ian returned to the almost empty lobby. He took a walk around and got a better feel for the hotel, its bar, restaurant and sitting area. The gym had a good mix of equipment and four treadmills. He would probably not have time for the swimming pool but its presentation of reclining lounge chairs below small palm trees all the way around the pool was sure to capture the attention of everyone.

Ian returned to the lobby and approached the concierge and asked about the night spots and if by any chance he could arrange to have a driver that would stay with him as he tried each place out.

Ian wanted to hit as many places as possible on his first night. He planned to make the round several times in hopes of making contact with the Los Zeta Cartel.

"Si, yes, my cousin would love such an opportunity. Can you wait about fifteen minutes for him to get here," the concierge whose name tag identified him as Diego replied?

"Diego, is he available for the week," Ian continued his inquiry?

A few minutes later, Ian looked at a person entering the lobby that he presumed was the cousin. He was dressed in a plain light blue T shirt, blue jeans, and light blue slip-on tennis shoes. His black hair, dark brown eyes and open smile immediately made him seem a good choice. Ian watched as he walked over and talked to Diego.

Ian stood up as the two approached him.

"Senor Linquest, I am Raul. I would be pleased to be your driver this week. How many hours each day do you want me to be available," Raul inquired.

His direct manner, inquiry and seeming confidence in his carriage and his voice pleased Ian.

Ian decided on the spot that he would hire Raul. Now it was just a matter of getting through the bargaining.

Ian would pay whatever it took but he always bargained so the recipient of the money would feel he had gotten a good deal.

"I am not sure. Why don't we agree on ten hours a day whether I need you or not? Some days it may be less and maybe there will be a time when it is more. What will it cost for such an arrangement," Ian inquired?

Ian watched as Raul thought about the situation and was pleased when he came to a quick decision.

"Ok Senor Linquest, fifty dollars each day including today, and you pay for the gas," Raul put forward his offer.

Ian knew he could bargain the price down significantly but chose instead to add some requirements that he knew would be easily accepted.

"Fifty dollars each day but you must call me Martin, take me to eat at the good Mexican restaurants you would want to go to, and show me all the night spots in Nuevo Laredo. You cannot drink alcohol during this week, not even a beer," Ian replied.

Ian was serious about the drinking. He did not want to end up in an accident as the two of them went from bar to bar.

"Senor, I mean Martin, you drive a very hard bargain," Raul replied as he feigned pain by putting his hands on his chest.

Ian could tell from the response and the look Raul gave to his cousin that it was good for him.

OK, I will pay you half now and when I make contact with Benito Salano-Salano you get the other half, but then your employment is over, and you will not contact me after that contact is made.

Both Raul and Diego's eyes went wide, and they inhaled in unison and both uttered,

"Jesús, Oh mi dios, eres loco," Diego uttered.

"Yes, I suppose I am crazy. I am here to see if I can get an interview with him for the Boston Herald about his personal life and aspirations.

"Martin, perhaps you should pay all up front, so I do not have to look in your wallet after they kill you," Raul joked.

Ian understood both the joke and the concern about getting paid.

"OK, I will give you three hundred now, an extra fifty dollars for gas and I will put another two hundred in an envelope with your name on it in the office safe. You can pick it up on Friday, but you must promise to stay out of my wallet," Ian finished with a joke.

Ian opened his black leather two chamber wallet with a hidden third pocket covered by the back flap. He counted out fifteen twenties and handed it over to Raul. He then counted out another fifty. Please count it and sign this receipt. I want the Herald to reimburse me later. Ian instructed.

He watched as Raul slowly counted and then signed the receipt.

Ian accepted the receipt and then walked across the lobby to the check-in desk and asked for an envelope. He put the other two hundred and a generous tip into the envelope and asked the receptionist to put this in the safe until Friday when a Raul Lopez would pick it up.

"Please wait here and I will bring the car to the hotel entrance," Raul said as he hurried toward the hallway leading to the back of the hotel.

The car sparkled in the lights shining down from the light pole. As Raul opened the front passenger door for Ian the cool interior air presented the faint smell of lavender. The interior was spotless. It was hard to tell the year of the car and it did not matter. It was in pristine condition.

Ian's appraisal of Raul went up dramatically.

Ian asked Raul if he had dinner yet. Raul had not, so Ian suggested that they go to the best Mexican restaurant Raul could think of but one that did not cater to the Gringos.

The night lights of Nuevo Laredo and what Ian considered an erratic driving style typical of his many experiences as a passenger in Mexico made the drive to Raul's favorite place stimulating.

The small square cement block building painted in a light yellow with four plain glass windows and a glass front door all trimmed in white, was located on the corner of two busy streets. The building wore a yellow panel around the roof with one forest green and one dark red stripe and proudly declared *"Polo Frito Fiesta"* with the words alternating red, green, red in color and on the front of the building the sign declared it as the best chicken in the city.

Ian followed Raul in and listened as he was greeted by the plump but very friendly woman behind the counter.

Ian took in the four well-worn but solid wooden tables along the front. The cooking was done in a grill behind the building and the mouth-watering aroma seemed to tempt the appetite each time the door was opened.

Ian followed Raul to the only available table at the end of the row.

A young version of the person behind the counter came to take their orders. Her broad white toothed smile, the swing of her hips and her greeting made it clear to Ian she was flirting with Raul. Raul looked at Ian, raised his left eyebrow, and smiled.

Ian sat back and enjoyed watching the interplay of the two young people. It was refreshing to see this dance take place in all corners of the world.

He agreed with Raul to try each style of the chicken and to sample the chicken salad. Raul ordered a soft drink and Ian asked for a bottle of tonic water.

The chicken was brought to the table on a plate lined with waxed paper with the chicken on top. Two small round plastic tubs offered two different white sauces to dip the chicken into. Ian liked the plain salt and pepper seasoned chicken the best. The hot wings were also very good, and the coated or breaded chicken was delicious.

Raul asked which he liked best. Ian decide that he liked them all and agreed that it was some of the best chicken he had eaten. He made the point that only his wife, Lesley, prepared a better chicken.

Raul turned out to be a good guide. He seemed to know all the night spot locations and the reputation each carried. Though each had a different atmosphere, all night spots had the same feel of people seeking some sort of relief from daily life, the goal of some connection with other people and the hope of finding one's purpose in life.

The discussion with the bar tenders and their common alarmed reactions when he inquired about meeting Benito Salano-Salano was almost a duplicate of Raul's reaction to the fact that he must be crazy.

However, in each case Ian left his Boston Herald business card with his cell number and his current hotel written on the back.

After visiting three-night spots, and leaving a business card at the bar, Ian decided it was enough for one night. He arranged to have lunch with Raul on the following day and then they would continue the visits to the bars.

The next morning Ian arose late, got up, went to the gym for a quick workout, came back to the room, took a quick shower and was in the lobby a few minutes before twelve.

Diego greeted him and asked how the previous evening had gone and if Raul was doing a good job.

"Raul won the day at the beginning by taking me to eat some of the best chicken I have ever eaten," Ian replied.

"Si I am sure he took you to Polo Frito Fiesta. Not only is the chicken very good but a very good-looking chicken that he likes works there for her mother," Diego said with a small laugh.

Raul's green car stopped at the front doors. The car was shiny and spotless. Raul must have cleaned it during the morning.

Ian said goodbye to Diego and walked out just as Raul pulled up to the hotel.

Raul suggested they take lunch at the El Ranchero restaurant he identified as an upscale place.

The exterior of the stucco building featured five arches topped by a second story with matching glass doors coming out to two small terraces that bracketed the outside seating area on the second floor.

The brown, red color of the arches and the black painted railing of the terraces and top deck topped with what appeared to be a giant plate with the years 1972-1993 arched over them impressed Ian.

Ian followed Raul in through the center arch leading to the entrance.

The interior was an onslaught of bright green, yellow, red, and blue colored mural scenes of Mexican life and key moments in history stretching around the seating area.

The tables were covered with light lime green table clothes. A second smaller tablecloth on top had dark green strips on an orange background.

The plain white panel ceiling was the only feature that seemed out of place.

The restaurant had a spacious setting with at least thirty tables.

Ian and Raul followed the receptionist to one of the tables roughly in the center of the room.

Ian decided that all Mexican restaurants carried the great smells of the foods they served. Steaks and beef dishes seemed to be popular at the El Ranchero. The sound of sizzling meat being carried out to the various tables immediately told Ian that the Fajitas must be good. He looked around several tables to get a better feel for the menu.

The sizzling Fajitas in their cast iron frying pans carried out on their wooden platters proved to be Ian's choice.

Raul and Ian were both drinking Pellegrino. The room was about three quarters full, but the high ceiling and the sound absorbing ceiling panels made quiet conversation possible.

A good choice of ceiling, Ian thought as he recalled his initial evaluation.

Ian ask Raul about his personal status. It turned out Raul was trying to work himself through school and was currently enrolled at the Instituto Tecnologico de Nuevo Laredo in their engineering program.

He had applied to several Universities in the US but had not been accepted at any of them. He was still trying to get into some US college in hopes of getting a path out of Nuevo Laredo.

Ian made a mental note to make a call to Dr. J and see if he could get Raul admitted on a scholastic scholarship. He was sure a reasonable gift to the engineering robot program would help in getting Raul admitted.

The next part of the conversation took Ian by surprise. Raul looked around as if there might be someone listening and then commented that one of his buddies knew where Ian could make contact with the cartel.

The food arrived, and Raul stopped talking until the waitress left.

"I will tell you more later in the car," Raul continued.

Ian was curious, but he preferred having the remainder of this conversation in the car as well. He initiated a conversation about Raul's family and his goals for the future.

The night visits to the various night clubs were a duplicate of the evening before. Ian had done his field work and visited most of the local pubs and coffee houses and asked questions about Benito. He was hoping to get noticed by the cartel and get invited to talk to the boss himself.

As the evening ended, Raul let him know that they had covered the majority of the entertainment spots.

Raul then shared the location of a restaurant where the cartel supposedly held many of their meetings.

It was only nine in the evening, but Ian decided to call it a day and asked Raul to give him a ride to that restaurant in the morning.

Ian walked into the quiet almost empty hotel lobby. Diego was still on duty and gave a furtive wave for him to come over.

"Senor Linquest, be careful, they have been in inquiring about you, and I think they went to your room. They left only a short time ago," Diego said in a hushed tone.

"Gracias Diego, it was good of you to let me know," Ian replied.

It was good to know that his inquiries had been heard.

Ian felt that giving Diego money for the information he had shared would be taken the wrong way, so he walked over to the check in desk and asked for an envelope into which he put two hundreds and put Diego's name on in with instructions to give it to him on the coming Friday.

Ian went to his room. Everything was as he had left it. The only way he knew that his room had been searched was the broken hair he had taped to the bedroom door.

He smiled. It seemed he had the attention of the cartel.

Sleep came easily, and he had a good night.

4 Laredo-Connection

*T*he next morning as he walked through the lobby, he noticed a different concierge was on duty. He wondered if Diego had purposely taken the day off.

Raul was exactly on time and arrived as Ian walked out of the lobby doors.

The early morning sky had that sleepy grey look, and the air had a moist feel. Ian knew that the cool of the morning would quickly dissipate and be replaced by the still hot air that had been yesterday afternoon.

"Buenos días Raúl, ¿cómo fue tu noche," Ian asked as he got into the front passenger seat.

"Thank you for asking. I had a great evening and even got my homework done," Raul replied.

The restaurant was only two minutes from the hotel. A tall imposing statue of someone named Juarez stood at the center of a traffic circle immediately in front of the restaurant that featured a windmill in what appeared to Ian to be a competition of height with the statue out in the circle.

Ian had Raul drop him off by the statue of Juarez and told him that he would call by noon if he needed transportation. He did not want Raul to be anywhere near the restaurant unless he was called back.

The smell of bacon and of fried beans in the restaurant immediately reminded Ian that he had skipped dinner the evening before. The big decision was whether to have two eggs with a waffle or a more traditional Mexican breakfast meal.

After a brief look at the menu and examining the orders of the people around him, Ian decided on the Barbacoa breakfast of enchiladas, coffee with cream and a bottle of water.

Ian was just finishing putting cream into his coffee and stirring it absent mindedly when a premonition made him look up as the door to the restaurant opened. Ian immediately recognized the person coming through the door as the Zeta leader known as Z-20 and nicknamed Pepino, *the hot one.* The birth name his mother had given him was Jorge.

The utter silence in the room screamed its warning as all the customers focused on their food or drink and averted their eyes away from where Z-20 was going.

A cold shiver went up Ian's back. There was no gun present, but Ian was at full alert and ready for anything. This was a guy that caused local journalists to quake in fear and caused some to disappear.

He watched as a second person stood by the door and Z-20 walked slowly and directly toward him.

"Good morning, Senor Linquest. I understand you would like to interview me. I am Benito Salano-Salano. What questions do you have for me," he said as he sat down?

"Good Morning, Senor Pepino. May I offer you a cup of coffee? I have just ordered breakfast. You are welcome to join me," Ian replied as he looked steadily back at Z-20 and pushed an empty cup toward him and lifted the coffee pot to pour a cup.

"An interview with you would be very interesting and put icing on the cake for my readers. I am trying to get a different perspective about the daily lives of the cartel leaders. My readers would love to hear about your daily family life and interactions. The drug statistics get boring after a while."

"So, you have at least done some homework on who we are. You know that I am the enforcer," Z-20 replied as he leaned toward Ian across the table trying to intimidate him with his persona.

His gaze was an effective way to cool any sort of passion and to sow fear into most people.

"Yes, I am aware of your reputation, and I hope to stay on your good side. I know the basics of the drug business. I am not interested in any of that."

I am interested in your personal life outside of your business. Do you go to church? Do you have a wife, or a girl friend? Do you play poker on Saturday night? My readers want to know the human side of the cartel bosses. These are the type questions my interview will focus on," was Ian's quiet reply.

Z-20 sat looking at Ian for several minutes apparently thinking. Ian hoped he was thinking good thoughts. Ian looked back steadily and waited.

"Don't show the enforcer any sign of fear," was the phrase that went through Ian's mind and there was no fear on his part.

Ian knew that if the enforcer made a move against him at this range, the enforcer would be dead before he could get his hands-on Ian or put a gun into use. The only worry Ian had was in how many support persons Z-20 had with him.

"Ok, tomorrow afternoon a car will pick you up at your hotel. You will be taken to meet with Benito. He said if you were legitimate, he would see you. I will be there as well. Do not bring any computer, phone, or recorder. You will work with pencil and paper only. Is that agreeable," Z-20 inquired?

It was clear to Ian he knew which hotel. His people were probably the ones that had searched his room and gone through his things. Ian hoped they had been thorough. He had worked hard to have the right information to convince them of his liberal leaning and his past reporting.

They could even go on his website and read past articles and comments. Ian was sure they had. Martin Linquest had a long history on the web.

"Pencil and paper, it is. I will be waiting. What time," Ian replied?

"Afternoon. Be patient, relax with a drink at the bar. Someone will come in and show you this coin," he said showing Ian a coin with Sapano emblazoned on both sides.

He stood up, gave Ian a hard stare that Ian returned evenly, Z-20 then turned and walked briskly away.

Ian looked around to see if anyone had taken notice of the event.

"Of course, we noticed," everyone screamed in their total silence and unwillingness to look toward his table.

His breakfast appeared as soon as the restaurant door closed.

The non-reaction at the coffee house was more chilling than the effect Z-20 had on Ian. People were so frightened they literally refused to acknowledge the existence of the person. In the process it seemed that Ian had become invisible as well.

The appealing smell of the pork enchiladas pulled Ian back and his gaze returned to his table. He topped off his coffee and slowly poured in some cream from the small white ceramic pitcher. The clink of his teaspoon against the side of the cup seemed to echo across the now silent dining area.

It was clear to Ian that the place would not return to normal until he left the premise. To them, he had become a potentially virulent germ ready to infect anyone who might get too near.

He purposefully took his time and enjoyed his meal before calling for the check.

Ian walked across the parking lot and then dashed across the traffic circle and sat down on the wall that created a pool at the base of the statue.

He called Raul, to let him know that contact had been made, thanked him for his services and told him to pick up the remainder of his money at the hotel desk.

Ian then sat and thought through the scenarios for his upcoming interaction with Benito.

Once he had thought through the variations Ian walked the six blocks back to the hotel. It was almost exactly noon as he walked across the lobby to the desk.

Ian instructed the desk clerk to allow Raul to pick up his envelope whenever he came in and he wanted to make sure Diego was given his envelope the next time he came in for work.

The attitude of the desk clerk had changed. She found it hard to talk directly to Ian. He was sure this was the result of the cartel's visit. She knew that he was being watched by the cartel and not sure she wanted to be associated with him or be too friendly to him.

Ian went up the elevator and put the key card up to the lock and heard the click as the lock activated. He was sure the guys who had come into the room had come in exactly the same way. Most probably with a card given to them by the young clerk who could not look him in the eyes.

Contact had been made and now it was time to relax.

Relaxing turned into a night long sleep. Ian could not recall getting into bed and was surprised when he woke up and looked at the door to see a chair wedged against the inside handle of the door.

He looked at the clock on the bedside table and let out a small groan. It was just past seven in the morning. He was terrible at waiting and he had until sometime in the afternoon before he was to be picked up.

On his way to breakfast he saw that Diego was at the concierge's position and gave him a slight nod as he walked past. Diego winked back but otherwise did not acknowledge him.

It was clear that Ian was now dangerous to be around. Ian understood and went on to the restaurant for a breakfast of two pancakes with butter and syrup, two over easy eggs with bacon or sausage and a cup of coffee with cream.

By late afternoon, Ian had worked out in the gym, sat in the ninety-two-degree hot tub where he spent some time determining that 35 degrees Celsius was approximately 95 degrees Fahrenheit.

Breakfast had lasted long enough, and it had been large enough that Ian again chose to skip lunch and he was now sitting at the lounge bar with a large bottle of Pellegrino and a glass as he waited for someone to walk up to him and show him the two-sided Sapano-Sapano coin.

Ian thought through various scenarios once again and concluded that success meant he would cross back across into the US no matter the outcome of the solution attempt. There was no failure scenario, only a success scenario. This realization made the next sip seem exceedingly sweet and fresh.

For the first time that day Ian actually relaxed, and he decided to order a gin and tonic with a twist of lime, without the gin.

Success or failure, Ian would cross the border and move on to the next cartel. There would be no, second chance or second attempt.

Three tonic waters later, a rather gentle, mild looking young man with slicked back black hair, a quiet voice put a Sapano coin on bar and then a moment later flipped it over to show Ian the Sapano on the other side. His mild voice softly said, "follow me."

Ian looked up from his tonic and knew he was looking at the deadliest person he had met so far on this trip. The black eyes were blank. This was a killer that had no emotions. A shiver ran down Ian's back. This was not someone Ian would trust. He would never allow him to be behind him.

Ian's immediate reaction was to observe the young man's movement and mannerisms. Ian decided that the weapon of choice for this young man would be a knife or straight razor used like a butterfly knife.

A shiver again ran down Ian's back. It was not the lion's den that he was going into but the devil's torture chamber.

The windows of the car were darkly tinted, and Ian could barely make out to the surroundings.

"Relax senor, it will be about thirty minutes before we get to our destination," the young man said quietly from the front seat.

Ian noted that they were indeed going down what he thought was highway two toward the compound he had located during his research.

They turned off the highway onto a hard dry dirt road.

The road back to the compound was several miles long and went through some rough terrain with sharp drop offs into deep dry ravines.

This part of the trip was slow going. It was a scenic dry desert with red flowers blooming from the ends of their paddle-like branches. The crevasses were greener than the surrounding landscape. The slow approach helped Ian get oriented to the many twists and turns. He was attentive and absorbing the surroundings as fully as possible.

"This country has a raw beauty all its own," he said in a friendly kind of way.

"Si," was the driver's brief reply.

The limo approached a walled compound and came to a stop to wait as three-inch-thick, ten-foot-high wooden gates rolled open to one half to each side. Once the gates retracted the car left the gravel road and entered a large smooth black cobble stone paved center courtyard.

A circular garden in the center with a flowering cactus was the main theme. The interior gardens were immaculate and manicured. Thick green grass framed the circular driveway.

The front door was probably forty inches across and eight feet high and the person standing in front of it obscured most of it.

Once the car came to a stop the hulk stepped forward and opened the back door for Ian.

His high voice did not match his build and Ian almost let out a chuckle.

"Slap yourself on the back of your head and behave. You don't want to make this guy mad," Ian thought to himself.

"I will need to pat you down," was the giant's only comment.

He held the same type of metal detector used at the airport security check points.

Ian dutifully spread his legs and held out his arms. The pad and pencil were in his left hand and nothing in his open right hand.

"Follow me," was all that was uttered by my young escort when the pat down was complete.

Again, Ian was comforted to be following versus having him behind. They entered a large room that seemed to be a library and gathering area. A billiard table was the central focus and shelves of books and large comfortable-looking leather chairs with small tables next to them went around the wall.

It was definitely a male oriented setting.

Ian conjectured that Benito was single and normally did not have women out for any length of time. He had seen no indication of a woman's touch.

"Please wait here," was the brief instruction.

Ian chose a chair facing the entrance to the room and his back to the wall. Ian flashed back to L.A. and another similar room. Three very bad people had died in that room. He hoped to be as successful here as he had been then.

This situation was much riskier than the previous one. Ian felt like he was being watched and was certain that he was.

The bar to the right of the entrance was well stocked and displayed some fine whiskeys and beers on tap. A bottle of Courvoisier Cognac and two classes were on the bar top.

It seemed to be prepared for Salano-Salano and him.

Ian always thought it interesting that it was the disgruntled Dutch settlers who found it difficult to preserve the French wine and through a series of distillations invented "Brandy" which comes from "brandewijin" meaning burnt wine.

Many of these Dutch settlers were smugglers too. Of course, that was a different time, and the goods were of a different nature.

Ian's musing came to an end as Benito walked into the room. He was as handsome as his pictures. In person he seemed like any other friendly good looking, black haired, black eyed, youngish looking handsome Mexican man.

Benito approached and introduced himself. Ian took note that he did not extend his hand in greeting.

It was clear to Ian that Benito was going to be polite, but not friendly.

"I am Benito. I understand you have been asking about me and would like to interview me," he said politely as Ian, and he looked steadily at each other.

"I am Martin Samuel Linquest," Ian said using all three names.

He knew in Mexico the names sometime would take on a meaning of their own.

"Yes, I am interested in doing an article on the personal side of your life. Your business side is well documented and has been written about exhaustively. However, my article will delve into who is Benito Salano-Salano, the person who built the church, who has donated substantial money to various charities.

Perhaps there are other stories of other good deeds that may not be known to the general public," Ian continued his introduction in a quiet even reply.

Ian was watching Benito's reaction closely. No one had entered the room with him. This was a bad sign for Ian because it meant they were being remotely monitored. For sure, there would be no aggressive action taken on Ian's part in this room.

"What can I offer you to drink," Benito asked as he indicated the bar.

"I would prefer either plain tonic or soda water, no ice," was Ian's reply.

Ian seldom drank hard liquor and, on this occasion, even a beer would not do.

A person came in through the door and went behind the bar. He opened a can of Canada Dry tonic and poured a shot of the Courvoisier.

It was clear they might be the only ones in the room, but they were not alone. Ian figured the help was probably in an adjacent room. It most likely opened directly into this one via one of the bookshelf walls. They were on an open stage. Their audience was just out of sight.

The pen may be mightier than the sword but here Ian stood with only a pencil. It was a weapon he had wielded many times in a very deadly fashion but in this case, it was hardly adequate.

Ian decided to focus on the interview.

"How do we do this interview," Benito asked.

"Well, I think perhaps the easiest way would be for you to describe all the good deeds you have done. Let them be stories from early on until now. I will listen and take notes. Later I will write a story from what I have heard and the notes I take," Ian replied.

"Will I be able to look at your notes," he asked?

"Yes, you can look at my notes before I leave, and I will send you the copy I turn in. I will also make sure you will get a copy of the paper that it is published in. Who knows, it may actually be picked up globally and you will be famous," Ian replied.

Apparently, I am already famous. I am just not well known as a good person he replied as he took a sip of the brandy.

Benito went back to his early days. His early school days were recalled fondly, and he recounted the wonderful time he had. He had been popular with the girls but had never met the right one.

"Not finding the right partner has been the continued disappointment in my life," Benito commented.

"In my early life, my family was not rich and did not have the money to send me to the University. I enlisted in the Army and qualified for the special force's unit. This was a good fit for me," Benito continued.

"I was very successful and rose to commander in a short period of time. Soon it became apparent to me that the sacrifices my troops were making in fighting the cartels was not supported by the corruption in the Army's top leadership."

"It was during a raid on the Gulf Cartel that it became clear to me that I could no longer sacrifice the men under my command and watch these senior army leaders take in their money with the blood of my men on it."

"It's like in the Star war movie, I went to the dark side. Here I have better control of my environment. My family now has the money to live well. I have been able to give money to the charities I believe do good and to the Church."

"Why don't we continue this interview over dinner," Benito abruptly suggested.

"Thank you, that would be great," Ian responded. Having skipped lunch, he was feeling hungry.

"Follow me."

Ian dutifully took his pad and pencil and followed Benito out the door, down the hallway to a large room with a long table large enough to seat twenty. Two places were set across from each other on one end.

Once again this was evidence to Ian that he was surrounded by an invisible but attentive group of people all working for Benito.

"Not in this house, perhaps not this time," flashed through Ian's mind.

The light conversation continued. Benito periodically would fill in another story.

Ian reflected on the great interview he was getting.

And the dinner was a delicious Argentine steak cooked rare and served with rice and Mexican beans. A separate mixed salad rounded out the dinner.

Ian relaxed, took notes, and enjoyed the meal. Nothing was going to happen as long as they were in this fortress of a compound.

Ian looked at this to be a failed problem-solving session. That was OK since he was starting to like this ruthless drug lord.

It was a delicious meal followed by a nice cup of coffee.

"I am out of stories that I can tell. The rest would most likely upset your readers." Benito said as he looked across the table to Ian.

"Thank you for your hospitality. I will send you a draft by tomorrow afternoon. After your approval, I will send it on to my editor," Ian said as he finished his coffee and stood up.

He was led back to the front door.

Ian was surprised to see that two cars were waiting.

He was taken to the lead car by the young man who had earlier escorted him.

This time Benito shook hands with Ian and said, "I am looking forward to your article."

"I'll send you all the material as promised. Later I will send you a first run copy of the newspaper," Ian replied truthfully.

He had every intent to do so. He was already thinking about how to get safely across the border.

Ian got into the back seat. Once again to his relief the young man got into the front seat.

Ian glanced back in time to see Benito getting into the car in back. Apparently, he had business back in town.

Ian's mind began to race and to envision a new scenario. Perhaps there would be an opportunity for his problem-solving on the way back to the highway.

He recalled one place ahead that would provide him with the opportunity he was seeking. Such a move would be dangerous, but it was the type of situation at which Ian excelled.

Ian silently opened his seat belt and prepared himself to act.

As the car took one sharp almost hair pin turn, around a small rise with a ravine on the left side of the car, Ian reached forward, grabbed the young man's chin with one hand and back of his head with the other. A quick twist ended his life.

Ian reached into the front pocket of the young man's suit and found the razor he had expected to find.

The driver was just reacting when Ian grabbed the steering wheel and twisted it to the left. Too late the driver realized the car was going to go over the edge and down into the canyon. He slammed on the brakes, but the momentum of the car would carry it over the edge.

Ian opened the back door, slit the driver's throat, and rolled out onto the rocky gravel road as the car disappeared.

He lay on the ground as the car behind came to a stop. Three doors opened, and three men approached him as Ian lay prone on the ground. He was on the edge of the road just shy of the drop down into the deep ravine.

The lead person was the very large guard who had searched him on arrival. As he reached down to turn Ian over, Ian grabbed the giant's wrist, put his right foot into his gut and hurled him over, head long down after the car.

The second person was just starting to raise his gun when Ian drove the pencil through his eye and into his head. Ian went swiftly around him toward Benito.

Benito was just raising his gun when Ian stepped in towards him, pushed his gun arm outward as the gun fired. The razor went across the back of the hand holding the gun, cutting all the tendons and the gun dropped to the ground.

There was a look of total surprise on Benito's face as Ian stepped past him as the razor slit his throat. By stepping past and behind him, Ian avoided the blood squirting out all around to the ground in front of Benito.

"Never talk. Carry out the required action and then breathe deeply," Ian recited his special forces instructor's saying.

The instructor had been a lifer that had softened just enough in his old age to become a decent trainer. In his spare time, Ian had learned and practiced every Aikido move useful in hand-to-hand combat.

Ian stepped past Benito and immediately verified there was no one else in the car.

Ian was looking for L-20. He had not seen him at the house. Ian figured that some other more important business had come up. Ian did not want to meet him anytime soon.

Ian threw the two bodies down the ravine where the giant grotesquely doubled over backwards on the top of the back bumper of the limo.

Ian closed all the doors on the still-idling second car and got in behind the wheel.

The total elapsed time for the problem-solving event was less than a minute. It seem like a life time and for some it had been.

Ian drove out of the lane at the same slow speed as before. He did not want to alert any guards that might be watching. He just hoped the fact that one car was missing would be totally overlooked by anyone looking out of the compound.

Ian drove a little faster once he was on the highway. Back in Nuevo Laredo, Ian parked the black car in the back corner of the Mac Donalds on the corner of Calle Venezuela and Cesar Lopez Avenue. Ian left the car running in hopes it would be recognized and since it was running it would keep people away.

Ian walked to the corner and flagged down a taxi.

Once back to the hotel, Ian walked across the lobby and took the elevator to his room. He made a quick check to ensure all his belongings were in his bag and two minutes later he was at the desk checking out.

He gave a small salute to Diego and went out to the cab that was waiting for him.

Ian took a taxi and headed to the shopping district at the foot of Bridge #1 that crossed over into the US.

The driver got the fair he asked for. Ian knew the driver was over charging and gave him a small tip. Ian hoped he would be quickly forgotten once the driver got a really good tip from some other gringo he had over charged.

There were a series of small booths selling "original and personally handmade dolls and other curios. Ian bought a small Mexican Doll.

He carried it for show and walked back across to the US. He thanked the border guard when the guard welcomed him back to the US after checking his passport.

A sigh of relief went through Ian as he went down the bridge steps to the corner of Salinas and Water streets.

He took a taxi back to the bus station and walked around it back to his car.

Ian smudged the front and back license plates. He was still in the disguise that he came across the bridge in. Ian got in and drove away from the back of the small bus station.

His destination was El Paso.

5 Recovery

*T*he snap of the broken neck, the stream of blood gushing like water from a garden hose, the giant guard folded backwards across the back bumper of the vertical limo down in the ravine, the second limo driver with a pencil through his eye, into his brain and finally the look of disbelief in Benito's eyes as his life pulsed out in a spray of blood, played out in an endless repeating loop in Ian's mind.

Benito's look of surprise had the greatest impact.

Benito's surprise had cost him his life. He should have been firing his gun long before Ian was able to disarm him and cut his throat with the straight razor.

Benito, who Ian had just finished interviewing and enjoying dinner with in what had been a delightful evening.

Benito who had told such delightful stories. Stories that were truly interesting.

Benito, who in those last few seconds of his life must have realized he had looked into the eyes of the devil.

Ian had originally planned to drive to San Antonio and take a bus that left at six in the morning for El Paso. Some premonition made him change his mind and he decided to drive.

He was still within the reach of Z-20. Ian was concerned that he might have the resources to watch airports and bus stations.

Ian decided the SUV was in good enough shape to make the trip with little problem if he held the speed down.

The constant replay of events was making it hard for him to concentrate on driving. He needed to stop somewhere soon.

He needed to take a hot shower and to take time to rest his exhausted mind and do something to let his guilty imagination remove the putrid stench of death that seemed to be lingering all around him.

Ian pulled into a rest stop long enough to search for a hotel up ahead and make a reservation. He noted he was still rational enough to look at several of the hotels his i-phone let him see.

He selected a hotel at Eagle Pass because of the picture of its workout room and what seemed to be a nice restaurant.

Rational criteria for an irrational crazy mind. The dark side of his brain was laughing. He wished he could go home where the bright light that Lesly exuded would push back the darkness. But home was not an option at this point on his trip.

Ian called and made reservations for two nights in the name of Robert Turan and gave the hotel the Amex card number.

It was lucky Ian engaged his GPS to guide him to the hotel. It got him onto state highway 83 and then brought him back from his self-torture long enough to get him on to 277 in Carrizo Springs.

Two hours later, mentally exhausted, Ian arrived at Eagle Pass and the hotel. The hotel foyer entrance appeared to Ian to be under a large rectangular white table with four blocky square legs. It was now almost midnight and the lights of the entrance guided Ian to its doors.

He parked his SUV in front of the four eight-foot-high vertical doors and stood for a moment next to the SUV before walking in. He needed a moment to gather himself and become the tired but friendly tourist from New Orleans.

He took a few moments to make sure he had the wallet belonging to one Robert Turan, a well-to-do descendant of the well-known Turan family. This was his new persona and he had to act the part.

The colorful orange couches, the pillows in the easy chair adjacent to the entrance, the bright lights, and the low whoosh of the two doors swinging swiftly open, all focused Ian's mind on getting registered.

For the moment he was in control as he walked up to the counter to face the smiling and for this time of night, too cheery clerk. Her white complexion, pixie cut blond hair and green eyes seemed out of place.

This was not Boston or New York but a small town of maybe twenty or thirty thousand in Texas, a stone's throw from the Mexican border. He had been expecting black hair, brown eyes, and tan skin.

Then her deep Texan drawl as she greeted Ian with a cheery *"Howdy"* coupled by the jeans and blue blouse with its top two buttons open, accented by a turquoise necklace transformed her to the out of place four pedaled bright yellow flower found in the spring on all the prickly pear cactus plants in Texas.

Standing barefoot Ian figured her to be five two but in her cowboy boots and her self-assured carriage she commanded the environment around her. Her name tag identified her as Katie.

Ian walked up to the registration counter greeted her with a *howdy Katie* in the best southern accent he could muster, stated his name, and presented his credit card. Ian got the smile he had been fishing for.

Here you are. Third floor, room 306, king size bed, work desk and business chair, couch, and kitchenette. You're all set.

She went on, "I always hate to ask but they tell me to, one key or two?"

"I only need one, when I lose that one, I will come for another," Ian replied.

He asked how late breakfast was served and was told ten.

Ian returned to his SUV and parked it in the nearest open spot. He pulled the plain dark blue soft sided suitcase with the name Robert Turan boldly printed in large black letters on a stainless-steel metal tag attached to the suitcase's woven top handle. He retrieved his backpack out of the back of the SUV and walked up to the two elevators and pressed the up button.

Ian stepped into the brightly lit interior as the right elevator doors opened immediately, as of course it would at the ungodly hour of twelve forty-five in the morning.

The elevator had a polished stainless-steel interior with a round oak wood railing that wrapped around at waist level. Ian turned to face the front and was surprised to come face to face with a stranger looking back at him from the closed elevator doors. He looked like hell.

The smooth slow ascent of the elevator identified it as a hydraulic lift type. Most people would be unaware of such minutiae, but Ian was always figuring out how the mechanical and electronic world around him worked. The doors opened slowly, and he stepped out.

He walked slowly down the yellow painted hallway, with its orange and tan patterned carpeting to Room 306 and placed the key card on the entrance lock. When the light turned green, he opened the door and turned on the room lights.

Cabinets with a microwave ran above a tan granite counter with a sink in the middle. A small refrigerator sat on the counter at the door end. Half of the left side of the entrance was a mirror, and the other half was a closet with sliding doors.

Ian slid the closet doors open. The entire interior was in white. An ironing board and iron hung on the right side. A metal suitcase stand was folded and leaned against the back wall. Three shelves with three small drawers below were on the left.

Ian opened the suitcase stand and put the suitcase on it. He put his backpack on the bottom shelf.

He then turned and stepped into the room onto the dark orange rug that seemed to have strings of light orange sperm swimming across the room toward the orange wall across from him. Ian wondered who would choose such a rug pattern?

The room was dominated by the white covered pistachio-green trimmed king size bed bracketed by lamps and oak bedside tables. It certainly caught the eye.

Above the couch facing the bed, two paintings of black, red, and grey hued desert sunsets added a sense that the couch was in a faceoff with the bed. The bed had large, long white pillows resting on a black headboard mounted on the wall and seemed to stare back across to the paintings in chaste innocence.

The scene led Ian to let out a chuckle as he fell, exhausted, across the bed. His mind was into wild interpretations of the simple world around him.

Ian awoke with a start as he mentally gathered his senses. He was stretched crosswise on the bed, still fully clothed. He had collapsed in both physical and mental exhaustion. He knew this was the aftereffects of the events of the day before. He looked at his phone to see that it was four forty-five in the morning.

Ian undressed and walked into the bathroom. The large walk-in shower stall featured a regular shower head and one hanging down from the ceiling. Ian began with the regular shower head.

The hot water spray on his face brought Ian slowly around. He felt much better. He switched to the overhead shower. He stood in the shower for a very long time. It was five thirty when he finally toweled off.

Once he had brushed his teeth and shaved. He was ready for a hearty breakfast.

The smell of sausage and bacon caused Ian to flash back to the events of the day before and then he recalled an event from his childhood.

He remembered a hard lesson he had learned as a boy about not getting too close to the animals that you would later put on the table as food. He had become attached to a runt pig that his dad had brought home. He had given the pig a name. The pig followed him around like a puppy. Eventually the piglet was a pig of butchering size. He tried to convince his dad to sell the pig instead of butchering him. The piglet ended up as bacon on the family table and was served for breakfast. The lesson, "don't get involved with the animal that is to be the meal."

He immediately flashed back to the events of the day before and the look of surprise on Benito's face. Ian had in a way gotten too attached.

Ian ate some sliced melon and a few grapes and left the breakfast area and the pancakes, eggs, and sausage. So much for my favorite breakfast, he thought.

He went to the small hotel exercise room with its single treadmill and universal weightlifting machine.

Ian spent the next two hours alternating between walking, jogging, and letting his mind process through its various emotions.

This was a harder lesson than the one he had learned as a boy on the farm. He would not repeat getting to know his target so personally again.

He took time to get ready for the next step of his journey.

Ian's focus switched to El Capitan of the Juarez cartel. El Capitan's location had been one of the hardest to find.

El Capitan's penchant for exercise and desire for the best equipment had been how Ian had "accidently or by luck" found out where he was located.

After El Capitan's son was arrested during a run in the park, El Capitan built his own gym inside his personal compound.

He had ordered the top line of Cybex exercise equipment.

Ian accidently learned of this through an acquaintance who liked to watch the show "The Biggest Loser" and had read on U tube that Vicente Carrillo Fuentes who was known as El Capitan had ordered the same equipment.

Ian contacted his support team and requested a search for the addresses of all equipment shipped to El Paso and Juarez. The next day the team identified a delivery company in Juarez where the equipment was sent. There was no local equipment delivery address online.

Ian would need to pay the delivery company a visit when he arrived in Juarez. They should have the delivery address in their files.

But he first had to get there.

It was time to be on his way, but he decided on one more day of rest and exercise. He would be ready when pancakes, with bacon and eggs were again palatable.

The following day after breakfast, he checked out of the hotel and made the several hour drive to a bed and breakfast located out on Purple Heart Boulevard in Juarez. This was the place he had sent many of the supplies he would need when he went on to San Diego.

He did not expect to use any of the supplies in Mexico.

The B&B owner recognized his name and said he had several boxes waiting back in the storage room. Ian asked him to keep them there for a couple days longer and made an excuse about visiting an army friend. He would ask for them before leaving.

Ian checked in, went to his room, and went to bed early.

6 El Paso-The Juarez Cartel

J uarez also long known by its old name as Paso del Norte, "Pass of the North," lay on the Mexican side of the river. El Paso on the US side with Juarez on the Mexican side made an almost perfect circle.

To the west the Sierra de Juarez mountains covered by a patch work of green and brown provided the southwest boundary. Franklin Mountain State Park poked its tip into the Northwestern part of El Paso.

Ian noted that Fort Bliss located in the middle of El Paso and Biggs Army Airfield provided the economic engine for the area.

The El Paso International airport took up the remainder of the Northwestern part of the greater El Paso area. El Paso, with a population of around seven hundred thousand, was actually the smaller of the two cities.

Juarez to the south in Mexico with more than a million people was a substantial and relatively modern city.

Ian chose to ride a bus into Mexico. This would reduce the risk of some accident exposing his presence. He would be the tourist looking for a quiet time. His hotel was a local low key one that offered personal family service. He did not want to utilize the more prominent and plush chain hotels.

The border guards on both sides of the border gave similar warnings.

"Have a good time but be careful, Juarez is a very dangerous place."

"No problem, I am only here for a couple of days of rest and relaxation." was Ian's reply.

Ian knew that his supplies had been delivered to the hotel in Juarez several weeks before.

Juarez was as modern city, perhaps more so than El Paso.

It appeared that the morning rush hour was nearing the end as he easily flag down a cab and gave the driver the hotel address.

He noticed new construction seemed to be everywhere. Juarez was enjoying robust growth and good economic times.

The ride had taken him away from the hustle and bustle of the town center. He seemed to have entered an area where working people made their homes.

The hotel located on a corner had the look of a double deck storage box rental building that was surrounded by an eight-foot-high wall. It was certainly not one of the high-rise, glittery western tourist hotels.

His team had responded to his request that his accommodations should be discrete and be one that locals would frequent. He hoped they had chosen well.

The plain cement courtyard was edged by red flowers and some small cactus plants that rose up through a layer of pebbles.

The hotel owner was very gracious and said Ian's boxes were already in the room he had requested. He stated that dinner was served at six in a family style setting in the dining room just behind the office area.

Ian thanked him, accepted his key card, and walked toward the end opposite the main office. He had a large end room near the quiet street.

The room was surprisingly spacious and bright. The yellow curtains stood out against the light brown color of the walls. The bed cover was embroidered with the symbol of the Mexican Eagle on a cactus with a snake in its beak. It was a tastefully done décor.

This was to be home for the next few days.

Ian checked out the supply boxes. They were unopened and everything seemed to be in order.

Ian put his things away. On this problem-solving outing he did not expect to have his room examined.

He was hungry and ready for a late breakfast, so he proceeded to go down to get his family style meal.

The dining room was a spacious area with several large tables made of at least four-inch-thick dark brown wood. It was finished in a clear glaze that seemed to be at least one-half inch thick.

The large chairs were of the same dark wood and were finished in the same clear glaze. The chair cushions were embroidered with different flowers.

Ian enjoyed the cozy feel of a place where friends gathered for their meals.

"Breakfast is offered starting at six in the morning. You are welcome to close the breakfast period. You must let me know if you want lunch," the owner informed him.

After breakfast, Ian walked across the hotel courtyard to a black wrought iron gate next to the main entry gate of the same design. He heard the lock open as he put his card up to the lock.

He walked out and turned left and walked toward where his map showed a local pottery shop that was located about four blocks away.

The street was a mix of individual homes and small businesses. The houses seemed well kept and their yellow, red, and tan exteriors seemed to have been coordinated. It was a giant mosaic made by the color of each home.

The effect was to make one smile and feel good.

The shop he went into was a combination cement, brick, roof tile and garden material supplier. It was much larger than the front implied. The front was equivalent to a four-car garage in width, but the depth was at least one hundred feet.

Ian walked past bags of cement and specialty stones. He could see out to a large back area that was stacked with bricks and tile.

One of the store's specialties was to make garden ornaments and objects to order. Ian sketched out a picture of an eight by eight by four-inch-thick block with a cone depression on one side that went down for two inches with a small hole through the center of the block.

"I would like two dozen of these blocks," Ian said as he showed the sketch to the shop owner.

The owner speaking in Spanish asked how the blocks would be used.

"Esto es fácil de hacer. ¿Para qué es esto?" the store owner inquired.

"It is for a garden landscape project. I will have water coming up into each cone. Can you make it from clay," was Ian's inquiring reply?

"Esto es simple, no hay problema," the owner replied.

Ian planned to pack the cones in each block with C4. The cone shape would function to focus the explosive force outward in a tight pattern.

Ian anticipated using them but was not sure exactly where or how many he needed.

He first needed to find the exact location of El Capitan. He could then finalize his solution approach and know exactly how many explosives were needed.

Ian's next stop was to go to the address of the exercise equipment shop that had delivered the exercise equipment to El Capitan. There he hoped to obtain the address that he needed.

He walked back to his hotel and caught a cab. The cab ride to the delivery address took about forty-five minutes.

Out of the cab window Ian saw a sign with Los Pablos's in big red letters. The restaurant's stylized blue peacock with yellow eyes with a dark blue center was accompanied by Los Pablos's No. 4 across the rest of the window.

A huge Hospital loomed directly behind it and in front of the restaurant, across the street was another medical facility.

It made sense that a concern in the business of selling exercise equipment was located in this area.

Ian decided that lunch would be a good idea. He went into the restaurant and ordered two beef tongue tacos with refried beans. This was a favorite taco that he normally only found in Mexico.

"Me sorprende que sé cómo comer lengua de vaca," the young waitress commented.

"Crecí en una granja," Ian replied in Spanish explaining that he had grown up on a farm and had learned to eat beef tongue when he was a young boy.

After lunch Ian walked out of the restaurant and turned to his left.

The equipment sales and delivery store was only two buildings away on the same side of the street. He walked by scanning the building for cameras.

He crossed the street and took in the entire red brick, two story structure that had about one hundred fifty-foot presence along the street.

It was a big place.

There were no visible cameras, but all the windows and doors had strong steel bars across them.

The other buildings did not seem to have any external cameras either.

Ian decided that everything he was seeing was good for him.

The only downside to the area was that it was well lit. It would be hard to walk up to the front of the building and not be seen.

Ian saw a driveway at the end of the building on his walk past the store.

The lot next to the driveway was empty.

Just past the lot was a sports bar.

Ian decided that an afternoon beer at the bar would be appropriate.

From the bar Ian was able to study the back part of the sports equipment building. He had what he needed because he now knew how to get into the building.

Ian called his cab which appeared almost instantly. The driver had parked in the restaurant parking lot.

"Back to the hotel," Ian instructed in Spanish.

The hotel shower was a large plain square covered in white tile with a thin black tile edging around the top. The hot shower relaxed Ian. He enjoyed the wide spray from the large shower head. He felt guilty about how much water he was using. He stood a long time under the hot water. He realized he was still recovering from his last solution.

By the time he had dried off and dressed it was time for dinner.

Ian locked his room and walked to the other end of the hotel to enjoy the evening meal.

After dinner, Ian made sure to call a different cab and instructed it to drop him off at the Hospital. Ian took up a slow jog on the sidewalk that went along the chain link fence that surrounded the hospital parking lot.

There were no other people out.

The restaurant was still open, and a few patrons were sitting inside. The sporting goods store was dark. The lights for the sports bar were on but no one was outside.

Ian turned and jogged back into the back-parking lot of the sporting goods store and then stopped.

He went to the truck loading dock hoping to find an easy way in.

Ian checked for and found that the store did have an older contact alarm system. Each door and window had a matching contact on the fixed surface. Breaking the contact between the two would set off the alarm.

This was an easy security system for Ian to work around.

His next concern was whether a motion detection system had been installed as a way to back up the older contact system.

Ian spotted what was probably a camera system. He would incapacitate it with a bright spotlight once he got in the door.

He got on his back, and very slowly opened the door.

He was looking up to see if there was a motion sensor.

He verified that there was.

He took a small bag and what folks were now calling a collapsible selfy handle and very slowly raised the bag and slipped it over the camera. If checked before it recycled there would only be black in the system.

Ian hoped this place still used a continuous tape system and not the newer digital system with memory storage.

Once in Ian used the same routine in the other two rooms in the front office area. He did not expect to go into the warehouse and loading dock area.

He wished he could have thanked the filing clerk. He or she was very organized, and Ian was able to find the information he needed in less than ten minutes.

Ian put the address on a sticky note that he found on the very neat desk with everything in its place.

It had taken thirty minutes to break in. It took a little longer to break out. It seemed to him he had gotten in and out undetected.

Ian jogged back to the hospital and took a cab back to the hotel.

The next morning after breakfast, Ian took a cab to an address several blocks away from the one on the sticky note.

It was clear to Ian that El Capitan lived in an exclusive part of the city.

Ian walked casually along the tree lined street to a cluster of new high-rise buildings.

The shops with their single purses, single pairs of shoes on widely spread shelves made it clear that these were up-scale boutiques selling upscale products.

Across a small cobblestone square the address on his sticky note was boldly emblazoned in large brass letters on the gate to a walled compound. To the left of the gate, there was a building with what appeared to be a gun tower on the flat roof. Ian took the building to be where the guards would be located.

Getting in would be a challenge. Getting out alive would require some major distraction.

Ian slowly walk causally by.

He spotted an internet café and decided he could get a closer look from a Google vantage point. He bought a cup of coffee and time on one of the computers. With Google, he got a view from above of the compound and the area around it. The back wall had a ravine running close by behind it. The compound walls were ten feet high with razor wire along the tops. There was another guard tower on the far back corner of the compound.

It was clear to Ian that he would not be able to climb in over any of the walls.

He would need to find another way in.

An idea for a major distraction came to Ian and he decided on a reconnaissance of the back wall. He was sure there would be a camera system. He needed to determine if it had a blind spot.

Ian left the internet café and walked toward the tallest building in the area. Perhaps he could utilize it to get a better view of the compound.

The black car parked just around the corner on the street off the square immediately caught Ian's attention. Though the windows were tinted, the car seemed to be occupied.

Ian changed his mind about the building and entered the restaurant that occupied the entire corner of the block. The smartly set tables with their white napkins folded into swans sitting on the black tablecloth with white placement clothes declared it as an upscale place.

Ian knew he was not dressed properly but proceeded boldly in.

He asked for a table by the side windows. While studying the menu, he watched as two "men in black" got out of the car and walked to the single, white metal door on the side of the building that had been Ian's goal. A few moments later two similarly dressed men came out, got in the car, and drove away.

As the black car drove away, a grey ford slowly made a U-turn from the curb and followed the black one.

Ian realized that the men in the black car were being watched by those in the grey car. It was not clear who was watching who. But there seemed to be too many watchers. He was not sure if the authorities were watching the compound and if the cartel was keeping tab of who was using the building. Or it could be the other way around. In either case, the building was too hot to use.

Getting in and out of the compound had just become a bigger challenge.

Ian relaxed as his chicken salad lunch arrived.

He recalled the beggar sitting on the sidewalk looking out onto the square. He had dropped a ten-peso coin into the beggar's hat.

An idea came to him.

He ordered a soft drink and steak sandwich to go.

After finishing his lunch Ian exited the restaurant and walked back into the square.

He slowed his pace to get a better look at the beggar. Ian was aware at how little attention one paid to the actual looks of a beggar. The body odor became noticeable at about a ten-foot distance. This alone would make people take a wider berth around the beggar.

The feeling of personal guilt was immediate. Ian approached and squatted down next to the cross-legged beggar. The beggar was about Ian's size. His hat out in front of him was the receptacle for the meager donations.

"Cual es su nombre?" Ian inquired the beggar's name.

"Jorge"

"Jorge, here is a beef sandwich and a soft drink for your lunch.

"Gracias," was the only word Jorge uttered as he looked at Ian.

"¿me vender tu ropa," Ian asked.

He asked if the beggar would sell him his clothes and if he would like a nice place to stay for a few weeks.

"Why would you offer such a thing," Jorge questioned?

"I lost a bet, and I must live like a beggar for a week," Ian lied to him.

"Ok, why me," he asked as he took a bite of the sandwich.

"Because you are the right size and you were sitting in a place that seems safe," Ian replied.

"Si, it is the most watched square in the city," the beggar replied.

"OK, where is this vacation place you are offering and for how long do I get to stay," Jorge continued as he took a swig of the soft drink.

"It will be at the Inn at Ciudad Juarez for two weeks. Golf will be at Club Campestre," Ian replied.

Ian knew that the hotel was a grand place. He was also aware that were several great restaurants around the hotel.

"For four weeks, several rounds of golf each week and free meals and you can have my clothes and my spot," he bargained.

"Well now you are getting greedy. I may need to find a different beggar that doesn't play golf. How about three weeks, two rounds of golf each week, all the food you want to eat, and I will set you up in some new clothes that make you fit in," Ian countered.

"Oh, and you have to tell me where you go to the bathroom or go to get something to eat when you are in the square." Ian countered.

Ian knew he could have let Jorge have exactly what he wanted but the bargaining was part of making the deal.

"Jorge, I am going to walk around the corner. Wait a few moments and meet me there," Ian instructed as he got up and walked slowly down the street.

Ian called a cab. Jorge and the cab arrived almost in unison.

Ian instructed the cab driver to go to a shopping center. There Ian bought Jorge several casual but very nice outfits. Ian included a sports jacket, a regular pair of shoes and some golf shoes. The beggars outfit went into some plastic bags.

Jorge walked out looking like a new person. Next, they stopped and bought a suitcase. Then at a pharmacy they bought personal hygiene products.

It was clear that the Inn located just north of the Campestre Golf Club was relatively new. Ian had chosen to offer it since it was so close to the golf course.

He had called in to his support team to make the reservation and to arrange for access to the golf course. The cab stopped at the front entrance below the massive entrance cover that once again reminded Ian of two tables stacked on top of each other.

Two porters opened the doors to let them out of the cab. Ian paid the cab driver, gave him a good tip, and asked him if he could wait for a few moments.

The two receptionists looked up as Jorge and Ian approached. Ian inquired about a suite with one king-size bed. He gave his name.

"Si, we made the reservation only an hour ago. You were lucky the executive suite you asked for was available. It has been reserved for the next three weeks."

Ian inquired about the payment.

"It has all been taken care of. Also, the money you requested to be made available has been transferred to the room account," she continued.

"Jorge, I hope you have good time. You have an honorary membership to the Golf club. It turns out that you can play every day if you wish. It is all part of the membership. You have a daily spending allowance of one hundred dollars and your room is paid for," Ian said as he got ready to leave.

"Ah, this is indeed a wonderful vacation. I hope my clothes and location work for you," Jorge said as he took the key card for his room and followed the porter toward the elevator.

Ian looked around the grand lobby, thanked the receptionist and walked out to his waiting taxi.

Ian returned to his hotel room with Jorge's smelly clothes. He wished he could clean them but decided against doing so. Ian shook out the clothes, put them on hangers and hung them on the shower curtain rail. He used some soap and water to wipe the inside of the shoes and the inside of the sombrero.

He would need to be just as repulsive as Jorge had been. The only thing he would do different was to use a cardboard box to collect the money anyone might give him. Ian would be hiding under the large sombrero Jorge had use to serve this function.

Ian washed his hands and went to have some dinner. A bottle of Madero was really an attractive thought.

After dinner he put on his jogging clothes and took a cab out to the compound area. He had chosen an address about one half mile away. He asked the driver to return in two hours to pick him up. He turned as if to walk up to the house he was standing in front of. Once the cab departed, he slowly jogged toward the compound area.

He went down into the drain ravine and came slowly up where it was the closest to the corner of the compound. He pulled on his camouflage top and then slowly crawled on his belly to the corner of the compound wall.

The cameras were fixed and were pointed along the top of the razor wire. It appeared that there was a blind spot along the base of the wall.

Ian wanted to make sure it was really a blind spot. He crawled along the base of the wall from one end to the other and then crawled back.

Nothing happened. Verification was complete.

He then went into the ravine and got out of his camouflage top and carefully went back to the point where the cab would pick him up.

Early the next morning after breakfast, Ian walked to the garden shop and picked up the blocks he had ordered on his arrival.

The shop owner greeted him as he walked in and showed him the twenty-four blocks. Ian examined them and thanked the owner for doing such a good job. He paid for all twenty-four but asked if he could leave twelve of them to be picked up later.

Ian packed the other twelve blocks carefully into his backpack. It was clear the load was at the maximum weight that he could carry. Ian staggered out of the shop and slowly made his way back to the hotel. He put the backpack into the hotel room closet.

It was time to go begging.

Ian dressed in Jorge's well-worn clothes and tried to make himself look as close as possible to the local beggar. He was sure he would stand out like a sore thumb, but this seemed to be the only option.

He had the cab driver drop him off just outside the square. Ian walked slowly out and sat down on the corner where he had found Jorge. He put his sign asking for donations in the small cardboard box and then leaned back against the wall with the sombrero on his head.

Ian realized that no one seemed to notice the difference in the beggar. He received a few coins and quietly thanked each of his contributors in Spanish.

It was hard to ask for money for breakfast or for lunch or for any reason. He came to realize how difficult it was to beg and even more difficult to sit in one place for so long. His backside hurt after the first day.

After three days, Ian had enough understanding about El Capitan's routine. El Capitan left early in the morning and returned in the early afternoon and then stayed in for the rest of the night.

The only other regular traffic in and out of the compound seemed to be the people that worked for El Capitan, a variety of delivery vehicles and the garbage truck. Delivery was done at the gate. Only the garbage truck was allowed in each day.

The garbage truck was one of those round bodied compression trucks that crushed the garbage that was dumped in. The procedure at the gate was for the garbage truck to stop at the gate and cycle through the compression cycle before being let in through the gate. It appeared that the same garbage truck came every day in the morning.

Ian realized that unlike the movies with their underground tunnel entrances, his only way in would be in the back of the garbage truck.

Ian had also paid close attention to the other people who were watching the compound and the people who were watching the watchers. He would need to set up a way to distract all of them.

On the last morning that Ian was planning to spend in the square, he brought several especially prepared radio-controlled explosive packs. He wandered past the cars on the side street and placed the charges on lamp posts that were near where the watcher's cars were located and one on the door used by the watchers in the building.

Ian had located the window to the room on the fourth level that was being used to watch the compound. He scaled up an inside corner of the building and went in an open room window and out to the hotel hallway. He walked cautiously down the hallway and placed his final charge above the doorway of the room the watchers were in.

Ian's plan was to distract the watchers. He had no desire to hurt anyone. His charges would do some damage but mostly they would just be loud, release a cloud of gas, be a surprise and cause confusion.

Ian spent the next three days following the garbage truck and learning where it was parked overnight.

He then went to a hardware store and rented an acetylene torch, a drill and bought some hinges and latches.

Ian spent most of the night modifying the inside of the garbage truck so he could step through the compression gate when it cycled and so he could get out the bottom when he was inside the compound.

Ian practiced opening the door that would allow him to step through the compression plunger as it cycled back and forth.

He also made several small holes in the side of the container, so he would be able to utilize his flexible optics to see where the driver and his helper were and what they were doing.

It was time to prepare the main distraction event at the compound.

Ian spent the next day in his room packing the dozen shaped charges with C4 and carefully inserting the small radio-controlled triggers through the holes in the block.

That evening he crawled along the back wall of El Capitan's compound and placed each charge at the foot of each wall pillar.

Ian took the time to hide the evidence of his digging and arranged the area to make his handiwork unnoticeable.

There were nine charges in all. Ian hoped the explosion would topple the entire back wall.

The toppling of the wall was purely a distraction to allow his escape in the opposite direction.

It was past three in the morning before he was retreating back into the drain ravine.

Ian was not through. He proceeded to where the garbage truck was parked for the night with his three extra explosives. He also carried his inside the compound mission backpack. He climbed into the back of the garbage truck.

He sat down and fell asleep.

The roar of the truck engine brought Ian out of his brief sleep. He was instantly on the alert. He hoped that the driver would not cycle the plunger immediately.

Ian poked his flexible camera out of the truck's side so he could see where they were going.

He was pleased that it appeared the truck was going to the compound first. That made sense since this allowed the guard to see an empty truck.

Ian was dressed in his camouflage gear and would be hard to see. The guard had not looked into the compartment before, and Ian hoped that the previous practice would be followed.

The truck came in through a gate to the side of the control room building.

It went through the compression cycle.

It then proceeded to the back of the compound.

Ian realized that the easiest exit was out the back of the truck. The garbage was loaded into the truck up front from the side. The back of the truck was about a foot from the back wall.

One of the garbage men rolled out one the large containers from the holding area. The truck mounted forklift system was lowered, and the container rolled onto the forks.

Ian patiently waited for the large container to begin its upward journey.

One operator was looking at the controls and the other with his back to him was looking up at the slowly moving container.

Ian put his hands around his two bags, got out the back of the truck and darted behind the main garbage area gates. He was relieved to find a small side door leading into the compound garbage holding area.

Inside there were two designated areas for the containers and there was one recycling area.

Imagine, a Mexican drug lord that was conscientious about recycling!

Ian crawled in behind the recycle bins. When the first big bin was put back in its place, he changed location and hid behind it.

The second big bin was emptied and returned.

The recycle was taken and put on the back of the truck.

The two men closed the garbage area and slowly drove away.

Ian was in, but he now had to wait until dark for his next step.

He was hoping to get into the exercise area before El Capitan returned.

The time in the trash bin area was put to use locating all the surveillance cameras. Ian's fiber optic eye at the end of a cable allowed him to look over the wall and study every inch of his surroundings. He hoped to get to the gym unnoticed.

Late in the afternoon a person that looked like one of the cooks came out from the house to dump some trash.

Once he entered the trash bin area, Ian knocked him out. He would have a terrible headache but would likely live to complain about his ordeal. Ian taped him up with duct tape and put him into the large garbage container. He would wake up later bound and gagged but he would be able to free himself with some effort.

Ian wished himself luck as he put on the cook's outfit and made the best adjustment to himself so he would appear to be the cook.

He then walked slowly back looking down and away from the cameras. He had put all of the needed supplies into a body vest. He carried his three extra explosive blocks as if they were cakes. He hoped the guards were not being vigilante about monitoring one of the cooks.

Once inside, Ian looked up the well-lit hallway trying to decide where to go.

He was relieved to find no additional technology facing him. He took his best guess at the location of the gym and headed that way.

His senses were at full alert. He was peeking furtively into doorways and was ready to attack anyone he met.

Luck is always the best ally. Ian opened a door and was rewarded with the sight of a series of Cybex exercise machines. He quickly stepped in and closed the door behind him. There was no one in the gym area.

A steam bath and a sauna were on the other side of the room. Ian moved immediately to the sauna and the steam room. Both were empty.

Behind the sauna was a hot water whirlpool big enough for a dozen people. It had a foot-wide ledge all the way around the pool.

Ian strategically placed his explosives. One would take out the steam room and the other would take out the sauna. The third he put in the corner besides the entrance door. He hoped it would go unnoticed.

The ledge around the hot water pool was a perfect place to wait. Ian could stand in the corner and remain unseen even if several men accompanied El Captain into the room.

Ian envisioned and worked through several scenarios that he might face. He hoped El Capitan indeed was an evening exerciser. It would be much easier to leave in the dark than in the light of day.

Ian continued to play through several exit scenarios.

He came to full alert as the door to the exercise area opened. He heard someone say "clear." Next, he heard the treadmill begin to operate.

Ian kept his eyes open but relaxed in the corner of the hot tub. He was breathing evenly and in a set rhythm. He was ready for hand-to-hand action if necessary.

Sometime later he heard, "Is the steam room hot?"

Ian was now at full ready. He could see a hand and arm as the control dial was turned.

"Make sure the sauna is ready. Get me out of the steam room in fifteen minutes."

"Fifteen minutes," someone repeated.

Ian heard the door to the steam room open and close. He put in his ear plugs, put on his thin leather gloves, and then moved into action.

Ian moved quickly but quietly. He looped the choke wire around the guard's throat as the door to the steam room closed. A quick jerk locked the wire in place. He sent the guard sliding out into the workout area ahead of him.

The second guard was just pulling his gun when the choke wire locked around his throat.

Ian pulled both guards over to the water cooler. They were already dead.

It was not a fair way to fight but the circumstance required the actions he was taking. Fair was not a requirement.

As Ian stood back up, the door to the steam room opened and El Capitan came out with his gun drawn.

Ian immediately understood how this man had survived so long.

"Vas a morir…," El Capitan began to shout.

Ian pressed one of the control buttons.

The explosion in the sauna, and the steam room hurtled Ian into the wall behind him. El Capitan was sliced into a thousand pieces by the shattered glass from the steam room door and the sauna.

Dazed but alive Ian went into an adrenaline high slow-motion action mode. He could feel some blood running down his nose.

He pressed a second control button.

He was sure the first explosions would have kicked off some sort of reaction but the explosions along the rear wall would awaken the entire compound and the surrounding neighborhood.

Ian picked up his final charge and left the exercise area and went toward the front of the house. He looked out the front window and saw a small army of men heading for the front door and another contingent heading around the side of the house.

He immediately exited out the side door to the other side of the hedge. He ran toward the front gate behind the bushes on the edge of the driveway. The guards ran past him on the building side.

His goal was the electrical substation that he saw ahead of him and to the left of the entrance gate.

He opened the gate to the substation and taped a charge to the main transformer. He lay down at the roots of the hedge. He pushed another two buttons on his control panel.

The shock and the noise of the explosion stunned him.

The bushes around him ceased to exist.

"Keep moving," his internal control system said as he listened to a whistling sound and figured some part of the transformer was coming down from above.

The second button that Ian had pushed set off the two bombs planted near the watchers that were out on the other side of the square.

Ian hoped the observers were now too busy trying to figure out what was happening to them to worry about what was happening in the compound.

At the entrance gate Ian slapped on another charge.

He stepped to the side to blast the gates open. At almost the same time the very large top from the transformer landed in the exact spot along the bushes where he had been just a moment before.

"Damn," flashed through his mind as he triggered the charge on the gates.

A single guard sat at the control panel. He stood up with a stunned look on his faced as Ian stumbled into the gate house control center.

Ian hit him in the throat and the guard went down gagging. Ian immediately placed his last charge on the control consul.

He stepped back and stripped the jumpsuit off and put on the wig and beard hoping to make himself look like the beggar frequenting the corner across the square.

The guard still had a pulse, so Ian did his one good deed of the evening and pulled him out of the building and halfway across the square.

He could hear the police sirens and just caught the lights in his peripheral vision as he pressed the last button to trigger the charge in the gate house. The windows and doors blew out. Once again, he found himself hurdled back on his butt.

He knew he would be sore the next day.

The police swarmed into the compound.

"Get out of here old man," one of the officers told him as he helped Ian up and gave him a push away from the compound. Another policeman was attending to the guard on the ground. An ambulance came roaring in as Ian made it to the street corner where the beggar normally sat.

He just kept walking. After several blocks he caught a cab back to the hotel.

The next morning every bone in his body seemed to ache. A long hot shower helped. After breakfast, Ian took a taxi back to the main bus station and caught a bus back across the border into the US.

He retrieved his SUV that he had put into secure monitored storage to ensure none of the gear he needed for San Diego would be stolen.

He left El Paso and about an hour later stopped for lunch.

The morning news was about a mysterious explosion that had destroyed the compound of one of the wealthy community leaders. The leader had died in the fire.

7 San Diego Launch

*I*an had selected San Diego as the launch location for the strike against the Tijuana Cartel. He had located the Cartel's headquarters in a waterfront warehouse in the Ensenada basin harbor located on the Baja peninsula. He figured that getting there by sea made the most sense.

The warehouse was located just across the harbor from the Mexican Navy base. Ian was sure some high-ranking officer in the Navy was getting a healthy addition to his government pay. There could be no other explanation for the cartel to locate so close to a military base.

The drive to San Diego provided some of the decompression time he needed. His GPS put the direct drive at ten hours and eighteen minutes. Ian figure it would be more like twenty hours. He would stop on the way for another hot shower to relieve his aching body.

Ian laughed to himself when he realized the town of Eloy was the most likely place to stop. He recalled the story of The Time Machine by HG Wells. The Eloi were the gentler surface victims of the underground sinister Morlocks. He thought he would probably be a Morlock if he had been in the story. He decided it was appropriate for him to stop at Eloy.

Again, he laughed at his own bad joke.

The terrain around Eloy was sand, with sparse patches of grasses, some that had some green and other patches dead and dry.

The overall feeling was one of a dry, desolate land where life struggled to take hold and repeatedly lost the battle.

Eloy was on Interstate 10. It was a few miles before hitting Interstate 8 that went west to San Diego. Ian got off the exit prior to the town.

Ian's critical eye really made him feel like a Morlock.

The hotel had an empty fountain with a blue center piece where the water should come flowing out. It was clear to him that conserving the water was more important than having a working fountain. The expanse of small gravel around the fountain was carefully raked into wave-like patterns spread around gardens of larger stone flower beds.

The light blue roof of the Inn was accented by the darker blue posts of the veranda on the first and second floors. The parking lot was totally empty. He figured he would have no problems getting a room.

Ian almost reconsidered his choice but decided that he could stand it for one night. He parked near the lobby entrance.

He looked around and wondered what the entertainment of the younger crowd would be in an area like this. It had to be bars and night clubs. He wondered where they were located.

The receptionist was a motherly looking middle aged, slightly overweight woman. Betty was written in black across a white well used name tag pinned to her blouse. Ian guessed Betty to be in the late forties or early fifties.

Betty was pleasant and seemed pleased that he had chosen the American Inn.

Ian asked for a room with a King-sized bed preferably on the second floor.

"I have one in the back where it will be quiet," Betty replied without even looking on her computer screen. Ian wondered where any noise might possibly come from.

Ian decided against dinner and chose to take a long, long hot shower.

His body was one big bruise. He had a cut on his forehead and had removed a few pieces of glass from his right cheek. He knew where and how he had gotten his various injuries, but he had never felt any of it until he was driving. The aches seemed to surface as his mind went over everything that he had gone through so far.

He decided it was not a very good idea to put himself in the middle of exploding C4 or to rely on only his explosive being the ones that would be around to explode.

He stood under the shower and let the hot water hit his backside. He whispered an Oh! and Ah! as he slowly turned and let the hot water run down his body. He would have loved to sit down in a hot tub and just lounge in the comfort of the hot water.

After the shower Ian made himself a cup of coffee.

He went smoothly and slowly through his Tae Kwon Do moves as he listened to the news and periodically sipped his coffee. He counted one hundred push-ups and then collapsed in a verbal groan.

His mind became focused on his next target. It seemed the route he had designed was constantly pitting him against the next more dangerous cartel. Each time he seemed to be going up one rung on the danger ladder. In the coming confrontation perhaps, it was not more dangerous but more bizarre.

This cartel was known to have dissolved over three hundred of their rivals in fifty-gallon barrels of sodium hydroxide.

He was sure those going into the drums were tortured first.

He hoped that dissolving was done after the person was dead. If not, then he figured this was one mean and nasty cartel.

Ian told himself to get this one right and not end up in one of their sodium hydroxide drums.

"This will be another explosive foray," he thought as he contemplated and thought through the next scenario. This time he would make sure he was not around when the explosives went off.

By nine thirty he was ready for bed. He was asleep as his head hit the pillow.

Ian awoke at five thirty in the morning. He got up, dressed, and went down to check out.

Betty had been replaced by Fred. They both seemed to have the same well used name tags. He wondered when they would be replaced.

When he asked about breakfast, Fred suggested Denny's as the preferred place. It was also conveniently located at the entrance to I 10. Ian thanked Fred and walked out to the SUV.

Ian drove to Denny's ready for a hearty breakfast and a cup of coffee.

He was rested and ready to get to San Diego to the Seaside Marina located near Sea World.

The drive was long enough for him to go through the entire upcoming solution scenario.

Four hours later Ian was pleased to be greeted by an increase in the number of cars as he neared San Diego. He had driven straight through lunch and was now getting into the San Diego region in the early afternoon just prior to the rush hour.

US I8 came to an end at the San Diego, Sea World Park area at Sea World Drive. Ian got off the drive and onto Quivira Way and located the Seaside Boat rentals office. He parked out in front of the office and went in.

When Ian inquired about the Whistling Nanny, the manager came out of his office to greet him.

"I am Tim Cocaine. And let's skip over the drug jokes. I understand that you are here to inspect your rental, the Whistling Nanny," Tim introduced himself.

Tim was a slender well-tanned body with sun bleached brown hair and looked to Ian like a surfer.

"Yes, I am, and I will skip all the jokes, but you might catch me chuckling a couple of times," Ian replied as he shook Tim's hand.

Ian took a liking to Tim's open and what seemed to be direct manner.

"Captain Bitterly," Tim began.

Ian smiled as Tim formally used Ian's new identity.

"I won't make fun of your name if you call me Matt instead of Captain Bitterly," Ian cut Tim off.

"Matt, the owner is really happy about this thirty-day rental. It is a very attractive deal. However, she personally asked me to make certain you know how to handle the Whistling Nanny," Tim went on.

Ian had rented the Whistling Nanny for thirty-days at two thousand dollars a day plus a hundred-thousand-dollar deposit. The Nanny was one of the better yachts available for rent.

Ian followed Tim out of the office and then along the pier. The Nanny was immediately noticeable. She was the largest vessel in the bay and moored parallel to the pier's right-hand side.

The two walked out toward her. The late afternoon sun still had several hours to reach the horizon.

The afternoon sun was reflecting off the Whistling Nanny's white side with a black strip in an almost blinding display of elegance.

Matt led the way onto the boat.

"Your supplies arrived a day ago. We can bring them down whenever you want," Tim commented as the two walked aboard.

The selection of the make and model of the Nanny came from his previous experience in dealing with the pirates off the coast of Africa. It was a Bavarian Cruiser that he had crewed on. His mission then was to put a hit on the pirates in that area. Ian had learned how to handle this boat under extreme learning conditions, and he knew the cruiser's capabilities. He had learned how to make it dance for him. He had come to love its capability and ease of handling. He hoped the Nanny would handle in the same manner.

Ian thoroughly inspected the Nanny. Ian was no sea captain and not an expert, but he wanted to see what condition the boat was in.

The Bavarian Cruiser was a luxury vessel with three spacious bedrooms. Two bedrooms located toward the back had queen-size beds and plenty of the living area and the third bedroom where Ian planned to sleep, and just as nice as the back two, was in the bow and featured a king-size bed.

The spacious kitchen with a gas stove and a sink was separated from a booth and table eating area by a stand-up countertop. A black leather couch with two companion chairs with fixed small end tables rounded out the general relaxation area that was in the middle of the main deck.

Ian was as impressed with the Nanny as he had been previously with the same craft in Africa. He took the time to inspect the immaculate engine compartment, the sail holds and all the rigging.

"I have got to know why she is called the Whistling Nanny," Ian asked Tim.

"It's a great story," Tim began with a chuckle.

"The current owner ended up with the boat as part of the divorce settlement with her husband. Her nanny had a romantic affair with the husband. The nanny felt guilty and admitted it all. The wife then took every penny her husband had in the divorce. She bought the boat and periodically sailed it up and down the coast while her kids were growing up. Her nanny became her deck hand, and the boat was renamed the Whistling Nanny," Tim shared.

Ian judged the Whistling Nanny just as luxurious as had been promised and it was in excellent shape.

"I like her looks, can I take her out for a trial run," Ian asked.

"Sure, if you don't mind me acting as your deck hand. I have instructions to verify your capability in handling the boat before letting you take her for the month.

I can connect you with some good deck hands if you want," Tim replied.

Thanks for the offer. My deck hands will be here the day after tomorrow. Let's take her for a quick run.

Ian removed the covers from the main sails and went forward to make sure the spinnaker was ready. The rigging was all automated and controlled from the control panel in front of the main rudder wheel.

Cast the lines loose," Ian said as the diesel engine purred to life.

Ian backed the Nanny slowly away from the pier and pointed her bow toward the harbor exit. They went smoothly out of the harbor using the diesel engine. He could have sailed her out, but he did not want to alarm Tim or make him think he liked hot dogging. Ian stayed on the diesel until he had left the channel. Then he turned toward the south, so he could catch the wind.

As the sail filled Ian turned off the engine. The Nanny responded like an eager dog pulling on the leash. It was clear to Ian she wanted to fly.

"I can feel her come to life and say thank you. It's been too long," Ian voiced his thoughts.

"She was out only two weeks ago," the Tim replied.

"So, you agree with the Nanny," Ian said with a smile as the head sail reached the top of the mast and the Nanny responded with new energy.

The Whistling Nanny began to earn her name as she seemed to leap forward with new life. The lines of the yacht were literally whistling.

"This is the first time I have been on her when the head sail was in use. I didn't know she could move this fast," Tim shouted.

"Going faster doesn't mean you have to speak louder," Ian said in a normal voice as he smiled at Tim.

Ian knew the exhilaration Tim was feeling because he was feeling the rush of elation energizing his soul like the cream sauce in a Fettuccine Alfredo gave life to the spaghetti.

It all tasted so good.

His soul found release.

For the moment life was pure.

Ian sailed the Nanny out about a mile and then turned and sailed her back toward the harbor. He would have loved to stay out until sunset, but he needed to get his supplies on board and positioned.

"That felt good. Thanks for coming out with me," Ian said quietly as the Whistling Nanny entered the harbor under sail and approached the pier.

"Tim sit down and relax. Let me show you how I plan to moor the Nanny at every pier."

Ian brought the Nanny up to the pier and stopped her and then stepped off and tied her up himself. He knew Tim would pass this on to the owner.

"I have never been with anyone that has handled the Whistling Nanny with such ease and control," Tim said as helped place the deck ramp.

Ian smiled and thanked Tim for the compliment and told him to let the owner know that the Whistling Nanny has a lover as her captain.

On the way back to the office, Ian looked for the security cameras along the pier. There were none but there was one on top of the office building that scanned the entire dock area and one that scanned the parking area.

Ian was pleased that the level of security was rather low. He would be able to lower the water scooter off the stern of the Whistling Nanny and be shielded from the cameras.

"Are there many people who sleep on their boats here at the marina," Ian asked as he looked around at the various boats that were tied up.

"Once in a while some folks come in and are passing through and request overnight type of docking. We put them out there on the far dock. You can see the dock is currently empty. We have an occasional request by those docked here permanently but most of the owners are upscale and prefer their own homes to their boats," Tim replied.

"If you want to stay on board the Whistling Nanny that is Ok," Tim continued.

"Yes, I would like to load my stuff on onboard and then spend time getting everything prepared for sailing," Ian replied.

Ian followed Tim into the office where he signed the papers acknowledging the good condition of the Nanny.

He inspected the boxes being held in storage and arranged for them to be delivered to the ketch.

"Thanks for taking me out for the sea trial," Tim commented as they shook hands.

The sun was now low in the sky as Ian walked back toward the Nanny. He put in a call to his deck hand Ted and to the food service that held the order for the food needed on the trip. Neither party answered and Ian left a message for each.

Ian wanted to have Ted come on board in a day and he wanted the food delivered the day after that. He wanted Ted to store the food so he could manage how it was used.

Ian sat on deck and enjoyed watching the sunset in the west. He felt relaxed for the first time in several weeks. The smell of the ocean and the more distant sound of the waves seemed to soothe him.

Just as the sun went down, Ian heard a request to come on board. Two young men in shorts and sandals, with their hats on backwards were holding two dollies loaded with boxes.

Ian acknowledged them and gave them permission to board. He had them place the boxes in the kitchen area.

The young men made several trips. Their last trip consisted of rolling a large wooden crate that held the water scooter.

"What is in this box. It weighs a ton," one of them asked.

"It's an underwater scooter," Ian replied truthfully. He was not concerned about their idle curiosity.

Ian tipped them well for their service.

After they had left, Ian went about putting away the supplies that had been brought on board. He went out to the Nissan and unloaded the supplies he had brought with him.

The dock area was still and quiet. Ian found the light switch for the lamp posts that lit the area around the Nanny and turned off the lights. He walked up to the dock and ensured the gate was locked.

The lights of the coffee house and the restaurants across the harbor reflected off the dark water. The harbor area had the mysterious look and feeling of a place waiting for some exotic event to occur.

Ian decided on checking out the view from restaurant and bar location and walked up the slight hill. Once there he looked back to where the Nanny was docked.

He felt relieved to see that the Nanny was barely visible. He could relax when he lowered the scooter over the side. It would be almost impossible for anyone to see what he was doing.

Ian walked back to the boat. It took him most of the next hour to remove the scooter from the box.

His team had designed the scooter to mount under the hull behind the keel on two suction mounted hooks.

The V shaped hangers with radio-controlled suction cups at the ends went on like an octopus's suction cup grabbing its prey. Ian tried to pull them loose.

Once satisfied with their holding power, Ian lowered the water scooter down into the water and maneuvered it over to the hangers and secured it. It locked easily and solidly into place. The scooter was now part of the Whistling Nanny.

He mentally complemented his support team for doing a good job.

Ian still had a substantial amount of C4 to deal with. He had left this in the SUV until he was ready to put it into a bullet shaped, waterproof container that attached to the scooter below the hull.

The only trace would be in the SUV. He made sure any trace on his body or clothes were removed.

Ian was just settling down with a cup of ginger tea when he got a call from Ted. They agreed to meet for breakfast at the near-by Bagel shop.

After breakfast they would take the Whistling Nanny for a trial run.

Ian felt good about the pieces of this next phase coming together. He needed to make sure the submersible would ride smoothly and be unnoticeable as the Nanny sailed.

Ted had come highly recommended for his sailing skills and evidently, he cleared the support team's review of his background because they cleared him.

Ian needed to spend a couple of hours making sure Ted was the person to spend the next month with and to learn how well they would work together. He hoped they would get along well.

Ian was up by six the next morning. He mentally went over the entire upcoming trip. He had three more problem solutions ahead of him. Each *"problem"* required a different approach.

The approach to the Tijuana cartel had been the most difficulty for Ian. Since it was down the Baja peninsula in Ensanada an approach from the ocean seemed best.

The Whistling Nanny was a key part of a rather elaborate cover for getting in and out of Ensanada.

The other part of the plan was the fact that he was hosting two couples from Iowa that he had specifically recruited. As part of a dream vacation offer, they had agreed to be his crew for four weeks.

Ian had made the cost very attractive for them under the pretext that they would be part of the Whistling Nanny's crew. He needed them as cover for his cruising into the areas he was going.

Though Ian felt a little guilty about the subterfuge, he knew he would indeed give them an experience that they would talk about for many years to come.

Ian came out of his contemplation and walked up for his Bagel breakfast.

Ian was not overly impressed with the place, but he was focused on meeting Ted. A multi-grained toasted onion bagel with cream cheese and a good cup coffee was all he needed.

The young lady behind the counter was polite and quickly filled his order.

A slender, tall well-tanned, younger man wearing a red sports shirt, black shorts and sandals entered a few moments later. He stopped looked around and walked straight toward Ian.

"Captain Bitterly," he said as he extended his hand.

"Ted, Good morning, call me Matt," Ian replied as they shook hands.

Ian had an immediate good impression.

Ian pointed out of the window to where the Whistling Nanny was moored. In daylight she was a grand sight. The biggest boat in the basin. Her sleek outline spoke of speed and adventure.

"That is a beautiful sight. This is the first time I will crew on this particular boat, but I have had similar experiences on boats not quite as fancy," Ted replied.

"Once you get your stuff on board we will cast off. You are going to have to suffer the overhead bed in the main deck area. It is probably the most convenient location though it will be the one in the middle of the action," Ian advised.

"I am parked in front of the rental office. Is there a place I can leave my car where it will not be towed away," Ted asked?

"I have the same problem. Let's go ask Tim the rental manager about parking and then we can take the Nanny out for a trial run," Ian said as he paid the bill and stood up.

Ian led the way into the rental office to find out where to leave their cars.

Tim suggested that the Platinum long-term parking service would be the best place to leave the cars.

Ian decided to get the cars taken care of first. His car would at a later date be taken care of by his support team. He would never return to the parking lot.

It only took a few minutes to drive up, park and then return by cab.

From Ted's reaction as they boarded the Whistling Nanny, Ian knew that this was the first time he had crewed on a true luxury vessel.

"She is gorgeous," Ted commented as he walked around inspecting and taking a measure of the boat.

"Are you ready to take her out for a trial run," Ian asked as he prepared to cast off.

"Sure, what do you want me to do?" Ted asked.

This time Ian sailed the Nanny out of the harbor area. Once out he had Ted take the helm. Ian sat back, relaxed, and observed how Ted sailed. It was clear to Ian that Ted was indeed capable.

Ian and Ted were back at the pier by noon. He was expecting the food delivery truck at one o-clock. He was pleased with how Ted had performed and how skilled he was at handling the Nanny. He may not have sailed on a top end vessel like the Nanny, but he was skilled in sailing.

"We seem to work well together, and you certainly are qualified on this Bavarian model," Ian said after putting Tim through all the variations of handling the yacht that he could think of.

Ian was just as pleased at how well the two of them got along. This was as important to him as how well Ted performed.

Ian guided the two bringing on the food and Ted put it way in the locations he desired it to go.

Afterwards Ian pulled out the coastal map and showed Ted the route he planned to take along the coast and into the bay of California.

Ted asked about preparing dinner, but Ian suggested having dinner at the Red Fish Fin Inn.

Just before dinner, Ian verified that the remainder of the "crew" was in San Diego. They had checked in at their hotel the evening before. Ian had arranged a day visit for them to Sea World.

The next day, Ian was sitting on deck with Ted enjoying a morning coffee when he saw two couples exit a cab and begin unloading their suitcases.

Ian took in the scene and knew immediately that the four were carrying much more than they would ever need on the cruise. He thought about Lesley's favorite travel agent who said that there were two types of travelers; those who traveled light and those who wished they had traveled light.

"Well, I see two couples up by the head of the pier. Let's go meet them and get them on board."

Ian had thought this cover through carefully and had recruited in only one Iowa location. He had wanted two couples who would be looking for adventure but who knew little about sailing.

He knew that having the couples on board provided a perfect cover. These two young couples were close friends. They had answered Ian's add that promised, "an experience of a lifetime at a price you can afford." The price for the cruise was outrageously low. Ian was subsidizing the true expense.

Once they inquired and agreed to the timing and the cost, Ian pulled the advertising ad. The reason given for the low price was that they would be required to be part of the active crew.

"Hello, you must be Mike and Emily and Jerry and Carla," Ian said as he walked up the pier ramp to where the two couples were standing looking around at the various sailing vessels.

They were staring at the Nanny. The ketch was three times as large as anything currently docked in the basin.

"Is that for us," Emily exclaimed.

"That is the Whistling Nanny and yes that is for the four of you," Ian replied.

Ted and Ian carried several suitcases and each of the couples carried some additional ones.

The two couples came on board and Ian escorted them to their rooms. Their looks of amazement at the luxurious nature of the boat warmed his heart. The cruise was the best buy anyone could ever have hoped to land.

"Do you have all your things on board? Do you have your phones, glasses, wallets, passports," Ian slowly listed all the things he could think might be forgotten?

An image of his Lesley passed through his mind, and he gave an inward chuckle. List checking was her specialty, he was the forgetful one.

"Have you had breakfast yet?"

"We talked about having breakfast, but we were afraid to miss meeting you," Emily volunteered.

It was only seven in the morning. Ian had counted on them having to get up early to get to the dock.

"Let me introduce Ted Nickson, second in command of the Whistling Nanny. Let's see if he can whip up a good breakfast for all of us. He cooks but you all will clean. This morning's limited menu includes eggs any way you like, pancakes, sausage, or bacon or both," Ian rattled off.

"Ted make sure there is enough for the two of us," Ian added.

"So is there an experienced sailor among the lot of you," Ian asked as if he didn't already know the answer.

He had sent them a primer on sailing when they had sent in his earlier questionnaire.

"That's an unfair question since we already gave you the answer," Carla said from her side of the table.

"Ok, fair enough. Have you all studied your sailing primer," Ian asked next?

"We did, and we took two small sailing boats out on the lake to practice," Mike volunteered.

Ted delivered breakfast to Emily and Carla. Each had ordered two eggs and sausage.

"Good for you. That puts you one step closer to becoming a qualified deck hand," Ian replied with a smile.

"Next question, have you selected a motion sickness treatment recommended by your doctors," Ian asked?

"Good," Ian said as he saw them nod yes with their heads.

"Do you each have your passport and tourist Visa for Mexico?" Ian inquired next.

"Please get them out and put them in the waterproof plastic zip lock bag by the radio," Ian instructed and pointed to where the bag was clearly visible.

"Let me see the Tourist Visa please," Ian requested as they got their passports out.

Ted brought the breakfast for Mike and Jerry. The two of them had ordered two over easy eggs, two pancakes and two sausages.

"Ted I'll take what they are having but put my eggs on top of the two pancakes and bring the butter and syrup to the table," Ian requested.

They had all signed a contract as working crew members. This had been Ian's stated reason for the low price for the cruise.

"You all agreed to and signed a contract to crew on this trip. You will learn to sail the Nanny and take assigned watches at the helm. Are you ready for this," Ian asked?

"Sure, but will you train us before you leave us alone," Mike inquired.

"Actually, until you get many, many hours at the helm either Ted or I will be sitting here at the table or out behind you relaxing but on watch with you," Ian replied.

"Each of you will cook one meal a day. My cookbook is available, and I have the ingredients for anything in my cookbook. It is a simple cookbook. If you know better recipes, please feel free to add them. You will be able to prepare steaks, fish, lamb, shrimp, and a variety of other seafood items. Are you ready for your cooking responsibilities," Ian put the question out?

These were foods on the survey they had returned to him as part of their purchase.

"Can we ask for help in preparing our meals. I mean can one of our group help me or Mike," Jerry asked?

"This is not a test. You are all free to do what you want during your time on board. Certainly help each other in everything," Ian replied.

Ted will do much of the work but each of you will join in to help as needed.

Ian stood up and took the two couples for a tour while Ted got the Nanny ready to sail.

Today each of you will take a turn in each position. Ted will take the Nanny out. After lunch we will stop for a swim around three or so.

Tomorrow we should make Ensenada by early evening.

Dinner tonight will be provided by the person on the list named to cook the evening meal. The entire cooking schedule is posted on the refrigerator.

Ted will help you cook the meals today. You can discuss among yourselves who will do the cooking first.

Any questions," Ian asked as he looked at each of them?

They were all smiles and chattering to each other. It was clear they were going to enjoy themselves.

Ian returned to the table and inspected the passports, their visas and made sure the passports were secured by the radio. He knew the coast guard from either or both the US and Mexico would stop them to check.

The sun was at its zenith before Ian had the two couples oriented, moved in and in general ready to go. He spent extra time getting them familiar with the Nanny and discussing safety out on the high seas.

Finally, Ian declared it was time to cast off. He made each couple cast off one of the mooring lines.

Ted, his red hat on backwards, his feet spread, standing in a relaxed manner with the Nanny's wheel in his left hand was the picture of a modern romantic pirate.

Ian raised a sun cover that went across the stern of the Nanny and sat back in the shade enjoying the smooth motion as the Nanny climbed the long period Pacific Ocean swells at a sixty-degree angle and then went smoothly down the back slope. It was a smooth mesmerizing ride.

Ian watched as Mike and Emily washed and put away the breakfast dishes while Jeremy and Carla looked through the cookbook trying to decide what they would prepare for lunch. By their enthusiastic chatter, it was clear they were immediately enjoying themselves.

A few minutes later the four of them were looking at the navigation chart that Ian had put on the table. Ian had penciled in the route he planned to follow and made some notations about the events he had planned along the trip route. The four were absorbed by where they were going and what they would see.

Ian knew that they would cross the border into Mexico sometime around the noon hour. Of course, at sea, it was impossible to tell one side of the border from the other. The map clearly showed the line separating the two countries. The ocean looked the same on both sides of the border.

Ian saw a ship approaching them from the forward port bow.

"Have you decided on what you are preparing for lunch," Ian inquired?

"Yes, we decided on having hamburgers and hot dogs," Carla replied.

"Get them on the grill. We are about to get company. I will offer them some lunch," Ian said as he pointed to what looked like a small destroyer escort.

He figured it would most likely be the Mexican Coast Guard.

"I believe it is the Mexican Coast Guard coming out to greet us. Take it easy and let me do the talking," Ian instructed.

Ian arranged his sailing permit and the passports. He had Ted lower the mainsail. Then they waited for the Coast Guard to come along side.

Ian had all his paperwork ready when the Mexican Coast Guard hailed them.

"Buen día, es bueno tener a que nos visite. Aquí están todos nuestros pasaportes, visas y documentos de los buques," Ian greeted the coast guard inspector as he came on board.

"This is a vacation cruise for my passengers. I am taking them to see the whales and I will do some underwater filming," Ian continued to explain in Spanish as he showed him his camera equipment.

The Coast Guard officer was cordial, chatted with each of the guests as he checked their passports and tourist visas.

Ian planned to do the filming and send it to his old acquaintance he had from the Elephants and Ivory documentary adventure. He hoped to get some footage that would blow Andrea's mind.

"Would you and your crew care for some American hamburgers or hot dogs," Ian extended his invitation.

Gracias, voy a aceptar perros calientes para todos mis marineros. Hay ocho de nosotros a bordo. Podemos enviarlos a la nave?

"Yes of course. Eight hotdogs to go with ketchup and mustard and of course napkins," Ian replied loud enough for Carla to hear.

Carla responded with a thumbs up.

The officer checked out the paperwork. Briefly looked around. He accepted the bag of hot dogs and wished everyone a good time.

Ian watched the Mexican Coast Guard cruise away.

Let's have lunch, relax, and take time for a swim, Ian declared.

The Mexican Coast guard disappeared over the horizon. They were headed in the same direction as Ian and his crew. Ian was sure they would be moored very close to the Coast Guard base in Ensenada.

Amazing as it seemed, the Tijuana cartel had their headquarters in a warehouse almost directly across the harbor from the base. This was just amazing to Ian. It gave new meaning to hiding in plain sight.

Ian figured some high-ranking Coast Guard officer was getting a healthy bonus to add to his government pay.

Ian had rented dock space for five days. He hoped to be able to approach the cartel's warehouse from the water side. The water approach would be risky, but Ian had more confidence in it than any other.

He had made sure he was arriving at the time of the month that had the darkest, moonless nights. He needed really dark nights to aid him in getting into the warehouse unseen. He was leaving nothing to luck but would take good luck willingly if it came his way. Ian felt luck was always good.

The coast came into view as they sailed almost directly east. The sun was low on the horizon behind them.

Ian had the Nanny within sight of the "Islas de Todos Santos," All Saints Island.

"The islands you see to the starboard has some of the best snorkeling in the world. You will have a great time learning to scuba near those islands," Ian shared.

The sun was just setting as the Nanny docked at the pier.

"Let's plan on a leisurely dinner and then we will spend tomorrow snorkeling and learning to dive. Tonight, we can spend time on instruction and each of you can examine your scuba tanks," Ian suggested.

This would give Ian a chance to examine the harbor and get a firsthand look at what he faced.

Ian pointed out the box shaped coast on the navigation map. The harbor area was on the Northeast corner of the box. This was where the cruise ships came in. It was the largest of three harbors in the Ensenada area.

When they came in, they immediately saw a cruise ship dominating the harbor. As they came in, Emily pointed to her right where the coast guard boat that had checked them out. It was moored next to a destroyer that made the coast guard boat look small.

Ian was at the helm taking the Nanny to the berth he had rented for the next week. He had called ahead to the Cruise Port office, and he could see someone standing at the end of the pier that he had rented.

The Nanny was the largest sailing vessel in the dock area. There was one other ketch almost the same size at the end of the next dock.

This part of the harbor held about a hundred ocean going power boats and a few sailing vessels. The cruise ship was docked in the large part of the harbor. It was directly in front of them and dominated the view to the west. It was the largest structure in the Ensanada area.

Ian brought the Nanny to a smooth stop and his "crew" tied her forward and aft mooring lines the way they had practiced it. The side bumpers had been deployed just prior to getting next to the pier.

"Great job," Ian called out as he cut the engine.

Ian called the crew together.

I just called my local tour guide, and she is ready to take you all out for the evening. You get two evenings out here in Ensanada as part of the tour package. This includes all you can eat and drink.

Do you want to skip dinner on board and go out into Ensenada early or would you rather eat on board?

It was no surprise to Ian that the unanimous answer was to go out.

He had hoped that would be the answer.

Ian assigned Ted to go with them. He called the local guide and asked her to meet the group at the entrance to the dock area.

Ian let everyone know he was going to stay on board.

Once they were on their way, Ian lowered the battery for the submersible over the side. He put on his scuba gear and slipped quietly into the water. He was going to transit the harbor in the dark using the GPS on his phone. This was a first for him.

He hoped to miss the giant tour ship.

The water in the harbor was clear. Since it was a very dark night it really did not matter. All Ian could see were the lights of the harbor.

Ian's eyes were on the screen of his phone located in a recessed shielded holder on the submersible. Ian marveled at the fact that he was crossing the harbor in pitch black darkness following a picture on his phone.

He had calculated the distance across the harbor at almost four nautical miles. At top speed he reached his destination in a little over thirty minutes.

Ian surfaced briefly to get a visual of the area and to make sure he was in the proximity of the right warehouse. He then dropped an anchor and secured his supply of C4 and the monitoring equipment to the floor of the harbor.

His return trip was significantly faster but in total the trip consumed a little over an hour.

Ian reattached the submersible to the hooks just behind the keel. Once on deck Ian stored his wetsuit and recharged his scuba tank.

He then took a leisurely shower and went to bed.

8 Tijuana Cartel

*I*an woke slowly up. It was two in the morning. The whispering chatter and quiet laughter let him know that the "crew" had returned from their evening out. He was sure he would have the early morning to himself.

Ian was up at six and by six thirty he was standing at the helm with a cup of coffee guiding the Nanny out of the Harbor. He had not bothered to get anyone up.

Ahead Ian had just sighted the All-Saints Islands when Ted came up the steps and back to the helm with his cup of coffee.

"You should have awakened me," Ted said groggily.

"I would have worried about you falling overboard," Ian joked.

"How was the evening outing," Ian inquired?

Ted replied that he had a good time and that the rest of the crew had a wonderful time.

Ian brought the sail down and let the Nanny coast down slowly. Then he dropped anchor. The northern island was about a thousand yards away and the Nanny was just shy of the coral reef that would provide good snorkeling and good scuba diving.

The Nanny, the sleeping crew are all yours Ian declared. I am going to prepare some breakfast and then relax out here until everyone is up and ready for the day.

About an hour later the two couples had awakened and were in the galley.

"After you have had breakfast, we will begin with some snorkeling. Once you have had a chance to see it from on top, Ted will be your diving guide below," Ian said as he finished his breakfast and went back on deck and sat under the awning.

The day went by slowly for Ian. He got everyone out either snorkeling or diving. Ted guided the diving while Ian worked with the snorkelers.

Ian took his waterproof laminated fish observation charts with all the tropical and commercial fishes out with him. He had the four snorkelers check off each specific type of fish as it was observed. Everything went smoothly until several sand sharks swam by. The four clustered around Ian as if he would provide a shield.

Ian had his professional camera in the water with him and took a series of pictures. He had more than a dozen pictures of the commercial fish and hundreds of pictures of tropical fish from barely visible in size up to those that were several feet long.

He was able to capture some great pictures of the sharks.

Ian called everyone on board for a late lunch and announced that the group had an evening dinner reservation at the Santo Thomas Winery. They would enjoy a tour and then a late dinner. Afterwards they could once again enjoy the night life.

He then let them know about their Saturday schedule for a tour to La Bufadora and on their return they would stop by the open-air market for some souvenir shopping.

"This is great. I was a doubter when we signed the contract for this vacation trip, but it has already exceeded my expectations," Mike commented.

Ian looked calmly back at the group with a smile and thought, "You are right buddy. If it is too good to be true it probably is not true." You are lucky that my subterfuge did not cost you.

It was clear the two couples were eager to party.

After the snorkeling and the diving there was still a good part of the afternoon left.

"It's time for some sailing lessons. Stand around me. Emily stand at the helm you get the privilege of getting the first lesson," Ian said as he stepped away from the wheel.

"Let's up anchor and get underway," he continued.

The lessons went on into late afternoon and everyone got their turn at the wheel.

"We all want to thank you for this experience," Carla said as Ian brought the Nanny up to the pier.

"Ted says his tip jar is by the sink," Ian joked with her.

"Kids, he is joking. I don't have a tip jar but if you want my bank account number, I will give it to you," Ted joined in on the banter.

Ian had already made sure Ted got top pay for this trip and had told him he got twenty percent more as a tip for putting up with him.

"Well, I see your guide for the evening is arriving. Go get ready and then hit the town," Ian instructed as he put out the gang way and went ashore to meet with the tour guide.

"Mi nombre es Mateo. Gracias por venir. Por favor, dar a estos jóvenes gringos una buena noche en la ciudad y disfrutar también," Ian greeted the tour guide and told her to show the group a good time and to enjoy herself as well.

"I am Andrea. And thank you for being so generous," Andrea replied as Ian led her on board.

It took another hour for everyone to be ready. Andrea enjoyed a drink and commented on how nice the boat looked.

The sun had set, and the night was quickly getting dark. This seemed to be a perfect night for what Ian had in his plans.

Once again Ian sent Ted with the rest of the crew. It was clear that Ted was bonding well with the other four.

Ian was planning to utilize the evening to get into the cartel warehouse and put everything into place.

The crew left the Nanny as the final light of the day died. Ian packed a waterproof bag with all the listening devices, timers, and fuses. He then lowered everything into the water and in his scuba gear he went under the Nanny and unhooked the scooter.

The clear screen of his I phone shining up from its shielded holder and his depth reading were the only visible things Ian could see. The cruise ship had departed so Ian was able to shave off a couple of minutes transit time.

Ian went across as fast as he could. He wanted to be in and out as quickly as possible. He hoped that lady luck was on his side this evening.

If possible, he planned to make an appearance and mingle with the rest of the crew. This would seal his alibi if he were to need one.

Ian hoped the Mexican Navy did not have any sophisticated listening or sonar equipment in use in the harbor. The low almost unnoticeable hum and vibration of the submersible made him nervous, but the crossing was uneventful.

Ian located the bag with the C4 explosives. He attached everything to the submersible and slowly approached the pier.

The large warehouse building had external guard towers looking out over the harbor, but it appeared they would not be able to see below the edge of the pier. Ian went under the pier as far as possible. The piers had maintenance hatches every few hundred feet. Ian anchored his load to a piling and went about finding a hatch. He was looking for a hatch that was close to one of the main doors from the warehouse out to the pier.

Ian looked through the slit of the slightly lifted hatch. The towers had a clear view of the entire pier surface.

"Good for them bad for me," Ian thought as he lowered the hatch.

At the second hatch, Ian located a door almost next to it. Getting the explosives and other equipment into the warehouse would be a challenge but doable from this location. He moved all the gear to the top rung of the ladder.

Ian would need to act swiftly when the guards were looking in some other direction.

He hoped they had been guarding the pier for so long that they were bored stiff by the lack of any action.

Ian spent at least twenty minutes getting to know the pattern of the guards. It appeared to him that these guards had done this for many nights and days. They spent a great deal of time out of sight, probably sitting and talking to each other.

It appeared that the tower lights were fixed but Ian was sure there would be movable ones that could be manually manipulated. There was no moon, so it would be as dark as it ever got in these parts.

His small mirror provided a means to monitor the two towers. Ian opened the hatch completely. He hoped it would not be noticed.

He moved immediately to the door. As he expected it was locked. He picked the lock as quickly as he could. He was swearing under his breath the entire time.

Ian found the alarm contacts and put a jumper across them before opening the door. Then he opened door only wide enough to squeeze in.

No alarm! He immediately let out his breath.

Ian stood completely still. He was looking at a warehouse full of pallets stacked on high rise racks. He scanned the ceiling for cameras and made note of the lighting. He located three cameras but was sure there would be others. The first one that would need to me neutralized was the one directly above his head.

Ian carefully turned the cameras so there would be a clear lane for him to get to the warehouse office area.

He moved slowly. He was looking for motion sensors. At this point any alarm would end his attempt to set up the trap he had in mind.

It was a relief to learn there were no internal guards. A human guard always increased the level of complexity. He would still maintain his vigil since one of the guards from the tower might make an hourly run. If that were the case Ian would need to be out of the warehouse in the next thirty minutes.

Ian thanked the gods that the door to the warehouse opened inward since this decreased the chance of detection as he brought in his gear.

Slowly and carefully, Ian moved his equipment into the warehouse. He gave a sigh of relief once he got all his material in.

He calculated it was now almost a half an hour into the work. He needed about fifteen minutes to conceal the explosive charges and then another fifteen minutes to get back out of the warehouse. He truly hoped the guards were lax about any rounds they might make.

There were two main meeting rooms and one grand office. Ian selected the positions for the various charges.

He also carefully placed and concealed the listening devices.

He had brought along a variety of camouflage material to cover the various charges. He covered the charge under the main desk with a cloth similar to the color of the wood under the desk. It was virtually invisible.

Ian admired his work and thought that perhaps he should have been an interior decorator.

All the explosives were surface mounted with either cone or starfish shaped deflectors. Each charge also contained a handful of steel fragments.

There would be carnage in every one of these rooms when the charges went off. However, Ian's intent was to keep the explosions contained.

The explosive charges were designed to be focused with just enough power to take out the target in its vicinity. He was hoping to minimize any collateral deaths of the office workers.

Ian was counting on his listening devices to locate the intended targets. He finalized the placement of the listening devices carefully around the rooms and office area.

Ian would have loved to install some video cameras to see his targets, but this was beyond what he was able to do while keeping the risk of discovery down.

Ian planned to periodically energize the listening system and then de-energized while he was waiting. He hoped this approach would ensure that the equipment would not be found.

For the next several days, he planned to be in and out of the harbor listening.

Finally done, Ian returned to the exit door. He held an empty waterproof duffel bag. He was ready to return to the ketch.

Getting back out of the building was as dangerous as getting in. Getting caught leaving would be the ultimate failure. A sense of relief went through Ian as he closed the hatch on the dock floor above him.

He waited several minutes to make sure he had not been discovered.

Ian got quietly into the water and bundled up the underwater float.

The trip back was anticlimactic and much faster than the trip over.

After securing the submersible and leaving his wetsuit and all his clothes with the scooter, completely nude Ian got on board the Nanny and immediately took a long hot shower. He did not want any C4 residue to be detected.

It was too late to join the rest of the crew. Ian's two couples could be heard laughing and singing as they came back from their night out. They found him sitting on deck and drinking a Negra Modelo.

Ian suggested a night cap that they all accepted. Ted went about getting the beers or wine.

They all opted for a Corona with a lime and were soon seated around Ian chattering away.

They had loved the trip to the winery and the dinner there and thanked Ian for the arrangement.

They had loved the Mariachi players and the general friendliness of the Mexican people. Just before going to bed, they asked about the coming two days of scuba, snorkeling and sailing.

"We will do a lot more of each in the next few days and will stop only when you say uncle. Don't forget that you will go to the blowhole La Bufadora and the market tomorrow. I will join you on that excursion. Sunday it will be all sunshine, swimming, and sailing" Ian reminded them.

Ian said goodnight to Ted and went into his room. He was looking forward to a good night's sleep. This time he would not be bruised and battered. He would just remain anxious.

The next day, Ian relaxed and took in the ride south on highway 1 and then across on highway 23 along the southern coast of All Saints Bay. The tour van turned south and cross the peninsula to get to the town of La Bufadora. The town had grown only because of tourism. It was little more than one or two buildings deep on either side of the road that led to the viewing area.

This was Ian's first time to see the blow hole. The van stopped and the six of them walked the rest of the way toward the viewing area.

Andrea, their guide, led them on a walk that took them to the highest lookout point above the blow hole. Below them they could see a hoard of tourists. They were the only ones on their higher level. The view was better than the tourist viewing area.

After watching the event for the third time, Ian was ready for lunch and the trip back to the market.

Periodically, Ian activated the listening devices in the warehouse. All was silent as he expected it to be for the weekend.

The van took them to the market where Ian strolled casually through observing the tourists and the shop keepers. Everyone was engaged in their particular shopping endeavor. He did some looking but had no interest in buying anything.

That evening the crew once again went out for dinner and drinks.

Sunday morning Ian sailed out to the north tip of the Banda Peninsula. Once there he gave a choice to his guests to go on a scuba excursion led by Ted or to snorkel with him.

Mike and Emily preferred to snorkel. Emily could not get over her phobia about breathing through her scuba mouthpiece.

Jerry and Carla on the other hand always maxed out their scuba time.

The morning passed quickly and sailing lessons filled the afternoon. Ian enjoyed letting the Nanny loose and augmenting the main sail with the head sail to put the Nanny to full speed.

Late in the afternoon, Ian brought the Nanny back to the dock.

This was an evening that was free for everyone to do as they pleased. Ian had decided to relax on the Nanny and was surprised when the rest of the crew joined him and asked if he would join them playing one of the games they had requested. It turned out to be a great evening where everyone was chatting, laughing, and sharing what a wonderful time they all were enjoying.

Monday morning the activity in the warehouse came to life. There was activity in the main office and the small meeting area. Ian had on what appeared to be an i-pod and earplugs as he sailed out of the harbor. This allowed him to monitor the warehouse as he played cruise captain.

Ian delayed the departure by slowly moving over to where he could get the boat fueled up.

"I'm making a small change in our plans. We will fuel up and then sail on down the coast. This will get us into the bay of California sooner. We can continue our scuba and snorkeling activities each afternoon and then do some more once we get into the bay. You will all take turns sailing the Nanny on the way there," Ian informed the group.

After fueling, he sailed out of the harbor about eleven in the morning.

Just before lunch the main warehouse meeting area became a beehive of activity. Ian was having a hard time keeping up with what was transpiring. A major cartel business meeting was getting ready to take place.

The conversation in the office was what consignments went to which location and who was going to be responsible to make sure they made it to their destinations and collected the money.

Someone had been lax in their performance. There was some sort of infringement by the Pacific Cartel and someone in the Mexican Navy wanted more money.

These conversations eased Ian's conscience about the upcoming event.

There seemed to be two groups working different issues. Both were high intensity discussions and arguments. There seemed to be a great degree of tension and hostility.

Ian decided it would be best to set off the charges while the two groups were separated. This would be the most devastating.

The Whistling Nanny was just beyond the mouth of the harbor when Ian activated the explosives.

What followed was not what he had expected.

The entire waterfront section of the warehouse blew out. It was followed by large flames and flying debris. Even on the Nanny the roar was deafening.

Ian knew immediately that the warehouse must have housed a lot of explosives of its own. What he had planted would never have caused the explosion that had just occurred.

So far almost every explosive he had set was augmented by the explosives possessed by the cartels.

"What in the world was that" Emily asked.

"I guess some sort of industrial explosion," Ian replied as the harbor fire department boats raced toward the warehouse.

Ted was at the helm taking the Nanny out, so Ian stood with the other four and watched the scene.

It was clear to Ian that everyone in the warehouse would be dead. Once again, the collateral damage was much greater than Ian had planned.

Ian turned and looked out to sea.

He felt bad about the lowly workers in the office area. They most probably had mediocre jobs and mediocre pay and were only trying to make a living.

The Nanny caught the wind and sailed smoothly out. About an hour later the Nanny rounded the Banda Peninsula and headed down the coast toward the tip of the California Peninsula.

An hour later, Carla pointed aft at what appeared to be the Mexican Coast Guard Vessel. It seemed to be closing the distance between them.

Ian instructed Mike to swing to starboard and lower the main to two thirds mast. The Nanny slowed down.

Ian watched as the Coast Guard adjusted their course to intercept them.

Ian walked over to where he had stored the controls to the submersible hangers and pushed the button to release and drop the submersible. He hated to lose it, but he figured this time there would be a more thorough inspection. He could not afford to have the submersible be found.

Shortly afterwards the Nanny was hailed and ordered to stop. Jeremy was on the helm, and it was clear he was very nervous.

Ian told everyone to relax and that he would do the talking.

It was the same boat that had stopped them a few days before. He saw that a diver was getting into the dingy that was going to cross over to the Nanny. The same officer that had come on board before was also on the boat, there was also another sailor with a dog.

Since the Baja coastline was in view, Ian knew that the Nanny was still in Mexican waters. He told the crew to relax and that he would handle everything.

"It is good to see you again but what brings you out," Ian asked in his best Spanish?

A major explosion occurred in the harbor this morning, you are the only boat that is leaving the area. We have been sent out to inspect your boat and to clear you of having anything to do with the incident, the officer replied as he came on board.

We heard and saw much of what happened. We gave you our itinerary when we last met, and we are on our way to the Gulf of California, Ian replied.

The handler and the dog came onboard at the same time.

"Do you mind if the dog examines the inside of the boat, and my diver examines the hull of your boat.

"Crew, it looks like this could take a few moments. Let's stop for lunch.

Should we prepare enough for your crew? I think you plan your timing so that you can have a good lunch, Ian joked with the inspector.

It was clear the inspector was feeling a little embarrassed. The diver in the water came back aboard the Nanny and removed his scuba gear.

He explained there was nothing on the hull.

This time the inspector accepted twelve hamburgers and an equal number of Cokes.

Gracious, and accept my apology for having interrupted your sailing trip," the inspector said as he and his crew got into their dingy and went back toward their boat.

"No es nada, y que son bienvenidos en cualquier momento," Ian replied.

Ian informed the crew that he wanted to make it to the Cedros Island where they would anchor off the San Benito Island.

I am going to take a nap; your job is to take your turns at the helm. Keep us on course and get us to our anchor point before the sun sets. Ian informed his vacationing crew.

Ted indicated he would stay on duty.

Ian had rented a dock space at Cabo San Lucas. He was surprised that everything was going on schedule. He had been concerned about being stopped by the coast guard and was gratified that they had found nothing and had not made him return with them to the harbor. He had sacrificed his submersible but that was a small cost as compared to getting caught with it.

Ian had again arranged for an evening out for his four vacationing crew members. He joined them for dinner and then sent them off with Ted to experience the night life. Once again, they had a local tour guide to accompany them.

Ian looked at the map on the table. Cabo San Lucas was at the southern tip of the Baja Peninsula. The Pacific Cartel was his next target. They were located just outside of Culiacan.

9 Baha Transit

*H*e would have a few days of rest and relaxation before working on the next solution.

The Gulf was a known location for whales and a host of other sea life. Ian hoped to enjoy this brief respite in between his more odious actions. Ian put his pencil on the map and made an asterisk at a point in the middle of the Gulf just across form the coastal city of La Reforma located on the eastern side.

Ian poured himself a cup of coffee and walked out on deck. He felt good about the four vacationing crew members. They were becoming a good crew and seemed to be enjoying every moment. Jeremy was stretching the Nanny and letting her run as fast as he could get her. He had become the best sailor.

The Nanny was slicing smoothly through the water as if it were sliding through soft butter.

Everyone else except Emily who was cleaning up from breakfast was sitting around enjoying the breeze blowing back their hair and the morning sun warming their souls.

The appearance of all of them had darkened or in Jeremy's case reddened from their time at sea. They would return home as totally new people. They would not only look good; they would be more confident and surer of themselves.

Ian walked up to the bow to look ahead.

He almost immediately spotted a large manta ray traveling in the same direction as the Nanny.

He called out to Jeremy to sail along in parallel to and stay with the manta. Ian went below and brought out his camera equipment and set it up and began filming.

With Ted's help Jeremy brought the Nanny slowly toward the manta.

Ian wanted to get as close to the manta as possible. Looking through his camera, Ian gave Jeremy navigation instructions that slowly brought the Nanny almost within reach.

The entire crew was now standing around him talking about the size and graceful beauty of the giant manta.

Ian continued filming until the manta turned and went down out of sight.

Ian was pleased with the film he had.

For the rest of the day and well into the evening Ian kept himself occupied editing the footage of the manta. He also integrated his earlier filming and picture taking. He was pleased with the results.

The next morning, Ian was enjoying a first cup of coffee when Ted let him know that they were almost at the point on the map where there was an asterisk and nothing more.

Ian had picked the northern most point to which he intended to sail. Here he planned to spend a day or two and then sail to La Reforma where he would leave the Nanny.

The asterisk was some thirty miles offshore from the eastern side of the Gulf and the water depth was sixty feet. This would allow the Nanny to drop anchor. Ian hoped to see some of the abundant and diverse sea life that had their home in this area.

Ian looked around three hundred and sixty degrees and saw only water. The sky was the light clear blue that always made him think of the paint he painted the baby room for the birth of his first son. In contrast the sea around him was a blue that seemed dark but when he looked down it was clear, and it seemed he could see the bottom.

"Drop the sails. Let the Nanny drift to a stop and check the depth and drop anchor if we are at about sixty feet," was Ian's reply.

Breakfast was being prepared by Jeffery. Ian was having his favorite breakfast of two pancakes with two over easy eggs on top and three sausages. He lifted the pancake and with his knife put in a slice of butter and then poured on a healthy helping of maple syrup. He then did the same on top.

Emily commented that she had never seen anyone eat pancakes in quite this manner and that it would kill him.

Ian admitted that he would try to keep that from happening. He figured his death would come from something much more direct and sinister.

Ian then shared the edited shots of the giant manta ray. He had merged in some footage from pictures he had taken of the fish he had taken during their earlier scuba and snorkeling sessions. The combination created a totally different world.

Carla and Mike both commented that they would never have believed they were seeing what they knew they had personally seen and that they would love to have a copy.

Ian shared his plan to let the Nanny stay anchored for a day or two and take in what the Gulf had to offer. He planned to spend time in the water around the Nanny with his underwater camera in hopes of getting some additional good footage.

He let them know that anyone that was interested could hang out with him.

Everyone wanted to go into the water. Ted volunteered to stay on the Nanny. Everyone went about getting their gear in order and then getting into their wetsuits.

Ian arranged his gear on deck. His camera was a small newly released professional underwater camera about the size of a romance paperback book. He had selected it on the recommendation of an underwater photographer friend that had lauded the quality of the pictures and the ease of handling the camera.

It was a great recommendation, but it really was the small size that would be more manageable in the water that had connected with Ian.

Ian led the way by dropping backward off the back platform.

He signaled the group to gather together. He took his shots from below them. The white hull of the Nanny could be seen clearly above them.

Almost immediately Ian spotted and began filming a curious Pacific Hawk Bill sea turtle, its black scale sections centered with orange fading to yellow patches and its white and black patched front legs swam directly toward them. It came within twenty feet and went down to a deeper level.

Ian turned to the other divers capturing their thumbs up gestures. Emily began to gesture with her finger to something behind him.

Ian had a momentary start but relaxed when he realized he was looking at another giant manta ray. Its head on approach gave him a great shot of the mouth bracketed on each side by two paddle like protrusions. A white sucker fish had attached itself to the top right side. The pair made their approach and like the turtle veered off and went by the group at a close but not a threatening distance.

Their presence indicated that the area they were in was active. Ian hoped the display of sea life would keep up.

Ian decided it was a good time to take a break. He signaled the group to go up.

"This is the life. I am glad we agreed to this vacation," Jeffery said as he relaxed in the sun and drank Pellegrino with some freshly squeezed lime.

"Look out there, I see a whale, Emily called from her seat on the bow.

Ian looked and realized there were three whales. They provided a sense of wonder and awe.

He acted immediately and got everyone into the water. Everyone was eager to see the whales up close.

A mother humpback whale approached the group. Her young calf was swimming as if hugging her side and a second young whale just slightly smaller than the mother swam a little behind but provided a shield for the calf.

Ian moved some distance away from the others so he could get them and the whale in the same picture. He captured some great shots that had the group and the whales and one with the hull of the Nanny behind the entire setting.

Then the mother came directly at Ian. To Ian it looked as if she would hit him but at the last moment she went sliding by to his left.

Ian instinctively put his left arm over the top fin and caught a ride with the mother. She seemed not to notice. It took all his strength to hold on and swing his legs over her back as if she was a horse. He positioned himself in a sitting position but holding on for everything he was worth.

Ian was getting some really great close ups of the young baby whale. The mother made a large circle around the four swimmers.

Ian released his hold as it appeared the whale trio was going to leave the area. He swam back toward the group in the water.

Ian was going to signal getting back on to the Nanny when he spotted a pod of killer whales coming toward them. He figured they were following the mother whale with her baby.

Ian once again swam away from the group so he could capture them with the approaching killer whales. Once again, the camera seemed to attract the attention. To Ian, it seemed they were coming straight at him. He took in a deep breath and slowly released it in a continuous stream of bubbles.

He got his nerves under control.

The lead killer whale came right toward him. Ian threw one leg up and over him and mounted him facing backwards with the top fin between his legs. He had his chest up against the top fin.

Ian kept the camera going as each of the accompanying killers took a turn coming up to him as if to get a closer look or a better picture pose. None of them seemed aggressive. Their path followed the same one taken by the mother whale and her young. They too made a circle around the four in the water.

Ian figured the killer whales were probably following some scent that remained in the water. He hoped that the mother whale and her young would outwit this group of hunters.

As the lead killer whale finished its circle one of the followers came up and nudged Ian from his seat.

He was happy that he had not been on their lunch menu.

Ian knew that he had taken some of the best underwater sea life footage that had ever been captured. He knew who he was going to grace with the footage.

This time he gave the signal for everyone to go up. He had used almost all of his air.

"I can't believe what you did out there. You must be crazy," Jerry said as everyone got back on board. The other three agreed.

"I thought the whale was going to take you out. Each time the killer whales came at you, I thought the game was over.," Emily added.

"I just wanted to get out of the water and not be eaten," Carla said as she dried herself off.

"Well yes, I have been called crazy before. It seems animals relate well to me and understand I mean them no harm," Ian replied with a smile.

Ian took the memory chip from the camera and immediately created several backups of the original footage.

He let everyone know he was going to process the pictures he had taken. He worked rapidly on a first cut edit to share with the folks on the Nanny.

Ian wondered what Andria Miller of his Elephants and Ivory adventure would think when she got this footage in her mail. Ian would bequeath it to her since he personally would never be able to put this out publicly.

Ian wondered if the animals sensed his internal calm or somehow knew of his secret profession. Ian had capture elephants, lions, and other fierce animals up close and personal, and none had ever threatened him. Ian admitted to having played subservient to the giant silver back gorilla, but he had never felt threatened. He loved the interactions he had experienced with the wild animals.

The raw film footage was a big hit on the Nanny. It was several hours long and was highlighted by the two rides. However, it also had footage of the twenty-foot giant manta ray and a brief shot of the smaller six-foot reef manta.

A lone Leather Back Sea turtle and a Pacific Hawkbill turtle made cameo appearances.

Close ups of a variety of fish rounded out the cast.

"Unbelievable," was the phrase that kept coming up as the couples watched the raw film.

"I was out there with you, and I didn't see half of what you caught on camera," Jerry commented.

"This is like watching some of those National Geographic nature films. Let's see it again," Carla added.

Ian wished he could spend his time doing nature films. Then he amended his thought since he realized he was not being totally honest with himself. He could do whatever he wanted, and he realized he was doing exactly that.

Many opportunities to do something less dangerous had presented themselves over the years. He had never taken those off ramps.

There was just something about pitting himself against the bad guys that trumped every other thing he had ever thought of doing.

Ian knew it was time for him to take action on the next cartel.

He had a smile on his face as he told Ted that he was promoting him to the status of Captain.

Ted said sure thing, but when Ian went on to explain that he had officially submitted papers to that effect with the State of California Ted had tears in his eyes. Ian told him the official paperwork should be in his mailbox by the time he returned the Nanny to its port.

He also let Ted know that he was going to depart when they got into port.

Ted was overwhelmed. Ian knew that achieving the level of Captain was one of Ted's personal goals. Ted was excited about finishing the trip as captain and assured Ian that the Nanny and its crew would safely return to California.

The next morning at breakfast, Ian informed the rest of the Nanny's crew that there was a personal emergency and that he would be leaving them at the next port. He let them know that Ted had officially been promoted to captain. The next celebration would be to celebrate Ted's accomplishment.

He listened politely to the praise of the four "vacationing crew members" and then suggested that they all have dinner and a beer together once they docked in La Reforma.

The Nanny was at the La Reforma dock by late afternoon.

The evening out was on Ian. He joined everyone for dinner and a few drinks. Then he said his goodbyes and promised them that he would keep in touch. He would but they would never know his real identity.

He then walked down the street to where an old pickup was parked. It was one of the support items Ian had requested from his invisible and remote team of helpers.

<u>*10 The Sinaloa Cartel*</u>

*I*an looked at the wind worn grey paint of the old pickup. It passed for an old local pickup that a subsistence farmer would be driving. The condition of the tires indicated it was in good shape.

He put the few possessions he was carrying with him in the bed of the truck. He tried the combination lock on the side of what appeared to be a beat-up metal box. He looked inside and counted the bundles of explosives, took note that the timers and remote detonation equipment were all in the box. Satisfied that he had what was needed, Ian closed the box.

He prepared to get into the heavily worn front seat. The spring sticking up from the middle of the driver's seat stopped him. Next time he would make it clear that the driver's seat was to be comfortable, and the spring should stick up on the passenger's side. He was sure someone was pulling a joke on him. He actually chuckled as he folded and put his jacket over the spring.

He then got in and pushed the shiny finger polished start button. The engine started smoothly, and the purr of the engine signaled that it was tuned and in good shape. The truck might appear old, but Ian was sure it was ready to go the distance at any speed he needed to go.

The truck reminded him of the old floor shift pickup he had often driven when he was only fourteen. It had been one of the vehicles other than the tractors that he had driven as a farm boy.

Ian took his time driving down highway 3-21. He was in no particular hurry. His destination was an old, secluded farmhouse just outside of the city of Culiacan. The farmhouse had been arranged by his unseen support team. He hoped it would be as safe a location as they had promised.

Culiacan was much like Pittsburg where two rivers merge to form the Ohio River. In this case the Tamazula and Humava Rivers met to form the Culiacan River. Unlike Pittsburg, Culiacan was not as industrial.

Culiacan was home to the Sinaloa Cartel. The Cartel headquarters was about five miles away on the other side of the city. The city, the cradle of Mexican drug trafficking since the 1960s, was prospering in spite of the fact that their main official business was growing and exporting tomatoes. It was clear to Ian that more than exporting tomatoes made the local economy boom.

The city was dotted with money changing outlets, jewelry stores and luxury car showrooms. It was an accepted fact that the drug business was good for the city and a blind eye was turned to the business of the cartel. The underlining theme was to enjoy the prosperity that the gringo drug users provided.

Ian had done his homework and was aware that the Sinaloa Cartel was led by "Shorty" Guzman an exceptional leader who though currently in prison still outmaneuvered his competitors and for many years the governments that sought to shut him down. Ian was impressed with his ability to constantly adjust to the changing situation and move the Sinaloa Cartel into a more powerful position.

To Ian, it appeared that even from prison, Guzman was managing the strongest Cartel in Mexico. It had a very strong presence in the United States and across the world and had a much broader presence than the other cartels. Ian had read reports that this cartel moved up to two thirds of the drugs trafficked in the US. That was a huge advantage in terms of the resources that he could mount against his competitors.

The Cheshire moon, its smile bright in the night sky provided just enough light for Ian to see the gravel road that he was looking for.

Ian turned off the highway and followed the narrow one lane drive. It was bordered with a rusty wire fence held up by steel poles in the same rusty condition. The dry grass appearing to be a sandy tan, reflected the moonlight. The way was dotted with cactuses sporting their colorful red to purple fruit. In the night light these fruits appeared to be almost black with black flowers on top.

The stucco, single level building with a flat roof was accompanied by what Ian thought of as a small, weathered plank out building similar to a small barn he would have found back in Iowa. Both buildings had seen better days but seemed sturdy and useable.

Ian stopped and opened the double doors to the barn. After opening the doors Ian found the light switch on the beam on which the left door was mounted. The light made the roof beams of the barn appear to be the black ribs of some ancient giant beast.

He noted the bales of hay stacked to one side and the pile of loose straw just to the right of the hay.

Ian drove the pickup in and turned off the engine. He decided to unload the explosives and put them under the straw. Then he took his suitcase and backpack, closed the doors to the shed and locked it.

He walked across the drive to the house.

It was time to take a shower and get a good night's sleep. He hoped the black tank of water on the roof would provide some hot water.

The night passed uninterrupted and the morning sun stream through the bedroom window was Ian's wake up call.

Ian got up and looked to see if there was any coffee or other food in the house. Indeed, the team had provided him with coffee, eggs, sausage, and some instant oatmeal.

After a cup of coffee and breakfast, Ian drove slowly into and through Culiacan. The building cranes rising above multiple construction sites signaled a healthy economy. Ian continued out to the eastern edge of town toward the warehouse that was the regular meeting place for the cartel.

He made his way around the area to a place where a few scraggly, windblown trees created a dusty oasis with a sparse but adequate covering of grasses and a few cactuses. Ian got out and scouted out the grass covered fields that surrounded the warehouse on all sides.

He found a small depression where he would be out of sight from anyone watching from the warehouse.

Ian decided it was time to complete his tour of the city. The homes of the cartel personal were located in a northwestern suburb area named Sinaloa. These were homes that the cartel members had raised their families. This gave rise to the name for the Cartel. This was an upscale neighborhood. Ian hoped his old pickup fit the image of one of the local gardeners and grounds keepers.

After his tour, Ian stopped at a local grocery. Once he had what he thought would be sufficient food for several days he returned to the farmhouse. He scrambled some eggs and fried some sausage and onions for his lunch.

Ian spent the afternoon assembling two dozen small explosive units. He wrapped them in aluminum foil and made them look like they were traps for mice and rats. He carefully placed the radio-controlled triggering unit in one end of each block. He made additional explosive units to put in the office areas.

The next morning Ian slept in and rested. Then in the late afternoon he went back out to the depression in the grass field and got under his camouflage covering. He kept watch on the white forty-foot-high warehouse that was almost the size of a football field. It dominated the landscape and blocked out most of the green patched, mangy tan looking mountains in the distant horizon.

He had learned the cartel's schedule on the first two days. Every afternoon three white SUV's drove in and parked in front of the warehouse office building.

The arrival of the SUV's seemed to be the signal for the workers to leave. Ian counted at least a dozen people going to their cars and pickups.

Ian recognized Abelel Lambasko as one of the persons in the group. He was one of Guzman's trusted leaders.

This afternoon Ian would wait until dark and then go into the warehouse to plant his bombs. He had located the surveillance cameras mounted on the top of the warehouse and had determined the safest approach was via the truck holding area.

Ian slowly crawled through the tall grass. It took him all afternoon to get across to where the trucks were parked. He waited until he was certain everyone had left and then walked slowly to the warehouse side entrance.

Once inside the warehouse, Ian stood still for a few minutes in the eerie red darkness. Ian examined the structural beams and was pleased to discover that the bottom of the warehouse had an exterior cement lip that held the metal wall siding up against the bottom of the support I-beams. This created a perfect, out of sight, place to drop the explosive charges.

In less than ten minutes Ian had walked around the periphery of the warehouse and dropped a charge behind each support beam. The building should come straight down.

The office area was built outside of the warehouse. Ian recognized this as the greatest challenge. The fact that the office was completely dark provided Ian the chance to get in and then blind the surveillance cameras.

He put on his night vision goggles and looked up from his prone position. He found the camera above the door connecting to the warehouse. He hooded it and then went in and did the same for each camera.

Once the cameras were hooded Ian quickly planted and camouflaged each charge. He purposefully excluded the main cubical work areas near the front entrance where the common office workers were located.

He took careful inventory and inspected each charge. Ian then just as carefully un-hooded each surveillance camera and retreated out of the office area.

Ian took in a deep breath of relief once he was back into the warehouse. He paused for a moment after making sure all was set; he exited the warehouse. He carefully made his way back to the field. He paused to roll up his tarp and police the area to remove all traces of his presence.

Once back in the truck he slowly drove away in the dark.

On the following morning before lunch, he packed up all is belongings. He cleaned up the small bedroom. He folded up his bed sheets and light blanket, swept the room and took all his belongings out to the truck. He cleaned the kitchen and emptied the refrigerator into a cooler he had purchased. Everything, even the trash, went into the back of his truck.

He backed his truck out of the shed and with a broom erased his tire tracks. With a pack of sanitizing wipes Ian made a last walk-through inspection in the house and the barn. He wiped every surface he might have touched.

His support team would send a team in to clean the house, but Ian was aware that he was in the heart of one of the most thorough cartel in the world. He could not be sure the cleaners would be cartel proof. He was confident that he had erased any trace of his presence.

Once in his truck, Ian drove a small distance from the cartel warehouse and parked. He took the time to eat a sandwich before hiking to where he had a clear view of the warehouse office area.

Late in the afternoon, the white SUVs made their appearance. Ian watched as the workers walked out to their cars and the occupants of the SUVs entered the building.

Ian waited a moment and then energized his listening device located in the large main meeting room. He listened just long enough to verify it was occupied before triggering the explosions.

The back portion of the office area seemed to push the warehouse wall away into the collapsing warehouse structure. A wave of tan dust rolled away from the base of the warehouse walls and the fleet of trucks fell over like dominos. The entire structure settled down and the roof was held up by the strength of the pallet racks standing below. The sidewalls had spread like the wings of a fat bird laying on the ground.

The three white SUVs remained out front, untouched. The three drivers were standing together looking startled and pointing at the transformation happening before their eyes. Their guns were drawn as if they were going to shoot.

Ian took one last look and slowly walked back to the old truck and headed south toward Apatzingan, Michoacana.

11 La Familia Michoacana

*I*an had researched the leader of La Familia, Natsario Morelo Gonzoles also known as *El Más Loco,* the crazy one. He and his leadership team all had a two-million-dollar bounty on their heads. This cartel financed politicians in their bid for election. The cartel also provided aid to the less privileged who needed help. This gave Nazario Moreno González, the Robin Hood and messianic like image among the poor and the support of many in the government.

Ian knew that this image was counterbalanced with the dozens of police officials the cartel had killed.

The police had once erroneously announced killing Moreno. Still at large *El Más Loco* was being aggressively hunted. He, however, remained in firm control of the cartel. And the cartel was fully functioning.

The twelve-hour drive from Culiacan to Apatzingan with an overnight stop in Guadalajara provided Ian with time to think through the approach he had in mind.

He did not want any close at hand encounters, but he might have to go into the office building where he thought he might find Natsario. This office building was in the heart of Apatzingán.

La Familia was integrated and influenced all elements in the state of Michoacana. It was a part of the fabric of the local business, politics, and everyday life.

Ian planned to select one family member to eliminate.

He would approach the selection in an opportunistic way. The first one he could single out would be the target.

He also knew that his action would not likely have a major impact on the cartel. They had strong family capabilities.

In Guadalajara, Ian cleared the trash and other materials from the bed of the pickup. There were two bags in the locked box in the back of the pickup. One held his clothes and the other the next weapon of choice.

The weapon was almost the identical weapon to the one he had used in Gaza. It was a high-powered sniper's rifle.

It was just past ten in the morning as Ian drove slowly along Jose Maria Morelos highway on his way into Apatzingán.

He passed the airport and wished he could catch a plane back home instead of continuing on. He missed talking to Leslie, but he could not take the chance of calling her. He knew that he needed to stay invisible.

The local traffic picked up as he turned right on Acatita and headed into Apatzingán's central district. Traffic came to a stop and Ian could see a police barricade ahead. He stopped and looked around.

He decided he would turn off and proceed on the back streets to the apartment building he had selected as a place where he could study the downtown area. It had a clear view of the downtown central park but was far enough away that he could study the downtown and not worry about being seen. There were several closer buildings, but they were occupied by business offices, and he would risk being noticed.

He hoped to enter and exit the apartment building he had selected without meeting anyone.

Perhaps he would see what the police barricade was about.

The apartment building was about two blocks away from where he parked on one of the side streets. He preferred to go on foot the rest of the way. He took a moment to check out his appearance. He had whitened his hair and was wearing an old grey sports jacket and a pair of worn slacks. He wanted to appear like an old man returning home from a trip.

Ian retrieved a battered suitcase from the back of the pickup. He slowly walked up the street. He hoped anyone watching would see a worn old man carrying a battered suitcase and ignore him.

He slowly walked up the hill leading to the old apartment building. In the distance he could hear what he thought was the popping sound of gunfire. He figured that might be the reason for the police blockade.

Ian found an open side door to the apartment building. Once inside he followed the hallway to the elevators.

He entered the right-hand elevator and pushed the button with the number seventeen barely legible to the eye. The old elevator creaked and groaned as it slowly took him to the top floor.

The hallway outside of the elevator passed by a series of apartment doors. Ian went to the end of the hallway and climbed the stairs to a locked service door that led to the roof. He easily picked the lock and stepped cautiously out onto the roof.

He looked quickly around. The black tar and gravel roof was bordered by a three-foot-high red brick wall. Four large black water tanks towered above him and dominated the majority of the roof area.

The rest of the roof area had an assortment of ventilation pipes and some boxes that Ian took to be fan units. The roof was deserted, and its appearance indicated it was seldom used.

Ian locked the door and then picked up a section of pipe and propped it under the door handle to make sure it could not be opened. He did not want anyone surprising him from behind.

He then crossed to the side of the building that faced in the direction where he still periodically heard the popping of gunfire.

Ian took off his jacket, opened the suitcase and placed it carefully on the open lid.

The interior of the suitcase belied the shabby exterior. The black foam interior cradled a two-inch diameter, foot long scope with a plastic glare cover of the same length. The long slender black barrel that reminded Ian of a sleek black shark was just below it and the back end of ten six-inch-long bullets created a poke a dot brass and silver pattern below the barrel. The padded plastic stock of the rifle on the opposite side from the scope balanced the layout.

Ian carefully assembled the single fire sniper rifle. This was a gun that any NRA maniac would fall in love with. He snugged the single bolt connecting the barrel to the stock. Then he gently positioned the scope on the front and back groves and pushed it down until he felt the spring-loaded balls snap into place. The scope mounting design was one that assured the exact positioning required for extremely long shots.

Ian slowly pulled out each bullet and put them in the depressions designed into the foam rubber. The long slender six-inch-long shell with the quarter inch diameter one-inch-long bullet head always caught him by surprise. They were truly a beautiful sight that attracted him as much as any well-built bikini clad lady and he considered them even more deadly.

Ian looked up at the clear blue, cloudless sky. A gentle breeze was blowing over the wall in front of him. He located the sun, confirmed the direction of the wind, and then looked out to those structures that were higher than where he was.

Ian was now ready to look over the wall.

Out to his left and about two blocks away was a building towering above the main downtown square. There he saw two snipers with their right sides visible to him. He was not sure if there were more snipers on that roof top.

Three snipers with their backs to him were visible on two buildings in front of and slightly below his elevation. Their building seemed to overlook the town square. He wondered why they were not shooting. They had a better position than he had.

Ian completed his slow and careful scan of the entire scene surrounding the battle area in the square several blocks away.

Ian had a clear view of eight black SUV's forming a barricade on one side of the square. A series of police cars and military vehicles were on the other side of the square. The police side had many more people moving about then what Ian saw by the black vans.

The two sides appeared to be in a standoff.

Ian sat back down and put a bullet into the chamber of the rifle.

Once again Ian felt the breeze and took in the position of the sun.

This time Ian put his jacket down, so he could comfortably kneel on it while he lay the rifle barrel on the top of the wall.

He looked through his scope at the various figures crouched down behind the black SUV's. Ian could not believe it when the third figure he focused on was none other than "El Chayo," the crazy one.

This was an opportunity that could not to be denied but he was at the extreme of his sniper capability. The shot must hit the mark. He needed to calibrate his shot.

Ian took careful aim at the zero of the license plate on the SUV "El Chayo" was hiding behind. He slowly squeezed the trigger.

The hole that appeared on the license plate was two inches to the left but at the same height as his aim.

Ian made a mental aim adjustment, chambered the next bullet, took a deep breath, and found his target. He once again smoothly squeezed the trigger.

"El Chayo" seemed to look up at Ian at the moment the trigger was squeezed. After what seemed to Ian to be an eternity, a small dark spot appeared in El Chayo's forehead and a moment later he went down.

Ian did not wait but loaded and fired one bullet after the another at the row of men behind the SUV's. Each body shot found its target.

Ian saw one of the police wave to the snipers as the army and police surged across the square. Ian was sure the snipers were all surprised. They would be looking around to see where the shots had come from.

Ian sat back down behind the wall and carefully removed the scope and repacked it. He then cleaned the rifle barrel before placing it back in its place. Finally, he pushed each empty bullet casing into their holding place. He noted that the firing pin was striking slightly off center as he closed the suitcase and made a mental note to adjust it when he next used the rifle. Then he laughed as he realized he would never use it again.

After ensuring the roof area held no evidence of his presence Ian closed the door to the roof behind him.

Ian had been totally calm for the entire period on the roof. Now in the elevator, he felt nervous that everything had been too easy, too fast, and too smooth. His senses were heightened as he anticipated facing someone with a gun as he exited the building.

Ian walked slowly out of the building and back to his truck. He expected to be called out or shot at, at any moment. He put the old suitcase into the back of the pickup and got in.

He sat for a few moments before putting his finger on the start button. The engine once again began to purr like an aroused cat. He was still parked after a few moments.

He noted that he had literally just driven into Apatzingan and had accomplished his goal in less than an hour. This would most likely go down as the fastest solution on this trip.

It was time to leave the area.

12 Beltran Leyva Cartel

*I*an was not sure this last target qualified as the leader of a major cartel. Four brothers originally formed the Beltran Leyva cartel when they broke away from the Sinaloa cartel after Joaquin Guzman betrayed them by turning in their oldest brother to the government. The brothers ordered the murder of Joaquin's son in retaliation and at the same time formed their own cartel.

Ian was aware that both personal dislike and business competition ruled the relationships between the cartels. The competition between the cartels provided more control and restraint of their actions than the actions by either the Mexican or US government. Each cartel monitored and pushed back on any encroachment into their territory or their market.

The Beltran Leyva cartel became known for their kidnapping, torture, and murder against various Mexican people especially Mexican law enforcement officials. This made them more of a target by the government than was exerted on the other cartels.

Even in its weakened state, the Beltran Leyva cartel was still running and distributing drugs in the US. It really was the classic story of the multi-headed snake. Cutting one head off just meant another would grow or another head would became stronger. The consumption of drugs in the US fed the various heads and US consumption of drugs was going up as the US economy got better. The market was adequate to make all the cartels rich.

Between the US and Mexican governments there was a seven million dollars bounty for the one remaining brother, Hector Beltran Leyva, "El Ingeniero", the engineer.

Ian's research indicated Hector was hiding in plain sight. He was living with an early childhood friend who had become a successful soap opera star. She was past her youthful prime but was still doing commercials on a local Mexico City television channel.

Her flat was in a very nice part of the city across the street from two prestigious hotels.

This was an affluent area of nice homes and apartments.

Ian was very familiar with the hotels and the area. This was where he stayed during his legitimate regular business trips to Mexico City.

Her apartment or condo was directly behind a Starbucks outlet across the street from the locally owned prestigious hotels, so Ian selected a room with a view of Starbucks.

From the top of the hotel, Ian could look down into the apartment pool area that was across the street behind Starbucks. He spent several days just watching the pool to see if the pool would attract his target. It would make it very easy if Hector were to come out for a swim. It was a clear and relatively easy shot from the roof.

Ian had no such luck.

Instead, Ian saw a person who took a morning walk out to Starbucks and then walked down a few blocks and back around Emilio Castelar street back to Anstotelos street and returned to the apartment building.

He was sure he had found his target. He waited and watched for another day to make certain he had found his target.

Then the following morning Ian was sitting in Starbucks when Hector came in. Hector was much thinner and trimmer than the mug shots Ian had studied or that graced the various newspapers, but Ian was certain it was "El Ingeniero."

Hector ordered a large cappuccino. Once he had been served, he left with it in hand and went for his normal walk.

Ian walked slowly in the opposite direction. He was carrying only an ink pen from the hotel room. It was all he would need.

Hector was concentrating on his coffee and his walk as Ian nodded to him and said good morning in English.

Hector nodded but didn't really pay attention. That was his last mistake.

Ian's left hand placed the pen into Hector's ear and his right hand came down like a sledge and drove it through. Ian quickly removed the pen and continued walking. He never looked back.

He walked to the hotel and went into the restroom where he washed the pen. He then went out to the lobby and distributed the pieces of the pen in the various trash receptacles.

Once back in his hotel room, Ian took a quick shower, packed his bags, and checked out of the hotel.

Ian took several taxis to get to the airport. He disposed of his remaining weapons, explosives, and other equipment each time he changed taxis. He disposed of the sniper rifle one piece at a time. He hated to destroy such a beauty but there was no other way. He had taken the time to ensure there was no remaining gun powder in the bullets he disposed of. No two component parts were disposed in the same trash container or in close proximity trash cans.

The third taxi he flagged down took him to the Airport.

The total time to get to the airport took several hours longer than normal. Once there he was able to book a flight to Dallas, Texas. In Dallas, Ian went to another airline and booked a flight home.

Ian was anxious to give Lesley a big hug.

He stopped to give her a call and let her know that he was on the way home.

Lesley knew Ian was gentle and kind in the open life he lived.

She had voiced her suspicion about the worst for the other.

Ian had never confirmed his alternate personality. He was afraid that if Lesley ever learned the truth of the actions, he perpetrated she might leave him.

All she had ever asked was if Ian was one of the good guys.

Ian had replied that he thought he was.

He hoped he was one of the good, result-oriented, problem-solvers.

He also hoped that he would not get another problem-solving assignment.

The End

Border Crossers

Introduction

*I*t is a troubled world. The human species has, like no other, risen to dominate the world. The rise is marked with amazing beauty and grace. It is also marked by cruelty to other humans and a disregard for the negative impact they have on their only home, the earth.

The beauty found in poetry and writing, the beauty found in paintings and sculptors is more than countered by the wars, the intentional environmental destruction, and the barriers each separate country imposes on its peoples and the neighboring states.

The belief of limited resources, the behavior of greed, the desire for wealth and the desire for control are all factors in the behavior exhibited by those who surface at the top of the heap. The ability of various leaders, in a myriad of areas, to convince those more interested in their immediate family well-being allows those interested in domination to rise to positions of influence and power.

Often their belief is that they have been ordained to be in charge or alternately they are smarter and should be in the lead.

The rise of the rule of law has created a situation where fairness is managed by laws developed by the representatives of the people. Even in the situation found in the United States that has three branches of government designed to maintain the system of fairness to all, slavery, and women's right to vote were initially missed. More recently the rights of gay or lesbian people are in question.

Human greed, cruelty, misbehavior, and disregard of the environment seems to increase asymptotically with the rapid rise of the population.

Justice is not always served. This situation is managed by a secret organization that funds and directs the actions of ***The Problem-solver***. This is a person whose principles, judgement, behavior, and actions guide him in how to resolve problems that otherwise would be left unchecked.

The problems are many. The problems are anywhere in the world. The problems are solved in the best manner that The Problem-solver determines.

See if you agree with the problem resolutions, that this Problem-solver, ***Ian Sinclair***, has chosen for his various assignments.

1 Border Crosser

*I*t was pitch black, the screaming, the crying, the pounding, the sound of bone shattering and the ungodly scraping of bone against steel reach Marial's ears. She held her six-year-old daughter's and her nine-year-old son's heads against her chest and prayed. She asked forgiveness for her sins as she took her last few breaths.

Her life in Guatemala had been hard and she had lost her husband when the rebels came into her village and raped her. He had defended her only to have his head cut off by a machete.

Her two children had been out playing and had survived.

She had chosen to try to escape the horror. The long road up through Mexico had been hard but she thought of it as the road to a place where there was hope. A place where she and the children would find peace. A place where they would grow and prosper.

She had traded the one small treasure, two ounces of gold that she and her husband had saved. It was their dream to leave their village. They had talked about making the journey to the promised land.

When she crossed the Rio Grande, she felt a surge of hope. When she ran and got into the back of the large white van, she felt a surge of hope. Hope continued to carry her as in the pitch black the van ran for hours. Then the van shuttered to a stop and hope began to ebb and was slowly replaced by fear and then fear was replaced by despair.

She sat quietly in the dark singing softly with her children in her arms. In the pitch black, her dreams were replaced with the nightmare she was now living through. She was sure that the nightmare had only one ending. It was an ending that she had never envisioned. She felt each of her children stop breathing. She knew she was next and once again asked for the forgiveness of her sins.

Ian watched as the news camera zoomed in on the back of a panel truck. It had been found by the Arizona highway patrol abandoned in the scorching hot Arizona sun. The external temperature had reached an ungodly one hundred thirteen degrees.

The truck was filled with more than thirty bodies. It was clear by how they were piled up trying to scale the interior wall of the panel truck that the occupants had used their hands or a boot trying to break out.

Ian was sure that to the end the occupants were desperately shouting, crying, and pleading to be let out. The backdoor was bent, and one occupant had broken his leg, and the bone was exposed in a grotesque angle. The hands with their fingernails ripped back clearly indicated to Ian the final desperate efforts to claw their way out.

Ian absorbed the scene as the camera pulled to a distant view and then zoomed in on a mother cradling a young girl and boy to her chest. The three seemed to be in a Cinderella sleep just waiting to wake up.

The reporter walked away with a cloth over his nose as he commented about the stench of death. Some bodies were already beginning to bloat. There seemed to be an even mix of men, women, and children. It was clear to Ian that this had been mostly family units trying to get into the US.

The woman holding her children to her chest became the focus of the reporting. The report was picked up by all the national news channels and it went viral on the personal chat sites. The picture went viral with multimillions of hits in just one evening.

Ian let out a groan when he heard a national news caster say, "We need action to be taken against those trafficking in across the border people smuggling. We especially need someone to take action against smugglers that abandon people in locked trailers. This has got to be fixed." This Ian knew was clearly a message for him to act. He was the problem-solver.

Ian watched several other major channels and listened to the same message, saw the same iconic picture of the mother holding her two children to her chest. There was no doubt. The message could not have been clearer.

Ian left the grand family room. It was the place where he spent each early morning with a cup coffee and listened to Morning Joe before tuning in on BBC, CNN and then going on to Fox. He liked to keep a balanced perspective on what was being watched by the rest of the world. So much of what was presented as news was actually biased opinion by one side of the political aisle or the other. The worst of the group seemed to be Fox

Ian went down the hallway to his study.

He walked in and took in the book lined shelves along the two side walls of what had originally been a large spacious home library but over the years had become his office. The mahogany desk with a black three-foot-wide all in one computer faced the rear window overlooking the tennis court and the lawn around it. The Library was where he spent many hours doing research.

Ian booted up the computer and began his search on the topic of smuggling people.

After a moment he opened the bottom left hand desk drawer and extracted a locked box from the very back. He opened and picked up an older phone that did not have GPS as a function. He slowly dialed a well memorized number. It was immediately answered. By the tone of the voice, he was sure the person on the phone had been expecting the call.

"Send me everything you have on smuggling people across the Mexican border. Set me up as an FBI agent with orders to go to Arizona. Give me the name of the current field agents name that manages that area. Arrange for me to get there in two days. And thank you," Ian said as politely as possible.

Early in his career as the problem-solver he had tried to be friendly, but he was soon calibrated on the fact that the people on the other end of the line were to remain anonymous.

Whoever they were and however many made up his support team was unknown to him. He had envisioned a large work area all full of people doing his bidding and he had also envisioned a gray-haired old lady with coke bottle bifocals sitting in a darkened closet like office. He would probably never know which of the two scenes was the closest. All he cared about was that his support team always delivered what he needed. His support team showed up in the field in various ways that helped him but once again he never directly saw any of them.

The requested material began coming in almost immediately. They must have anticipated his request. He reviewed the information from past reports on the smuggling and movement of those coming across the border. It was very thorough and detailed.

He learned of an earlier abandoned truck full of people. It had not made the news.

The fact that two trucks had been abandoned in the last two months seemed to indicate carelessness, disregard or perhaps it was the result of an increased pressure by local law enforcement that frightened the drivers and caused them to abandon their trucks.

Smugglers always preferred to remain anonymous. Getting caught was one of their greatest fear. Subsequent publicity meant exposure and scrutiny which meant that their bosses were as likely to kill them as anyone.

The US border patrol preferred to keep the media at arms-length which meant they whenever possible kept their actions and findings under wraps.

Inadvertently this penchant to keep press coverage low caused the police to aid the smugglers.

Ian looked up the local law enforcement officers in Phoenix. Phoenix was where the Highway Patrol, the Local county sheriff and the FBI regional offices were located.

He reviewed the background and assignments of the local FBI Phoenix office chief. He seemed to have a well-rounded background including a stint in the Army. He appeared to be a solid individual with personal integrity.

The human smugglers had to get past the security, monitoring and patrolling done by Homeland Security. In fact, the border patrol units of the Homeland Security organization were highly trained and highly motivated. Ian's assessment was that they were good at their jobs.

He also suspected that some of them must play some part of the smuggling operation. The crossers had to get past the field teams and that indicated some sort internal agents working for the cartels. These agents most likely were bribed and receiving some sort of monthly amount of money.

The local sheriffs and State Highway Patrol seemed to be vigilant in their efforts to intercept the cars and trucks involved in the smuggling. They seemed to focus on looking for those being smuggled. It was unlikely that they had any direct involvement, but he would at this point not rule it out.

Ian suspected that there were a few bad actors in these organizations that would cause the good side to get a black eye. He was certain that there was one or more bad apple in the local law enforcement agencies.

He listed the ways people could be crossing the border and not be getting caught.

There could be participation by local law enforcement personnel. There could be a group of border guards that would look the other way. In all cases it appeared that those doing the smuggling had help on the US side of the border. Help that with the right incentive would let the smuggler get the people seeking to get into the United States get past the border security.

Ian knew he needed to go to the field and get firsthand knowledge to understand the true situation.

He had already asked for his FBI persona to be reactivated. He was Herman A. Lunquist, senior FBI investigator.

Ian reviewed his past history as Herman. It had continued to be updated and he laughed about some to the more current compliments and his work performance evaluations. Someone on his support team was having a good time fabricating and building his history.

He had many personalities on record but only a few got reactivated as often as Herman had been. For his Journey into the Heart of Russia, he had become a naturalist. In taking care of the Three Bad Pennies in the Gaza, he had become a cameraman.

This was a natural build because he had taken on the role of a cameraman on a team of National Geographic photographers out to document the Elephant Ivory trade plight. For fighting the Pirates off the coast of Africa he had become a sailboat captain.

Ian let Lesley know that he had an upcoming business trip out west. She immediately knew what kind of business and as always gave him a kiss on the cheek and told him to be careful. Over the years Lesley had come to accept the fact that Ian would remain a problem-solver for most of his life. She constantly reminded him that they had the small fortune most people dreamed of having and that they did not need the money.

Ian gave her a hug and thanked her for loving him.

Herman Lundquist had a high status as an FBI agent. He called Mike Lancaster the local FBI branch manager, introduced himself and let him know that he was coming to do some field work in his domain. Mike had agreed to meet him at the airport and escort him to the local FBI office.

As he came to the end of the airport concourse and walked out of the security area Ian spotted Mike almost immediately. Mike was roughly six two with dark hair that was cut almost in a short military style. Ian put him in the handsome category. He smiled as he thought that in his dark suit he could have starred in the movie, Men in Black.

Ian could tell that Mike was nervous and probably wondering why he, a senior FBI investigator, was there. In the car on the way to the office Ian explained that he had been sent to work with him because the FBI hierarchy was feeling pressure about the fact that two loads of people had died in the back of trucks and there seemed to be no solution in stopping it.

Mike thanked Ian for clarifying his presence and that he could see the reason he had been sent. He wondered what Ian was going to do.

Ian admitted that initially he planned to get a lay of the land and see if anything popped up that would help him determine what he could possibly do that had not been done so far.

The FBI office was in the local Federal building in the heart of downtown Phoenix.

On their way up from the basement parking lot, Mike informed Ian that an office had been arranged for him and that they would share Mary Gems as their secretarial support.

They approached Mary's desk where Mike introduced Herman Lundquist.

After some small talk and asking about her family, Herman asked if she would set up breakfast or lunch meetings with the leaders of the Highway Patrol, the Sheriff's office, and the Homeland Security Leader.

Herman made the point that he wanted his meetings to be on an informal basis. He did not want formality to become a barrier. He wanted everyone to know him on a more personal basis and feel somewhat relaxed around him.

Mary agreed to do so but made the point that the Homeland Security Leader was located in a small town about two hours away.

He suggested that meeting be arranged to meet the Homeland Security Leader's timing.

Mike next led Herman to an office next to his.

Herman commented that he hoped not to be at the desk at all.

Next Mike walked to a small room with a coffee pot, a shelf full of cups, a small refrigerator and stainless-steel sink.

"This is as good as it gets here in the office. If you want something better, May's restaurant just down the street makes a great breakfast and lunch and serves a variety of soft drinks, iced tea as well as great cup of coffee," Mike fired off in rapid order.

Herman could tell that Mike was still nervous.

He had a good feeling about Mike. He could see them working well together.

Herman followed Mike out of the coffee room

He asked Mike to bring him up to date on the investigation of the deaths of the people found in both of the abandoned panel trucks.

Mike said that the trucks were registered to two separate local truck rental companies. The rental companies had contracts on file for the trucks and everything was in order. The persons renting the trucks and their driver license information were fake. The information on both rentals led nowhere.

The FBI was working with the state and states around to see if they could determine who the drivers might have been. The trail at this moment was cold.

The records of the companies were being reviewed to determine how many other times a truck had been rented under a fictitious name. The net had been cast wider and truck rentals from all rental companies were being scrutinized.

Mike commented that it would take time to get through this investigation.

Herman commented on the impressive and solid approach Mike was pursuing. He went on to describe how great it would be if the two of them solved this current case and put an end to trucks being abandoned.

He asked Mike to speculate what action he would take if he could take any action he wanted. What would he do?

There was a soft knock on the door just as Mike was about to answer. Mary opened the door and informed them that she had set up breakfasts for the next three days for the two of them.

Herman thanked Mary and she closed the door.

He then suggested that he and Mike continue their discussion over lunch.

Mike led the way to May's. He said that he recommended the Reuben special.

After lunch Mike dropped him off at the downtown hotel.

Ian checked in and went up to his room. After a long shower, he sat down and turned on his computer and thoroughly reviewed the information he had on each of the law enforcement leaders.

Mathew Martin was the leader of the highway patrol. In his mid-fifties Mathew had served in the Marines. He had a wife and three children, all now in their late teens and early twenties. He had an impressive record and had quickly risen in the state's highway patrol organization. It made no sense to Ian that he would be involved.

Bill Peters was the local sheriff. He too had the same family profile. He had an Army background and had been elected sheriff four times. He was known for his active participation in getting downtown Phoenix renovated and well-lit, so people could safely enjoy their time in the city.

It made no sense to Ian that either these two would be involved.

He, however, did not rule out the fact that someone high in their organization might be involved.

The next morning, he walked to May's diner. The appealing smell of fresh rolls, bacon and was trumped by the smell of coffee. As the waitress poured his coffee it immediately captured Ian's mind and made his stomach growl. He sat down and looked around. He had arrived early, so he could watch the customers come in.

Someone in a dark blue city police uniform with a gold badge on the chest came in and sat in a far corner booth. A moment later a person in a tan uniform with State Highway Patrol embroidered where the sleeves met the shoulder came in and joined the person in the corner. They both looked over at Ian.

Ian took in the two seasoned, well-aged older men sitting in full uniform at the booth. He stood and walked over and introduced himself as Herman Lunquist. He had planned to meet first with the highway patrol leader, but it was clear they had talked to each other. The Highway Patrol leader introduced himself as Mathew Martin and then introduced the City Police Chief, Bill Peters.

Mathew said he preferred to be called Matt, said that the two had talked and decided that they would meet the investigating FBI leader together.

Herman thanked them for having breakfast with him.

At that moment Mike walked in and came over to the table. He apologized for being late.

Ian noted that Mike seemed to be treated as one of them.

Herman was the odd one out and was the one they all seemed to be wondering about. He surprised the group by asking about their families and the age of their kids. He had the statistics of each family, but he was interested in listening to how each of the people at the table related to their family.

The discussion that followed made it clear to him that "Matt" and Bill were old and good friends. He made note that these were family men, proud of their work and solid in their integrity. This made it easier for Ian. If there was corruption in their organization, it would involve those below these two. The problem would be deeper in the organization, but he would not be fighting the organization leaders.

After breakfast, Ian accompanied by Mike went on tour of the border and to the office of border security to see how they operated.

The drive to the office of border security took over an hour. Ian used this time to get to know Mike. He listened as Mike described coaching his two sons in soccer, baseball, and basketball. Mike did not want his sons to play football because of his own experience and the injuries that were only getting worse with age.

They arrived at the Homeland Security office and met with Ricard Butterfield the regional director. Rick, as he wanted to be called, showed Herman a map and the way the area was patrolled. He invited Herman on a drive through tour along the border.

Herman gladly accepted. Rick led the way to a large, air-conditioned trail buggy and for the rest of the day he, Mike and Rick drove the route that his border guards patrolled.

It didn't take Ian long to figure out that the guys in the field needed directions from the drones that flew overhead.

They and their dogs made great teams. The dog handlers all took to Herman once their dogs allowed him to scratch them behind their ears. Their dogs showed them that Herman was OK. They commented that Herman was one of a handful of people that the dogs accepted.

Ian laughed and replied that his wife thought he was a dog too.

The team described how they went about their normal daily patrol. Their manner was professional, thorough, and very conscientious.

After learning about how the field teams were guided, Ian asked to tour the drone control office and understand how they interacted with the ground team.

Rick said the tour would need to be the next day around noon. He was joining Matt and Joe for his usual midweek breakfast at May's. He asked whether Mike would be there.

Mike answered in the affirmative and looked at Ian to see what his response would be.

Herman answered that he wouldn't miss it.

The next day after breakfast Mike and Ian followed Rick back to the Border Patrol offices. Rick led the way in and walked Ian and Mike through the normal observation shift and the communication with the border patrol vehicle surveillance and the dog patrol teams.

It was clear the drone handlers had the best vantage point to see almost everything. A mole on this team could easily provide the information that would misdirect those on the ground.

On the drive back, Ian asked Mike to check on the background of all the drone operators.

Ian again guided the conversation to Mike and his family.

Mike described his home as strategically located between the Middle School, where his youngest son and middle daughter attended, and the High school where his oldest son was now in his junior year.

The family church was just beyond the middle school. The family doctor was located across from the High School and a hospital was just a stone's throw north of the high school.

He and his wife belonged to a health club less than three miles away. Mike described it as a convenient arrangement for the entire family.

He had a large two story, five-bedroom home on a corner lot that faced third street and was blessed with a dead-end street to its right. That meant a quiet back yard and a street with almost no traffic on one side.

Mike made a point of mentioning the nine-foot interior ceilings of the house that kept the air conditioning bill reasonable. He liked the fact that the large size of the house and the relatively small size of the lot made the yard work reasonably easy and the entire package affordable.

Mike extended an invitation to Ian to a family grill out. He explained the grilling would happen out in the backyard, but because of the heat everyone would be taking shelter in the air-conditioned back patio.

Ian said he would love to meet his family and looked forward to the grill out.

Ian spent Saturday sleeping in late, taking a swim and working out. He took in a movie and spent some time reviewing the case.

Sunday morning early Ian took a walk-through downtown Phoenix. The heat of the day was building when he flagged down one of the few cabs and gave him Mike's address. He sat back and enjoyed the short ride out.

The grill out and meeting the family put Ian in a good mood. Then toward the end of the day Mike received a call. He beckoned Ian over and quietly shared the fact that the border patrol had lost a large group of border crossers but had seen a light grey or perhaps dirty white panel truck leaving the area.

Ian and Mike agreed to meet early before going to and figure out what to do before going to breakfast.

That evening Ian began to study the routes that he would choose if he were transporting illegal aliens and wanted to minimize his chances of getting caught. Based on the mileage of each of the two confiscated trucks that had been previously used Ian plotted various routes. He decided to check these routes with Matt and Bill at breakfast on Monday morning.

Ian met Mike at the office and suggested that they have breakfast at Mays. He had questions for both Bill and Matt.

Mike was especially interested in Ian's study on possible travel routes and wondered why his team had not done something similar.

Ian pointed out that he had no clue about travel in the region, but he didn't know what else to do so he was doing what he always did best. He created his own sandbox to play in and hoped there was no cat shit in it.

There seemed to be one route that best fit the miles. It also ended just shy of Interstate 40, which was a main East-West traffic corridor. Ian had used a red pen to trace Highway 80 north, to 75, to 78, to 180 then on to 32, 36 and finally 117. This brought both trucks very close to Interstate 40. It was a slow tedious route, but it certainly kept the trucks off the main thoroughfares.

Ian figured that it was probably around this area where a transfer to other modes of transport would be made. There could be may second leg routes depending on the mode of transportation that had been arranged. There were endless dispersal scenarios that Ian could think of.

Matt and Bill concurred on the route Herman liked best. They figured it was as good as any and asked what good knowing this would now do for those who had died.

Herman agreed that it did nothing for them, but he felt it might help to be ready for the next time. And he pointed out that Rick had let Mike know on Sunday that a white panel truck had left the border.

Ian decided to drive and feel out the route he had mapped. He figured his chances were very low of finding anything, but the drive would occupy him and give him time to decide on the next steps he needed to take.

He asked Mike if the office kept any cases of water handy and found out that indeed they had extra cases on hand. He asked that several cases be put in the trunk.

Mike said he would have one of his guys put it in the back of the car Ian was being issued and asked if Ian was expecting to find a truck load of people.

Ian replied that he had no clue, but he was going to be Boy Scout ready.

Ian walked out to the assigned car, checked the trunk, and threw in his small personal needs bag.

Ian left Phoenix and began what he decided was a scenic drive through the scraggly pine covered mountains surrounded by a wide skirt of sage, cactus and tumble weed stretch of barren desert. Ian encountered almost no traffic. An occasional car or truck going the opposite direction broke the otherwise monotonous drive.

He was thinking through what he had learned so far and almost missed what he was looking for. He was almost all the way to Interstate 40 when a white panel truck stopped on the side of the road caught his eye. He slowed down as he drove past.

He saw no one.

The truck seemed to be deserted. A red flag went up in Ian's shocked mind. Unbelievably it was the exact scenario he had imagined.

Ian decided to go back to the truck and take a closer look. He parked just past the truck on the opposite side of the road and carefully approached the truck. He looked out to the right of the truck to see if the driver was out in that direction. The underside of the truck was clear. It seemed the truck was deserted.

It was just not possible went through his mind.

He walked up to the cab and stepped up on the sideboard to look inside.

Almost immediately there was pounding on the panels from inside the back of the truck. He walked to the back of the truck. The doors were locked.

Ian pounded on the backdoor and in Spanish he told them to wait a moment. He would open the back doors.

The truck had a cross lug nut wrench but no straight bar. Ian went to his car and came back with the hockey stick style lug wrench most cars carried. The lock was a standard case quarter inch shank. It snapped on his first hard twist.

A swoosh of hot air from inside hit him as the doors came open. Ian was almost overwhelmed by the smell of sweat and urine. He was immediately angered by these conditions. The relief of finding everyone alive was the only thing that placated Ian. He helped those inside get out.

The people needed help and they needed water. Ian knew that his earlier premonition that caused him to ask for the two cases of water now confirmed why he was still alive today. He always seemed to have these premonitions.

Ian passed the water out and told everyone to drink slowly so they would not be sick.

He got everyone out and had them sit in the shade of the truck.

Ian saw a white van approaching slowly from the direction of Interstate 40. He took a bottle of water and went to the front of the panel truck. He stood leaning against the front of the truck. The heat of the radiator hitting his back added to the heat of the sun. He could feel the beads of sweat forming on his forehead.

The oncoming van stopped about twenty feet from the truck. Two men with guns drawn got out and approached him.

They asked what the hell Ian was doing letting the people out of the truck.

Ian calmly told them to take it easy and that he had stopped to see if he could help. Ian pointed to the engine compartment. He told them that he was a mechanic in Phoenix and just happened to be driving back from a job he had just finished. Ian went on to claim that he had fixed hundreds of engines of this type and that he could help them.

The taller of the two said they would fix their own truck and Ian should just get on his way.

Ian took note that the group along the side of the truck were now standing and quietly watching. The presence of the group seemed to distract the two gunmen.

The two had finally reached the distance when Ian could go into action. He waited until the two took their next step forward.

The taller of the two took the step forward that Ian had been waiting for. Ian threw his water bottle at him and took a long step forward. He deflected the gun hand with his left hand while at the same time stepping down hard on the arch of his right foot. He kept the gunman's body between him and his partner. The final stiff finger stab to his throat took him down.

As the taller gunman was just beginning to crumble, Ian delivered a round house kick to the second gunman's temple area and followed it with a downward fist blow to his nose. The second gunman fell down on his knees holding his nose with two hands and then toppled over. Both gunmen were out.

Ian quickly picked up the two guns and checked the two for any other weapons. Both were carrying large hunting style knives.

Ian threw the knifes back into the on-looking crowd.

He asked the on lookers to take off the men's boots and pants and to throw them both into the back of the truck.

Ian was surprised by the energy and enthusiasm the crowd displayed as they picked the two up and took off the articles Ian had specified. They literally threw them into back of the truck. There was a cheer when the doors were shut. It was clear that the two had earned the displeasure of the people they had left locked in the truck.

Ian would interrogate the two but first he had to disperse the people that were now looking to him for guidance.

2 Imelda

*E*lisa lay against her mother's side. She was hot and thirsty. She and her mother had been riding in the absolute black darkness in the back of a truck for a very long time.

The truck started jerking and then stopped.

When they had first jumped into the truck Elisa had been happy because they had escaped the patrol dogs. Her friends had told her the dogs ripped people apart and ate them. But now she was hot, thirsty, and really scared. She could not even see her mother's face, and the air smelled really bad. She kept her head on her mother's chest and listened to her mother's heartbeat. Her mother kept praying and singing, which really worried Elisa.

Imelda hugged her daughter. The heat was unbearable. They had not been given any water or provisions. She and the others in the group that were in the truck with her had crossed the border into the US during the night.

They had come through a hole cut in a fence as the guide brought them across the river and then they had jogged for about a half mile to where the truck was waiting for them.

Imelda When she picked up Imelda so the two of them would not be left behind, she had dropped her bag with all her valuables. They had all jumped into the back of the truck and the doors were shut. It was hot, and the ride was bumpy and bruising until they reached what must have been the highway. Then it was a long monotonous ride in the pitch-black interior of the truck.

The heat and the bad smell seemed to go up simultaneously. She hugged Elisa to her chest and said a quite prayer.

She was on the way to meet her husband in Cincinnati, Ohio. He told her he had a small place to live and was working for the state as a gardener in a local state hospital. They had agreed it was time for her to bring Elisa and come live with him.

Now as she sat in the back of the truck she wondered if their lives back in Oaxaca had been all that bad. Carlos and she had been friends since they were kids. Their families lived on adjacent small farms and did fairly well. They grew most of their own food and raised a few goats and sheep. Their chickens provided eggs and meat.

It was a simple life. It was a good life for a poor family. But it held little hope that the future would be any different than the past.

The two had married shortly after getting out of high school. Carlos went to work for a local building materials supplier. He got his pay partly in goods and a small amount in cash.

He got permission from both of their families to build a small home on the boundary property where the two farms came together.

Carlos and Imelda had sketched out a small single story two-bedroom home. A tiled entry hall split the home with one bedroom on each side. The bathroom and shower were on the left back corner. The kitchen was the biggest room in the house and featured a large table at its center. A window over the sink looked out to the outdoor cooking area.

Every day Carlos would bring home a few bricks or bags of cement. Every weekend the two would work at building the next part of their home. It took them almost a year to build their home. The two had worked together every evening. This was a fond memory for Imelda. They had grown closer together with each brick they cemented into the wall. Each was a gold brick that strengthened their love for each other.

There was a big party to celebrate the completion of the home. They moved in and immediately they felt a new surge of hope for the future. Imelda became pregnant only a few weeks later. Her pregnancy was another cause for celebration.

The next big event was the drilling of the well and then having electricity brought to the house. Each was followed by celebration.

Life was good.

Elisa was born in December. Dark brown eyes, a full head of black hair, blessed with all her fingers and toes, she was a perfect child. It was the most joyous of times. She was their Christmas baby.

Carlos was a consummate father. Always good with his work roughened but skilled hands, he made a crib by hand for Elisa and a rocking chair for her. Both were treasures Imelda cherished.

For a few years, their lives seemed to be going smoothly and making progress.

Then the economy went bad. Carlos lost his job. No matter how hard he tried he could not find another.

He was despondent and had a feeling of hopelessness. Their few chickens and small garden kept them from going hungry but there was no income and they had little money in reserve. Carlos was despondent and shared his feeling of hopelessness.

A friend of Carlos told him about working in the US and how several of his friends were up north and sending money home to their families. The jobs were not hard to get and if one lived economically the money was enough to send home and to save.

Shortly afterwards Carlos made up his mind to cross the border to the US. His friend's friend lived in Cincinnati and vouched that there were abundant jobs to be had.

Carlos experienced an easy trip. His crossing went smoothly, and he quickly made his way to Cincinnati. Once he arrived, he called back home and told Imelda how easy it had been. Only the border crossing itself had been somewhat challenging and scary, but the rest of the trip was no different than taking a trip into Mexico City. His calls and a few letters shared the various part time jobs of gardening or working on small construction projects. The money he sent home was more than enough for Imelda to live on and to provide some extras for Elisa.

Life on the farm was again good but Carlos was missing.

When he landed a permanent job, he asked her to come to Cincinnati. He felt the US offered a better chance for their family to get ahead. Elisa would get a good education and have the chance to go to college. Carlos was thinking ahead about what was good for his family.

Imelda shared her decision to go to Cincinnati with both sets of grandparents.

At first both grandparents asked her not to go. They understood the bleak future that staying in Mexico meant for Imelda, but they wanted to have their only granddaughter close at hand.

All of them saw how much both Imelda and Elisa missed Carlos and they then became supportive and wished her good luck. Imelda turned down their offer of money and instead left most of what she had saved with her mother.

She and Elisa were now into their second week of travel. Elisa had been especially afraid of the border crossing. They made the crossing with a group of about twenty people made up mostly of young men. Counting herself there were four women in the group. She was the only one with a child.

When border guards seemed to approach them with dogs, their guide told them to run as fast as they could to a white panel truck waiting for them. Imelda had dropped all her belongings, as she scooped up Elisa so she could run and keep up with the rest.

They all jumped into the truck and the doors were closed. The truck lurched forward and went speeding away. It was pitch black in the truck and everyone remained quiet. Someone with a cigarette lighter flicked it on and they all got a quick look around the empty truck. There was no water or food.

Imelda now had a new worry. She had no money, and she did not have a way to get to Cincinnati.

Occasionally there were some whispered conversations. Otherwise, there was only darkness and silence.

Imelda softly hummed some of Elisa's favorite songs. They were together and soon she hoped that somehow, they would get to Cincinnati.

Then the truck sputtered, shuddered, jerked and came to a stop. Everyone got ready to get out, but the doors did not open.

Fear slowly crept into Imelda's mind. She hugged Elisa to her and made a prayer to the Virgin Mary asking that the doors would open.

Someone pounded on the side of the truck. Another group kicked at the back door.

Imelda just kept praying.

It seemed they had been still for a very long time when suddenly the truck leaned as if someone was getting into the driver's side of the truck.

Almost everyone began pounding on the side of the truck walls and yelling at the top of their voices.

Imelda just kept repeating, "please open the door."

The rattling of the lock on the back door caused everyone to suddenly become silent.

Then in what Imelda considered the best bad Spanish she had ever heard; someone call out and let them know that he was going to open up the backdoor.

She knew it was not either of the two who had been driving the truck. They were Mexican and spoke perfect Spanish.

Imelda crossed her herself and thanked the Virgin.

As the doors opened, the people in the back rushed out. It was hot out in the sun but there was fresh air to breathe.

Imelda led Elisa out and into the shade that was on the desert side of the truck.

She was surprised to see a total stranger, a gringo, helping them.

She watched as he went to the trunk of the car across the road. He had two young men carry two cases of bottled water across the road.

He took the first two bottles and gave them to her and Elisa.

He kept a third for himself but did not open it.

Imelda had tears in her eyes as she thanked him.

Everything went silent as they heard a van was coming toward the front of the truck.

Imelda watched as the generous man that had opened the door went to the front of the truck. All he had was a bottle of water in his hands.

Two men got out of the truck. Imelda realized they had their guns aimed at the person that had freed her.

This time her prayer was for him.

It seemed that the person she was praying for had no idea about the danger he might be in.

Imelda moved behind the front left wheel of the truck and put Elisa behind her. She listened to what was being said.

Suddenly the man moved so swiftly that she almost missed what was happening. The two men with guns were down, moaning and bleeding. The strange man had both their guns and was asking the two be thrown into the back of the truck. He told the crowd to take of their shoes and pants before locking them in.

She was surprised to hear herself shouting when he asked for some help in throwing the two men into the back of the truck.

Imelda leaped up to help but she was pushed aside by the rush of several of the men. She suddenly realized that she did not like the two men on the ground. She had paid a lot of money and had been treated worse than a pig.

She wanted to give the stranger helping her a hug.

Imelda came back to her bleak reality. She was in trouble. She had no money. No clothes but what she had on. She was hungry, and she had a young daughter who was clinging to her in fear.

Her mind kept returning to one thought, "How was she going to get to Cincinnati? She went from a high at getting out of the back of the truck and getting water to an extreme low despair.

She once again said a prayer.

3 *Deliverance*

*I*an looked down the empty road toward the way he had driven out toward Interstate 40. He turned toward the Interstate and looked at another stretch of road in that direction. It was all empty and going one way as going the other. He had the two culprits locked in the back of the van and thirty or so people standing in the shade of the truck.

The day was coming to its peak temperature. He was sure it was more than one hundred degrees in the shade. The two in the back of the truck would already be feeling the much higher heat inside the truck. Ian would wait a little longer before he interrogated the two. They would be more willing to cooperate after exposure to the stench and to the oven like temperature.

He had to disperse the border crossers. Ian was not interested in turning the group in. He inquired about who could drive the van parked in front of the panel truck. Several hands went up. Ian picked the oldest of the volunteers who he took to be near his thirties to do the driving.

He then asked how many were expecting rides when they got to the interstate. He noted that most of the hands were in the air.

Most notable to Ian was that the women did not raise their hands. The woman with the young girl was hanging her head.

He figured she realized she was in trouble.

Ian inquired about the names of the women and of the young girl. The distress in the mother's voice made it clear to Ian that she needed help.

"I am Imelda, and this is my daughter Elisa. She is turning eight this year," Imelda spoke up. I had bus tickets to go to Cincinnati, but I lost my backpack and all my belongings when we had to run for the truck. The driver of the truck was to take us to the bus stop.

Imelda's plight helped Ian make up his mind.

He told the women they would ride in his car. They should continue standing in the shade until he got the men on their way.

The men all managed to squeeze into the van. It would be a hot ride, but it was only a short distance to the Interstate. The van made a U turn and went back toward the Interstate.

Ian walked back to the car and opened all the windows. He told Imelda to sit in front with Elisa and to relax while he went and asked the two in the back of the truck a few questions.

He walked back to the truck and picked up his tire iron. He walked around to the far side and poked several holes in the side wall.

Ian asked if they were still alive. There was an immediate plea for him to let them out. Ian said that it would continue to get hotter as the sun hit its peak. If they wanted out, they would have to tell him who they worked for.

He was met with silence.

He hit the side of the truck with his tire iron and said goodbye. He wished them a good life for as long as it could last.

Ian heard one of them say it was an official in the highway patrol. They did not have a name.

Ian replied that they would not live very long if he left, and he was leaving if they did not give him a name.

"Wait, Wait, we get our orders to rent a truck and where to go over the internet. We do as instructed. We pick up the border crossers and drive to the designated location. Once the border crossers are on their way, we return the rented truck. Our pay gets transferred into our bank accounts. We never see or talk with anyone.

"How do you know it is a high-ranking official in the Highway patrol," Ian asked.

When we were first recruited the person said that he had the cover of the highway patrol at the highest level.

Ian asked for their email names and wrote them down.

He next asked if they had been the drivers of the truck found with dead people in the back. He expected the denials they gave. He would check there whereabouts later.

Ian quickly verified the email names they had given him.

He then unlatched the door and told them to get out. He told them to walk toward Interstate 40. They were to walk there and disappear from the area.

They asked for their pants and boots.

Ian laughed and said that they had on what they were going to walk in. He had looked around and realized that the clothes had been taken by the men who had left.

As they began the walk the tallest one complained about his broken foot and crushed Adam's apple. The shorter one complained about his broken nose and the lump on the side of his head.

Ian replied that they had met the devil, and they should be happy to be alive and not down burning in hell.

Ian stood and watched them until they were at least a thousand paces down the road.

He put in a call to the Highway patrol to pick up the two men walking toward the interstate in their underwear. He instructed they be taken back to headquarters and held.

He then returned to the car. He started the engine and put the air conditioner on high and closed all the windows. Then he made a U turn and went toward the interstate.

The flashing red lights of multiple highway patrol cars surrounding the van and the men standing in a row with their hands up clearly showed the fate of the men who had driven up in the van.

Ian looked at Imelda and told her that the men would be processed, and many would be allowed to go to their US destinations. Some would be returned across the border.

Ian proceeded on and got onto the Interstate going east.

Imelda asked where Ian was taking all of them?

He replied that it would depend on what they told him. He asked for the names of the people who connected them to the border crossing guides and that they tell him where they were going. He was watching the three in the back. He repeated the question in Spanish.

They all started to talk at the same time.

Ian stopped them and asked Imelda to tell her story first.

Imelda assured Ian that it was not a gangster but a family friend who knew someone who could get her connected with a border crossing guide.

Ian made it clear he was not interested in any family friends. He described the scene of a truck just like theirs but full of people who had died of the heat. They had been discovered only a few weeks back. There was a mother, daughter and son all huddled together. They had died in her arms.

Imelda had tears in her eyes as she hugged Elisa and told him she was on the way to Cincinnati to meet her husband.

Imelda whispered thank you God. She wished she had her rosary.

Ian let her know that he would put her on a bus that would take her to her husband.

Each of the other three gave the names of their contacts in Mexico and where they were planning to go. It surprised Ian to learn that one was going to Minneapolis to meet other family members. One was on the way to Auburn, Maine to live with her best friend. And the last was on the way to Washington, DC where she had been offered a job at a local hotel.

Ian told them what was going to happen. They would spend the night at a nice hotel. They would have a pleasant evening meal at some family restaurant. He would buy each of them bus tickets to their destinations. Tomorrow they would get on their buses and make the remainder of the trip on their own

Imelda asked why he was doing this for them.

Ian explained that he did not always know why he did what he did, but he smiled and said that this time it was because Elisa smiled at him.

It was so true.

Ian never tried to reason why when he made these types of decisions. He figured someday he would either meet the devil or be standing at the pearly gates trying to explain his grievous sins.

Let's stop and get all of you some basic clothes to wear. Imelda, you, and Elisa go into Target and buy two outfits each and some shoes as well. Buy a small suitcase for each of you. And get anything else you need such as toothpaste and toothbrushes. Pay cash Ian said giving her enough money to cover the shopping.

"You three go separately to Sears, Kohl's and Burlington Clothes factory," Ian instructed the other three as he gave them cash as well.

Once they had departed, Ian dialed his support number and requested reservations at the Ambassador Suites, the bus tickets for each of the women and one thousand dollars in cash. He asked that everything be sent to the Hotel.

He did not want to buy the tickets at the bus station because it would make his activities too traceable, and he wanted enough cash to hand out.

Ian also called into the office to let Mike know that he had been on the road driving the routes he suspected the border crossers took. And had intercepted the truck. He let Mike know he would be back by noon the next day and that he wanted to interrogate the drivers of the panel truck.

Imelda and Elisa were the first to return. They walked toward the car pulling their very practical matching dark blue suitcases. They were smiling and talking to each other. It was great to see the two finally relaxed and happy. Elisa was wearing her new "just do it" sneakers.

Ian had a couple of throw away phones in the glove compartment. He took one out and handed it to Imelda. He instructed her to call her husband and let him know that she and Elisa were safe and on the way home. He told her not to say anything more than that and that once there she could tell him the whole story. He looked at Elisa told her to say hello but told her say anything either.

Ian could hear the happy ring in Carlos's voice as he talked to Imelda and Elisa.

Ian watched as the other three met each other on the sidewalk. They were chattering as they walked back to the car. Each had bought a different color roller board.

Ian stopped at an restaurant for a quick dinner. The endless salad was a hit. Everyone found something on the menu they liked. Elisa especially seemed to like the buttered bread sticks. It was clear that they had all been hungry.

One of the women asked why he was being so kind. Ian replied that sometimes good things happened, and they just needed to accept it and later they should be kind to someone else. He really did not have a good answer but in his mind, he linked his actions to the much darker and deadly actions he often took when solving problems.

Ian told them that they all had room reservations at the Ambassador Suites under names he had given them. They should pay cash. He instructed the three to go first, that they were friends returning from vacation, sharing one room and for the night they were Maria, Eli, and Fran. He told them not to talk too much and that they should just check in, go to the room, enjoy a good shower and catch a movie. He instructed them to stay in their room until morning.

He said that he would check in next.

Imelda and Elisa were to come in last. He said that their names were Angela and Justine and that they were on the way home.

He said they would all have breakfast at seven on the ground floor and told them to their evening.

Ian moved the car to a parking space and got out, took his overnight case that he carried in the trunk and headed for the lobby.

Imelda and Elisa were on the sidewalk coming in slowly behind him.

A shower and a cup of coffee, the evening news and he was ready for bed. Ian called home and talked with Lesley and let her know all was well. Hearing her voice and listening to her tell him about her day put him at ease.

The next morning, they all met for breakfast on the first floor.

Ian had already checked out. The clerk had handed him a grey envelope that had been dropped off for him. The bus tickets and money were inside.

The five looked totally refreshed and quite local in their new clothes. It was clear by their consumption that they really enjoyed their breakfast. Ian could tell Elisa was having the time of her life.

He knew that years later she would remember only the good part of her journey and would have to think hard about how frightened she had been only a few hours earlier.

Imelda was quiet. She was so relieved to be safe. She still found it strange to get the help that she was getting from a stranger. Her prayers had been answered.

He made sure everyone had checked out. They all enjoyed a long morning breakfast. Ian then led the way to the car. There he handed each their tickets and ten twenty-dollar bills. Elisa got her own ticket and her own ten twenty-dollar bills.

Each said gracias and asked how they could pay him back.

Ian told them that there was no way to pay him back but that someday they would be able to do something good for someone else. When that happened, they should do it. He told them that doing so would make them feel very good about themselves.

He knew it made him feel that way.

As she got out of the car at the bus station, Elisa asked if she could write to him.

Ian would be living in the same city, but he knew that it would not be safe for him to stay in contact with her. He lied and told her that he would keep in touch with her and gave her a hug.

He got back in his car and began his drive back to Phoenix. He was going to find out if there had been someone in the highway patrol office involved by the fact he would know by finding the two drivers alive.

231

<u>*4 The Devil and the Drivers*</u>

*I*an took the same route back as the one he had taken out from Phoenix. The white panel truck was gone. He had expected it to be.

As the miles clicked over, Ian was more certain of a high probability that there was a connection in one of the law enforcement agencies. He pondered how he might determine who that person might be.

He came to the conclusion that there needed to be a connection or helper in the border patrol organization. He was more confident in finding that person. His focus area was on the drone monitoring team. He thought that person might need help to coordinate their actions.

Ian arrived at the federal building and parked his car in the basement next to all the other non-descript government vehicles.

He decided first to find out what had happened to the group of people he had helped and then were caught at Interstate 40.

The sergeant on duty at the highway patrol desk looked at his computer screen and let him know that they had been sent to homeland security for the normal entrance processing. Each would have their day in court.

The sergeant went on to let Ian know that two of the people picked up were still in the holding cell. He chuckled and said that they had been picked up walking barefoot and only in their briefs. They had admitted to driving the panel truck that had hauled the border crossers away from the border. They wanted a lawyer and were threatening to sue because they claimed some policeman beat them up. They were in a sorry state and their feet were bleeding when they were picked up. He went on to share that they were to be transferred to the city jail because the city had jurisdiction since the two lived here in Phoenix. The police would be picking them up sometime in the afternoon.

Ian asked the sergeant not to let the transfer happen until he heard from captain Martin.

He let the sergeant know that he planned to return immediately afterwards meeting with the captain to talk with the two being held.

The sergeant told him good luck on getting them to talk. They have refused to talk until they got a lawyer.

Ian had doubted the two in the holding cell about some high-ranking official in the highway patrol being the leader. When Ian learned of the transfer to the city police a red flag went up.

The fact that the two had survived the night in highway patrol custody immediately transferred his suspicion as to where the higher contact resided to the city police.

He went to May's restaurant to get some coffee.

He approached Mathew's support, Marilyn, with her favorite cup of latte from May's and handed it to her as he walked past her and told her he had to talk to the boss.

She informed him that she was supposed to stop him but made no move to do so but instead took a sip of her latte and raised one eyebrow and said thanks. She knew she was not going to stop Herman.

Herman handed an angry looking Matt a cup of May's plain black coffee as he excused himself on the phone and hung up.

What the hell, I told Marilyn to keep everyone out. Then he stopped.

"Thanks, I suppose you bribed your way in with a latte for Marilyn. What's up?" Matt said as he took his coffee. He was surprised that he was getting to like Herman.

Ian apologized for his disruption but came right to the point that someone in the Phoenix police department was involved in managing the transport of the border crossers.

He went on to explain that the Highway Patrol had the two drivers of the transport in a holding cell. They were scheduled to be picked up by someone from the police department in the afternoon.

Ian then put forward the theory that the two would never reach the city jail alive but would be killed during their escape attempt.

Matt made the comment that he had just started to like him and now he came in with this story.

He wanted to know how Ian could possibly have gotten such information since his department had tried to question the two and had gotten nothing from them.

He went on to say that Ian did not seem to be such a trusting person that the two would just volunteer the information to him.

Ian gave a small laugh. He shared the fact that he had locked the two up in the back of the panel truck and threatened to keep them there until they cooked to death. It was hot enough that they gave him just enough information. He had then released them.

Your men picked them up along the road soon after. You saw and treated their condition. That was also my doing.

Matt simply said Oh! That explains their police brutality claim.

"So how do you figure it is somebody high up in the Phoenix police department and not someone in the Highway Patrol. Why not me," Matt inquired?

"Well, the two in the holding cell informed me that someone, high up in the Highway Patrol department had hired them. Since they are still alive today, I figured it wasn't you or anyone in your organization," Ian said with a smile.

"What if they had died during the night," Matt asked?

Herman smiled and said that then instead of bringing coffee he would have entered to arrest him.

Matt chuckled and commented that the coffee tasted even better.

Ian pointed out that the two in the holding cell had no clue as to the actual person or persons who hired them might be. They got their orders and their pay via the internet. They could easily have been misdirected on purpose.

"What kind of help are you asking for," Mathew inquired?

"I want the two men to wear a wire and I want your department to follow the city police transport and listen in on the conversation that goes on during transport."

Matt first defended Bill, the chief of police. And said that there was no way he would be involved and do such a thing. He did not need money and had grandchildren that he spent all his free time with. Matt said he thought that the idea was crazy.

Ian replied that he did not think it was Bill but asked that he be kept out of the loop in the near term. He was sure that the culprit had to be someone Bill trusted. Ian pointed out that they would know almost immediately if there was someone in the sheriff's office and at breakfast tomorrow Ian would personally apologize to Bill if he was wrong.

Matt said he would support him, but he did not think that the two in custody would agree to wear a wire. If they did wear a wire and made it safely to the city jail, he would have hell to pay with Bill.

Ian agreed and again said he would put himself in front of that train if he was wrong. He said he would not have asked if he did not believe he was right.

Matt was under the impression that the two would not agree to wear a wire. They have been stonewalling ever since they arrived, and insisted they wanted a lawyer.

Ian replied that he would convince them to wear a wire. And asked that Matt call Mike and have him come over.

Ian walked back downstairs to the desk sergeant. He asked to be taken to the holding cell.

The desk sergeant stopped in amazement as the two inside the cell jumped up and stood up at attention. He looked at Ian and commented that there was something about him that these two respected. The two had so far refused to stand because the condition of their feet.

Ian approached the cell and simply said hello. He asked about their claim that they had been mistreated. He asked if there was some complaint, they would like to share with him?

They both shook their head to indicate no. The strained look on their faces almost made him laugh.

The sergeant commented that the two had been a pain when the highway patrol tried to question them. They had refused to even talk. You say hello and they immediately stand at attention.

Ian had made a point of learning the sergeant's name. He now let Bob know that he needed a few moments alone with the two. He asked for about ten minutes. After that the folks who would outfit the two with wires should come in to do so.

Bob commented that it was a little unusual but said that if he needed anything he should just press the buzzer on the wall.

Ian told the two in the cell to sit down and listen. He asked them if they knew that they were being transferred to the city jail. They said they had been told that.

Ian asked if they believed they would live to see the inside of the sheriff's jail cell.

Eduardo, the tall one, asked Ian who he was.

Manuel the shorter one reminded him that than Ian claimed to be the devil.

Ian replied that he certainly was willing to play the part of the devil but in their case, he was trying to save their lives. He pointed out that he was interested in the person or persons at the top of the ladder that paid them.

He told them they would be dead by late in afternoon if they did not cooperate. Whoever the people in the police department may be, they will kill you as you try to escape.

Eduardo asked why they would try to escape. They had received good treatment so far.

Ian told them they would be taken somewhere to the edge of the city and told to go home. After they stepped out of the police van, they would be shot in the back with the cover story that they were trying to escape.

Ian let the silence stand. Then he stood and reached for the buzzer, and he told them good luck getting to heaven.

Manuel asked what they needed to do.

Ian informed them that they needed to wear a hidden microphone so he could hear what the men picking them up were saying. He said he expected those transporting them would probably be friendly and tell the two that they were going to be dropped off outside the city limits. They would be instructed to go home, get their stuff and to move on. They will tell you they will send instructions to you later. Or they will tell you some other similar story. However, when they let you out of the police van, they will shout out "stop" and as you run or turn around to look at them, they will shoot you.

How do you know this Eduardo asked?

Ian replied he would do something similar if he were the person in the police department managing the operation.

Eduardo then said they would cooperate. He wanted to know how Ian would help them afterwards.

Ian replied that they would be held accountable for their deeds, and they faced up to thirty years in jail, however he would make sure they got the best possible deal for their cooperation and would probably only get a fraction of that time. He would also recommend a minimum-security prison.

Eduardo looked at Manuel. The two were silent for a moment and then agreed to wear the wire.

Ian gave a nod and let them know that they would soon be outfitted with the microphones.

Ian left the cell as the officers that were there to outfit the two with the wires walked in.

He went to the sergeant and asked where he would take the two if he was planning to kill them and make it look like and escape.

The sergeant gave a good chuckle and smiled. He went on to explain that the scenario that Ian had just described was the talk at almost every beer drinking outing that the local law enforcement held.

One group had the scenario playing out somewhere south of East Dobbins Road out on South Central Avenue. Another group talks about going out on the 303 or the 74 west of I 17. A third group talks about going out on 87 north. He made the point that it was all drink and all talk.

He then made the point that almost any short drive outside the city would do. There were many secluded out of the way places.

The sergeant asked if he had passed the test.

Ian pointed out that looking at the city map he figured the police van should go southeast down North West Grand Avenue. Ian was trying to figure out where it was most likely to go if the police van deviated from that route.

The sergeant put his finger on the map and said he would take them out on that road.

Ian asked the sergeant to make sure that the drivers of the city police van did not know what was going down.

He was pleased to hear the sergeant exclaim that if there were any crooked cops in Phoenix, he wanted them caught and punished.

5 A Short Ride

*I*an walked slowly up the stairs. He could hear the coon dogs yelping as they got the scent of their prey. He could see the stars overhead as his gas head lantern lit the way before him. He could feel the adrenaline rush. He was closing in for the kill. His adrenalin level was at its peak.

Ian knew that it was only a matter of time. He realized he did not know how many people worked for Mike. By now Mike should be in Matt's office. Matt had mentioned he would have his team ready to go. Ian needed at least four different cars to follow the police van. He did not want the driver to notice he was being followed.

Matt was sitting with Mike discussing the logistics of moving the various cars along the direction the city police transport van would take. Mike was in control of four cars and the chief said he had as many.

Ian asked Matt to be in charge of positioning the eight vehicles and that he would just be along for the ride. He also requested that the people in all the vehicles be in street clothes.

Matt gave a small laugh. He said the sergeant downstairs figures you are the one in charge of everything that is going down and he said to help or get out of the way.

Ian looked at Matt and Mike. He could see that they too had the adrenaline rush going. He suggested that a quick lunch would help all of them.

During lunch Ian kept the conversation on family and events going on in the city. He wanted to keep the focus away from the coming action.

At three the dark blue van with Phoenix City Police painted on the sides pulled into the State Trooper's pick-up area. The shackled, Edwardo and Manuel were led out and put into the back. As per protocol seat belts were put on before the doors were closed.

Ian watched as the van went down toward North West Grand Avenue. It was headed in the right direction. He wondered if he was wrong.

A few moments later a call came in letting them know that the van had turned off Grand Avenue and was headed south down 19th Avenue.

Ian was listening in on the conversation that was going on in the city police transport van. The conversation with Edwardo and Manuel was almost verbatim to what Ian had told them they would hear.

He was sure the two were now paying very close attention to what was going on.

The transport turned east on West Dobbins. It appeared that Ian would be buying Bob, the sergeant at the desk, a beer. Bob had said that the southern scenario would be the one he would choose.

Ian listened as Matt instructed three of the cars to head south on South Central. He positioned two cars north of the intersection.

The cars tailing the van kept switching so that they would not be discovered.

Matt and Ian were following behind all of them as Matt directed the flow of the cars like a chess master playing in a tournament.

The van made the expected right turn and headed south on South Central avenue.

Matt instructed the three lead cars to go just past where South-Central crossed Phoenix South Mountain Park. He was counting on the fact that the park provided the right conditions for the planned killing.

Matt had all the cars closing in from behind. His car was up front.

Ian continued listening to what was going on in the van. The van drove into a secluded area at the entrance to the park and came to a stop.

The tailing highway patrol vehicles parked, and everyone ran out to surround the city police van. It seemed to him they were generating a hell of a racket. Ian was surprised they had not been discovered.

Ian was standing by a tree directly behind the van. He did not need his headset to hear Eduardo and Manuel being told to get out and find their way home.

Ian heard the escape call going into the city police dispatch office. The two transport policemen were just raising their guns to fire when he stepped out and shouted that they were under arrest and for them to put their guns down.

The two foolishly turned and fired at him. He took one bullet in the chest, but the other shot missed. He knelt and returned fire. He was sure they were wearing bullet proof vests like himself, so he shot each of them in the leg to get them down.

Since he was sure they were wearing bullet proof vests like himself, he shot both of them in the chest. He wanted them alive, but he wanted them to feel the pain he was going to feel from the bullet that had hit him.

Matt and Mike rushed over to Ian. They were amazed that the forty-five-slug embedded in the vest had not knocked him down.

They were more amazed that Ian had taken down the other two in such a fashion that they would live to be prosecuted.

Ian knew he would have a large chest bruise accompanied by an ache once the adrenalin rush subsided but at the moment his adrenaline was covering any pain.

Mike took over the scene. An ambulance was on the way to take the two wounded policemen to the hospital. He assigned two of his agents to stand guard over the two policemen going to the hospital.

They were instructed to only let himself, Matt, or Ian in.

Ian asked to have a word alone with the two he had shot.

Ian walked over to the two who were still laying on the ground. He let them know that he knew they had help back in the city police department. They needed to make a choice to save their skin or get the maximum time of around thirty years for shooting an FBI agent and they would get the maximum time for being accessories to the death of thirty people in the back of the van discovered a few weeks ago.

Ian waited for a count of thirty. OK, keep quiet, it's your funeral. I am sure those above you will make sure you never get to talk. They will transfer your money in the offshore bank accounts to their own and freeze you out. Then they will make sure you never get to trial.

Ian watched the surprised look on their faces. It had just occurred to them that they might be killed.

Ian was standing to leave when he was asked about the deal. They would give him information for a good deal.

Ian got back down on one knee. He told them it would be a deal that kept them alive, off death row and perhaps an assignment to a low security prison. He told them they would go to jail and would serve some significant time but they would stay alive.

The two looked at each other then asked what Ian wanted to know.

Ian told them he wanted the name of the top guy.

They both whispered the name Bradley Peterson.

Ian said thank you and stood up. He looked over at one of the agents and told him to read them their rights and stay with them in the ambulances. Guard them well and keep them alive and arrange lawyers for them.

One of the highway patrol officers asked what to do with Eduardo and Manuel.

Matt responded that the two should be taken back to the station and put back into the holding cell. He would deal with them at a later time.

Matt and Mike approached Ian. They wanted to know the name that the two policemen had given him.

Ian watched Matt as he gave out the name of Bradley Peterson.

Matt was surprised and said so. He commented that Bradley was second in command and that he was considered next in line to take over the sheriff's office.

Matt said he would give Bill a call and tell him to isolate Bradley and not let him destroy any records. Damn this is not going to be pretty Matt continued.

Ian was ready for the killing blow.

He suggested they all go to Bill's office and confront Bradley together. Ian made a call to his help number and requested a quick rundown on the finances of Bradley Peterson.

As the three arrived at the city police station, Ian received a call back on the finances for Bradley. Bradley was living very well for someone making one hundred thousand dollars a year. So far there seemed to be no indication of anything unusual in his bank accounts. They were not sure where he had gotten the money for a the very high-level life style he was living.

Ian told the group to check for transactions with any offshore account.

Bradley was sitting in Bob's office when the three walked in. Bob immediately commented that the request he had fulfilled was very unusual and he hoped there was a very good reason.

Ian looked at Bradley and formally put him under arrest for conspiracy against the US government.

There was silence in the room.

Ian was acting as if the case was clear and complete. He went on to list the fact that Bradley had aided and abetted the crossing of thousands of illegal aliens. It was most likely that he would be indicted for the deaths of more than thirty people found in the back of a panel truck, perhaps both trucks. He informed Bradley that he had been identified by two of his participating members who had turned state's evidence.

He asked Bradley what he had to say?

Bradley replied that the charges were preposterous. He refused to say anything until his lawyer was present.

That's fine, the FBI is already in the process of confiscating your computer and all your records, your secretary's computer and records, your associate's computers, and records. They have also entered your home and secured your home computer and any records you had there.

The FBI has also moved to freeze all your offshore bank accounts.

Your cooperation would be useful, but I prefer you refuse so that you get the death penalty, Ian continued as he leaned in almost nose to nose to Bradley.

Ian did not have most of the information he had just rattled off but he was in the mood to play poker and go for the winning hand via a bluff.

Bradley stood up and said he would consult with his lawyer and got up to leave.

Ian blocked his way and asked whether he had understood that he was under arrest and that his lawyer would need to come to him. Meanwhile he would cool his heals behind bars.

Ian turned to the two police officers standing in the room and told them to handcuff Bradley and read him his rights. The two looked at each other and finally one of them took his handcuffs and put them on Bradley. The other read Bradly his Miranda rights.

Ian turned to Bill and asked him if any of his officers had left early today. Whoever left is probably one of the guys working in dispatch. Ian went on to conjecture that there would be four or five individuals involved.

Ian's phone rang, and he held up his hand to stop the two police officers that were escorting Bradley out.

He went into an excited conversation and commented how much easier it was going to be to wrap up the investigation. He went on to thank the person on the line for making the connection to the offshore accounts happen so quickly. Ian instructed the person online to contact Mike Lancaster in the Phoenix office as soon as the bank accounts were secured.

Everyone in the room heard Ian's end of the conversation. The person on the other end wondered what was going on. He had been ready to tell Ian that it would take a while to identify and track down the offshore accounts.

Ian went on to comment how much easier it was going to be having made the link to the offshore accounts. Looking directly at Bradley he commented that it would have been smarter to use different offshore banks.

Ian walked over to Bradley and put his lips close to his ear and whispered, "if you don't talk, you won't live to see morning. I am an assassin sent to eliminate any obstacle to the resolution to this problem and I have just been cleared to assassinate you. If you talk you live."

Ian then pulled away only far enough to stare directly into Bradley's eyes. Then he turned and sat on the edge of Bob's desk.

Ian asked Bradley if he had anything to say.

"Alright, I am involved but Sam Henderson has been the mastermind of the operation. I provided a shield for the operation," Bradley confessed.

Ian was pleased with Bradley's reaction. Ian's threat had been real.

Ian turned to Mike and asked him to have a couple of his agents document Bradley's confession. They were to take down everything he knew about the operation and its finances. Have the remainder of those involved in the operation picked up.

Mike commented that the offshore bank link had really been found very fast. He had never heard of being able to track money so fast.

Once Bradley was out of the room, Ian let everyone know that the call had been to inform him that it would take a couple of days to a few weeks to track the accounts and that it would probably be impossible to tell where in the US the funds were coming from or going to. They needed more information from this end.

Everyone in the room agreed with Mike that it was one hell of a bluff. They all agreed that Ian was barred from their Saturday poker games.

Ian let that stand. He knew that it was his death threat that had tipped the scale.

He looked around and commented that they were almost done.

When asked what remained, Ian pointed out that someone in Homeland Security had to be involved. The successes of the crossings were not an accident. The person or persons involved were as guilty of the deaths of two truckloads of people as the driver and those arranging the border crossings.

6 Securing the Border

*A*rt sipped on his Black Russian watching his young bikini clad companion diving, swimming across the pool then walking sexily back to the low diving board and doing it again. She was on her third round, and he was on his third drink. He figured that they were both about to change what they were doing. He knew that she would stretch out on a beach towel and spend most of the afternoon working on her tan. He was going to go into his office and work on finding the next weak person that he would recruit to help him in making sure his clients had a way to smuggle their clientele into the US.

He knew that he was living the high life, but he wished he could be doing so in New York City versus in Mexico City. He had fond memories of his early years in the Bronx. He still had many friends in the mafia's family business.

He unfortunately was a wanted man there. He had disciplined one of his collection clients a little too severely and had killed him. He had fled the state and later the country.

His boss in New York had put him in contact with one of the top lieutenants of the Sinaloa cartel. That introduction had opened the door to a relationship that had enriched him beyond his expectations. From the start he had been given access to the money that let him bribe and corrupt the protectors of the realm while at the same time he received a rewarding cash flow into his bank account.

It was not long before he was able to buy the home where he had now lived for several years. They had been good years that saw him make friends with many of the cartel's members. He was generous with his parties but kept them low key, which pleased the cartel leaders.

He got a monthly percentage of the money made by smuggling people north into the US. He never questioned the amount or even kept track of it. He focused on making sure that the crossings were facilitated and kept open as agreed to.

His mother, bless her soul, always told him that he would be successful, but he was sure that she would be surprised that his success would be in Mexico and not in New York City. She had always encouraged him and told him he would be as good as his father. He knew that he currently was about ten times as successful as his father had ever been. He had more money and more influence than his father had ever had.

Today he was reviewing the situation along the border. He had one reluctant player that was reacting to the news of the people that had died in the transport that had been abandoned in the middle of the desert. He personally had put out his feelers to see if the two drivers could be identified and eliminated. He had been reassured by his cartel contacts that it was in the works and only a matter of a very short time. He knew that the kind of news coverage that truck was getting was very bad for business. It made everyone un happy.

The word was out that drivers should know that the cartel would take care of them even if they were arrested.

He needed to do some repair work with the folks in the US border patrol that he had under his wing. He booked his flights and got ready for his very early morning flight.

He left from Mexico City at six in the morning and by noon he was in his favorite restaurant in Nogales for lunch. He sat enjoying his steak as he thought through how he was going to handle the situation.

He had gotten the hint of a problem from the scheduler, who he thought of as a pompous ass but who was easy to manage because he was in it for the money.

The potential problem was with the person that he actually liked but who was too emotionally connected to the plight of those trying to get into the US. The deaths of the people in that deserted truck had put him over the edge. His personal guilt was weighing heavily on him.

Art figured that he would need to use the threat of bodily harm to keep him in line. He would offer money as well, but he figured that money alone would not work. He decided that a missing bodily part of the loss of an eye would be the threat he would use.

Once lunch was over, he called for his driver who he used when making the trip. It was a short drive to Sasabe.

Sasabe, in Arizona was the actual location where he made contact with his border patrol people. He had purchased and had the interior of an old home there remodeled. It was literally next door to the bar where he connected with his border patrol people. He used a fake passport to cross over and after getting situated in his house he would walk over to the bar where he usually had dinner and watched some sports show until his contacts came in.

The young women, there were usually only a couple, appeared to be of Mexican or Indian heritage and usually approached the few young men that came in for drinks. He had come to recognize several of them and always bought them a drink.

He had made the trip because his drone operator had disobeyed a requested diversion and had cost them the crossing of a group of paying customers. He needed to get him back in line because he had to get that group across and on their way.

He was now also looking to activate his back up that he had been paying for more than a year. The cost of a backup was minimal, and he considered it a drop in the money bucket. He did not want to have two people active in the same location. He hoped to rectify the situation and hoped that the backup might get a change of assignment to some other location along the border.

He was nursing, a white Russian, when, Josh, his drone operator came in. He knew he was facing a person who had a very guilty conscious when the drink he chose was a plain sparkling water, when in the past it had always been a Margherita, no salt.

He listened as Josh spilled out his heart-felt sorrow about the truck load of people that had died such an inhumane death in the back of that truck in the desert. He confessed that the scene of the mother holding her two children to her breast was incised into his brain. He could not get it out of his mind and every day and night he saw it.

Art sympathized and said he understood the anguish. He felt bad for the people in that truck but for him it was due to two drivers who had abandoned their post. A sorry state of affairs but so was life. He then put down the hammer and threatened Josh with bodily harm if he ever broke his promise of doing as asked. He waited a moment and then offered the honey with a fifteen percent raise in the reward.

Josh shook his head, took a long drink and agreed to do as instructed. He thanked Art for the increase in the money but reminded him that he did not take the money but was having it sent to several charities and asked him to make sure they all got an even increase.

That reminded Art why Josh was one of his favorite people that he had corrupted. He thought of Josh as an ethically corrupted person. He nodded and said that he would see that the increase would be evenly distributed.

A day later he had a similar meeting with Ethan, the schedular for the patrol dog team. Ethan was his pompous self. Art thanked him for his heads-up warning and rewarded him with a five percent reward increase and told him to keep up the good work. He had contemplated not giving him anything but had decided against that. It was business and he let the percentage amount reflect his personal taste or distaste for the individual.

The next day he left and returned to his home in Mexico City.

7 The Scheduler

*E*than watched as Bradely met two men who arrived just before noon and after a brief conversation lead them into the building. He made it a point to walk out and go past the three and say good morning. The older white-haired person was dressed casually whereas the younger one looked like he was formally dress to impress someone who would decide whether to hire him. He stopped long enough to watch them go into Bradley's office. He wondered what was going on. The next day was scheduled for the crossing of the next group of border crossers. He hoped that it had nothing to do with that. He did not need his smoothly organized world to be disrupted.

He figured he was one of the luckiest guys in the world. He had grown up in one of the most beautiful areas in the US and seen what he considered the five wonders of the world all in the state where he had been raised.

In his youth he had walked the same trail as Lewis and Clark and had white water rafted there.

He had visited the Little Big Horn where the Battle of Little Bighorn was fought and where Custer died fighting several thousand Lakota, Cheyenne, and Arapaho warriors. He figured he was smarter than Custer and he would have defeated the Indians.

He and his parents had hiked through the Bighorn area and had been lucky enough to spot three Bighorn sheep. He had run toward them, and they had taken several leaps and run away.

As a scout he had taken many hikes through the Montana Rockies. Hikes that he figured were some of the best hiking in the world.

One vacation was spent in Glacier National Park hiking, camping and swimming in one of the coldest lakes he could remember. He had continued the swimming even though he came out blue each time.

In college he met, dated and married a beautiful woman and now had a family of four with one girl and one boy. His wife was a great cook and great at getting the family involved in the community.

He had become an ordained Evangelical minister and currently presided over a congregation of three hundred people. He really enjoyed delivering the sermons and watching the perishers kneeling down in front of him.

What he considered his one failing was his inability to find a job that fit his status. He had interviewed with all the large financial companies as well as the prestigious banks. He failed to understand why he had not received any offers.

The one offer he did receive came from the US border patrol organization with which he had interviewed on a lark.

His current role as a team scheduler for the border guards and their dogs was challenging but he knew that it was well below his true potential. He should be somewhere several levels above the position of his current boss, Bradley.

He felt great about his finances and was sure they were in great shape.

He had his government salary that came in just above six figures.

Surprisingly his salary for being the primary minister in his church was almost equal to the government salary. He had not realized that ministers made as much as they did.

He had been recruited by some Mexican cartel to adjust the border guard schedule to create holes in the coverage allowing the coyote guides to bring groups of people into the US without having to face the security patrols. The income from it was variable since he got paid for each group that made it through. There had been several months where that income was well above the sum of his other two incomes.

He justified that part of his behavior and correlated it to his role as minister to improving the life of the people that got into the US and besides it didn't hurt anyone.

Until recently everything along the border worked like clockwork. The hiccup had been the group of people that had died locked in the back of a truck out in the desert. He figured it was the cost of taking that kind of risk. They, not he had made that choice, so his conscience was clear.

He became aware that there was another person that was very emotionally affected by that situation. He had called the tip line that his cartel handler had given him and let him know about the situation. He didn't want some bleeding heart to ruining a great thing.

He figured that at the upcoming meeting with his handler he would get recognized for tipping him off and would likely get a hefty reward.

Meanwhile he made sure to adjust the scheduling and placement of the key ground teams so that a clear corridor was available to get people across the border at the designated times.

He thought about the meeting going on in Bradley's office and felt sure that none of them would have a clue how the border crossers were getting across the border. He figured that none of them were that smart.

It was not complex, but it was invisible unless someone was able to correlate all the times and the placement of the border guard teams.

He was sure his life was set and the only thing he had to worry about was figuring out how to get promoted to the right level.

8 Drone Operator

*I*t all started one evening as he sat watching the Arizona Diamondbacks at the sports bar. Trey was approached by a man that introduced himself as Sam.

Sam had done his homework and knew Trey was sympathetic to the plight of the border crossers. He proposed a working relationship that offered a little extra money and a lot of personal satisfaction of helping people get to their dream. All he had to do was to misdirect the border patrol he was guiding. It would only take a few minutes, and no one would ever know. He pointed out that those entering the US were all fleeing from some bad people and were trying to better their lives.

The statement, "no one would ever know" alarmed Trey. How did Sam know so much about him? Trey replied that he would think about it.

A few weeks went by, and Trey had almost forgotten about the offer. Then he was on duty as a group of crossers refused to stop when confronted by the border guards.

They scattered and began to run and one of the guards pull out his gun and began to fire. Two to the crossers were hit. One was just wounded in the leg but a young boy in his early teens died on the scene.

Trey had watched the entire confrontation from his drone camera.

That incident made up his mind that he wanted to help the border crossers.

That weekend Sam again made contact with him at the sports bar.

Since that time, Trey had been aiding in the crossings by miss-positioning the guards.

This had been several years ago, and the operation ran smoothly and Trey felt that he was actually doing good.

Then he saw the news report about the dead border crossers piled in the back of a panel truck. He vowed he would not misdirect the border guards again. He knew that most border crossers who were trying for a better life in the US would be sent back. Those who truly were seeking asylum in fear of their lives would be processed and get their day in court.

He had played god and at least fifty people were dead.

He was not in it for the money and did not even bring money up when he was recruited. When finally asked about money, he inquired about the amount. It was to be two thousand a month. Trey agreed that is was significant, but he personally did not need or want it.

Trey pushed a piece of paper across the table to Sam. There were three organizations on it: Red Cross Relief Fund, United Appeal, and Catholic Social Services. He bargained for more by asking that each organization get a thousand dollars each month and that a confirmation post card be sent to him.

Sam readily agreed to the arrangement. He would have paid double that amount if he had been asked.

The redirecting went on smoothly until the abandoned truck with all the bodies had made the news. Trey was shocked and wondered if he had contributed to the deaths of the people. In his mind he was sure that he had.

Two trucks abandoned in the middle of the desert. The sun making the metal skin of the panel truck's metal exterior hot enough to fry an egg. People abandoned to die in the suffocating oven like heat. Humans so desperate that they broke their bodies against the backdoors in an attempt to break out. Humans so desperate that their fingernails ripped out in their attempt to claw their way out.

These were constant elements of Trey's nightmares. But the scene of the two dead children being lovingly held to their mother's dead chest played in both his sleep and daylight cycles. He could not shake the vision and the knowledge that he was part of putting those people through the hell of their last few hours of their lives.

Trey knew he was on the verge of a mental breakdown. He loathed himself. He had succumbed to the lure of easy money for helping those poor border crossers. He truly was sympathetic to their cause. He now believed he had made a deal with the devil. He had sold his soul for a small bag of gold. He could not forgive himself.

He went to the bar several times hoping to make contact with Sam. But it never happened.

The reality of his situation hit Trey hard. He took vacation and drank himself into a stupor for two weeks.

He vowed he would not misdirect the border guards again.

He had played god and at least fifty people were dead.

Trey returned to work and followed his conscious for the following week. Then the signal for misdirection came into him.

He ignored it and the group coming across was apprehended.

He got a call at his home that night. He was told that if he missed the next misdirection signal, he would lose the sight of his left eye and the loss of one finger. If he did as he was told, he would get a ten percent bonus for each event.

Trey immediately understood that he was indeed working for the devil, and he was in a trap. He would suffer dearly for not following orders.

He wrote down the phone number from which the threat had been made. He did not know how to trace it to a source but a friend of his probably could.

Trey imagined finding the culprit and taking some sort of action to eliminate him.

He realized immediately that he did not have the courage to follow through. He knew he was being threatened by one of the cartels in Mexico.

He could accept them killing him. He deserved being killed. He could not imagine or accept the torture they were threatening.

Two days later he again got the signal to misdirect a specific border security team.

Trey diverted the border guards just to the west of where the crossing was to occur. The truck was parked only a mile from the boarder in a small ravine. It was visible from the air but the team on the ground did not see it as they passed only a few hundred yards away.

Trey complied but it came to him that someone else was also on the take. Each time the misdirection was targeted at a specific team and at a specific time. He had never thought about this key fact. Someone else in the organization who knew the schedule and location of the security teams had to be involved.

Trey began keeping track of which schedulers were on duty on the days he got the misdirection signal.

Again, Trey came to the realization that when he figured out who it was, he was not sure what he would do.

He wondered if he could leave the region and not be found.

A few days later the FBI toured the drone control facility. Trey listened as the supervisor explained the interaction of the drone operators with the various border patrol teams.

He figured his days were numbered. It was clear to him that the older FBI agent was in charge. He listened intently and asked the kind of questions that made it clear he understood how easily it would be for a drone operator to misdirect the action on the ground.

Trey thought about the old saying about being between a rock and a hard place. He figured he was between hell and if extremely lucky a long term in jail if he could avoid a death sentence.

At this point jail seemed to be the safest place to be. Trey thought about his complicity and the thought of a death sentence silenced him.

Trey succumbed to drinking himself asleep each night. He awakened in the morning to his nightmares. His work life was miserable. He barely ate. He was a mess.

Trey knew that the noose around his neck was tightening. He did not know how much longer he could take his self-inflicted pressure.

He made a point of documenting everything he knew about the situation.

He had made up his mind. He was going to take his own life. It was the only pain free way to escape the situation he was in.

He wondered if his parents would understand. He was their only child. He took the time to write them a letter explaining his situation and said he loved them and hoped they would forgive him.

All that remained was to work up the courage to do it and he knew that deep inside he was a coward.

He was at work and in the process of again misdirecting a field team of border guards when he again observed the FBI agent come into the Border Security office.

Trey immediately knew what he was going to do.

First, he walked over to the shredder and put in the suicide letter to his parents.

9 Closure

The several-hour ride to the Homeland Security offices somewhere out in the desert provided Mike and Ian time to talk.

Mike asked what Ian had whispered to Bradley to get him to confess so fast.

Ian shared that he had reminded Bradley that it was going to be a long night and he was not going to have to give up his belt or tie, but much could happen to him before the sun came up. Bradley's imagination did the rest. Ian left out the part where he told Bradley he was the assassin sent out to kill whoever was behind the truck incident.

The drive through the bleak desert terrain of patches of tumble weeds, cactuses and some dry looking grasses seemed to compliment the stones, blowing dirt or maybe brown sand and a wide dead looking terrain. The sky was cloudless. Ian figured it was too hot for any moisture to rise and condense. He wondered when the last rain had been.

He was glad to let Mike do the driving since it gave him time to reflect.

He relaxed and concentrated on how they would flush out the guilty party or parties at the Homeland office. Ian suspected that there was more than one person involved. He expected at least one person to be a drone operator. Such a person would be able to misguide the group personnel, so the border crossers could pass by, but timing was a key factor. That meant someone scheduling the teams on the ground was most likely to be involved.

They were to again meet with Tom Hemsley, the station supervisor. Ian hoped Tom was not involved. It would really be a bad situation if he were.

Tom was standing by to receive the FBI agents coming to meet with him. He had worked with Matt and Bill and had attended a cookout where his family and their families had shared a picnic table. Their kids had played and now his kids were always asking when there was going to be another police picnic in Phoenix. He had met Mike the FBI regional leader at that picnic.

On the other hand, the FBI agent that was currently helping Mike, scared the bejesus out of him. His penetrating gaze and his direct and rather aggressive manner made Tom nervous. He knew it would not be a good idea to get in his way.

Tom had one of his crew scouting for an incoming car. He did not want any surprises. He would meet the two in the parking lot before bringing them into the building. Once they entered everyone in the building would know and wonder why the two had come back again.

Ian saw the Homeland Security agent riding an RTV alongside of the highway. He figured him for a scout out verifying the incoming traffic.

Ian let Mike know that Tom knew that they were arriving. And it appeared that he was nervous about their arrival.

Mike conjectured that perhaps they should have told him more about their purpose in coming. It would have been easier if they could totally count on him and his immediate reports and got their help.

Ian pointed out the situation they had just experienced. What would have happened in their interactions at the sheriff's office if Bob had shared any information with Bradley.

Mike looked at Ian and decided never to play poker or chess with him. He knew Ian would not cheat. He would just figure out how to beat you. It was clear to Mike that Herman Lunquist never left anything to chance.

Mike agreed with him. His personal connection with Tom and his family gave him confidence that Tom was in the clear.

He did not know how but he was confident that Herman would find the guilty.

Ian saw Tom standing under the building entrance canopy on the edge of the parking lot. Tom pointed to an empty parking space almost directly in front of the canopy. Matt parked in the space to which Tom pointed.

Tom greeted Mike with a handshake and a man hug. Ian liked him for doing that. Ian was a hugger with people he knew.

Tom gave Ian a formal and firm handshake.

Before escorting them in, Tom wanted to know why the FBI was back and in such a cryptic fashion.

It took all his inner strength and control, but he glanced at Mike and then focused on Herman.

Ian smiled. Tom's actions made it clear to him that Tom stood by his people. He was a protector. He would be devastated if one of them were involved in helping the smugglers to smuggle people across the border that he was sworn to patrol and enforce. This was going to be as hard on him as it had been on Bill

Ian quietly told Tom that one or more of his people were corrupt. He had come to determine who in the drone team was involved and who on the scheduling team was involved. Ian figured that the two positions would be the minimum number involved in the border crossing scheme.

He asked Tom if that was a problem.

Tom got angry and asked how the hell he was so sure any one of his people were involved.

Ian calmly replied that it was more than one and that it was the only explanation that fit the situation.

Mike decided to break the tension. He explained what had just transpired in Phoenix where the second in command of the police department had confessed to hiring the truck drivers and having the trucks rented.

Tom stood silently for a moment. Then he muttered, "Jesus this is going to play hell with our organization if some of our folks are involved. They are likely to get shot by their angry coworkers."

Ian pointed out that it was time for them to go in and figure out how to spot the perpetrators.

Tom nodded and led the way into the building and up to his office.

From his window desk on the second floor Trey saw the trio walking in. He knew the jig was up. He was glad. He walked over to the shredder and shredded the suicide letter he had delayed in sending to his parents.

He was going to turn himself in. He would not wait to be interrogated. He wasn't sure what the penalty was for what he had done but it couldn't be worse than the sleepless nights and continuous anguish that he was now experiencing. He figured it was one step above suicide.

He got up, walked to Tom's office where the three were meeting and knocked on the door.

Ian was surprised as Trey walked in and simply said that he was the one they were looking for. Someone turning themselves in had not been on Ian's list of how to find the perpetrator.

Ian stood up and asked Trey to take his seat. He turned so he could see Tom's reaction.

Ian asked Trey to explain why the FBI would be interested in him.

Trey held up a thumb drive and explained that he had documented all he knew about how the border crossings were managed. He explained that he periodically received a divert signal and the time and place of the diversion of the ground guard team to be diverted. Trey commented on the fact that he had come to the conclusion that one of the schedulers had to be involved.

Ian asked how long Trey had been doing this and how he had been recruited.

Trey said it was all detailed on this thumb drive.

Ian thanked Trey for the documentation but said he wanted to hear it in Trey's own words. He asked Tom to record Trey's confession. He asked Mike to read Trey his Miranda rights. He took the thumb drive and gave it to Mike.

Trey had tears in his eyes. It was hard for him to see. The flood of emotion was overwhelming him.

He began to cry.

Through his crying he explained that the vision of the dead mother holding her two dead children to her chest would be with him forever. If there was a hell, he said he was sure to go there. He was sure that truck had been one of the ones used when he had diverted the ground crew.

Ian looked at Tom and asked if there was a secure room where Trey could be put.

Ian wanted some time to review what was on the thumb drive, so they could determine their next steps.

Ian asked that Tom, Mike, and he together review the contents of the thumb drive.

After locking Trey in a secure room, Tom plugged the thumb drive into his computer and opened the only file that was on it.

It was clear that Trey had provided a detailed account of his recruitment. He had provided the time and dates of all the diversions. Trey had come to the realization that a person in scheduling had to also be involved and had narrowed it down to two people.

Ian scanned all the information. He came to a much more startling theory.

Trey had not done it for the money, but the scheduler most probably had done it for money. The cartels had billions of dollars with which to work. Sam, or whatever his real name was, had most probably recruited multiple people. Why stop at one. There was money to be made. He would want to have backups. He would recruit as many people as possible.

Ian realized that there were probably sleeper candidates that were ready to step in when he arrested those people currently involved.

He looked at Tom and could see that he was angry about what was transpiring. Ian knew that if he were in Tom's position, he would be wondering who else was on the take. This was probably Tom's most dreaded situation.

Tom personally knew one of the two, Ethan, as a true family man and an upstanding member of his church. He picked Josh as the most likely one to be recruited. He was the one that was forever coming up with an excuse for being late to work and he dressed in a slovenly manner.

The selection made little sense to Ian. He had known too many family men who had let their ego and desire for personal goods sell out their families.

Ian walked out of the office and put in a call to his support team. He asked them to check out the two schedulers. He asked them to especially look at the bank accounts and spending habit changes. They were also to look through the background clearance checks and see if there were any gaps in the information.

He returned and asked Tom to bring in the person he suspected.

A young looking, man that probably got carded every time he ordered a drink came through the door. Ian stepped forward and shook hands with Josh. He appeared to be sixteen but was probably in his early thirties. He sported a scraggly beard and a head of hair that was greased and made into spikes. What Ian took to be a punk head.

It was clear that Tom did not especially like Josh and that Josh knew this and probably presented himself in the way he did as a way to irritate Tom.

Almost instantly Ian figured it was the family man that would be the culprit. Josh seemed too confident and together to be the one.

Ian also concluded that Tom was a biased judge of character.

Mike watched Ian's interactions with Josh. Ian pressed him on how he scheduled his teams. He pressed him hard about the timing and placement of the teams and who he shared this information with.

Ian then probed into Josh's personal life. Was he single? Yes, did he have a girlfriend? How often did he go out? Where did they go out? Was he getting laid?

Josh remained cool and collected. He calmly answered Ian's questions and even joked with Ian about his poor love life and the fact that there was no place to go in this forsaken part of the world. He did not seem disturbed. He laughed at the last question and answered, "not enough."

Ian thanked Josh for answering his questions and made a point that there would be a follow-up the following day.

As Josh was leaving, he invited Ian for a drink if he was staying in town that evening.

Ian turned to Tom and asked him to bring in Ethan for his interview.

Mike came to the conclusion that Ethan was in for a really thorough grilling. It was clear to him that Josh had passed the grilling he had undergone, with flying colors.

Ethan reminded Mike of Bradley who had been confident that he was above suspicion.

Ian asked similar questions to what he had asked Josh. The answers Ethan gave were always logical and often supported with examples of his family and church life. He put on the air of a loving father that focused on his family life.

Ian decided it was time to use the one threat that he knew would work.

Ian leaned in close to Ethan's ear. He whispered a curse, "you god damn soulless son of a bitch. I have your offshore bank account number and the times you refilled your account. I know exactly when you were recruited. I am not an FBI agent. The government does not desire to be embarrassed and has sent me out to eliminate anyone who does not confess to their deeds. You have to the count of twenty and then I leave and tonight you die."

Tom was looking at Mike. He mouthed, "What is he saying?"

Mike just shrugged and tilted his head. He had the gist but had no clue as to the actual words. He watched as Ethan's face went white. To Mike this was the face of someone who was guilty.

Ian stepped back. Ethan put his elbows on his knees and leaned his face into his cupped hands. It was clear that he was crying.

Ian counted slowly to twenty. When he said twenty out loud, Ethan fell to his knees and cried out, "Please forgive me. I just wanted to be a better provider for my family."

Tom looked at Herman with newfound respect. He told Ethan it was not their role to forgive. He would be tried for his misdeeds. A judge and jury would decide his fate.

Ian asked Mike to read Ethan his rights. He looked at Tom who was looking a little pale and appeared to be in a state of shock.

Ian knew that if Tom was kept employed, he was now in line for reassignment to the most remote location possible.

Ian asked that Trey and Ethan be held in custody. He and Matt would transport both Ethan and Trey to Phoenix where they would be arraigned.

Ian knew the follow-up investigations would go on for a long time. He looked at Mike and commented that he would have his hands full for the foreseeable future. He was sure that his coming promotion would help.

The next day, the drive to Phoenix was eerily quiet. Ian was sitting in the back seat with Ethan who had his handcuffed hands on his lap.

Trey sat quietly in the right front seat looking out the window. It was clear that he had found whatever peace he would have for the rest of his life. He seemed calm. Ian figured confession had freed his soul.

Ethan on the other hand went from whimpering to full sobs. He was still wrestling with his demons. Ian would make sure he was put on suicide watch.

The expanse of the desert seemed to go on forever until it met the black and dark green of the Rockies. The blue of the cloudless sky seemed appealing until the heat of the day hit your face.

Ian decided the best thing for him to do was to doze lightly. Mike seemed to be fully concentrating on his driving. There was silence in the car.

Mike had called ahead and made arrangements with Bill to have space available for the two they were bringing in. He also let him know that each had obtained the services of a lawyer. The lawyers were going to meet their clients the next day. The two would be arraigned on Friday.

Mike planned to hold a news conference in the morning. He asked Herman to take the lead.

Ian declined. He led Mike to believe that it would ruin his future in solving cases like the one they had just solved together.

Mike found this a little hard to believe but he knew the news conference to share the success would certainly help his career. He remembered Herman asking him what he hoped for. Mike knew solving this case would certainly lead to a promotion. He wondered how it would affect Herman.

At breakfast Bill and Matt asked why Herman was not taking part in the press conference.

Mike made the point that publicity would make it harder for him to be effective in the future.

Matt looked at Ian and quietly mouth the work "bullshit".

Ian smiled and simply said that the dancing in the spotlight was Mike's job. He said his job was done and it was time for him to move on. He made the point that there were many other problems that still need to be solved.

Bill looked at Ian as he took a sip of his coffee. He made the comment that he did not believe Ian worked for the FBI.

"Let's just say I am called on to solve the problems that are defying solution in a normal manner. I work for whoever needs my help" Ian replied. I am a problem solver.

"Well, whoever you may be, thanks for getting to the bottom of this situation. I would have never believed anyone in my organization would have been involved in such a scheme. I will forever be in your debt," Bill said from his side of the table.

"Well, I am on the way home and that is always a treat. My wife is the best cook in the world," Ian said as he got up.

He was on the way to meet a helicopter at Montezuma Castle National Monument. It would take him all the way home and to the arms of his lovely Lesley.

"I thought he was single," Ian heard Matt say to Bill as he walked out.

Ian smiled. He had never discussed his personal life with anyone. They had reached their own conclusion.

The End

Of Rhinos and Horns

Introduction

It is a troubled world. The human species has, like no other, risen to dominate the world. The rise is marked with amazing beauty and grace. It is also marked by cruelty to other humans and a disregard for the negative impact they have on their only home, the earth.

The beauty found in poetry and writing, the beauty found in paintings and sculptors is more than countered by the wars, the intentional environmental destruction, and the barriers each separate country imposes on its peoples and the neighboring states.

The belief of limited resources, the behavior of greed, the desire for wealth and the desire for control are all factors in the behavior exhibited by those who surface at the top of the heap. The ability of various leaders, in a myriad of areas, to convince those more interested in their immediate family well-being allows those interested in domination to rise to positions of influence and power.

Often their belief is that they have been ordained to be in charge or alternately they are smarter and should be in the lead.

The rise of the rule of law has created a situation where fairness is managed by laws developed by the representatives of the people. Even in the situation found in the United States that has three branches of government designed to maintain the system of fairness to all, slavery, and women's right to vote were initially missed. More recently the rights of gay or lesbian people are in question.

Human greed, cruelty, misbehavior, and disregard of the environment seems to increase asymptotically with the rapid rise of the population.

Justice is not always served. This situation is managed by a secret organization that funds and directs the actions of ***The Problem-solver***. This is a person whose principles, judgement, behavior, and actions guide him in how to resolve problems that otherwise would be left unchecked.

The problems are many. The problems are anywhere in the world. The problems are solved in the best manner that The Problem-solver determines.

See if you agree with the problem resolutions, that this Problem-solver, ***Ian Sinclair***, has chosen for his various assignments.

1 Lazy Lady

*T*heir escape from the pirates was the most dramatic event in Maurice's and Ted's lives. Matt's handling of the battle was a lesson in preparation and in how to totally devastate your opponent. Only a few of the twenty some attack pirate boats disappeared in what seemed to be a crater created by the explosion of every boat.

Then the command ship attacked and once again it seemed that they were going to be captured by a ship armed with a deck cannon that put a shell on each side of the Lazy Lady.

Then Maurice watched as Matt pressed a button and the entire front end of the giant on coming ship blew up as if it had been hit by some unseen rocket.

She rejoiced when Matt asked Ted to hoist the main sail and the jib, and she felt the Lazy Lady come to life and seemingly leap forward in joy.

They sailed into Cape Town where Matt left them.

A short time after they docked Matt left them to return to the US.

She and Ted sailed the Lazy Lady out of Cape Town to continue on their around the world sailing tour. They sailed north along the coast of Africa. They stopped at almost every port for a day so that they could enjoy the various historic sites but mostly because it allowed them to enjoy the wide variety of dishes and did not have to cook or clean. This took them several months and then before entering the Med, they returned to the US to celebrate the births of grandchildren and spend a few days with the new children.

They were known to the family as the grandparents that sailed the world. Maurice accepted the title with pride and offered to pay the airfare for any family member that desired to join them on the Lazy Lady.

After being away for more than a month they returned to the Lazy Lady that they had come to considered home. Each time they returned they would talk about the time they were saved by Matt from being taken hostage by the Pirates of the coast of East Africa. They would laugh at the fact that they had never asked and now did not know his last name. They would have loved dearly to communicate with him and share the highlights of their journey.

They sailed into the Mediterranean and did a counter clockwise tour. They stopped in Algiers, Tunis, Tripoli and when four months later they got to Alexandria, they once again flew back to the US to celebrate Thanksgiving.

After enjoying the family and all their grandchildren they decided to stay for Christmas. This allowed them to play Santa parents and spoil their brewed of grandchildren.

On their return they continued on and went to see Jerusalem where they spent more than a week visiting all the religious sites.

They then sailed to Beirut and from there sailed to Cyprus. They stopped briefly in Antalya, Turkey to rejuvenate and get the Lazy Lady refreshed.

Then it was on to Athens where they spent a week visiting all the historic sites that they had studied in high school and college.

Then up northward up eastern side of the Adriatic Sea with brief stops in several of sea ports. The longest stay was at the very northern part when they reached Venice. They toured Venice for a week and then sailed nonstop to Catania, Sicily before going on to Naples.

There they once again left the Lazy Lady while they flew home for several grandchildren's graduations from high school and college. This was only a brief visit, and, on their return, they sailed to Fiumicino where they anchored for a week as they visited Rome. Their next stop was Livorno where they stopped so they could take a road trip to Florence.

The sailing continue for the rest of the year as the two visited Genoa, Nice, Marseille Barcelona and Valencia.

They left the Mediterranean and sailed north and stopped in Lisbon.

From there they sailed straight to Dublin where they stayed for more than a month to tour Ireland. It was during this period that they once again flew back to the states.

They continued their sailing for yet two more years and would spend time visiting many of the cities in the UK, spent a month in Amsterdam and then took a boat tour down the Rhine to Switzerland and back.

They chuckled when they lined the Lazy Lady with a row of potted flowers.

They waited until summer to sail into the Bering Sea and hit many of the ports like Helsinki, Stockholm and Copenhagen.

Their last stop on the way back to the States was Edinburgh where they spent several weeks relaxing and touring the countryside.

Once they made New York they took another family break and flew back to LA to celebrate in Pasadena where the majority of the family now lived.

After a few weeks they flew back to the Lazy lady.

Once they returned to the Lazy Lady, it took them another five years to bring her through the Panama canal and up the coast of Baja California. They finally docked the Lazy Lady and arranged for her complete overhaul.

The Lazy Lady was taken out of the water and literally refurbished and restored to the point where she was once again like new. Her engine and the appliance were all replaced.

They then sailed on her for almost another ten years and then when they could no longer do so on their own. They arranged to once again refurbish the Lazy Lady.

It was during this last time of renewing the Lazy Lady that after checking with their sons, they decided that the person who had rescued them from the pirates off the coast of Africa should be the new owner of the yacht that he had saved from the pirates.

Maurice had looked ahead and every year for the last five years she had held a family goodbye party. She had done much of the baking and preparation for the first party but for the other four years had the party catered. These parties let everyone involved deal with the fact that there was an end point to everyone's journey.

Shortly after, both went into Hospice care where they shared the same apartment for what they knew would be their final journey together. They had settled all their accounts and knew that they had shared a wonderous life together.

Their two sons who were now nearing their own retirement and their children who were now all grown adults themselves and who had children all stopped by to say their goodbyes.

Their wealth was significant but not exceedingly huge, most of their estate was in the business that they had passed on to their sons. However, there was still a sizeable amount that was in trust with specific instructions of how that was to be handled.

The biggest challenge that they had worked through was how to pass the Lazy Lady on to the one person who they agreed should be the one to inherit it.

They only knew him as Matt, so they put an advertisement in the personal section of several newspapers in major cities across the US that simply gave their names and the fact that they had been saved from being captured by pirates by someone sent to save them. They wanted to reward that person and needed to get in contact with him to make sure he accepted the ownership of the Lazy Lady.

They kept that Ad active for more than three years and were giving up hope when they received the call that they had waited for what to them seemed to be an eternity. They learned the name of the person they would pass the Lazy Lady to. It was less than a year later that they both took that name with them to eternity when within a month of each other they passed away.

The person who had contacted them was Ian's handler. He had met with Maurice's and Ted's lawyer and had made all the legal arrangements for the transfer. Not a month later he was online with Ian letting him know of their passing and the fact that they had left him the Lazy Lady as a measure of their gratitude.

The contact with Ian had more to do with a problem requiring his special touch than about the yacht. It had to do with a high stakes kidnapping that needed to be resolved. It needed the special touch of the Problem-Solver.

Ian knew immediately that he would put the Lazy Lady to work as part of the solution that he had in mind.

2 Rise to Power

General Ingraditi was frustrated by the situation of the current Army Command. He controlled much of the country, but his two longtime nemesis seemed to currently have the upper hand. For years he had been hounded by General Mumbada and his longtime friend General Wesbow who controlled about forty percent of the country. The two were inseparable and were able to fend off his many attempts to derail them and take complete control of the army.

He was upset with the support they were given by a group of wealthy businessmen that had great influence with the general assembly. It was a delicate situation that he knew he would win in the near future when it came to head that very likely might be a bloody confrontation.

He had the loyalty of the larger part of the army but that only meant that he could defend the territory he currently controlled and keep his adversaries at bay.

He knew that the richest part of Nairobi was in the hands of General Mumbada and the part of the army that had his loyalty. As long as that was the case, he would have to put up with General Mumbada.

As General Ingraditi lamented, needing to put up with his adversary, General Mumbada, followed by his longtime friend, Vice General Wesbow walked slowly down the line of soldiers they were inspecting.

The last two soldiers were dressed in very expensive black suites that had been awarded to them for their superior service to the army. The general lightly brushed the thousand-dollar suits and congratulated each of the soldiers for their superior service and shook their hands. He was sure that his reward-based recognition was loved by his army. He knew that they were loyal to him more than the parts of the army controlled by his superior.

He and General Wesbow were friends since their childhood when they were in grade school. At that time Kenya was still in the control of Great Briton and was known as British East Africa. The two of them were disturbed to see the British and European farmers prospering by growing coffee and tea on the rich Kenyan land while the general population was struggling to make ends meet. The two came to despise the inequity of the situation and throughout their younger years they and their friends played games where they rid the country of foreigners and became the leaders who took Kenya to higher power in the world.

He and Lionel Wesbow remained friends as they grew older. They had parents that pushed them to do well in school and later to get into the Army. The two went to and graduated from a school similar to the US army's West Point Academy.

He had the framed degree stating that Maurice Mumbada had graduated first in the class of 1976 proudly displayed on the wall of his office. He knew that Lionel had a similar degree that stated he had graduated second that he had hung in his office.

It was a time where the country's many clans and forty some differing languages kept the various clans apart from each other. In 1963 after facing internal rebellion, the British relinquished control and the following year Kenya became an independent nation.

Kiswahili became the common language. That was the language that the two had grown up with. They were fluent in English which put them in a great position as they made their way up the army ranks.

In the following years they focused on what it took to get ahead and made sure that both were at the right place at the right time. They were both rewarded with the promotions that they sought.

There was always the one person to whom they were both junior to and who seemed to be promoted just ahead of the two of them.

The two now in controlled of most of the western part of the country and wide strip that extended down to the Indian Ocean.

General Ingraditi, who they supposedly reported to controlled the eastern and northern part of Kenya.

Their reporting relationship with Ingraditi was frosty but they made sure that it would not reach the point of direct confrontation.

The area they controlled included Nairobi that was several million people strong and the entire area they controlled included sixty percent of the population.

They recognized that their main strength was the support of a group of wealthy businessmen that were prospering by having them look the other way to their across the border self-serving business dealings.

General Ingraditi controlled more territory and had to interface with four boundary countries whereas he only dealt with the politics of dealing with two border countries.

They felt certain that they had enough power that they could take control of the entire country, but it would put them at risk of a battle between the men loyal to them and those loyal to General Ingraditi. It would entail an internal battle that would not be good for them or the country. It was clear to them that it might increase their ability to add to the billions to what they already had in their Swiss bank accounts.

They decided they were in a strong position and should continue to wait to make their upward move when the opportunity presented itself.

General Ingraditi gave them the idea of how to increase the cash flow to their bank accounts. He periodically kidnapped some important business man and then demanded a ransom. When the ransom was paid the business man was released. The timing of the kidnappings varied but they were far enough apart that the public attention span waned, and another kidnapping did not alarm the population.

They liked that idea, but they planned to do the same on a grander scale. The opportunity to do so presented itself a few weeks after they had agreed to the ransom idea.

The Society of Geographic Exploration contacted General Mumbada and asked for his support for a four-member film crew that they wanted to send into the country to document the condition of the black rhino population. They were seeking his support so that the team would be able to safely travel around the various parks to photograph the rhinos in their natural habitat.

He and General Wesbow immediately set into motion a plan to kidnap the team and then demand five million dollars for the release of each film crew member.

A few months later when the film team arrived, they were met by a specially assigned army squad that was assigned to take them to a holding location until the ransom was paid. The kidnapping was a nonevent. A black van met the team as they exited the airport with all their equipment.

The driver and his companion helped load all the equipment and suitcases into the van and then drove to a destination outside of Nairobi where the team was to be held.

Soon after, General Mumbada learned that there was a nasty interaction with the female team leader when she insisted, they be taken to their hotel. He was told that she had a bruise that covered her right cheek where she had been backhanded. He asked for the soldiers name who had hit the leader and he also sent word that the film crew was to be treated well. He had them separated and locked in two separate rooms of the barracks where they were being held.

He and Lionel discussed how they would handle the four when the ransom was paid.

He publicly announced the film crew's abduction and said that the army was in pursuit of the kidnappers who were demanding a ransom of five million dollars per person for their safe release. He assured the news channels that the team would be found and rescued by his men.

General Ingraditi learned of the kidnapping as he listened to a news report. He was shocked by the amount of ransom that was being demanded. He was also sure that his two nemesis and strong competitors for control of the army were the ones behind the kidnapping.

He sent them a cryptic message stating, "it is not me so it must be something the two of you have cooked up. I am staying clear of it."

He was not staying clear. He set forth a plan that brought his army units closer to Nairobi in preparation of arresting both General Mumbada and General Wesbow. It seemed that the two were getting greedy and that they would no doubt think about gaining more power as well as more money.

General Mumbada and Wesbow were glad to get the message and figured that they had clear sailing and would soon be able to send a significant amount of money to their Swiss bank accounts.

They were disappointed when they news from The Society of Geographic Exploration saying that the US would not allow the organization to meet the ransom demands. This worried them but they figured it was just the first step in the ransom demand dance. They agreed that they should reiterate the ransom demand that threatened harm to the film crew if the demand was not met.

A few days later they received a reply to the ransom demand that asked how the payment should be delivered. The message was signed, Matthew Parker ransom settlement specialist.

They figured that the company had hired an outsider to deliver the ransom money.

They had never heard of a "ransom settlement specialist" but they were pleased that the ransom was to be paid. They hoped that this specialist would arrive at the airport with the ransom money where their men would quickly put this would be specialist out of business when they took control of the ransom money.

They organized a team to seize the ransom money. They had come to the conclusion that eliminating the film crew would make it easier for them to close out the kidnapping situation.

It was clear to them that their kidnapping case had grown roots and would yield the millions that they had hoped. They congratulated each other on having come up with such a lucrative idea.

They decided that a celebration outing was appropriate and visited the most expensive restaurant in Nairobi and celebrated their success.

The two would not have been celebrating if they had known who Mathew Parker was and how he solved the problems that he was assigned and the many years that he had successfully done so.

While they celebrated Mathew Parker was on his way to solve the problem they had created.

3 Old Friends in Trouble

What began as a trip to another great photo journalism trip to get out into the wilderness and capture the plight of the black rhino on film turned into a nightmare as soon as the team arrived in Nairobi. They had been assured they would be met with help and assistance and instead they were met by group of men they took as soldiers who loaded their things into the back of a black van and whisked them away.

Andria had her hand over the bruise on the side of her face where she had been back handed when she had demanded to be taken to the hotel where the team had reservations. It became clear to her that they had been kidnaped but she felt that a forceful approach was how to handle the situation. That aggressive approach proved to be very wrong.

She and Mary now sat in one room guarded by one of the members of the abductors. Her head ached but what she was now more worried about was Mike and Iri the two male members on her crew. She hoped that Mike would not lose his temper. He was prone to letting his anger get the best of him.

As she thought about who had lost their anger she laughed.

Her laugh seemed to bring the guard to action, and he wanted to know why she was laughing.

She answered him saying that she was just thinking about what would happen to all of the people who were involved in doing the kidnapping.

Mary sat silently across from her and with her head cupped in her hands. Mary commented that so far there was not much to laugh about. She asked how the face felt.

Andria wondered how, while coming out of the airport, they could be so easily get abducted. She figured that it was the work of whoever was in charge of the area. Clearly the abductors were in some sort of military uniform. The public aspect of where the kidnapping took place seemed to support her supposition.

She thought back to how the trip had started out. The team had been enthused when they had received their assignment to go to Kenya to the Lewa Wild Life Conservancy to film the black Rhino in its natural state. They were to produce an article about the good work being done there to repopulate the rhino population. The team had discussed the great time they all had when they filmed the documentary on elephants and then produced the story, "Of Elephants and Ivory." They figured that this story would be, "Of Rhinos and Horns."

They had gone out and celebrated their good fortune.

Andria thought about the irony that she had to hire a camera man to fill a vacancy on the team. That had been how she had first met Mathew Parker. She had hired a young camera man named Iri that Mike had taken under his tutelage to bring him up to speed.

Being kidnapped and told that they would be released when the ransom that was being asked was paid was of great concern to her. She wondered whether the company would pay the five million dollars per person that was being demanded. She hoped so. She and the team had generated one hundred times that amount with the documentary films they had produced.

That thought brought Matt back into her thinking. Matt, the person who had surprised her and the team with his escapades when they were filming, "Of Elephants and Ivory." He had demonstrated an uncanny skill at moving around within reach of the elephants that in turn seemed to accept him.

A few years later she had received some amazing film footage that she was very sure he had taken. They were amazing pictures of a myriad of fish, whales, killer whales, turtles, and manta rays. She and the team view all of it multiple times and were blown away when they watched him ride the mother whale. The were overjoyed at the close up that he got of the baby whale. Then they were more amazed when he caught a ride on the back of a killer whale and was able to get a upshot of each of the other members of that pod as each individual came up to check him out.

His shots of the gaping mouth of a shark and then a similar one of a giant Manta Ray coming straight at him had caused everyone to let out loud exclamations of surprise. She figured only Matt would have that kind of gumption and courage, but his face never made it on film.

The collection of fish and underwater scenes were beyond what the team had ever imagined could be captured on camera.

They had made that gift into a documentary that earned all of them a raise and she had received a promotion.

She wondered where Matt was and wished he were here because she was sure that he would figure out how to get all of them out of the mess they found themselves in.

Andria was soon to be surprised at the role that her "Old" friend, Mathew Parker was to play in getting her out of the mess she was in. Not only would she be surprised but she would once again be blown away with the actions he would take in accomplishing getting the team to safety.

Ian, alias Mathew Parker, had been writing one of his many fiction stories when on the news he heard the announcer discussing the kidnapping of a Geographical film crew. He immediately focused in on the report. The pictures of the film crew were that of his old friends when he had played the part of Mathew Parker and had become a camera man on the crew. He had ended up taking very close up pictures of the elephants. His problem-solving actions had temporarily ended the extensive poaching and harvesting of elephant tusks.

At that time, he was sure that his "solutions" were only temporary and that by now the poor elephants were probably in the same jam they had been in at that time.

This time his old team mates had gone to Kenya to make a similar documentary on the Black Rhinoceros. He figured this time the bad guys were more than just poachers and wheeled more power. He looked to the army to be involved.

The abduction had been on the curb of the airport when they had exited with all their equipment. Those in charge of the area must have at least looked the other way for that to happen.

He knew he would soon get his activation call. He began to think through what action he was going to take.

He was in the middle of his thought process when he got a rare call. It was a surprise in that it was his long-time handler that was on the other end of the secure line where usually it was some unknown voice that gave him the briefest and usually cryptic message possible.

His handler informed him that he was indeed being activated to solve the problem that his old friends faced.

His handler added that he had some sad news about Maurice and Ted Daimler, the two people he had saved from the Pirates off the coast of Africa. They had recently passed away within a month of each other. Their sons had inherited their furniture business, but they had left their sailing yacht, "The Lazy Lady," to him. He added that they had the boat sailed to South Africa and it was now docked at the last place where the three of them had been together.

His handler said that he was being given that information in case it would be of help in handling his new assignment.

Ian thanked him for the information and said that an idea had just popped into his mind.

There was a chuckle on the other end and his handler added "just don't kill too many of the perps," and then the line went dead.

The idea that had popped into his mind caused Ian to make a call to another old friend that he hoped would be available to help him.

Ted was sitting at home in Tampa wishing that his slow boat captaining business would come back to life. He was now known for his capabilities and was often asked to handle some of the best sailing yachts that were anchored in the Tampa Bay area but recently things had been quieter than usual. Even the occasional call to captain some of the very large power yachts had dried out.

His musings made him wonder what had happened to the person that had launched his career as the captain of the "Whistling Nanny". His career had soared after that job and a very prosperous life had followed.

When a few days later after having wondered about his long-ago acquaintance, he answered his phone and almost fell out of his chair when he heard the voice of Mathew Bitterly. It was hard for him to pay attention to what was being said because he had figured he would never hear from him again. Over the years he had come to realize that Mathew was most likely an alias for a much more clandestine profession. A profession that he still wondered about.

Once he gathered himself, he finally realized that he was being asked to Captain a yacht named the "Lazy Lady" that was currently located in South Africa. He was ecstatic.

It took him a minute to respond that it would be great to do so. He then asked what type of yacht the "Lazy Lady" happened to be. He laughed when he learned that it was a duplicate of the Whistling Nanny and replied he would love to sail her.

He took down all the information and the flight information that Matt provided. It took him several days to travel to South Africa to where the sailing yacht was moored. He decided to handle the yacht single handedly. He was impressed how the Lazy Lady looked and smelled new. It was clear that she had been refurbished. He took her out and as he put her through her paces the years melted away and it seemed like only yesterday when he and Matt had sailed the Whistling Nanny.

Once he had the yacht underway to Mombasa, he let Matt know.

Ian, now Matt, was figuring out how he could get out to the field and make contact as soon as possible. He had been given the phone connection with the kidnappers, so he decided to become the person who was to finalize the ransom negotiations with them.

He placed the call and conveyed the fact that the company was sending him out with the ransom money in cash and that he would deliver it and would hand it over when the four abductees were released to him.

The ease with which the kidnappers agreed and gave him the location where the exchange was to take place let him know that it was a set up and that he and the four would be killed when they tried to leave that location. He also figured he might be stopped at the airport just as Andrea had been.

He of course did not have any connection with the company that Andria and her team worked for and the money to be used for the ransom was coming out of his bottomless offshore account that he had used for more than thirty years. It was an account that always had a minimum of one million dollars in it but had access to whatever amount he needed. The amount of money that he had withdrawn for this problem-solving session was not the highest, but it was close. He wondered what the person managing the bank account thought when he withdrew these large sums of money.

He decided to get into the Kenya surreptitiously. He flew into Dar es Salaam in Tanzania. From there he flew on a private charter into Nairobi where it landed on a private airfield.

He arrived several days earlier than he had shared with the abductors. He wanted time to walk through the situation he would face.

He scouted out the exchange location so he could figure out how to counter act what he knew would be a trap.

He went to the specified location and decided to take the position nearest to the statue in the park where the exchange was to take place. It had a wide area to the front of a statue of Absko Njeri, who had saved the country and had guided it throughout his life time. Ian noted that the life time was very short since Absko died at the age of forty-one. He took the location as a signal that he needed to be able to control the situation so that he would not follow Absko.

There was a large flat brick covered area out in front of the statue, and it had a long set of stairs behind the statue that went down about a football field in length to a lower parking area.

He called his support team and requested the delivery of sixty bars of radio controlled fused C4 with a remote-control App for his phone that could be used to trigger the C4. He said he needed the order in the next twelve-four hours and that the order was to be placed in the bushes behind the statue.

The next night, he placed C4 in a semi-circle under the bricks out about fifty feet, and another semi-circle closer in at thirty feet. He then went out in the cobble stone street and placed C4 where the trucks or vehicles would park. He then placed the C4 down the sides of the steps coming up from the lower parking lot. He set up a trip wire near the top of the steps but counted on the ability to set off the C4 via his phone.

He made sure that the statue base would provide the cover that would be needed when he set the C4 off.

He hid the money that he was to exchange in bushes just behind the statue.

It was near morning when he finished setting everything up.

He then went to the airport so he could make it appear that he had come in as per his instructions.

At the airport he found his way in through a service area and went to a set of lockers where four empty suitcases were located and strapped the four together. The four cases were the same as the ones with the money in them that were back at the statue. Each case had its own set of wheels which would carry them toward the kidnappers as the exchange happened. His empty ones were already carrying C4 in them that were timer controlled.

He went to the curb and got into a cab that was at the back of the long cab que line.

The driver was about to refuse him, but the hundred-dollar bill Ian held out to him caused him to smile and ask where he wanted to go.

Ian gave him the location and the driver pulled away from the curb.

Ian looked back to see if they were being followed and was relieved that they were not. He was sure that by jumping the line he had gotten away from whomever had been sent to meet him and most likely take the money they thought he would be carrying.

He paid the driver during the transit and asked him to drive up to the statue and then leave immediately.

He had just gotten the money cases, the empty cases arranged, and his phone app activated when a large black SUV followed by two armed trucks came roaring into the area in front of the statue.

Ian watched as they parked exactly where he had hoped they would. Once they parked at least thirty soldiers lined up in front of the lead SUV.

Ian thought about his handlers comment about how many people he shouldn't kill and now wondered how many he would.

Two men dress impeccably in black suites sporting white boutonnières addressed him with a bull horn.

Ian replied with a much smaller voice amplifier and warned them not to send the troops up the back way and to keep the troops out front at least twenty meters away from the statue.

He then pointed to the four cases that he had brought out and said that each had five million dollars in them. He then rolled three of the cases back behind the statue.

He suggested they get the exchange under way.

He watched as one of the two men in black communicated with someone that was remotely located.

Ian hoped it was to keep the men in the lower parking lot from coming up the stairs. He backed up to the point where he could take a quick look down and was pleased to see the steps were empty.

He watched the other leader call back to a person standing by the side back door to the SUV.

The door was opened, and Mike stepped out and reached in to help Mary exit. Then a young man that Ian would later learn was Iri stepped out and reached and helped Andria out.

Ian could see the bruise that colored one side of her face and knew that she had angered someone.

He asked that she be the first to be sent across to him.

One of the men in black as Ian now thought of the two, said they would determine the order of the exchange. He pushed Mary to the front and asked for the first five million dollars.

Ian replied that when she made it to the statue, he would push the first case with the money across. He was pleased to see that Mary was given a push and began walking across.

When she was at the statue, Ian simultaneously pushed her behind the statue and pushed the first suitcase toward the two men in charge.

He then pulled a second suitcase to the side of the statue.

He asked Mary to keep her eyes on the stairs and let him know if anybody was coming up.

The first suitcase was opened to make sure that the money was inside.

Ian made the point that he was keeping his end of the bargain and that they should continue the exchange.

Mike was the next to be sent across.

When he reached the statue, Ian again pushed a suitcase with the money across.

It was again checked.

Ian told Mike to get the weapons out of the bushes and get ready to fight for his life. He was glad to hear Mike say he was ready to take down as many as he could.

Ian was surprised when the two in charge said they would send both the remaining persons across together and that he should push the last two cases to them.

He figured that immediately after this exchange the action would start.

Ian went behind the statue and selected two empty cases that were loaded with the C4 versus.

He waited until Andria and Iri were near him and then reached down and activated the C4 timers in the empty suit cases and pushed them towards the kidnapers and at the same time shoved the two behind the statue as the anticipated gun fire from the group of soldiers began.

He was hit but his body armor saved him.

He lay down and took out both of the men in black and watched as the two suitcases exploded and leveled the first line of soldiers.

The next line of soldiers ran forward firing their weapons.

When they reached the most distant ring of C4 he set that ring off and eliminated the second wave. The third wave was getting ready to follow one of the trucks that had a fifty-caliber machine gun mounted on it when Ian set the C4 under it off and lifted the truck several feet into the air before it blew up from whatever ammunition it was carrying.

The carnage was not complete. The remaining soldiers ran toward the statue. They all reached the thirty-foot ring of explosives and were totally annihilated when Ian set that group of C4 explosives off.

Mike was shouting that the troops from below were running up the stairs.

Ian went to where Mike was shooting downward taking out the lead soldiers. He told him to let them come up.

Mike looked at him and asked if, he was sure.

Ian smiled and said that he wanted all the soldiers from the parking lot to make it onto the stairs.

He asked Mike to guard his back and make sure there were no survivors in front of the statue.

He waited until the stairs were full and then he set off the line of explosive charges he had put on each side of the stairs.

Andria shook her head and thanked him for coming to save their bacon. She commented that he was delivering the carnage that in her anger she had dreamt of.

Ian smiled and replied that he would love to catch up on old times, but they needed to make their escape.

He went out to where the suit cases with the five million dollars were sitting and pulled them to the back of the statue.

He pulled the other two with money in them and place all four together.

He asked each of the team to carry their own five million dollars and to follow him to the van in front of the statue.

Andria laughed when she realized she had been traded for with an empty case loaded not with money but with C4. She commented that Matt was a true gambler.

Ian said that he had the cases with the actual money ready to go if each case continued to be examined. He had made the switch at the last moment when the kidnap leaders had suggested sending over two cases at once.

He chuckled and ask if she had a problem with how he gambled since it had worked out so well.

4 Race through the City

*I*an asked if they should take the black SUV.

Andria immediately said they should because it had all the camera equipment in it.

Mary spoke up and commented that it had comfortable seats.

Mike added that he thought it was bullet proofed.

Ian looked across the area at all the bodies and cringed at the carnage he had caused. He remembered his handler's comment about not killing too many of the abductors. So far, he had started out with a huge body count, and he was not yet out of Kenya. He was sure that none of the soldiers had expected to be mowed down by the brick and stone shrapnel caused by the explosions.

He asked everyone to select a weapon and pick up as much ammunition as possible as they made their way across to the SUV.

He went to where the two men in black suits were laying and picked up one of the phones. He hoped to be able to listen to the field communications of those that would come to the scene.

He picked up several of the rifles and was very pleased that one was a sniper's rifle. He stopped and checked it out and as he was picking up the bag of ammunition for it that the soldier had carried, he realized that the soldier had a case on his shoulder that held the scope for the rifle.

Ian figured that the find of a sniper's rifle might well be worth more than the money that he had brought for the ransom. It might well be the weapon that would save them.

He turned the van around and headed back the way the kidnapers had driven in. At the first intersection he took a right and just as he was about to make a left at the next intersection, he saw a convoy of soldiers speeding in toward the statue area. He knew that he had been very lucky with the departure timing. He made the left and then at the next intersection he took a right. He kept up his zig-zagging route up for several miles. Then at what seemed to be a major road he headed southeast. His goal was to get out of Kenya and to do so he needed to get to Mombasa where he had sent Ted with the Lazy Lady. He knew that he had to get out as quickly as possible because of the carnage he had left behind. He was beginning to suspect that it was the army that was in charge of staging the kidnaping.

Everybody in the SUV had been quiet since they had driven out of Nairobi. Then he had to divert from going south because he saw a roadblock where the military were checking out cars. He immediately took a small east bound road and drove away from that area.

This, however, put them well away from the direction he had hoped to be going. What made it worse was that the road was taking him east by northeast which was taking him farther away from where he wanted to go.

Getting food supplies and then finding a place to get some rest was what he figured needed to happen next.

He looked on the map and decided to go to Ol Donyo Sabuk National Park where he hoped they would be able to stop for the night. He knew he had to stay out of sight for the next few days.

A large grocery store in the suburbs caught his eye and he stopped there. He asked Mary and Iri to go in and get enough food for a week. He suggested that they get a variety of food that did not need to be refrigerated or kept cold but would fit everyone's appetite. He added they should get plenty of water and a variety of soft drinks.

He set out to obtain a new license plate. He found a screw driver in a tool box in the back of the SUV.

He had asked Andria and Mike to stay in the van but keep a look out in case they were being followed.

He removed the license plate on the SUV and went out hunting for a new one. He found a van parked by a dumpster that provided him the opportunity to switch plates.

Mary and Iri where just coming out of the grocery store pushing two fully loaded grocery carts when he returned. Iri was wearing a large brimmed, grass woven hat.

Ian knew that such a hat would be great if he were out in the hot Kenyon sun. He asked Iri to go back in and buy one for him.

Once Iri was back and they were all in, he asked Mike to drive so he could think through how they were going to get out of the country.

Andria shook her head and commented that she wondered who he really was, but she was so happy to see him that it really didn't matter who he was.

Ian, i.e. Matt, smiled and said that he was the problem-solver that had come to the aid of his old friends to solve their problem.

Iri commented that he was glad to have him as a friend.

Mike drove down a long dirt road into the middle of the park.

Every few miles Ian had Mike pull under the cover of a large oak or maple-like tree to put the van out of sight. On one such occurrence a helicopter flew by overhead confirming that there was an all-out search for them.

Deep into the park Ian directed Mike to a stand of trees that overlooked a small lake and had him pull well under the trees so that the van was not visible from the sky. He did not want it spotted from the air.

He opened one of the empty money cases to see if there was anything in the case that might be of use. He first defused the C4 and then examined the case. He found that the case was lined with a wire mesh. He figured that it was meant to keep the money from being detected.

The wire gauge was heavy enough that by folding it and doubling the wire, it was strong enough to serve as a fishhook. He then unwove part of the mesh to form a long continuous wire that was more than twenty feet long.

He decided that he was going to go fishing.

He looked down to the lake and was pleased to see weeping willow trees lining the lake bank. He saw several that were just right to become a fishing pole.

He found a box knife in the toolbox and walked with his line and his hook and led the way to where he saw a young slender willow that he felt was long enough to serve as a pole. He cut the small tree down and trimmed off the small limbs and leaves and created a clean ten-foot pole. He then looked around for something to serve as a bobber and for some sort of bait.

Mike walked over to a large flat stone and lifted it to expose a large number of very large ants tending to large plump larvae. He carefully picked up about a dozen and gently put the rock back in place.

Andria found a dry round seed pot and tested it out in the water. It floated, so she brought it over to Matt.

Ian took the seed pod and with a short piece of wire attached it to his line.

He accepted two ant larvae and put them on the hook.

He walked to the edge of the lake and threw his line out. He was surprised when almost immediately the bobber went under, and his pole bent.

He played the fish slowly in toward the shore and then walked backward uphill and dragged the fish up on the shore where both Andria and Mike worked together to capture it. It was a beauty that was about as long as Andrea's combined forearm and hand.

The sun reflecting off the scales made the top fins glisten a purple and black color and the scales formed a mesh of white and black that looked much like the mesh that had lined the money suitcase.

It would make a fine meal.

Mike commented that it was large enough that once grilled they would all be able to have a nice piece.

Ian suggested they try for another so that everyone could get a larger portion of fish.

Fishing seemed to release the tension that had embraced the group. Everyone tried their hand and without exception they all caught one.

It was clear that it had been a long time since anyone had fished on the lake.

Iri caught the biggest fish which turned out to be a huge catfish that had been sucking on his hook but had not given any hint of being on the line until Iri tried to pull his pole out of the water. He thought he had hooked a stump or had snagged his line on rocks on the bottom of the lake. He walked backward up the slope away from the lake and was surprised when the catfish started to fight to keep from getting pulled out.

It took him, Mike, and Andrea to get the fish up the slope.

Ian liked how the team had come back to life. They sat around and grilled fish on a variety of sticks that they had retrieved and made into skewers.

He listened as each of them shared a fishing story or gave advice on the best seasoning to bring out the flavor of a fish. He preferred his simple routine of salting the fish after each bite and putting it back out over the fire while he was chewing on the bite he had taken.

He had already decided where he was going to sleep. He pointed to a limb of a giant native silky oak that was about one hundred feet away from where the van was located. He suggest that Andrea and Mary fold the two back seats as flat as possible and that Iri was most likely short enough to be comfortable in the very back of the SUV.

He pointed Mike to another limb in the silky oak, but Mike said he preferred to incline the passenger's seat as far back as possible and sleep there.

Ian stripped the seat cover from the SUV's back seat and climbed into the tree and lay with his feet against the trunk and relaxed along the slight incline of the limb.

The night temperature dropped down to a cool fifty degrees. The temperature in the van dropped down to a comfortable level. Ian was glad to have the hat to cover his head to keep the dew off his face.

He woke up early and decided to see what he could find around the camp.

About halfway around the lake, he came across a black rhino family.

The bull was huge.

His horn was a beautiful black two-foot curved sickle-shaped arc that looked like it came to a very sharp point.

The cow was about two thirds his size and had a short stubby horn. She was shadowed by a calf that was about the size of a yearling cow.

He knew immediately what he was going to do.

He returned to camp and woke up the team and said they should grab the camera equipment and follow him because he had a surprise.

He took out his personal hand held, reflex lens digital camera and led the way to where the rhino family was located.

He spotted some droppings and decided to use the trick that had worked so well when he had put elephant manure on his clothing to get in close with the elephants. Once he had rubbed the harder rhino dropping on his clothes, he slowly walked out away from the tree that he had been hiding behind.

He wanted to get close enough to get some really close up shots that he knew Mary would like. As she referred to them as, "shots that made it easy to edit."

The cow must have seen his movement and walked slowly toward him. He was ready to bolt for the tree, if necessary, but he stood still. After a moment she snorted and turned away to take a bite of some green grass. The baby rhino came much closer but when it sniffed Ian it too turned away and went to its mother. It had come right up to him, and he knew that he had some great shots of the little one.

He followed the three as the bull led the way to a shady spot under a huge oak tree and lay down. The cow did the same and the little one pushed his nose between her legs to get his morning meal. The cow obligingly raised one leg so that her two tits were available to her calf.

Ian made his way slowly around the three and got close ups from his three hundred sixty excruciatingly slow walk.

When he got back to the tree trunk, he stepped behind it and took a deep breath. He made a production of lifting his camera lens cover in the air and displayed it to Andrea and then put it on. This was an old joke that went back to the time when they filmed the elephants.

He walked away from the scene keeping the large tree trunk between he and the three rhinos. Once he felt he was far enough away he turned and walked back to where the rest of the team was situated.

He handed Mary his camera and said that the pictures were hers, but he wanted his camera back.

Mary commented that with his and Mike's pictures she would be able to produce an entire set of pictures and that once she mixed in some shots that she had from other excursions she would be able to put together an entire story.

Andria commented on how crazy he still was but that she was sure his close ups would save the trip from being a total loss. She then held her nose and commented that he really needed to take a bath.

Back on the army airfield two side gunners, the pilot and co-pilot were just lifting off as the film team was out filming the rhinos. They had been given the coordinates where they would find the van with the group fleeing the army.

The pilot commented that it was going to be like shooting sitting ducks. He was homing in on the beacon that was sending out a strong signal.

He was flying in low and fast.

The two gunners were arguing with which one of them should get to have their side facing the van and be first to take out the people on the ground.

The pilot laughed and said he would give each of them equal time shooting the sitting ducks.

He was coming in low and at his top speed.

He began his first pass and as he took a long slow turn to the left to give his favorite gunner the first pass.

Suddenly his oil level gauge alarmed, and he saw dark grey smoke bellowing from the engine compartment.

He realized the chopper had been hit. He hoped desperately that he would be able to make it back to the airfield.

Little did he realize that he would make it less than halfway back when the engine would freeze, and the rotors would stop. His expertise saved the crew but all of them were injured when he brought it down for a hard landing.

When Ian got back to the van, he took out a light jogging outfit and walked down to the lake where he stripped down and carried all of clothes into the lake with him. After getting out and putting on his jogging outfit he spread his clothes out on some bushes to dry.

He returned to the van and was getting his suitcase organized when he heard the sound of a helicopter.

He looked up and barely visible on the horizon he could see the dark green of what he figured was a military helicopter coming directly toward them.

He assembled his sniper's rifle and took a position under the oak tree and looked through his scope. It was clear to him that it was indeed coming straight at them.

He waited until the chopper was just within the range of his sniper's rifle and to the point that he felt comfortable to shoot. He was trying to incapacitate the copter in such a fashion that it would need to return to some place where it could safely land.

His first shot hit but it did not do what Ian wanted it to do.

The second shot hit the engine compartment and must have hit the oil pan or done some other damage because smoke started coming out of the compartment.

The helicopter turned and went back along the route that it had come.

Ian shouted that it was time for them to leave. He ran down and rescued his clothes and returned to the van.

He asked that they all check the van to see if they could find a tracking device. Mike was the one that found it attached to the top of the back wheel well on the driver's side. He was able to pull it off.

He asked how Ian had known that there would be one.

Ian responded that the helicopter was coming straight at them and must have been following a signal.

Ian trimmed the two-sided tape on the tracking device and said he would be back shortly. He instructed the team to get ready to leave.

He jogged back to where the rhinos were still napping. He boldly walk to the back of the bull and clued the tracking device to his back haunch. He figured it would stay in place for a couple of days and then would drop off.

He jogged back to the van and had Mike take a small road that went directly east.

The small road seemed to go on forever.

During the transit Ian put in a call to his support team and requested a new transport.

He specified that it be white, bullet proof, have tinted windows all around and have comfortable seating for five.

Andrea laughed and asked what kind of rental company offered delivery services in the Keyan outback.

After several hours Ian was beginning to worry when the small road ended in a large parking lot where there were several vans and other cars that were mostly parked under the trees around the lot and not in the parking spaces so they could be in the shade. Ian pointed to a white SUV on the other side of the lot parked in a spot that was on the lot but in the shade of a huge tree.

Andrea commented that she could not believe that he had ordered a specific vehicle in the middle of an isolated park and a few hours later had it waiting for him and conveniently parked in the shade.

He had Mike pull up parallel to it and they transferred all their belongings into their new transport.

He then put the black SUV farther under the large tree so that it would be hard to spot from the air.

Mike commented on how much better their new SUV drove.

Everyone else made some sort of comment about its comfort and the great view they now enjoyed.

Back at the army airfield the command was shocked to get the mayday call from the helicopter that had been sent out to eliminate the escaping film crew.

The command group had been expecting a successful kill report and had a site cleanup crew standing by to be sent to the location to clean up the carnage. Instead, they sent out an ambulance to the coordinates sent in by the copter pilot.

They decided to send out the new gunship helicopter that sported a gatling gun. It had arrived at the beginning of the month and had yet to see action in the field. They assigned all three pilots trained to fly it to take it out and find the van by homing in on the tracking signal.

Shortly after the chopper left the field, they called back to say that the signal had led them to a rhinoceros that was standing in the middle of the forest.

A variety of theories of how the tracking device could possibly end up on a rhino ensued.

Everyone knew that some brave or very stupid person had to be responsible.

When the airfield commander called General Mumbada he was told to have the helicopter search the highway for an SUV or large vehicle going south to Mombasa and take out any vehicle capable of carrying five people and a be able to carry a significant amount of luggage.

The order was sent out and the gunship went towards the highway.

The pilots was enjoying taking the new gunship into action. The three carried on a continuous chatter about how great it felt.

They had all qualified on the gunship and were eager to see how it performed in actual combat. They viewed their current assignment well short of combat but figured it would give them the feel of how it could take out their chosen target.

The pilot pointed to white SUV driving south toward Mombasa. It was the only vehicle for as far as any of them could see so they agreed that they should take it out. They swooped in and the gatling gun put out a stream of bullets that hit the passenger side but amazingly did not stop the vehicle.

The pilot radioed in that they had found their target, and he was going in for the kill.

He took a long sweep around and lined up for the kill shot. He was surprised when he tried to fire, and the gatling gun seemed to disintegrate and send shrapnel back at the window. He was just about to swing away when he saw a star-shaped hole appeared in the window in front of him, and the pain in his chest caused him to lean forward. He watched in amazement as the highway seemed to be coming toward him as his vision slowly ceased.

Periodically Ian would stand up through the sunroof and scan the horizon. He did this every fifteen or twenty minutes and thought that perhaps they would not be found but about three quarters of the way towards Mombasa he spotted a helicopter making its approach. Looking through his sniper scope, he realized that it was one of the newer gunships that sported a fifty-caliber gatling gun that fired six thousand rounds per minute.

The sight of such a formidable craft cause his veins to run cold. He knew they were in deep trouble.

He let everyone know that they were about to be attacked.

He asked Iri to hand him a bullet every time he put his hand back for one. He then stood up and positioned himself.

He told Mike to zig zag down the road and to constantly change speed.

The Helio got one round off and hit the SUV on the passenger door and cracked the bullet proof window next to where Andrea was sitting.

Ian fired three shots at the barrel section of the gatling gun as it came in for a second round. He then put three shots through the window and took out the pilot. It appeared that the Helio was going to crash directly into them.

He shouted to Mike to gun it and go straight down the highway.

He watched as the Helio hit the edge of the highway directly behind them, slid across and then blew up when it went into the ditch.

Andria sat back up straight and then touched the cracked bullet proof window and commented that if she lived to tell the story of the filming of the Black Rhino, she would add the adventure that she and her team had so far lived through.

Ian smiled and asked if it would be as good as her last two documentaries.

Andria smiled and said that the last footage of whales, dolphins and Orcas that he had sent her had gotten the team raises and she had been promoted.

This time she was only hoping to make it out alive.

Ian nodded and said that alive would be good.

He then said they would need to change their mode of transportation but this time they would need to do it the old-fashioned way and stop at some car lot and buy whatever they could so they could continue to the coast.

He had Mike stop at the first lot that they found where there were several cars on the lot.

There was one newer pickup that had an extended cab that fit the bill. The camera equipment and luggage was put in the back and a tarp was put over all of it. The cab was roomy enough that everyone was comfortable.

The lot owner asked about the SUV and Ian said that it was his to keep but that he should take it to the repair shop to have the passenger door repaired and suggested that he change the color of the SUV as well.

The owner smiled, nodded and seemed to understand that the van was hot.

They arrived to Mumbada and drove to where the Lazy Lady was anchored just off the beach.

After all the luggage and equipment was off loaded, Ian said that he had business that needed finishing in Nairobi, and he was driving there and would return when that was over.

It was about a five-hour drive, and he arrived there early in the morning.

5 General's Greed

General Mumbada was furious that he had lost more than forty men and two helicopters to whomever had come to the rescue of the kidnapped film crew. He had just purchased the helicopter gunship that had been shot down at a cost of fifty million dollars. He had been planning to use it if and when he decided to take over the country. He pounded his desk and shout out, "fifty million dollars. I want the head of the person who shot it down." He now faced not only the loss of many men and two invaluable helicopters, but he was also out of the twenty million dollars ransom.

How the exchange of the prisoners for the twenty million dollars could have gone so wrong was beyond comprehension. The carnage out in front of the statue and on the steps down to the lower parking lot had shocked and astounded him. He had been in some battles, but he had never seen so many bodies in such a small space.

He had been told a moment prior to the carnage that there was only one person present with the ransom money.

He thought that if he had a few people like him in his army he could take over Kenya and the rest of Africa. He wondered how one person could possibly have done so much damaged but worse he had gotten away with both the kidnapped people and the money. He had left a trail of death and destruction that shocked both he and Lionel, his second in command.

His men had found the tracking device that he had planted on the black SUV out in the middle of the Ol Donyo Sabuk National Park reserve. Later they found the black van abandoned miles away parked under a tree just off the normal parking lot used by hikers.

He had sent out his prized new gunship to look for any cars that were heading south on B8. It had found one and had gone in for the kill. But later he learned that it had somehow been shot out of the sky.

A gunship that he knew was one of the most formidable weapons in the sky had been brought down by someone in the SUV!

He could only believe it was the same person who had caused the carnage at the ransom exchange.

It all seemed impossible.

He slammed his hand down on his desk and shouted out in anger.

He and Lional discussed how they might still capture this mysterious, deadly person and decided to monitor the coast for any major navy vessel that might be waiting for this person.

They set up a meeting with the General of the Airforce to get him to cruise the coast to check for any foreign naval vessels or any smaller boats making their way away from the port of Mombasa.

Some how they needed to eliminate this destroyer of their well laid plans.

He was also worried about what General Ingraditi might do to take advantage of the situation.

As it turned out General Mumbada had a right to be worried.

General Ingraditi was indeed monitoring the situation. He had gone to the square where all the bodies of the dead soldiers were still being removed. He walked the area and realized that whoever had orchestrated the events that took place was a formidable adversary that if left alone might solve his problem with his two adversary generals who had gone well beyond what was acceptable for anyone in the army.

They would need to be dealt with, but he figured it was worth waiting to see how much more they would lose trying to carry out their current kidnapping scheme.

A short time later, his informant reported that two helicopters had been lost in pursuit of the escaped camera crew. He knew that one was the newest gunships that the army had acquired at an exceedingly high cost that he had objected to.

This cemented his decision to standby and monitor what took place.

Ian arrived in Nairobi in the wee hours of the morning. On the way he had called his support group and asked for the name of the person who was in charge of the army that controlled Nairobi and what his normal daily schedule was. He also asked for information about the person second in command, and he wanted pictures of both.

The information came back to him as he drove into Nairobi. He drove to the work address he had been given. It was an old colonial structure that looked like a library with four columns out front. It had a large loop in front that came in directly from a main thoroughfare. A block away to one side there were tall glass front, glimmering business office buildings.

As he looked around, he realized that there was only one two story building on the other side that might provide him a place to shoot from.

The taller buildings on the other side of the circle were all better sniper locations, but he figured they would be traps for him because he would have to come down several stories and then exit into very busy streets. The much smaller building would make the shot extremely difficult, but he would be able to depart in seconds and drive away in a direction that would not expose him.

He drove to the smaller three-story building and entered the parking lot in back and then he drove his escape route. He found a large bus station where he could abandon his pickup in a multilevel parking lot that was down the street from the station.

He went into the bus station and bought two tickets. One to Kampala to the west and another to Mombasa in the south. He wanted to be able to openly get on the bus to Kampala, get off of it once it had gone a few blocks and then come back and get on the bus going to Mombasa. He hoped that action would for a short time misdirect anyone that might be trying to track him.

He then returned to the two-story building and sighted in his rifle for the range that he would be shooting across.

The rifle had a silencer, so he took a practice shop at a red soft drink can that was illuminated by the street light. The can flew up into the air and let him know that his shot came in a little low.

He figured he had just enough height to shoot over the heads of the guards that he was sure would surround the general. His target was the general and he didn't want to hit one of the soldiers.

It would need to be one of his better shots.

He then napped through most of the early morning but was up early to monitor the situation in front of the general's office building. It remained quiet throughout the early morning until people began arriving for work.

He arranged his bullets so he could take several shots if necessary.

He had concluded that it would be too dangerous for him to take the rifle with him, so he planned to abandon everything on the roof when he left.

He was not worried about leaving the evidence behind. In fact, he figured it would create work that would cause any decision makers to wait to get what they believed to be critical information and then they would be confused when they found no fingerprints on the weapon and learned the weapon belonged to one of the dead soldiers killed in front of the statue during the ransom exchange.

He watched as a black limo, followed by a military truck with a mounted fifty-caliber machine gun, entered the square.

He loaded his rifle and got ready.

He watched as six soldiers stood three on each side of the limo's back door as it was opened.

His peripheral vision caught a similar limo also followed by an armored truck entering and parking behind the first two vehicles.

He kept his eyes on the first limo and the person stepping out from it. When that person was totally out, and he verified their identity, he slowly squeezed the trigger.

He did not wait to see what had happened but automatically reloaded.

He raised his scope to catch the second person getting out of the second limo. He verified that it was the second person he had on his short list of two. He followed the same procedure and watched as a second shot successfully found the target.

His shots had been silent, his location at the top of the less-than-ideal building had proved to be the best one for him. There was no return gunfire.

He made his move to escape.

One thousand and one.

He put everything down and crawled across the roof.

One thousand and two.

One thousand and three.

One thousand and four

He was to the back to the fire escape.

One thousand five.

He slid down the fire escape

One thousand six.

He got into the pickup, started it.

One thousand seven.

One thousand eight.

One thousand nine.

He drove away.

One thousand ten.

He took a deep breath and thought, "get away time ten seconds."

He drove to the bus station, went past it and turned into the public parking garage across the street and parked his pickup in a back far corner, got out and walked back to the bus station where the bus to Kampala was just loading.

He handed the bus driver his ticket and took the first seat behind him and put his overnight bag on his lap.

He chatted with the bus driver letting him know that he was going to his brother's wedding.

The bus left the station and two blocks later, he let out a loud groan and explained that he needed to get off because he had left his wallet in his car.

The bus driver stopped to let him off but said that he could not refund the ticket and that would need to be done at the station.

Ian thanked him for stopping and giving him the information and gave him a tip.

He then got out and casually walked back to the station and got on the bus that would go to Mombasa. This time he took one of the back seats near the back door.

After the bus was on the way, Ian placed a call to his support team and put in an order for the armament he wanted to take on board the Lazy Lady.

He then put his seat back and fell asleep.

The bus stopped for lunch, and he had a half of a grilled chicken with a side of French fries, took a short walk and then got back on the bus.

He had called ahead to let Ted know that he was on the way and would arrive late in the afternoon and that he would have a significant amount luggage to bring on board.

General Ingraditi learned about the assassination of Generals Mumbada and Wesbow and moved immediately to take firm command of their sections of the Army. He sent out communiques to all the military leaders announcing his consolidation of the Army under his command.

He visited the offices of both Mumbada and Wesbow and noted their proud display of their graduation degrees.

He smiled as he thought about the fact that they had gone to the next world as number one followed by number two.

It was the order that the two had gone throughout their lives. He was sure this time their greed had led them to make choices that had resulted in their one-two demise. They had underestimated a very deadly opponent.

He had no plans to pursue that person and hoped that he and the team of photographers would leave the country. He was sure that the person that had come to their rescue had also come with the means of escape, and he had no plans to get in the way.

Ted shared the news with the rest of the team that Matt was on his way back and that he had asked that he be prepared to bring a fair amount of luggage on board.

Andrea commented that the luggage that Matt was talking about would most likely be weapons.

Ted shared the fact that he had captained for Matt several years earlier and the only weapon he had ever seen him use was a camera.

Andrea laughed and said that Matt had always been the best with whatever weapon he had in his hands and that he used his camera with the same expertise that she was sure he could use whatever weapon he had in his hands.

She added that she had now witnessed what he could do under almost any situation and figured him to be one of the world's most deadly, dangerous, gentle, friendly persons she had ever met.

She asked if anyone wanted to bet on what Matt's luggage would be.

Ian arrived in Mombasa and left the bus station and got in a taxi. He got a call that his order was at the location he had specified.

He had the taxi driver drop him off in the beach side parking lot entrance and after paying him he walked toward the pile that he saw just past the far end at of the parking lot.

He took inventory and found that he was short one shoulder grenade launcher. A note on the pile explained that they had not been able to get a third one in the time frame he had specified. They had augmented the number of grenades for the grenade launchers.

He called Ted to pick him up.

Once all the boxes were brought on board he asked if supper was yet to be served because he was starving.

Mary said that they were having a pepperoni-cheese pizza with extra cheese that would be out of the oven in a few moments. She added that she had made a small side salad and a large pitcher of tea to round things out.

Andrea asked if whatever he had gone back to Nairobi to address had been resolved successfully.

Ian nodded and said that he figured their trouble with being hunted was over.

Andrea asked if that was the case why had he brought enough fire power on board to take on a fleet of ships.

Ian smiled and asked why she thought it was armament.

She laughed and said because what was in each box was boldly written on its exterior.

Ted had listened to the exchange and realized that he was seeing another side of Matt that he had not seen on their first time together.

He wondered what Matt had been up to when they had sailed the Whistling Nanny and then he remembered the gigantic explosion as they left the harbor in Ensenada. He now wondered if Matt had something to do with that explosion that had been unbelievably loud even a mile out to sea.

Ian ate his pizza and afterwards went up on the deck and proceeded to unpack the various weapons.

He put the two self-propelled grenade launchers and the extra grenades at the very back of the yacht.

He then unpacked his new sniper's rifle, assembled it and then tried several shots out at stones he saw on the beach.

Andrea and the rest of the team watched and were amazed at how good he was.

Once he was satisfied, he unpacked a series of weapons for each person on board.

He threw out several plastic bottles and asked everyone to shoot at the bottles. He took note that Mike and Ted were proficient with the rifles they had chosen, The rest were able to get a few shots close to the bottles with varied success.

He figured he had two capable marksmen, and the rest were willing shooters.

He thought about the saying, "you make tea with the leaves you have on hand."

In this case he had to make do with the army that was on board the Lazy Lady.

He asked Ted to take the packing material to the beach and to pick up the target bottles on the way.

He then explained that he was preparing to interact with the coastal pirates that would most probably try to take them as hostages for ransom and the Lazy Lady as a prize.

Andria commented that the trip to film black rhinos seemed to have a continuous set of twists and turns that tested their survival skills.

It seemed to her that they had just gotten out of the frying pan but had jumped into the fire. She added that she did not want to be hostage to any other Africans, pirates or otherwise.

Ian smiled and commented that she was the one that had signed the filming contract. He then asked if she had read the fine print to see if it had a "do not kidnap or no pirates allowed clause" that she might have missed.

She nodded and said that she had not read her contract that carefully.

<u>6 Pirates</u>

General Ingraditi reviewed the arial panoramic stream of images that his helicopter had captured of the short but dramatic battle between the four pirate vessels and a single sailing yacht of about the same size.

He was sure he was now seeing the actions of the same individual who had vanquished more than forty attacking soldiers, had taken down two helicopters and had so efficiently assassinated Generals Mumbada and Wesbow.

The report about the assassination had stated that it had taken almost an hour to find the location of where the shots had been taken because the assumption was that a sniper would have chosen one of the tall buildings that allowed for a clear direct shot.

The folks in the field explained that shooting from the three-story building put the two shots in the extremely lucky category.

The general figured that there was nothing about luck that was involved. It had not been luck that had so far ensured the escape of the camera crew and whoever was rescuing them.

Now as he reviewed the footage coming in from his helicopter that was flying along the coast, he was not surprised so much as he was amazed.

He marveled at the first bomb that was clearly a homemade device being hurdled at the first boat and was taken by surprise at seeing the boat seemingly stand on its nose and drive itself half way down into the water. The second and third boats each suffered a similar fate. The fourth boat stopped to pick up the few survivors that were in the water.

He knew these were not novice pirates but ones that had in the past attacked and taken over huge merchant ships and held them for ransom. It was clear they had not expected to face the type of defensive actions that devastated them. The fourth attack ship had stopped to rescue the pirates on the first three boats. The boats did not sink and would most likely be salvaged.

The unscathed yacht sailed on.

He knew that his decision to discontinue having the army pursue the film crew had been the correct one. He was sure that he would need to mend some political fences as part of resolving the whole kidnapping incident but that was a small price to pay for now having complete control of the army and subsequently the entire country.

He knew he would be able to lay the blame on two deceased generals.

He was now the top dog, or as many Kenyans would say the Pride's Male Lion. He would make sure that he would be Kenya's Lion.

He took the initiative to leak key portions of the video of the pirate attack as a means of closing the chapter of what had happened in Kenya.

On the morning after they left Mombasa Ian saw the approaching pirates. He realized that there were four large high-speed boats and that he would need more firepower than he had laid out.

He figured he would not have time to reload a rocket launcher, so he retrieved a block of C4 and carefully wrapped a nylon cord around it that extended out about three feet.

He cut a foot off a broomstick and tied the cord to it. This would allow him to swing the C4 in a loop and then release the entire contrivance as he launched it at the bow of the nearest of the oncoming boats.

He decided to use the homemade bomb first and then follow up with the self-propelled grenades.

The rate at which the boats were closing in surprised him. He asked Ted to take the Lazy Lady to its top speed and make rather wide zig zags so he could get the oncoming boats to close in close to each other as they pursued them.

He asked Mike to stand by in case a pirate got on board. He suggested everyone else go below.

As the boats closed in, he watched as the boat that had been in the lead for some reason dropped back.

Ian had no way of knowing that the captain of that lead boat had seen something that brought back the memory of the horrible explosion that had wiped out most of the members of the group of pirate boat operators of which he was one of the few who miraculous survived and that the name "Lazy Lady" was forever burned in his mind. It had been many years ago, but that day and that name was forever burned in the mind of the pirate boat captain.

That golden name often woke him from a nightmare that had him drenched in sweat. He had survived but the hard life of a fisherman had kept him in the pirate trade. Since then, he had moved up in the quality of his attack boat that had three crew members, two gunners and himself. He dropped back from the lead and called the boats with him to cease their pursuit, but they insisted that they had their quarry and were going in for the capture. He watched as one after the other the boats were destroyed and most of the men on those boats killed. It was a repeat of the first time he had interacted with whoever sailed the "Lazy Lady."

He thanked the stars for having dropped back.

His boat and he and his crew were unscathed.

He stopped to pick up the survivors of which there were only three.

When the lead boat began to fire Ian shot the gunner at the machine gun position then he picked up his makeshift bomb and after getting a few swings and judging the distance to the bow he launched the C4 in a high arc. As he watched, it seemed that the pirate boat moved in to catch the bomb on its bow.

The explosion completely tore off the bow, and it looked like the boat was trying to stand on its nose as its speed drove it down into the sea.

The boat directly behind it swung out and began to fire. Mike responded with rapid cover fire while Ian picked up the self-propelled grenade launcher and aimed it for the second boat's bow. The grenade took out the bow and that boat made it halfway into the water before bouncing back out up like a cork, but it came up and was engulfed in flames.

The third boat seemed to follow the same approach and as Mike took the initiative and shot the gunner, Ian fired the second grenade and took out the third boat that repeated what seemed to be a bow first plunge.

The fourth boat stopped and focused on rescuing the men on the first three boats as the Lazy Lady continued sailing on.

Ian noted the helicopter that had been following the action halted its forward progress, hover for a few moments and then turn and fly back toward Mombasa. He wondered if it was an army helicopter and how much of the battle had been recorded.

Andrea had retreated to the kitchen area, but she decided to take up Mike's field camera and crawled out to capture what was taking place. It was hard for her to focus on the action because she kept ducking as if she was the focus of the shooting. She was sure that Mike would have had a steadier hand on the camera.

After the action was over, she came out on deck with Mike's camera and said she had captured the entire engagement and figured she would be able to make it a part of the story that she was planning to call of Rhinos and the Horns of Injustice.

Ian suggested they swing in close to Zanzibar to take them as far off the coast as possible so they would not draw the attention of any other pirates since he was short of ammunition. He had reloaded the two rocket launchers and figured he could handle another round but preferred to savor his win rather than take a chance of a repeat performance and getting someone onboard wounded or worse, killed.

He asked Ted to sail into Dar es Salaam where the team would need to clear Tanzanian customs before catching a flight home.

Ian knew that it would be tricky for him. He would need to use his US passport to be able to show ownership of the Lazy Lady. This was something that he did not want to expose to the team.

He went to the bow for privacy and made a call to his support team. He arranged for a hotel for the team members, located a bank where the millions that he had for each team member could be deposited and for flight reservations and tickets back to the US.

He added the request that all the equipment and suitcases automatically clear the customs inspection at their landing location.

He instructed that the information be sent to Andrea Millar and gave her phone number.

He put in the request for his own and his captains entrance and exit paperwork with the Lazy Lady from Tanzania be immediately issued.

He then returned to the kitchen area and joined the rest of the team.

Somehow their arrival to the Zanzibar port and the pirate attack had become known. A Military boat came out to escort them in. It took them to a peer at the Dar es Salaam port. There were several news crews waiting when they docked, the team was surrounded and bombarded with question on how they had survived the pirate attack.

Ian used this distraction to clear customs and to certify his ownership of the Lazy Lady. He had no plans to disembark but planned to leave as soon as approval to leave was granted.

A call to his support team as they were being escorted in proved to be wise. They had cleared both his arrival and immediate departure after offloading his passengers. They confirmed that they would give Andrea a call as the Lazy Lady left port.

Ted supervised the offloading and once everything was cleared, he cast off.

Andria had been overwhelmed by the onslaught of the news crews all shouting over each other as they asked about the pirate engagement. She turned to see where Matt happened to be and realized that he and Ted had the Lazy Lady heading out of the harbor.

Tears came to her eyes because she figured she would never be able to thank Matt, or whoever he was, for having come to her and the team's rescue. She waved and was pleased to see flashing from what she figured was a mirror.

Her phone buzzed in her pocket, and she read a rather long message explaining that she, her team, their belongings had all cleared customs and that she should proceed to a hotel that had been reserved for her and her team.

She then realized that the four suitcases with five million dollars in each were all lined up with the name of each team member written in black on them and they had the custom clearance papers taped to them.

She had no idea how Matt had pulled that off, but she figured that now it was up to the four of them to get the money put into a bank that she had also been told about.

Later they could move the money to whatever country they planned to live in. She wondered where the money had come from, but she also knew that it was now each team member's money to use as they pleased.

She shook her head as she thought about the fact that they had been kidnapped, had managed to get enough footage to produce a story about the black rhino and were going home with enough money that they could easily retire or do whatever they desired.

It was more than she could process, and she decided to gather the team and get all their things moved to the hotel.

She looked out to where the Lazy Lady was just a dot.

Ian used his binoculars to watch the crowd on the pier. When Andrea turned to look for the Lazy Lady, he used his cell phone to reflect the sun to flash her a goodbye. He wished he could have stayed with the team, but he had accomplished his mission and the problem had been solved.

It was time for him to get back to his Leslie.

Ted figured that the person he knew both as Captain Bitterly and more recently as Mathew Parker were both fictious names. He asked Matt whether he would ever know his real name.

Ian laughed and used the old expression that if he learned his real name he would have to be shot.

He added that instead of worrying about who he was, he should think about how he was going to use the bonus he was getting for doing such a great job as the captain of the Lazy Lady. He was only being rewarded with half of what the camera crew had received because he had only been in on half of the fun that the rest had experienced. But if he accepted the bonus he would have to stop asking about names.

Ted asked what half amounted to and almost fell over when he learned that it was two and a half million dollars. He figured that Matt by any other name would always be Matt to him. The trip across the Atlantic took an entirely new meaning about getting a bonus and how it felt to get a bonus that made him rich.

On the way across the Atlantic, Ian arranged for Ted to take care of the Lazy Lady and keep her active as part of his business.

When they got to Tampa, he thanked Ted for having been a good sailing partner.

They celebrated with a beer and then, he walked down the pier and took a cab to the Airport, took a flight and was soon back to Cincinnati. When he got to the escalator leading to the baggage claim area he looked up and the sunshine of his life was standing at the top smiling down at him.

This was his reward and one that had put the light in his mind on high so that the dark of his mind was manageable and worth more than all the gold in the world.

7 Conclusion

*A*ndria stood staring at the name on the back of the sailing yacht She had returned to the states and she and the team had put together another outstanding story that earned all of them the best of the year award from the company that was accompanied with a shopping spree reward. They had also all received a very generous cash bonus.

When asked what she planned to do next she let her boss know that she was leaving to get a PhD in photographic journalism.

Her boss congratulated her and said that the company would grant her a stipend that would cover her tuition to whatever university she selected on the condition that she document her PhD experience and let them have first refusal of her dissertation.

She accepted.

She was accepted to the University of South Florida. It had been one of her top choices because of its location on the Gulf of Mexico coast.

She had become an avid sailor, and on most weekends, she went out sailing with her friends and more recently with a special professor that she was dating.

She had been walking along the boardwalk that made its way along the harbor when in the distance she saw a yacht that seemed familiar, so she had gone down to the dock and walked out on the pier.

Now she was a statue with her feet anchored fast as she stared at the name painted in gold on the aft of the sailing yacht.

It was a very familiar one that was forever emblazoned in her mind.

She was looking at the name, "*Lazy Lady*."

She was frozen in her spot because she had tears running down her eyes and was afraid to move. Finally, after wiping away her tears, she walk toward the yacht. She wondered if there was anyone on board. As she got nearer, she saw Ted sitting and looking at her.

Ted had been watching the person at the end of the pier.

She looked very familiar, but he was not sure that he was seeing who he thought he was or if his eyes were playing a trick on him.

She finally continued coming toward the Lazy Lady.

He raised his beer that he was sipping and called out to her and suggested she come on board so they could talk about old times.

Andria teared up again.

It was hard to believe that she was once again on the Lazy Lady.

She asked if Ted owned her.

He shook his head and said that the owner was none other than their Matt or whatever his real name might be. He admitted to checking who the person to whom the boat was registered at the marina's main office, and it was registered to a Matthew Bitterly Parker.

He added that the middle name was the one that was used out on the west coast on another of Matt's problem-solving assignments when he had first met him and was the second in command on a twin of the Lazy Lady.

He said that Matt had given him a sizeable bonus for the recent adventure they had on the Lazy Lady on the condition he quit trying to find out his name and with the stipulation that he take care of the Lazy Lady.

He said that he had adhered to both.

He then asked if Andria would care to spend a few hours sailing.

Andria nodded, trying to find her voice to say yes.

Once they were underway, she asked if she could take the wheel and sail her.

As she sailed the Lazy Lady a warm melancholy feeling swept through her. She had relived the adventure in Kenya and the escape that they had made many times.

Now to be sailing the Lazy Lady was like a dream come true.

Later in the afternoon as she was sailing back into the harbor, she asked if she could schedule another outing so that her significant other could experience sailing with her on the Lazy Lady.

She had told that person the entire story of her adventure associated with the filming in Kenya and then the escape on the Lazy Lady.

She was sure that he would love to go out on her.

Ted smiled and said that most weekdays were open, but the Lazy Lady did not get to be lazy on weekends and was booked out for more than three months.

Andria called her significant other and asked if he had any open days. It turned out that he had no classes on Thursdays and used that day to grade papers or prepare for a new lecture topic.

Andria booked the following Thursday.

Ted asked her whether she preferred seafood or red meat for the late lunch meal. He then added that breakfast was made to order and if she wanted a full day out, she would need to be on deck at eight in the morning.

Andria smiled and suggested they stay with seafood and that he should surprise her on what that might be. As she was getting ready to leave, she asked what the cost for such an outing might be.

Ted held up his bottle and said that two cases of beer and two bottles of wine would cover the trip.

Andrea gave him a hug and said she and her significant other would be on time.

Ted watched as Andrea walked away. He was feeling great about her finding the Lazy Lady.

He was just about to call it a day and go home when his phone began to chirp. It was the call of the loon and he had assigned that call to only one person.

Ian had received a brief call from one of his unknown team members informing him that Andria had found the Lazy Lady and asked if there was any concern about the matter. He thanked the caller for the information and said that there was no issue.

He then called Ted to see how sailing with Andria had gone.

Ted answered and was surprised about the question. He asked if he was being watched.

Ian assured him that he was not being watched but that Andria was and would continue to be watched for a few years until whomever the watchers were became satisfied with her safety.

Ted asked whether their Iowa participants on the trip where he had first sailed with him were being watched.

Ian responded that they had been watched for almost a year, but they were never directly in danger like Andrea and her team had been.

Ted then asked if he had been watched.

Ian explained that he had been scrutinized and thoroughly vetted before he had been hired for their first trip together.

Ted laughed and said that so far, he had loved every minute of the experiences he had with Mathew Bitterly Parker and looked forward to another adventure in the future.

Ian chuckled and said that at the right time he would host a reunion of the Kenyan Four and their significant others on the Lazy Lady.

Ted said that he would look forward to the reunion.

Andrea returned to her apartment and spent most of the evening talking about the her sailing the Lazy Lady. She could not get over having gone for a walk and then having spotted a sailing vessel out of all the sail boats anchored in the harbor that turned out to be the Lazy Lady.

That evening she called Mike who now was living in Seatle and let him know about finding the Lazy Lady and taking her out for a several hour sail.

Mike asked if she had run into Matt.

Andrea let him know that Ted did not know where Matt was or how to get in touch with him. She asked if he was open to taking a vacation on the Lazy Lady in the coming summer. By then they might be celebrating her getting her PhD.

Mike agreed that he would love to do that. He figured that the rest of the team would all enjoy such a reunion.

A day later Ian got another call informing him of the planned reunion that would take place in the coming summer. He thanked the caller and said he would wait for them to give him the time, date, and the names of all those that were going to attend.

He said that he wanted to arrange his arrival to the Lazy Lady by helicopter after she passed under the Sunshine Skyway Bridge.

Less than a year later his handlers gave him a call.

Ian was expecting a call focused on a new problem and was pleasantly surprised that the caller gave him the date when his helicopter ride to the Lazy Lady was scheduled. He chuckled and asked what else there was.

His caller told him that the Lazy Lady had been booked for a wedding and a graduation ceremony of an Andria Miller to an Andre Mikles. The date was to be July 15.

Ian asked that a deed for the Lazy Lady be prepared that made Andria the owner with the stipulation that Ted Nickson was to be kept on as the Captain until he decided to retire. He also wanted to have a case of beer delivered to Ted with a message letting him know to expect one additional surprise guest that would arrive in an unusual way.

His caller said, "done" and then hung up.

Ian let Lesley know of the situation and asked if she wanted to go with him.

Lesley said that she would be a fish out of water at the event and that he should plan on attending on his own. She added that for once she would not be home worrying about what danger he was facing.

Ian decided not to share how he planned to board the Lazy Lady.

Andrea worked hard to close her PhD dissertation. The wedding arrangement was the simple part. She did not plan on a wedding dress and chose to have a simple wedding cake. She hired a catering company to prepare for a rather extensive lunch menu, bring it on board and then limit the number of servers to two people.

Her wedding and PhD celebration invitation list was as short as she dared make it. Her parents and Andre's parents were at the top of her list. They were followed by her team members. Andre had his long-time friend be his best man and his brother as a groomsman. She had asked Mary to be her matron of honor.

Ted had been surprised when she asked him to perform the wedding and let her know that he was honored to be asked.

The final list added up to fifteen people and with the two caters there would be seventeen on board.

She cleared the number with Ted to make sure that was acceptable.

Early in the morning on the day of the wedding, Ian left Cincinnati and flew to Tampa. Once there he was met and escorted to where a military helicopter was waiting for him. One of the crew members explained how "T" lift that would lower him to the deck of the yacht worked. They practiced that from twenty feet up before taking him out to the yacht.

The sun was rising when Andria and Andre arrived at the pier where the Lazy Lady was moored. They stood at the head of the pier and greeted their wedding guests and sent them down to where Ted was taking them onboard. The caterers arrived and took the food onboard.

Finally, it was time to depart.

She went to the wheel and stood with Andre at her side as Ted untied the Lazy Lady and jumped on board.

Andrea used the engine to carefully navigate out into the harbor's open area and then raised the main sail. She cautiously sailed out toward the Sunshine Skyway Bridge.

As they were approaching the bridge Ted came to her and asked to take over.

She was surprised but they had been sailing for about an hour and she figured that it was good time to mingle with the rest of the family and friends.

Ted had received a message from Matt that he was making a surprise arrival once the Lazy Lady passed under the bridge. He saw a helicopter hovering on the other side of the bridge and after passing through and sailing for about three football fields he lowered the sail as the chopper came in and hovered about forty feet in the air.

Everyone on board was looking up wondering what was happening.

Andrea started laughing when she saw Matt being lowered from the helicopter.

Ian looked down and waved. He stepped off on the bow and waved up to the pilot as the copter raised the lift, swayed, and then flew away.

Andrea ran up to the bow and gave him a hug, led him back in to the kitchen area and introduced him to Andre, his brother and his parents and then her parents.

She explained that she was alive and here to be wed because of Matt and that his dramatic arrival matched all his other escapades with her and her film crew.

When it came time for the wedding ceremony, Andrea approached Ian and asked if he were a captain and if so, would he take part in the ceremony.

Ian smiled and said that he was not a certified captain but that he was an ordained minister and would be honored to be part of performing her wedding.

Andrea smiled and shook her head and said that seemed such a dichotomy to what he had done in saving her.

Ian nodded and agreed that it even seemed strange to him.

Ted took the sails down and tied the boom off and then stepped in front of the wheel area and ask the bride and groom to step up to his level.

He had Mendelssohn's wedding march playing on the ships sound system as they stepped up to him.

He appreciated the smile on Andrea's face as she stepped up toward him.

Ian was standing at his side and together they performed the wedding.

Andrea was ecstatic as she and Andre exchanged vows and accepted each other's gold wedding rings.

She knew that she had found her soul mate.

And she was especially happy that Matt had arrived in time to perform the wedding.

Ian watched as the two kissed and then stepped down into the kitchen area and received congratulations from everyone on board.

Andrea and Andre cut the small wedding cake and gave each other a bite.

She then led the way to the table where all the gifts were located. She picked up the very official looking certificate. When she realized what it was, she stopped and walked over to Matt and asked if he was serious about giving her the title to the Lazy Lady. She said that having Ted as a perpetual captain was also a great gift.

Ian smiled and said that the Lazy Lady needed to be sailed more often than he had the time to enjoy her. And that he had found the two people that would do just that.

Andrea found it hard to concentrate on the remaining gifts that had been graciously given to her.

The rest of the day was a daze. She kept coming back to the title to the Lazy Lady to make sure it was real.

She realized that she could not read the previous owner's signature and smiled at the fact that even on paper Matt managed to shield his real name.

She picked up the wedding certificate and almost laughed as she took in Matt's long squiggle that was signed below Ted's signature.

Ian enjoyed the rest of the day mingling with the old team and in discussions with both pairs of parents. He felt good about having given the Lazy Lady to Andrea. He planned to buy himself a similar boat if Leslie took to sailing but until then he would enjoy the home where the two of them had spent many wonderful years.

Once they were back to the dock, the partying continued.

Suddenly, Andrea realized that Matt was missing.

She looked up the pier to the very end where she spotted him.

Ian spotted Andrea standing looking his way and with his phone he reflected the sun and sent her a farewell signal. He then turned and walked over to where a taxi was waiting for him.

The End

About the Author

Ronald E. Mueller
remwriter95@gmail.com

Ron grew up in what is now Flint River State Park in Southeast Iowa. The 170-year-old house Ron lived in is built into a hillside. It faces a 125-foot-high cliff towering over the little Flint River. The house and the land talked to him about; the passing of time, the struggle to conquer the land, the struggles people faced and the wonder of nature.

He climbed the cliffs, crawled into the caves, dove from the swimming rock, collected clams from the bottom of the pond, gigged and skinned frogs for their legs. He trapped muskrats for fur, hunted raccoon in the dead of night, and with only a stick hunted rabbits in the dead of winter.

His young life was outdoors, and nature tested him.

He walked to a one room stone schoolhouse uphill both ways. A stern but warm-hearted teacher, Mrs. Henry was instrumental in shaping his character as she shepherded him from the fourth to the eighth grade.

It was a great way to grow up.

Ron graduated from Burlington, High School, went to Vietnam in the Navy. He graduated from The University of South Florida with a master's degree in engineering, worked for thirty eight years for Procter and Gamble, traveled around the world thirty times.

He has remained happily married for more than fifty years. His daughter and his two sons are all successful and his three grandchildren have all graduated.

His wife has humored and supported him as he became a full time professional story teller.

He has come to realize that he is, what is known as, a Cozy writer. Excitement and adventure but little guts and gore. His heroine or hero suffer a little but live happily ever after.

His experiences inter-twined with snippets of fantasy lend themselves to the adventures he leads the reader through.

<u>Books by the Author</u>

<u>Fiction Series</u>
The Alex Evercrest Series
The River Front
The Girl on The Grill
Missing
Maggot
Racist
Votive Candles
Windy City
Country Road
Pool of Blood
Sins of the Daughter
Body Parts
The Skull Collector
The Vanishing
The Shadow Fighter
Moonshine
Grief's Trajectory
The Magic Touch
Northern Lights
Alex Evercrest Heroine
Alex Evercrest Collection Two
New Direction
A Family Affair
Disruption
Aftermath
The St. Lebuinnus Church Murder

A Brian O'Neil Novel
Hawaiian Phoenix
Moon Curser
Death Broker

The Problem Solver Series
Solutions
Drug Lords
Border Crosser
The Problem Solver Collection

<u>The Taelo Series</u>
The Early Years
The Golden Feather
Journey of Discovery
Dangerous Passage
Condor Clan Slingers
Circumvention
The Journey of Sages
Collection
Future Leaders Journey

<u>A Taelo Story:</u>
White Swan and Quiet Pheasant
The Child's Name
Floating Cloud
Quiet Rabbit
Busy Bee
Little Otter & Talking Wren
Broken Spear
Burley Bear & Meadow Flower
Taelo Story Collection

<u>Science Fiction</u>

The Savitar Series:
Journey's End
Savitar
Confluence
Savitar Series Collection

Bram Nielson Series
The Fold
The Message
Fold Wormhole
Negative Fold
Ripples in Time
Bram Nielson Collection

<u>Single Science Fiction Books:</u>
Current Past and Future
The Event
The Door
Viajante 7

https://www.remwriter95.net/